A Text Book of

EMBEDDED SYSTEM

(17626)

For

Semester - VI

Third Year Diploma in Computer Engineering Group

As Per MSBTE's 'G' Scheme Syllabus

PRAMOD B. BOROLE

M. Tech. (Electronics),
Lecturer, Electronics Engg. Deptt.
V.J.T.I., Matunga,
Mumbai

MANOJ KAVEDIA

B.E. (EXTC)
Lecturer, Electronics Engg. Deptt.
Smt. S. H. Mansukhani Institute of Technology
Ulhasnagar

GANESH B. AKOLIYA

M.E. (Digital Electronics),
H.O.D. Electronics & Telecomm. Deptt.
Thakur Polytechnic
Kandivali (E), Mumbai : 400 101

RITA A. VORA

M.E. (EXTC),
Lecturer, Electronics & Telecomm. Deptt.
Thakur Polytechnic
Mumbai : 400 101

NIRALI PRAKASHAN
ADVANCEMENT OF KNOWLEDGE

N3282

EMBEDDED SYSTEM

ISBN : 978-93-5164-315-9

First Edition : February 2015

© : **Authors**

Published By :
NIRALI PRAKASHAN
Abhyudaya Pragati, 1312, Shivaji Nagar,
Off J.M. Road, PUNE – 411005
Tel - (020) 25512336/37/39, Fax - (020) 25511379
Email : niralipune@pragationline.com

Typeset By :
DECENT TYPESETTERS
parasrambhia@hotmail.com
📱 - 98920 65565

DISTRIBUTION CENTRES
PUNE

Nirali Prakashan
119, Budhwar Peth, Jogeshwari Mandir Lane
Pune 411002, Maharashtra
Tel : (020) 2445 2044, 66022708, Fax : (020) 2445 1538
Email : bookorder@pragationline.com

Nirali Prakashan
S. No. 28/27, Dhyari,
Near Pari Company, Pune 411041
Tel : (020) 24690204 Fax : (020) 24690316
Email : dhyari@pragationline.com
bookorder@pragationline.com

MUMBAI
Nirali Prakashan
385, S.V.P. Road, Rasdhara Co-op. Hsg. Society Ltd.,
Girgaum, Mumbai 400004, Maharashtra
Tel : (022) 2385 6339 / 2386 9976, Fax : (022) 2386 9976
Email : niralimumbai@pragationline.com

DISTRIBUTION BRANCHES

NAGPUR
Pratibha Book Distributors
Above Maratha Mandir, Shop No. 3, First Floor,
Rani Jhanshi Square, Sitabuldi, Nagpur 440012,
Maharashtra, Tel : (0712) 254 7129

BENGALURU
Pragati Book House
House No. 1, Sanjeevappa Lane, Avenue Road Cross,
Opp. Rice Church, Bengaluru – 560002.
Tel : (080) 64513344, 64513355,
Mob : 9880582331, 9845021552
Email:bharatsavla@yahoo.com

JALGAON
Nirali Prakashan
34, V. V. Golani Market, Navi Peth, Jalgaon 425001,
Maharashtra, Tel : (0257) 222 0395
Mob : 94234 91860

KOLHAPUR
Nirali Prakashan
New Mahadvar Road,
Kedar Plaza, 1st Floor Opp. IDBI Bank
Kolhapur 416 012, Maharashtra. Mob : 9850046155

CHENNAI
Pragati Books
9/1, Montieth Road, Behind Taas Mahal, Egmore,
Chennai 600008 Tamil Nadu, Tel : (044) 6518 3535,
Mob : 94440 01782 / 98450 21552 / 98805 82331, Email : bharatsavla@yahoo.com

RETAIL OUTLETS
PUNE

Pragati Book Centre
157, Budhwar Peth, Opp. Ratan Talkies,
Pune 411002, Maharashtra
Tel : (020) 2445 8887 / 6602 2707, Fax : (020) 2445 8887

Pragati Book Centre
Amber Chamber, 28/A, Budhwar Peth,
Appa Balwant Chowk, Pune : 411002, Maharashtra,
Tel : (020) 20240335 / 66281669
Email : pbcpune@pragationline.com

Pragati Book Centre
676/B, Budhwar Peth, Opp. Jogeshwari Mandir,
Pune 411002, Maharashtra
Tel : (020) 6601 7784 / 6602 0855

PBC Book Sellers & Stationers
152, Budhwar Peth, Pune 411002, Maharashtra
Tel : (020) 2445 2254 / 6609 2463

MUMBAI
Pragati Book Corner
Indira Niwas, 111 - A, Bhavani Shankar Road, Dadar (W), Mumbai 400028, Maharashtra
Tel : (022) 2422 3526 / 6662 5254, Email : pbcmumbai@pragationline.com

www.pragationline.com

info@pragationline.com

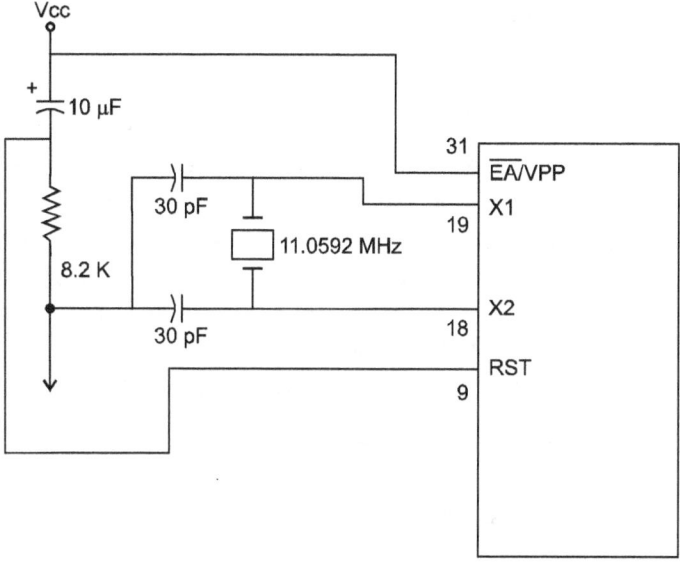

Fig. 1.4 (a) : Power on Reset Circuit

- This is often referred to as a power-on reset. Activating a power-on reset will cause all values in the registers to be lost. It will set program counter to all 0s.

- Fig. 1.4. (a) and 4. (b) show two ways of connecting the RST pin to the power-on reset circuitry. Fig. 1.4. (b) uses a momentary switch for reset circuitry.

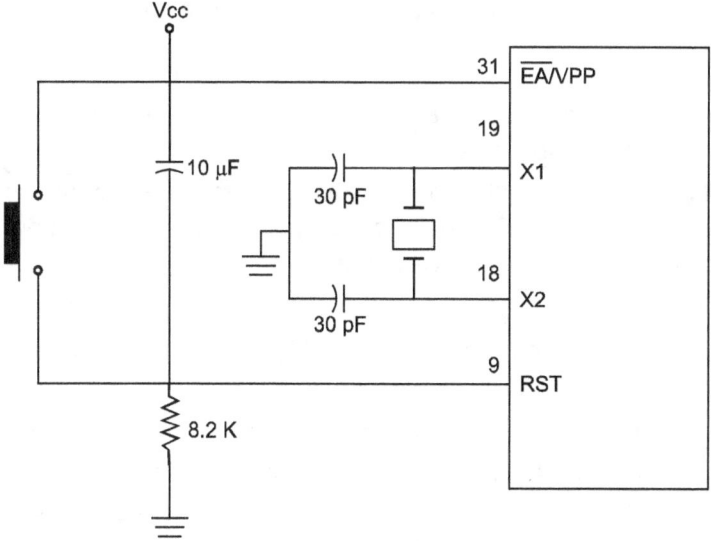

Fig. 1.4 (b) : Power on Reset With Momentary Switch

- In order for the RESET input to be effective, it must have a minimum duration of two machine cycles. In other words, the high pulse must be high for a minimum of two machine cycles before it is allowed to go low. Here is what the Intel manual says about the Reset circuitry. "When power is turned on, the circuit holds the RST pin high for an amount of time that depends on the capacitor value and the rate at which it charges.

- To ensure a valid reset the RST pin must be held high long enough to allow the oscillator to start up plus two machine cycles. Although, an 8.2 K-ohm resistor and a 10-µF capacitor will take care of the vast majority of the cases, you still need to check the data sheet for the 8051 you are using.

- Table 1.3 provides a partial list of 8051 registers and their values after power-on reset.

8051 Registers	
Register	**Reset Values**
PC	0000H
ACC	0000H
B	0000H
PSW	0000H
SP	0007H
DPTR	0000H

Table 1.3 : Value of Register after Reset

Note :

- The value of the PC (program counter) is 0000 upon reset, hence it fetch the first opcode from ROM memory location 0000.

- In order for the RESET input to be effective, it must have a minimum duration of 2 machine cycles. In other words, the high pulse must be high for a minimum of 2 machine cycles before it is allowed to go low.

ALE/PROG (Pin 31) :

- Address Latch Enable output pulse for latching the low byte of the address during accesses to external memory.

- This pin is also the program puke input (PROG) during Flash programming.

- In normal operation ALE is emitted at a constant rate of 1/6 the oscillator frequency and may be used for external timing or clocking purposes.

- Note, however, that one ALE pulse is skipped during each access to external Data.

Preface ...

This book has been written keeping in mind the 'G-Scheme' curriculum designed by MSBTE w.e.f. June 2014 for the students appearing for Third Year Diploma in various branches of Computer Engineering.

We are happy to introduce the book entitled **'Embedded System'** for students of Polytechnics in Maharashtra.

This text can serve as a self learning tool for diploma students. The language of the book has been kept simple, straight forward and easy to understand specially for Marathi medium students. In this text, we have adopted top-down approach. We have presented 89C51 microcontroller in embedded system point of view. The concept specific to 89C51 have been explained in detail with several examples. Students can download Keil software from www.keil.com and develop 89C51 based embedded software.

Our special thanks to Shri Pradeep K. Furia, Shri Dineshbhai Furia, Shri Jignesh Furia of **Nirali Prakashan** for giving personal attention and bringing out this book in so decent form and fast as well. We are also thankful to Mr. Shashikant Patel, Mr. Jayanth Dedhia and staff of Nirali Prakashan. We would like to thank Mr. Paras Rambhia and Mr. Hardik Vira of Decent Typesetters for their quick follow up of matter and excellent computer typesetting work.

Authors

Syllabus ...

Chapter 1 : 8051 - Microcontroller [Hrs. : 08, Marks : 16]

1.1 Introduction to 8051 family Microcontroller

1.2 8051 Microcontroller

- Salient features
- Pins description,
- Architecture of 8051
- Special function Register (SFR)
- Memory Organization
- I/O Ports, Timer/counters, Interrupt structure
- Serial Port Interface
- Boolean Operation
- Power Down Operation

Chapter 2 : Instruction Set of 8051 [Hrs. : 08, Marks : 16]

2.1 Instruction Set of 8051

- Programmers model of 8051
- Operand types
- Assembler Directives
- Addressing modes
- Data transfer, Arithmetic, logical, Control transfer instructions
- Simple programs such as addition, subtraction, multiplication, division in assembly and 'C'
- Execution of program using cross compiler like Keil IDE, SPJ, RIDE

Chapter 3 : I/O Ports, Timers/Counters, Interrupts and Serial Communication Programming [Hrs. : 10, Marks : 16]

3.1 Port Structure and Simple I/O port programming

3.2 Timer/Counter Programming in assembly and C

3.3 Serial Port programming in assembly and C

3.4 Interrupt programming in assembly and C

Chapter 4 : 8051 Interfacing Application [Hrs. : 08, Marks : 16]

4.1 Interfacing of seven segment display and LCD display Interfacing diagram and pin out of 2x16 LCD

4.2 Interfacing of 4x4 Keyboard, ADC and DAC- interfacing diagram and programming.

4.3 Interfacing of stepper motor- interfacing diagram and Programming function

Chapter 5 : Embedded Systems [Hrs. : 08, Marks : 18]

5.1 Introduction to Embedded System, Processor in system, different Hardware Units, advantages, Applications, Software embedded into system, System-On-Chip, Concept of Device Driver

5.2 Software and Hardware development tools , IDE, Compiler, Debugger, Simulator, Emulator, In circuit Emulator(ICE), Target Board, Device Programmer

5.3 Embedded software development cycle

Chapter 6 : RTOS & Inter-process Communication [Hrs. : 06, Marks : 18]

6.1 Concepts of RTOS, Need of RTOS in Embedded systems

6.2 Multitasking

6.3 Task synchronization and Mutual Exclusion

6.4 Starvation, Deadlock, Multiple process

6.5 Basics of Inter-process Communication

Total – Hrs. : 48, Marks : 100

Contents ...

$\mathcal{C}hapter$ **1** ...

8051 - Microcontroller

Specific Objectives

➢ Students will be able to

   ❖ Draw the architecture of 8051

   ❖ Identify the functions of different pins of 8051

   ❖ Identify status of different flags.

1.1 INTRODUCTION TO 8051 MICROCONTROLLER FAMILY

- In 1981, Intel Corporation introduced an 8-bit microcontroller called the 8051. This microcontroller had 128 bytes of RAM, 4 K bytes of on-chip ROM, two timers, one serial port, and four ports (each 8-bits wide) all on a single chip. At the time, it was also referred to s a "system on a chip."

Fig. 1.1 : Intel 8051

- As shown in Fig. 1.1, the 8051 is an 8-bit processor, meaning that the CPU can work on only 8 bits of data at a time. Data larger than 8 bits has to be broken into 8-bit pieces to be processed by the CPU. The 8051 has a total of four I/O ports, each 8 bits wide. Although, the 8051 can have a maximum of 64 Kbytes of on-chip ROM, many manufacturers have put only 4 K bytes on the chip.

- There are two other members in the 8051 family of microcontrollers. They are the 8052 and the 8031.

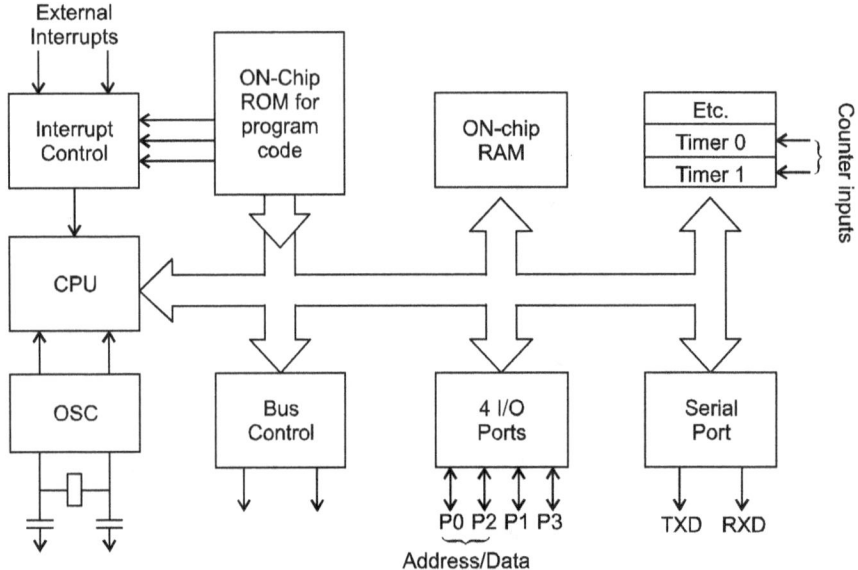

Fig. 1.2 : Block diagram of 8 bit microcontroller

8052 microcontroller :

- The 8052 is another member of the 8051 family. The 8052 has all the standard features of the 8051 in addition to an extra 128 bytes of RAM and an extra timer. In other words, the 8052 has 256 bytes of RAM and 3 timers. It also has 8K bytes of on-chip program ROM instead of 4K bytes.

8031 microcontroller :

- This chip is often referred to as a ROM-less 8051 since it has 0 K bytes of on-chip ROM. To use this chip, you must add external ROM to it. This external ROM must contain the program that the 8031 will fetch and execute.

- Contrast to that the 8051 in which the on-chip ROM contains the program to be fetched and executed but is limited to only 4 K bytes of code.

- The ROM containing the program attached to the 8031 can be as large as 64 K bytes. In the process of adding external ROM to the 8031, you lose two ports. That leaves only 2 ports (of the 4 ports) for I/O operations. To solve this problem, you can add external I/O to the 8031.

Comparison of Different 8-bit controller :

Features	8051	8052	8053
ROM (on-chip program space in bytes)	4K	8K	0K
RAM (bytes)	128	256	128
Timers	2	3	2
I/O pins	32	32	32
Serial port	1	1	1
Interrupt sources	6	8	6

Table 1.1 : Comparison of 8051, 8052, 8031

1.2 MICROCONTROLLER 8051

- 8051 is manufactured using N-Channel Metal Oxide Silicon (NMOS) and Complementary Metal Oxide Silicon (CMOS) construction in a variety of package types. An enhanced version of the 8051, the 8052, also exists with its own family of variations and even includes one member that can be programmed in BASIC and C. Packaged in 40 pin package with following features:
  - ➢ 8 bit CPU
  - ➢ Internal ROM and RAM
  - ➢ I/O ports with programmable pins
  - ➢ Timers and counters
  - ➢ Serial data communication
  - ➢ Interrupt control
  - ➢ Oscillator circuit.

1.2.1 Salient Feature of 8051

- The 8051 microcontroller is a very popular 8-bit microcontroller introduced by Intel in the year 1981 and it has become almost the academic standard now a days. The 8051 is based on an 8-bit CISC core with Harvard architecture. Its 8-bit architecture is optimized for control applications with extensive Boolean processing. It is available as a 40-pin DIP chip and works at +5 Volts DC. The salient features of 8051 controller are given below. The salient features of 8051 Microcontroller are:
  1. 80C51 based architecture with 8-bit CPU.
  2. Processor with support Boolean operations on bits.
  3. Memory addressing capability 64k ROM and 64k RAM.
  4. 4 KB on chip program memory (ROM or EPROM).

5. 128 bytes on chip data memory (RAM).

6. 8-bit data bus.

7. 16-bit address bus.

8. 32 general purpose registers each of 8 bits.

9. Two -16 bit timers T0 and T1.

10. Five Interrupts (3 internal and 2 external).

11. Four Parallel ports each of 8-bits (PORT0, PORT1, PORT2, PORT3) with a total of 32 I/O lines.

12. One 16-bit program counter and One 16-bit DPTR (data pointer).

13. One 8-bit stack pointer.

14. One Microsecond instruction cycle with 12 MHz crystal.

15. One full duplex serial communication port.

16. 1000 times write/erase.

17. Compatible with MCS-51 products.

18. Compatible with TTL and CMOS digital technologies.

1.2.2 Pin Description

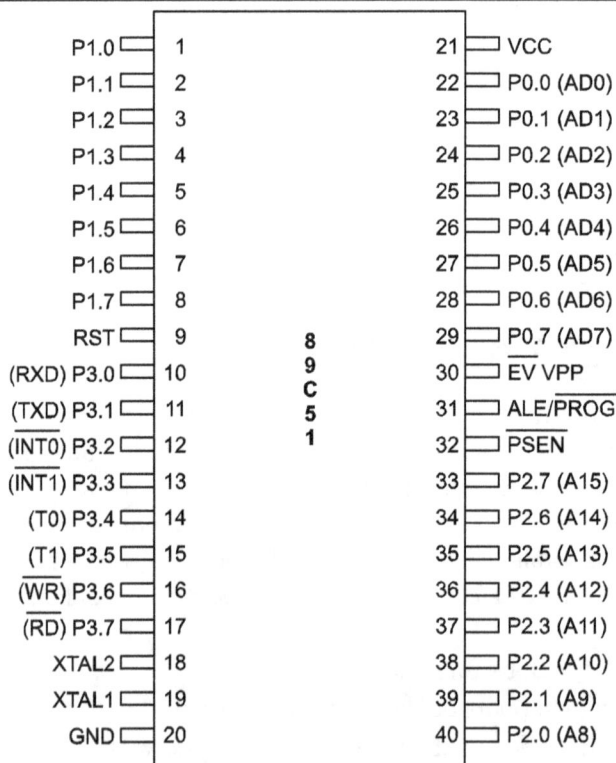

Fig. 1.3 : Pin Diagram 8051/8951

VCC (Pin 21): Supply voltage.

GND (Pin 20): Ground.

Port 0 (Pin 22-29) :

- Port 0 is an 8-bit open drain bidirectional I/O port. As an output port each pin can sink eight TTL inputs.

- When 1s are written to port 0 pins, the pins can be used as high independence inputs.

- Port 0 may also be configured to be the multiplexed low order address/data bus during access to external program and data memory. In this mode P0 has internal pull-ups.

- Port 0 also receives the code bytes during Flash programming, and outputs the code bytes during program verification. External pull-ups are required during program verification.

Port 1 (Pin1-8) :

- Port 1 is an 8-bit bidirectional I/O port with internal pull-ups.

- The Port 1 output buffers can sink/source four TTL inputs. When 1s are written to Port 1 pins they are pulled high by the internal pull-ups and can be used as inputs.

- As inputs, Port 1 pins that are externally being pulled low will source current (IIL) because of the internal pull-ups. Port 1 also receives the low order address bytes during Flash programming and program verification.

Port 2 (Pin 22-29) :

- Port 2 is an 8-bit bidirectional I/O port with internal pull-ups.

- The Port 2 output buffers can sink/source four TTL inputs. When Is are written to Port 2 pins they are pulled high by the internal pull-ups and can be used as inputs.

- As inputs, Port 2 pins that are externally being pulled low will source current (I_{IL}) because of the internal pull-ups.

- Port 2 emits the high-order address byte during fetches from external program memory and during accesses to external data memory that uses 16-bit addresses (MOVX A, @ DPTR).

- In this application it uses strong internal pull-ups when emitting 1s.

- During accesses to external data memory that uses 8-bit addresses (MOVX @ R1); Port 2 emits the contents of the P2 Special Function Register. Port

2 also receives the high-order address bits and some control signals during Flash programming and verification.

Port 3 (Pin 10-17) :

- Port 3 is an 8-bit bidirectional I/O port with internal pull-ups.

- The Port 3 output buffers can sink/source four TTL inputs. When 1s are written to Port 3 pins they are pulled high by the internal pull-ups and can be used as inputs.

- Port 3 pins that are externally being pulled low will source current (I_{IL}) because of the pull-ups.

- Port 3 also serves the functions of various special features of the AT89C51/8051 as listed below :

Port Pin	I Alternate Functions
P3.0	RXD (serial input port)
P3.1	TXD (serial output port)
P3.2	$\overline{INT0}$ (external interrupt 0)
P3.3	$\overline{INT1}$ (external interrupt 1)
P3.4	T0 (timer 0 atonal input)
P3.5	T1 (timer 1 external input)
P3.6	$\overline{WR}$ (external data memory write strobe)
P3.7	$\overline{RD}$ (external data memory read strobe)

Table 1.2 : Alternate Function of 8051 Port 3

- Port 3 also receives some control signals for Flash programming and Programming verification.

RST (Pin 9) :

- It is an input and is active high (normally low). Upon applying a high pulse to this pin, the microcontroller will reset and terminate all activities.

Memory :

- If desired, ALE operation can be disabled by setting bit 0 of SFR location 8EH. With the bit set, ALE is active only during a MOVX or MOVC instruction.

- Otherwise, the pin is weakly pulled high. Setting the ALE-disable bit has no effect if the microcontroller is in external execution mode.

PSEN (Pin 32):

- Program Store Enable is the read strobe to external program memory.

- When the AT89C51 is executing code from external program memory, PSEN is activated twice each machine cycle, except that two PSEN activations are skipped during each access to external data memory.

EA/VPP(Pin 30) :

- The 8051 family members, such as the 8751/52, 89C51/52, or DS89C4xO, all come with on-chip ROM to store programs. In such cases, the EA pin is connected to V_{cc}. For family members such as the 8031 and 8032 in which there is no on-chip ROM. code is stored on an external ROM and is fetched by the 8031/32. Therefore, for the 8031 the EA pin must be connected to GND to indicate that the code is stored externally. EA. which stands for "external access," is pin number 31 in the DIP packages. It is an input pin and must be connected to either V_{cc} or GND. In other words, it cannot be left unconnected..

XTAL1 and XTAL2 (Pin 18-19) :

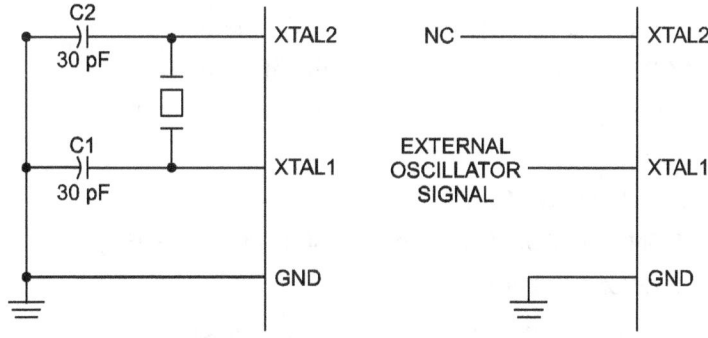

Fig. 1.5 : Clock Circuitry

- The 8051 has an on-chip oscillator but requires an external clock to run it. Most often a quartz crystal oscillator is connected to inputs XTAL1 (19) and XTAL2 (pin 18). Fig. 1.5. Show s connection of clock to 8051.

- The quartz crystal oscillator connected to XTAL1 and XTAL2 also needs two capacitors of 30 pF value. One side of each capacitor is connected to the ground as shown in Fig. 1.5

- The speeds of the 8051 refer to the maximum oscillator frequency connected to XTAL. For example a 12-MHz chip must be connected to a crystal with 12 MHz frequency or less.

- If frequency source is not crystal oscillator, but a TTL oscillator circuit, it will be connected to XTAL1; XTAL2 is left unconnected, as shown in Fig. 1.5.

1.2.3 Architecture of 8051

- 8051 is manufactured using N-Channel Metal Oxide Silicon (NMOS) and Complementary Metal Oxide Silicon (CMOS) construction in a variety of package types. An enhanced version of the 8051, the 8052, also exists with its own family of variations and even includes one member that can be programmed in BASIC and C. Architecture is as shown in Fig. 1.6. with following features :

  - 8 bit CPU
  - Internal ROM and RAM
  - I/O ports with programmable pins
  - Timers and counters
  - Serial data communication
  - Interrupt control
  - Oscillator circuit

- The 8051 architecture consists of these specific features :

  - Eight-bit CPU with registers A the accumulator and B.
  - Sixteen-bit program counter (PC) and data pointer (DPTR).
  - Eight-bit program status word (PSW).
  - Eight-bit stack pointer (SP).
  - Internal ROM or EPROM (8751) of 0K (8031) to 4K (8051).
  - Internal RAM of 128 bytes.
  - Four register banks, each containing eight registers.
  - Sixteen bytes, which may be addressed at the hit level.
  - Eighty bytes of general-purpose data memory.
  - Thirty-two input/output pins arranged as four 8-bit ports: P0—P3.
  - Two 16-bit timer/counters: T0 and T1.
  - Full duplex serial data receiver/transmitter: SBUF.
  - Control registers: TCON, TMOD, SCON, PCON, IP, and IE.
  - Two external and three internal interrupt sources Oscillator and clock circuits.

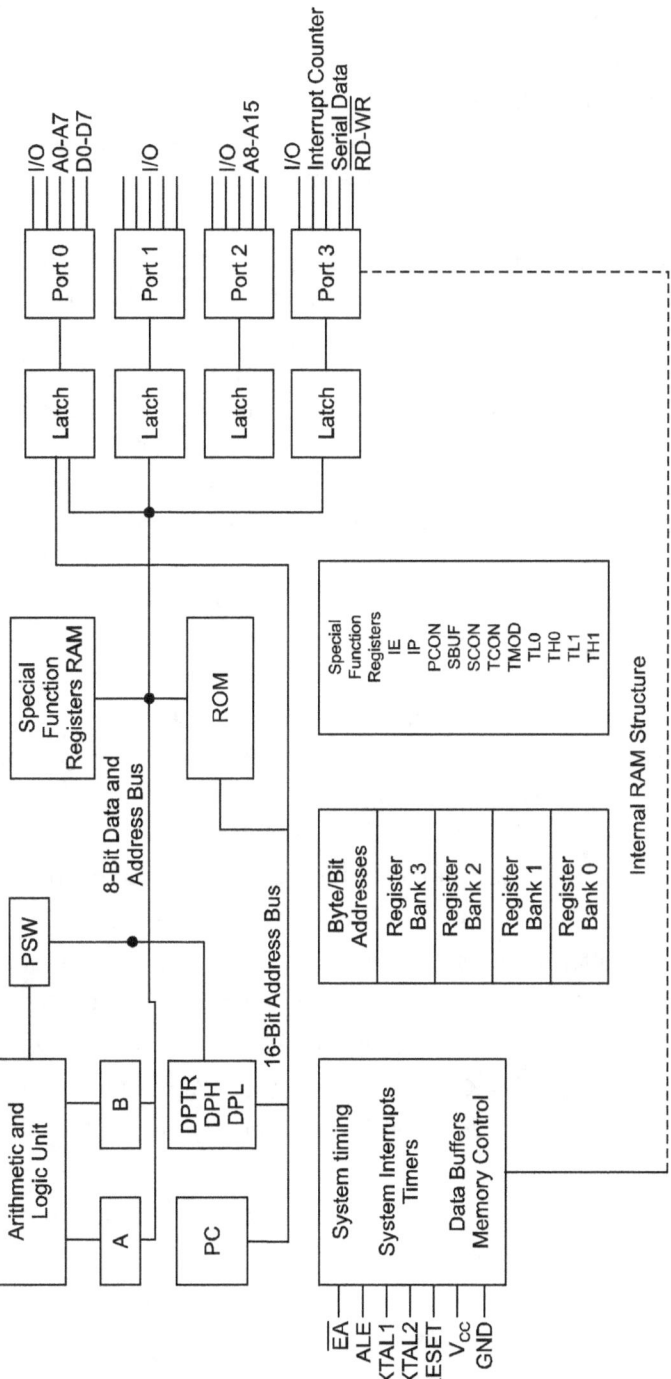

Fig. 1.6 : Architecture of 8051

Central Processor Unit(CPU) :

- CPU is the brain of any processing device. It monitors and controls all operations that are performed in the Microcontroller.
- User has no control over the work of CPU. It reads program written in ROM memory and executes them and do the expected task.

Interrupts :

- Interrupt is a subroutine call that interrupts Microcontroller's main operation or work and causes it to execute some another program which is more important at that time.
- The feature of Interrupt is very useful as it helps in cases of emergency. Interrupts gives us a mechanism to put on hold the ongoing operation , execute a subroutine and then again resumes normal program execution.
- The Microcontroller 8051 can be configured in such a way that it temporarily terminates or pause the main program at the occurrence of interrupt. When subroutine is completed then the execution of main program starts as usual.
- There are five interrupt sources in 8051 Microcontroller. 2 of them are external interrupts, 2 timer interrupts and one serial port interrupt.

Memory :

- Microcontroller requires a program which is a collection of instructions. This program tells Microcontroller to do specific tasks. These programs require a memory on which these can be saved and read by Microcontroller to perform specific operation.
- The memory which is used to store the program of Microcontroller, is known as code memory or Program memory . It is known as 'ROM' (Read Only Memory).
- Microcontroller also requires a memory to store data or operands temporarily. The memory which is used to temporarily store data for operation is known as Data Memory and we uses 'RAM' (Random Access Memory) for this purpose.
- Microcontroller 8051 has 4K of Code Memory or Program memory that is it has 4 KB Rom and it also have 128 bytes of data memory i.e. RAM.

Bus :

- Basically, Bus is a collection of wires which work as a communication channel or medium for transfer of Data.
- These buses consist of 8, 16 or more wires. Thus these can carry 8 bits, 16 bits simultaneously. Buses are of two types:
  - Address Bus
  - Data Bus

Address Bus:

- Microcontroller 8051 has a 16 bit address bus. It used to address memory locations. It is used to transfer the address from CPU to Memory.

Data Bus:

- Microcontroller 8051 has 8 bits data bus. It is used to carry data.

Oscillator:

- Microcontroller is a digital circuit device, therefore it requires clock for its operation. For this purpose, Microcontroller 8051 has an on-chip oscillator which works as a clock source for Central Processing Unit.

- As the output pulses of oscillator are stable therefore it enables synchronized work of all parts of 8051 Microcontroller.

Input/Output Port:

- Microcontroller is used in embedded systems to control the operation of machines. Therefore, to connect it to other machines, devices or peripherals we require I/O interfacing ports in Microcontroller.

- For this purpose, Microcontroller 8051 has 4 input/output ports to connect it to other peripherals.

Timers/Counters: Microcontroller :

- 8051 has 2 16 bit timers and counters. The counters are divided into 8 bit registers. The timers are used for measurement of intervals , to determine pulse width etc.

1.2.4 Special Function Registers (SFR)

- Some SFRs marked with an asterisk * are bit addressable. This feature allows the programmer to change only what needs to be changed, leaving the remaining bits in that SFR unchanged.

- The 8051 operations that do not use the internal 128-byte RAM addresses from 00h to 7Fh are done by a group of specific internal registers, each called a Special-Function register (SFR), which may he addressed much like internal RAM, using addresses from 80h to FFh.

- Not all of the addresses from 80h to FFh are used for SFRs, and attempting to use an address that is not defined, or empty, results in unpredictable results.

- The SFR names and equivalent internal RAM addresses are given in the following list :

Name	Function	Internal Ram Address
A	Accumulator	0E0
B	Arithmetic Register	0F0
DPH	Addressable External Memory	83
DPL	Addressable External Memory	82
IE	Enable Interrupt Control	0A8
IP	Interrupt Priority	0B8
P0	Input/Output Port Latch	80
P1	Input/Output Port Latch	90
P2	Input/Output Port Latch	0A0
P3	Input/Output Port Latch	0B0
PCON	Power Control	87
PSW	Program Status Word	0D0
SCON	Serial Port Control	98
SBUF	Serial Port Data Buffer	99
SP	Stack Port	81
TMOD	Timer/Counter Mode Control	89
TCON	Timer Control	88
TLO	Timer 0 Low Byte	8A
THO	Timer 0 High Byte	8C
TL1	Timer 1 Low Byte	8B
TH1	Timer 1 High Byte	8D

Table 1.4 : SFRs and SFR address

- SFRs are named in certain opcodes by their functional names such as A or TH0 and are referred by other opcodes by their addresses, such as 0E0h or 8CH.

1.2.5 Memory Organization

Program and Data Memory :

- The 8051 is organized so that data memory and program code memory can be in two entirely different physical memory entities. Each has the same address ranges. Fig. 1.7. shows memory organization of 8051.

Internal ROM :

- The internal ROM occupies code address space 0000h to 0FFFh.

- The PC is ordinarily used to address program code bytes from addresses 0000h to FFFFh.

- Program addresses higher than 0FFFh, which exceed the internal ROM capacity, will cause the 8051 to automatically fetch code bytes from external program memory.

- Code bytes can also be fetched exclusively from an external memory, addresses 0000h to FFFFh, by connecting the external access pin (EA pin 31 on the IC) to ground.

- The PC does not care where the code is the circuit designer decides whether the code is found totally in internal ROM, totally in external ROM, or in a combination of internal and external ROM.

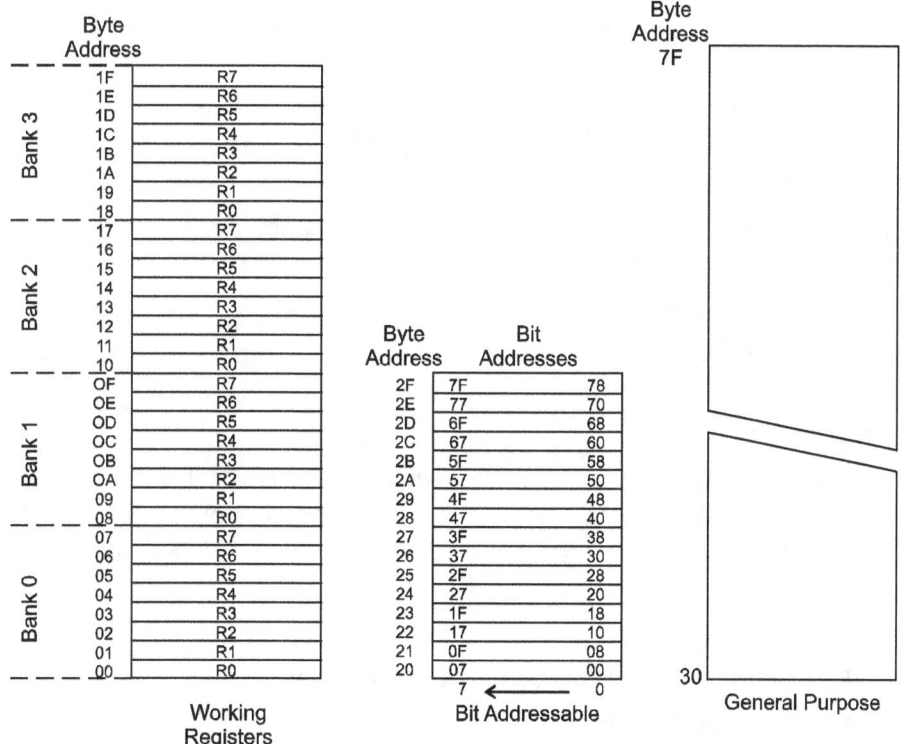

Fig. 1.7. Internal memory Structure

Internal RAM :

- The 128-byte internal RAM, which is shown generally in Fig. 1.7 Total 128 Bytes are organized into three distinct areas :

  1. Register Bank

  ➢ Thirty-two bytes from address 00h to IFh that make up 32 working registers organized as four banks of eight registers each. The four register banks are numbered 0 to 3 and are made up of eight registers named R0 to R7.

  ➢ Each register can be addressed by name (when its bank is selected) or by its RAM address. Thus R0 of bank 3 is RK0 (if bank 3 is currently selected) or address 18h (whether bank 3 is selected or not).

  ➢ Bits RS0 and RS1 in the PSW determine which bank of registers is currently in use at any time when the program is running.

  ➢ Register banks not selected can be used as general-purpose RAM. Bank 0 is selected on reset.

  2. Bit Addressable Area

  ➢ A bit-addressable area of 16 bytes occupies RAM byte addresses 20h to 2Fh, forming a total of 128 addressable bits.

  ➢ An addressable bit may be specified by its bit address of 0Db to 7Fh, or 8 bits may form any byte address from 20h to 2Fh. Thus, for example, bit address 4Fh is also bit 7 of byte address 29h.

  ➢ Addressable bits are useful when the program need only remember a binary event (switch on, light off, etc.).

  3. General Purpose Ram

  ➢ A general-purpose RAM area above the bit area, from 3Dh to 7Fh, addressable as bytes.

External memory :

- The data pointer Rp (R0 and R1) is used to point internal and external data memory. In external memory access, it places contents of Rp on port0 (lower byte of address) and contents of port2 latch (higher byte of address) on port 2 lines.

- In this case, external data memory functions as a paged memory. It is divided into 256 pages and the size of each page is 256 bytes. The Rp is used to access a location within a page while port 2 latch is used to select the page.

- DPTR is used to point external data memory only. It places contents of DPH on port0 and contents of DPL on port 2.

1.2.6 I/O Ports Structure

Input Output Ports :

- There are four ports P0, P1, P2 and P3 each use 8 pins, making them 8-bit ports i.e. total 32 I/O lines. All the ports upon RESET are configured as output, ready to be used as output ports. To use any of these ports as an input port, it must be programmed.

- Each port has a D-type output latch for each pin. The SFR for each port is made up of these eight latches, which can be addressed at the SFR address for that port.

Port 0 (Bit –Byte Addressable – Address – 80H)

- Port 0 is an 8-bit open drain bidirectional I/O port without internal pull-ups. As an output port each pin can sink 8 LS TTL inputs.

- Port 0 requires external pull-ups.

- Port 0 is also the multiplexed with low-order address/data bus during accesses to external memory.

Port 1 (Bit –Byte Addressable – Address – 90H)

- Port 1 is an 8-bit bidirectional I/O port with internal pull-ups. Port 1 pins that have 1's written to them are pulled high by the internal pull ups, and in that state can be used as inputs.

- As inputs, Port 1 pins that are externally being pulled low will source current because of the internal pull ups.

Port 2 (Bit –Byte Addressable – Address – A0H)

- Port 2 is an 8-bit bidirectional I/O port with internal pull-ups. Port 2 pins that are written to them are pulled high by the internal pull ups, and in that state can be used as inputs.

- As inputs Port 2 pins that are externally being pulled low will source current because of the internal pull ups.

- Port 2 outputs the high-order address byte during fetches from external Program memory and In this application it uses strong internal pull ups when outputs are 1's.

Port 3 (Bit –Byte Addressable – Address – B0H)

- Port 3 is an 8-bit bidirectional I/O port with internal pull ups. Port 3 pins that have 1's written to them are pulled high by the internal pull ups, and in that state can be used as inputs.

- As inputs, Port 3 pins that are externally being pulled low will source current because of the pull ups.

- Port 3 has various different functions as listed below :

Pin	Label	Usage	SFR Needed
P3.0	RXD	Serial Data Input	SBUF
P3.1	TXD	Serial Data Output	SBUF
P3.2	INT0	External Interrupt 0	TCON.1
P3.3	INT1	External Interrupt 1	TCON.3
P3.4	T0	External Timer 0	TMOD
P3.5	T1	External Timer 1	TMOD
P3.6	WR	External Memory Write Pulse	-------
P3.7	RD	External Memory Read Pulse	-------

Table 1.5 : Alternate function of port 3

1.2.7 Timer/Counters

- Microcontroller applications require
  1. The counting of external events, such as the frequency of a pulse train,
  2. The generation of precise internal time delays between computer actions.
- Both of these tasks can be accomplished using software techniques, but software loops for counting or timing keep the processor occupied so that other, perhaps more important, functions are not done.
- To relieve the processor of this burden, two 16-bit up counters, named T0 and TI, are provided for the general use of the programmer. Each counter may be programmed to count internal clock pulses, acting as a timer, or programmed to count external pulses as a counter.
- The counters are divided into two 8-bit registers called the timer low (TL0, TLI) and high (TH0, TH1) bytes. All counter action is controlled by bit states in the timer mode control register (TMOD), the timer/counter control register (TCON), and certain program instructions.
- TMOD is used for two timers and can be considered to be two duplicate 4-bit registers, each of which controls the action of one of the timers. TCON has control bits and flags for the timers in the upper nibble, and control bits and flags for the external interrupts in the lower nibble.
- For T0 and T1 Interrupt are assigned, which when activated transfer the program control to vector memory Location (T0-000BH , T1-001BH).

- When Counter start counting the internal / external event it increment with every clock pulse , when the counter has reached the value FFH and on next pulse it will roll to 00H , the timer Flag(TF0,TF1) set which activate the interrupt.

- 8051 timer are operated in four different mode ,both timer can be programmed independently, which are as follows:

  1. Timer Mode 0 – 13 Bit Timer.

  2. Timer Mode 1 – 16 bit Timer.

  3. Timer Mode 2 – 8 bit auto reload mode.

  4. Timer Mode 3 – Two 8bit timer using timer 0.

1.2.8 Serial Data Input/Output

- Computers must be able to communicate with other computers in modem multiprocessor distributed systems. One cheaper way to communicate is to send and receive data bits serially.

- 8051 has full duplex serial communication facility provided by pin P3.0(RXD) and pin P3.1(TXD).Along with this pins 8051 also uses

- Register SBUF to hold data.

- Register SCON controls data communication,

- Register PCON controls data rates,

- The serial data flags in SCON, TI and RI, are set whenever a data byte is transmitted (TI) or received (RI). These flags are ORed together to produce an interrupt to the program. The program must read these flags to determine which caused the interrupt and then clear the flag.

- The serial communication feature support four mode of serial communication

  1. Serial Data Mode 0–Shift Register Mode

  2. Serial Data Mode 1–Standard UART

  3. Serial Data Mode 2–Multiprocessor Mode

  4. Serial Data Mode 3–Same as Mode 2

1.2.9 Interrupts Structure

- A computer program has only two ways to determine the status that exist in internal and external circuits.

  1. Using software instructions that jump to subroutines on the states of flags and part pins.

2. Responds to hardware signals, called interrupts, that force the program to call a subroutine.

- Software techniques use up processor time that could be devoted to other tasks; interrupts take processor time only when action by the program is needed; Most applications of microcontrollers involve responding to events quickly enough to control the environment that generates the events (generically termed real-time programming).

- Interrupts may be generated by internal chip operations or provided by external sources. Any interrupt can cause the 8051 to perform a hardware call to an interrupt-handling subroutine that is located at a predetermined address in program memory.

- Five interrupts are provided in the 8051.

    ➢ Three of these are generated automatically by internal operations

        1. Timer flag 0-TF0,

        2. Timer flag 1-TF1 and

        3. The serial port interrupts (RI or TI).

    ➢ Two interrupts are triggered by external signals provided by circuitry Connected to pins INTO and INTl (port pins P3.2 and P3.3).

- Along with TF0, TF1, RI, TI, INT0 and INT1, some register are needed for interrupt programming those are

    1. The Interrupt Enable register IE

    2. The Interrupt Priority register IP), and

    3. The Timer Control Register (TCON).

- Interrupts with a high priority can interrupt another interrupt with a lower priority, the lower priority interrupt continues after the higher is finished. If two interrupts with the same priority occur at the same time, then they have the following ranking:

    1. IE0,

    2. TF0,

    3. IE1,

    4. IT1,

    5. Serial Interrupt.

Interrupt Vector Address, Priority :

Interrupt Identity	Symbol	Priority	Vector Address	Port Pin
Reset	RST	Highest	0000H	9
External Interrupt 0	IE0	1	0003H	P3.2
Timer Interrupt 0	TF0	2	000BH	Internal
External Interrupt 1	IE1	3	0013H	P3.3
Timer Interrupt 0	TF1	4	001BH	Internal
Serial Interrupt	TI or RI	5	0023H	Internal

Table 1.6 : Interrupt Vector Address, Priority

1.2.10 Boolean Operation

- Microcomputer is powerful in numerical calculation on bytes. This is useful in numeric processing. Bit addressing is very convenient way to change a single bit of a byte, in a control register for instance, without changing other bit of the same byte.

- However, controllers deal with bits, not byte. The controller is used to turn ON or OFF the switch, motor, relay and indicator. It is also used to test 'low' or 'high' state of a sensor and logic device.

- The 8051 provides a separate processor to handle bit as a data type. The bit processing can be done 'by using byte process, but the remaining 7 bits of a byte are wasted and affected.

- The Boolean processor provides many feature like direct bit manipulation, testing of individual bit and logical bit manipulation etc. This processor provides 17 Boolean instructions.

ANL C, b	ORL C,/b	CLR C	Mov b, C	RL A	RLC A
ANL C, /b	MOV C , b	CLR b	SETB C	RR A	CPL b
ORL C, b	SWAP A	CPL C	SETB b	RRC A	

Table 1.7 : Bitwise Instructions

- It provides multiple addressing modes, subroutine, and two level interrupt structure for Boolean processor based programs. In Boolean processing, carry flag functions as a one bit accumulator for logical operation and data transfers.

- The Boolean instructions are one, two or three bytes long depending on what function they perform. It can operate directly upon 144 general purpose bits of RAM. These bits can be used as software flags or to store one bit variable.

Internal RAM Bit Addresses :

- In 8051 every bit of bit addressable areas has 8 bit address which makes programming very flexible and efficient.

- Hence complete bytes should not be affected for manipulation of one or two bits of data. The relation between byte and bit addresses is shown in the following table

Byte Address	Bit Address
20	00-07
21	08-0F
22	10-07
23	18-0F
24	20-27
25	28-2F
26	30-37
27	38-3F
28	40-47
29	48-4F
2A	50-57
2B	58-5F
2C	60-67
2D	68-6F
2E	70-77
2F	78-7F

SFR	Direct Address	Bit Address
A	0E0	0E0-0E7
B	0F0	0F0-0F7
IE	0A8	0A8-0AF
IP	0B8	0B8-0BF
P0	80	80-87
P1	90	90-97
P2	0A0	0A0-0A7
P3	0B0	0B0-0B7
PSW	0D0	0D0-0D7
TCON	88	88-8F
PCON	98	98-9F
Bit Addressable Register and SFR		

Table 1.8 : Internal RAM Bit Addresses

- For example, the address of bit 5 of internal RAM byte address 25h is 32h, the bit address of bit 5 of RAM address 21h is 0Dh, and bit address 47h is bit 7 of RAM byte address 28h.

1.2.11 Power Down Mode

- Normally in a CPU the microcontroller is inactive for the most part and just waits for some external signal in order to takes its role in a show. This can cause some problems in case batteries are used for power supply. In extreme cases, the only solution is to set the whole electronics in sleep mode in order to minimize consumption shown in Fig. 1.8.

- A typical example is a TV remote controller: it can be out of use for months but when used again it takes less than a second to send a command to TV receiver.

- The AT89v51 uses approximately 25mA for regular operation, which doesn't make it a power-saving microcontroller. Anyway, it doesn't have to be always like that, it can easily switch the operating mode in order to reduce its total consumption to approximately 40uA. Actually, there are two power-saving modes of operation:
  - ➢ Idle Mode and
  - ➢ Power Down Mode.

Idle mode :

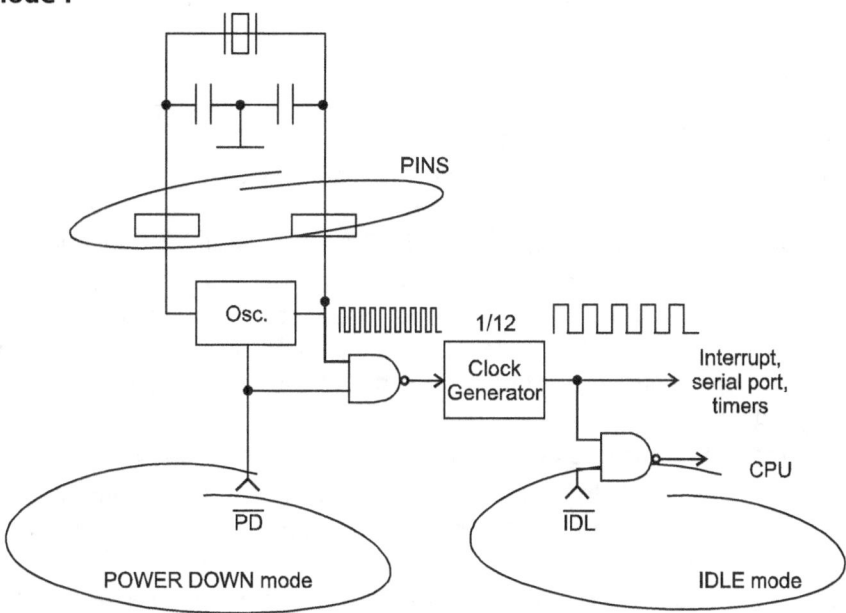

Fig. 1.8 : Power Down Mode of 89c51/8051

- Upon the IDL bit of the PCON register is set, the microcontroller turns off the greatest power consumer-CPU unit while peripheral units such as serial port, timers and interrupt system continue operating normally consuming 6.5mA. In Idle mode, the state of all registers and I/O ports remains unchanged.

- In order to exit the Idle mode and make the microcontroller operate normally, it is necessary to enable and execute any interrupt or reset. It will cause the IDL bit to be automatically cleared and the program resumes operation from instruction having set the IDL bit. It is recommended that first three instructions to execute now are NOP instructions. They don't perform any operation but provide some time for the microcontroller to stabilize and prevents undesired changes on the I/O ports.

Power Down mode :

- By setting the PD bit of the PCON register from within the program, the microcontroller is set to Power down mode, thus turning off its internal oscillator and reduces power consumption enormously.

- The microcontroller can operate using only 2V power supply in power- down mode, while a total power consumption is less than 40uA. The only way to get the microcontroller back to normal mode is by reset.

- While the microcontroller is in Power Down mode, the state of all SFR registers and I/O ports remains unchanged. By setting it back into the normal mode, the contents of the SFR register is lost, but the content of internal RAM is saved.

- Reset signal must be long enough, approximately 10mS, to enable stable operation of the quartz oscillator.

Clock and Oscillator :

- This circuitry generates the clock pulses by which all internal operations are synchronized. Pins XTAL1 and XTAL2 are provided for connecting a resonant network to form an oscillator. A quartz crystal and capacitors can be used as shown in Fig. 1.9. The crystal frequency is the basic internal clock frequency of the microcontroller. Typically 1 MHz to 16 MHz is the oscillator frequency.

- Serial data communication needs frequency of the oscillator because of the requirement that internal counters must divide the basic clock rate to yield standard communication bit per second (baud) rates. If the basic clock frequency is not divisible without a remainder, then the resulting communication frequency is not standard.

- Ceramic resonators may be used as a low-cost alternative to crystal resonators.

- The oscillator formed by the crystal, capacitors, and an on-chip inverter generates a pulse train at the frequency of the crystal, as shown in Fig. 1.9.

- The clock frequency f, establishes the smallest interval of time within the Microcontroller called the pulse P, time. The smallest interval of time to accomplish any simple instruction or part of a complex instruction, however, is the machine cycle.

- The machine cycle is itself made up of six states. A state is the basic time interval for discrete operations of the microcontroller such as fetching an opcode byte, decoding an opcode, executing an opcodes, or writing a data byte. Two oscillator pulses define each state.

- Program instruction may require one, two, or four machine cycles to be executed, depending on the type of instruction. Instructions are fetched and executed by the microcontroller automatically, beginning with the instruction located at ROM memory address 0000h at the time the microcontroller is first reset.

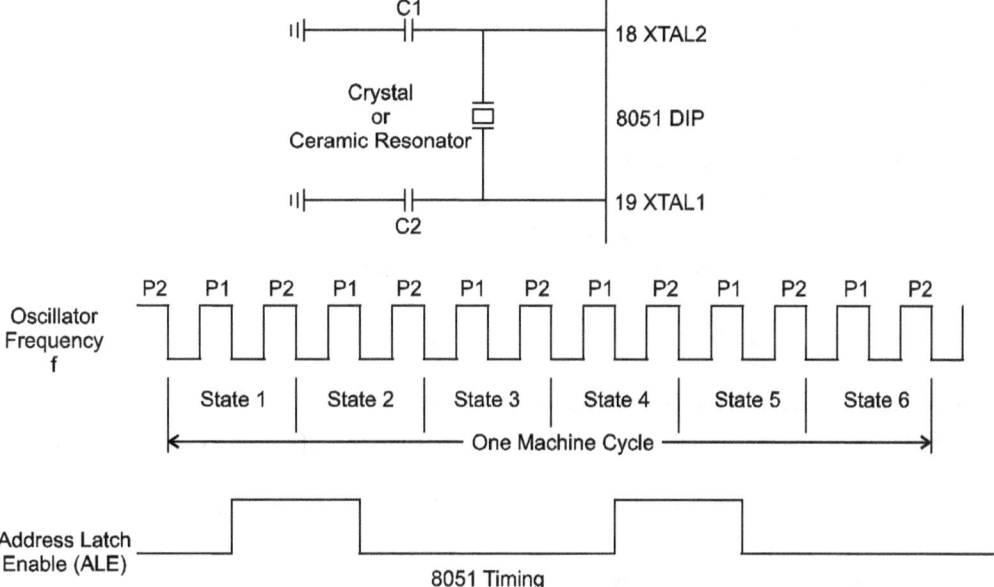

Fig. 1.9 : Timing diagram

- To calculate the time any particular instruction will take to be executed, find the number of cycles, C. The time to execute that instruction is then found by multiplying C by 12 and dividing the product by the crystal frequency.

  Tinst = (C * 12d) / Crystal Frequency

- For example, if the crystal frequency is 16 megahertz, then the time to execute an ADD A, R1 one-cycle instruction is 0.75 microseconds. A 12 megahertz crystal yields the convenient time of 1 microsecond per cycle. An 11.0592 megahertz crystal, although seemingly an odd value, yields a cycle frequency of 921.6 kilo hertz, which can be divided evenly by the standard communication baud rates of 19200, 9600, 4800, 2400, 1200, and 300 hertz.

- From the Fig. 1.9. it is clear that there are two ALE pulses per machine cycle. The ALE pulse, which is primarily used as a timing pulse for external memory access, indicates when every instruction byte is fetched. Two bytes of a single instruction may thus be fetched, and executed, in one machine cycle. Single- byte instructions are not executed in a half cycle, however. Single-byte instructions "throw-away" the second byte (which is the first byte of the next instruction.) The next instruction is then fetched in the following cycle.

Important Points

- It is an 8bit microcontroller.
- 8 bit accumulator, 8bit Register and 8bit ALU.
- On chip RAM 128 bites (data memory).
- On chip ROM 4 Kbytes (program memory).
- Two 16 bit counter/ timer.
- A 16 bit dptr (data pointer).
- Two levels of interrupt priority.
- Total 3 internal and 2 external interrupt.
- 4 byte bi-directional input/ output port i.e. 32 I/O lines.
- Power saving mode (on some derivatives).
- 16 bit address bus:-it can access 2^16 memory locations:-64 kb (65536) each of RAM and ROM.
- It is an inclusion of Boolean processing system, have an ability to allow logic operations to be carried out on registers and RAM.
- 8bit data bus:-it can access 8bit of data in one operation.
- UART (this serial communication port makes chip to use simply as a serial communication interface).
- It has four separate Register set. (Each contains 8 Registers (R0 to R7)).
- 16 byte bit addressable memory.
- 80 bytes general purpose memory.
- 8051 can process 1 million one-cycle instructions per second.
- Fully duplexed serial data receiver/transmitter (SBUF).
- Control register TMOD, TCON, SCON,SMOD, PCON, IP and IE.
- Oscillator and Clock circuit.

Practice Questions

1. Enlist the features of 89C51 microcontroller.
2. Draw the block diagram of 89C51 microcontroller.
3. Explain port 0 of 89C51 I/O ports.
4. Explain interrupt system of 89C51 microcontrollers.
5. Describe program memory and data memory.
6. Distinguish between RISC and CISC microcontroller.
7. Distinguish between Von Neumann and Harvard Architecture.
8. Describe all the flags of 89C51.
9. Can you use DPTR to access internal ROM?
10. Describe the memory structure of 89C51?
11. Draw format of PSW register and explain each bit.
12. Explain DSP and multicore processor.

MSBTE Questions

Summer 2012

1. Draw the port 3 structure of 8051 with neat label. Also list its alternate function of port 3.

2. Give any four applications of embedded system with example.

3. Draw and describe internal memory organization of 8051 etc.

4. Give an over view of 8051 family.

5. Draw PSW of 8051. State the function of each bit.

6. Draw the architecture of 8051.

7. State function of pin V_{PP}, PSSEN, PROG, ALE.

Winter 2012

1. Enlist any 8 feature of 8051 µc.

2. Write an alternate pin function of port 3. State function of each pin.

3. Draw the internal architecture of 8051 µc and state function of ALU and Boolean processor.

4. State difference between microprocessor and microcontroller.

5. Enlist any 8 special function register of 8051 microcontroller.

Summer 2013

1. Draw and describe memory organization of 8051 microcontroller.

2. Draw and describe format of PSW of 8051 microcontroller.

3. State the function of the following pins of 8051 microcontroller.

4. Draw internal architecture of 8051 microcontroller and state function of ALU and Boolean processor.

Winter 2013

1. List ports available with 8051 and state its alternate functions of port 3.

2. Draw pin diagram of 8051 and state function of each pin.

3. Draw the functional block diagram of 8051.

4. Explain detail of memory organization of 8051.

Summer 2014

1. Enlist any 8 features of 8051 µc.

2. Draw internal memory organization of 8051 µc.

3. Draw PSW of 8051 and state function of each bit.

4. Draw the architecture of 8051.

5. State function of pin V_{PP}, PSSEN, PROG, ALE.

Winter 2014

1. State function of $\overline{PSEN}$, $\overline{EA}$, XTAL1 pin of 8051.

2. Draw structure of internal RAM of 8051 and show how to select register bank.

3. List alternate function of port 3 pin.

4. Draw architecture of 8051.

✍ ✍ ✍

Chapter 2...

Instruction Set of 8051

Weightage of Marks = 16, Teaching Hours = 08

Specific Objectives

➤ Students will be able to

❖ Use the different types of instructions,

❖ Interpret addressing modes of instructions,

❖ Write syntax of the instructions.

2.1 INSTRUCTION SET OF 8051

- CPU can access data in various ways. The data source can be any of the following ways :

  1. Register.

  2. Memory.

  3. Immediate.

- There are various ways of accessing data; these various ways of accessing data are called Addressing Modes. 8051 supports five addressing modes those are :

  ➤ Immediate addressing mode.

  ➤ Register addressing mode.

  ➤ Direct addressing mode.

  ➤ Register indirect addressing mode.

  ➤ Indexed addressing mode.

- The instruction set is divided in to 5 categories. They are as follows :

  ➤ Arithmetic instructions.

  ➤ Logic instructions.

  ➤ Data transfer instructions.

> ➢ Boolean variable manipulation instruction.

> ➢ Program and machine control instruction.

2.1.1 Programmer Model

- The programming model of the 8051 is shown Fig. 2.1.

  > ➢ The 8051 consists of 8-bit and 16-bit registers and 8-bit memory locations. Using instructions, registers and memory can be accessed and operated.

  > ➢ The 8051 contains 34 general purpose or working registers. (4 Banks of 8-bit registers, and A, B registers).

  > ➢ Each register is referred with either symbolic name or the 8-bit address.

  > ➢ Each register, other than program counter, has an internal 1-byte address assigned to it.

  > ➢ The registers, which are marked with an asterisk '*', are bit and byte addressable.

  > ➢ Software instructions are generally able to specify a register by its address, symbolic name, or both.

  > ➢ A pin out of the 8051 packaged in a 40-pin DIP is shown in chapter-1 Fig. 1.3. The full and abbreviated names of the signals for each pin.

  > ➢ It is important to note that many of the pins are used for more than one function (the alternate functions are shown in Table 1.3 Chapter-1).

  > ➢ Programming instructions or physical pin connections determine the use of any multifunction pins. For example, port 3 bit 0 (abbreviated P3.0) may be used as a general-purpose I/O pin, or as an input (RXD) to SBUF, the serial data receiver register. The system designer decides which of these two functions is to be used and designs the hardware and software affecting that pin accordingly.

Program Counter and Data Pointer :

- The 8051 contains two 16-bit registers :
- Program Counter (PC) and
- Data Pointer (DPTR).
- Each is used to hold the 16-bit address of a byte in memory.

Program Counter :

- Program instruction bytes are fetched from locations in memory that are addressed by the PC. Program ROM may be on the chip at addresses 0000h to 0FFFh, external to the chip for addresses that exceed 0FFFh, or totally external for all addresses from 0000h to FFFFh.

- The PC is automatically incremented after every instruction byte is fetched and may also be altered by certain instructions. The PC is the only register that does not have an internal address. It cannot hold the address of the data memory.

Data Pointer (DPTR) :

- The DPTR register is made up of two 8-bit registers, named DPH and DPL, which are used to provide memory addresses for internal and external code access and external data access.

- The DPTR is under the control of program instructions and can be specified by its 16-bit name, DPTR, only each individual byte name, DPH and DPL. DPTR does not have a single internal address.

- DPH and DPL are each assigned an address. DPH is 83H and DPL is 82H. It is used as base register in Base Relative and Indirect Addressing mode.

A and B CPU Registers :

- Two of these, registers A and B, hold results of many instructions, particularly math and logical operations, of the 8051 central processing unit (CPU).

- The other 32 are arranged as a part of internal RAM in four banks, B0-B3, of eight registers and comprise the mathematical core.

Accumulator :

- The A (accumulator) register is used for many operations, including addition, subtraction, integer multiplication and division, and Boolean bit manipulations. It is used as pointer for look up table along with DPTR.

- Accumulator is also used for parity computation, testing zero, for rotating the data using rotate instruction.

- The A register is also used for all data transfers between the 8051 and any external memory. It is used for external memory expansion. It used as memory location and it is bit addressable. Memory address for accumulator is 0E0H.

  Example : MOV A, #40h or MOV OE0h, #40h.

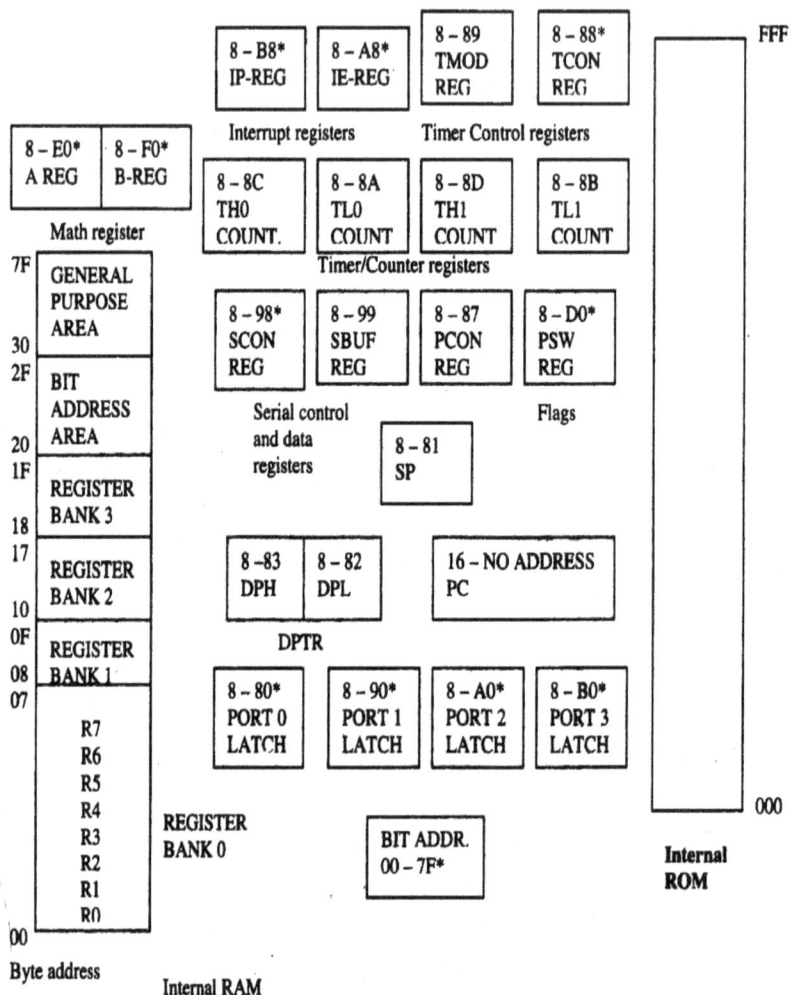

Fig. 2.1 : Programmer Model of 8051

B register :

- It is special MATHS register. The B register is used with the A register for multiplication and division operations and has no other function other than as a location where data may be stored.

- It used as memory location and it is bit addressable. Memory address for accumulator is 0F0H. Data cannot be directly transferred in B register. It is accessed using address only.

   Example : MOV 0F0h, #40h

Flags and the Program Status Word (PSW) :

- Flags are 1-bit registers used to store the results of operation performed by program instructions. Some can test the condition of the flags and make decisions based on the flag states. The flags are grouped :

1. In the program status word (PSW) and

2. The power control (PCON) registers.

Program Status Word :

7	6	5	4	3	2	1	0
CY	AC	FO	RS1	RS0	OV	X	P

Table 2.1 : A Program Status Word (PSW)

- The 8051 has four math flags affected by mathematical operations and three general-purpose user flags. These flags can be set to 1 or cleared to 0 by the programmer. The math flags include :

  - ➢ Carry (C),

  - ➢ Auxiliary Carry (AC),

  - ➢ Overflow (OV), and

  - ➢ Parity (P).

- User flags are named FO, GFO, and GF1; they are general-purpose flags that may be used by the programmer to record some event in the program.

- The program status word is shown in Table 2.1.

- The PSW contains 4 math flags, 1 user program flag F0, and 2 register select bits (RS1, RS0) that will select which of the four general-purpose register bank is currently in use by the program. The remaining two user flags, GFO and GF1, are stored in PCON.

CY	It is a **carry** flag. Internal hardware or software sets it. It is used in arithmetic, logical, jump, rotate and Boolean operations. In Boolean operation, it functions as an acc.
AC	It is also called half carry or **auxiliary carry**. It is used in BCD arithmetic operations.
FO	It is **user-defined** flag. The user defines the function of this flag. The user can test, clear and set this flag through software.

RS1, RS0	These flags are used to select only one bank of 8 registers. In default mode, it selects bank. The user can use only one bank of registers at a time. The programmer can use different banks for different programs.

RS1	RS1	Register Bank
0	0	Bank 0
0	1	Bank 1
1	0	Bank 2
1	1	Bank 3

OV	It is used in signed operations only. It is used to detect **overflow** in the signed arithmetic operations.
P	It is a **parity** flag. It shows the parity of data stored in the acc. If the number of 1's present in the acc is odd, then P flag is set. This flag is reset for even number of 1's present in the acc. The parity of the data including parity bit is always even. Hence, this flag can be used as even parity flag.

Table 2.2 : Program Status Word in Detail

The Stack and the Stack Pointer :

- The stack is an area of internal RAM that is used in along with certain opcodes to store and retrieve data quickly. The 8-bit Stack Pointer (SP) register is used by the 8051 to hold an internal RAM address that is called the Top Of the Stack (TOS). The address held in the SP register is the location in internal RAM, where the last byte of data was stored by a stack operation.

- When data is to be placed on the stack, the SP increments before storing data on the stack so that the stack grows up as data is stored. It is automatically incremented or with execution of PUSH and CALL instruction.

- As data is retrieved from the stack, the byte is read from the stack, and then the SP decrements to point to the next available byte of stored data. It is decremented by POP, RET, RETI instruction.

- The SP is set to 07h when the 8051 is reset and can be changed to any internal RAM address by the programmer, using a data move command. Stack Pointer is not used to store and retrieve the data from external Memory.

- The stack is limited in height to the size of the internal RAM. The stack has the potential (if the programmer is not careful to limit its growth) to over write valuable data in the register banks, bit-addressable RAM, and scratch pad RAM areas. The programmer is responsible for making sure the stack does not grow beyond predefined bounds!

- The stack is normally placed high in internal RAM, by an appropriate choice of the number placed in the SP register, to avoid conflict with the register, bit, and scratch-pad internal RAM areas.

Arithmetic and Logical Unit :

- It performs addition, subtraction, multiplication, division, logical AND, OR, EXOR, rotate, clear and complement operations. It manipulates 8-bit and 16-bit data. It consists of Boolean processor.

- The Boolean processor can perform bit set, test, clear, complement, move and all logical operations. It also performs internal data transfer operations. It makes condition branching decisions. It increments or decrements 8-bit registers. It can also increment or decrement 16-bit registers.

- It calculates the address of jump location in relative branch executions. It compares two bytes through subtraction. To execute one form of compare instruction, it increments the PC three times, reads three bytes of program memory, computes a register address with logical operations, reads internal data memory twice, makes arithmetic comparison of two variables, computes a sixteen bit destination address and decides whether or not to make a branch within two microseconds.

- The Boolean processor can be used for control applications.

2.1.2 Elements of Assembler

- Simple assembler is basically like any other language which means that it has the words, rules, and syntax. Basic elements are as follows :
  - ➢ Labels.
  - ➢ Operators.
  - ➢ Directives.
  - ➢ Comments.

Symbols/Keyword :

The asm keyword :

- This is an additional keyword, which allows you to insert assembly language statements directly into your C program. This keyword, when used, must appear as the first word of a line. Everything following this keyword - up to the end of line - is directly copied into the .ASM output file. It is to be noted that, no syntax checking is done by the compiler on this assembly language statement; it is done later on by the assembler.

The peripheral keyword :

- This is a keyword used to specify the address of a standard peripheral. In order to use these library functions, the compiler must somehow know the address of the peripheral being used. This keyword allows you to do so. The syntax is as follows :

peripheral periph_name = periph_addr

where periph_name is the name of the standard peripheral (e.g. "LCD") and periph_addr is its address written as a constant hex number (e.g. "0x4000").

Example :

Peripheral LCD = 0x4000;

The BIT Keyword :

- The BIT keyword is an additional (non-ANSI) keyword. It can be used to define pseudo variables of bit type. For example, suppose you are using bit 0 of P1 for some purpose, say to switch on a motor. Then you might like to assign a symbolic name to P1.0. Exactly this can be done using the BIT keyword. The syntax for using it is :

BIT identifier_name value

- Note that a BIT statement is NOT followed by a semicolon. The identifier can be any legal identifier name, which is not previously declared. The value must take these forms :

sfr_name.bit_addr

where sfr_name can be the name of any bit accessible SFR of 8051 and bit_addr may be any value between 0 and 7.

- Here are some examples of correct and incorrect BIT statements :

BIT motor p1.0　　　　　/* correct */

BIT limit_switch p3.6　　/* correct */

BIT motor p3　　　　　　/* wrong, because the bit_addr is missing */

BIT something dpl.2　　　/* wrong, because "dpl" is not a bit accessible SFR */

Declaring Variables at Specific Address (in Internal/External RAM) :

- This compiler allows the programmer to declare a variable at a specific address. The syntax for doing so is as follows :

var_type @addr var_name ;

or

var_type @Iaddr var_name ;

where 'var_type' is any legal data type (except bit) and 'var_name' is any legal identifier name and addr is any hexadecimal constant. In the first case, the variable 'var_name' is assigned an address = addr in external RAM, and in the later case, the variable 'var_name' is assigned an address = addr in internal RAM. Thus, in a variable declaration, if the variable type is followed by @ followed by a hexadecimal constant address, then the variable will reside at the specified address in external RAM. On the other hand, if the variable type is followed by @I (there should not be any space between @ and I) followed by a hexadecimal constant address, then the variable will reside at the specified address in internal RAM.

Example :

unsigned char @0x6000 dat_8279 ;   /* i.e. &dat_8279 is 0x6000 in external RAM */

unsigned char @0x6001 cmd_8279 ;   /* i.e. &cmd_8279 is 0x6001 in external RAM*/

int @0x2d var1 ;   /* i.e. &var1 is 0x2d in Internal RAM */

Assembler Directives :

- An *assembler directive* is a message to the assembler that tells the assembler something it needs to know in order to carry out the assembly process. For example, an assemble directive ORG the assembler where a program is to be located in memory.

- Directives are written to the column resaved for instructions. There is the rule allowing only one directive per program line.

EQU Directive :

- By means of this directive, a numeric value is replaced by a symbol. For example, MINIIMUM EQU 99

  After this directive, every appearance of the label "MINIIMUM" in the program, the assembler will interoperates as number 99 (MINIIMUM = 99).

- It is only once possible to define symbols in this way. So, the EQU directive is mostly used at the beginning of the program.

SET Directive :

- Similar to the EQU directive, by means of the SET directive, a numeric value is replaced by a symbol.

- Significant difference is that with this directive it can be done for unlimited number of times :

  UpperLimit SET 45

  UpperLimit SET 46

  UpperLimit SET 57

BIT Directive :

- By means of this directive, bit address is replaced by a symbol (bit address must be in the range of 0-255). For example,

  TRANSMIT BIT PSW.7   ; Transmit bit (the seventh bit in PSW register) is assigned the name "TRANSMIT"

  TPUT BIT 6   ; Bit at address 06 is assigned the name "OUTPUT"

  RELAY BIT 81   ; Bit at address 81 the name Port0 is assigned the name "REPLY"

CODE Directive :

- By means of this directive, an address in program memory is designated as a symbol. Since the maximal capacity of program memory is 64 K, the address must be in the range of 0-65535. For example,

  RESET CODE 0   ; Memory location 00h called "RESET"

  TABLE CODE 1024   ; Memory locution 1024h called "TABLE"

DATA Directive :

- By means of this directive, an address within internal RAM is designated as a symbol (address must be in the range of 0-255). In other words, any selected register may change its name or be assigned a new one. For example,

  TEMP12 DATA 32   ; Register at address 32 is named as "TEMP12"

  STATUS_R DATA D0h   ; PSW register is assigned the name "STATUS_R"

IDATA Directive :

- By means of this directive, indirectly addressed register located in the specified address changes its name or is assigned a new one. For example,

  TEMP22 IDATA 32   ; Register whose address is in register at address 32 is named as "TEMP22"

  TEMP33 IDATA T_ADR   ; Register whose address is in register T_ADR is named as "TEMP33"

XDATA directive :

- This directive is used to name registers within external additional RAM memory Address of such defined register cannot be greater than 65535. For example,

  TABLE_1 XDATA 2048 ; Register stored in external memory at address 2048 is named as "TABLE_1"

ORG Directive :

- This directive is used to define location in program where the program following a directive is to be placed. For example,

BEGINNING ORG 100

...

...

ORG 1000h

TABLE

...

...

Program begins at location 100. The table with data will start at location 1024 (1000h).

USING Directive :

- This directive is used to define which register bank (registers R0-R7) will be used in the following program :

  USING 0, Bank 0 is used (registers R0-R7 at RAM-addresses 0-7)

  USING 1, Bank 1 is used (registers R0-R7 at RAM-addresses 8-15)

  USING 2, Bank 2 is used (registers R0-R7 at RAM-addresses 16-23)

  USING 3, Bank 3 is used (registers R0-R7 at RAM-addresses 24-31)

END Directive :

- This directive must be at the end of every program. Once it encounters this directive, the assembler will stop interpreting program into machine code. For example,

  ...

  END

  ...

  End of program

DS Directive :

- This directive reserves space in memory expressed in bytes. It is used, if the segment ISEG, DSEG or XSEG is currently active.

  Example 1 :

  DSEG　　　　　　　　; Selects part of RAM with direct addressing

  DS 32　　　　　　　　; Actual value of address counter is incremented by 32

  SP_BFF DS 16　　　　; Reserves space for serial part buffer (16 Bytes)

  IO_BUFF DS 8　　　　; Reserves space for I/O buffer in size of 8 Bytes

  Example 2 :

  ORG 100　　　　　　　; Starts at address 100

  DS 8　　　　　　　　; 8 bytes are reserved

  LAB ......　　　　　　; Program continues execution (address of this location is 108)

DBIT Directive :

- This directive reveres space within bit-addressable of RAM (size is expressed in bits). It can be used, only if the BSEG segment is active. For example,

  BSEG   ; Bit-addressable part of RAM is selected

  IO_MAPDBIT 32   ; First 32 bits occupy space provided for I/O Buffer

DB Directive :

- This directive is used for writing indicated value to program memory.

- If several values are indicated one after another, then they are separated by commas.

- If ASCII array is indicated, it is enclosed with single quotation marks. This directive can be also used, only if the segment CSEG is active. For example,

  CSEG

  DB 22,33, 'Alarm',44

  when written before this directive, the label will point to the first value in the array.

DW Directive :

- This directives has the same purpose as DB directive, but it is followed by two-byte value (the high byte is written first, the low byte afterwards).

Control Directives :

- These directives are recognized by having the dollar symbol ($) as the first letter. These commands are used to define which files are to be used by assembler during compiling.

- It is used to determine where executed file is to be stored as well as the final appearance of the compiled program.

- Although, there are many directives belonging to this category, only few for them are really important :

$INCLUDE Directive :

- The name of these directives tells enough about its purpose. During compiling, it enables assembler to use data stored in another file. For example,

  $INCLUDE (TABLE.ASM)

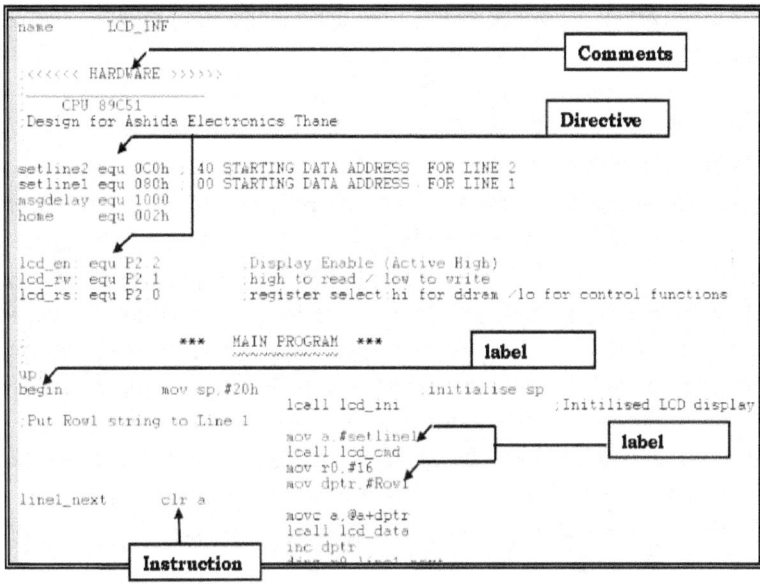

Fig. 2.2 : Use of Directives in a program

2.1.3 Addressing Mode

- Addressing mode defines the way of the data source or destination address is specified in the mnemonics that moves the data.

2.1.3.1 Register Addressing Mode

- In this addressing mode, source and destination register are specified in the opcode itself. Hence, the length of instruction in this addressing mode is One byte.

D7	D6	D5	D4	D3	D2	D1	D0
Opcode			Destination		Source		
Opcode			Rd		Rs		
One Byte							

- Register can be used as part of the opcode mnemonic as sources or destinations of data. Registers A, B, DPTR, Carry bit and R0 to R7 may be named as part of the op-code mnemonic.

- Instructions are of two categories in Register Addressing mode :

  1. Single Operand : Only one register is used in such instruction. For example, INR R0.

2. Two Operand : Two registers are used, one as source and another as destination. For example, MOV A, R0.

2.1.3.2 Immediate Addressing Mode

- In Immediate addressing mode, data source is part of an instruction. Since the data is part of instruction memory, the operand is also located in program memory.

- The operand may be of 8-bit or 16-bit, hence instruction can be of 2 bytes (8-bit operand) and it can be of 3 bytes (16-bit operand).

- The mnemonic symbol of immediate data is pound sign (#). This addressing mode instruction can be used to load data in any register including DPTR.

Opcode	8-bit operand
First Byte	Second byte
Format for 8-bit Operand – 2 Byte Instruction	

Opcode	8-bit operand	8-bit operand
First Byte	Second Byte	Third Byte
Format for 16-bit operand – 3-byte instruction		

2.1.3.3 Direct Addressing Mode

- In this mode, the address of data memory location is specified in the instruction itself. In this mode, source, destination or both data can be stored in the memory. In this addressing mode, at least one data should be stored in memory. The address of the data memory is always 8-bit long.

- The length of the instruction will be of 2 bytes. If one data is in memory, whether it is source or destination, it requires one 8-bit address.

- The length of the instruction will be of 3 bytes. If both source and destination data are in memory, it requires two 8-bit addresses.

- In this mode, all internal registers, other than PC, can be used as data memory location. These types of instruction are not used for accessing external data memory.

- All SFR, ports, internal RAM locations, register banks can be used as memory address.

- Internal RAM address is starting from 00H-7FH and SFR addresses are starting from 80H–FFH.

- If, by mistake, # sign is missing, then, instead of considering data as part on instruction register, it will considered as data.

Opcode	8-bit Address
First Byte	Second Byte

Format for 8-bit Address – 2 Byte Instruction

Opcode	8-bit – Destination Memory Address	8-bit – Source Memory Address
First Byte	Second Byte	Third Byte

Format for 16-bit Address – 3 byte Instruction

2.1.3.4 Indirect Address Mode

- In this addressing mode, address of data memory is stored in a pointer. At least one data should be stored in memory. In this addressing mode, registers R0 and R1 are used to store 8-bit address and DPTR is used to store 16-bit address.

- This address mode can be used to access data from both internal as well as external memory location.

- The instructions with 'X' in mnemonics (MOVX) are used to access external data memory and the instructions with 'C' in mnemonics (MOVC) are used to access internal and external program memory.

- The length of the instruction in this addressing mode is one byte because address is not directly specified. The pointers holding the address of the memory location are preceded by 'at' i.e. '@' sign.

- If, by mistake, @ sign is missing, then, instead of considering register as pointer (Address register), it will considered as data register.

- It is also called register indirect addressing mode because register is used to point memory where data is stored.

- SFR cannot be addressed by this addressing mode. Similarly, external memory address beyond lower 256 bytes cannot be addressed.

D7	D6	D5	D4	D3	D2	D1	D0
Opcode							
One Byte							

2.1.3.5 Indexed Addressing Mode

- This mode allows a byte to be accessed from the program memory, whose address is calculated as the sum of a base register (DPTR or PC) and index register, accumulator.

- For example, the instruction MOVC A, @A + DPTR will fetch the byte from the program memory, whose address is calculated by adding the original 8-bit unsigned content of the accumulator and the 16-bit content of the DPTR. This method is generally used for look up table programming.

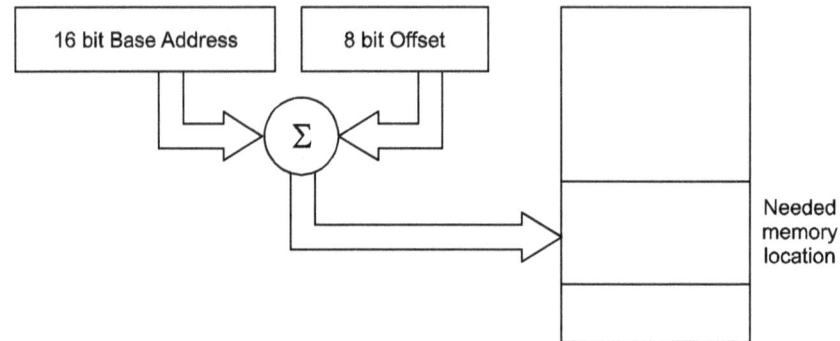

Fig. 2.3 : Indexed Addressing

Symbols and Their Meaning :

Symbol	Explanation
Rn	Register R7-R0 of the currently selected Register Bank.
Direct	8-bit internal data location's address. This could be an Internal Data RAM location (0-127) or a SFR [i.e., I/O port, control register, status register, etc. (128-255)].
@Ri	8-bit internal data RAM location (0-255) addressed indirectly through register R1or R0.
#data	8-bit constant included in instruction.
#data 16	16-bit constant included in instruction.
Addr16	16-bit destination address. Used by LCALL and LJMP. A branch can be anywhere within the 64 K byte program memory address space.
Addr11	11-bit destination address. Used by ACALL and AJMP. The branch will be within the same 2 K byte page of program memory as the first byte of the following instruction.
Rel	Signed (two's complement) 8-bit offset byte. Used by SJMP and all conditional jumps. Range is –128 to +127 bytes relative to first byte of the following instruction.
bit	Direct Addressed bit in Internal Data RAM or Special Function Register.

Abbreviation	Explanation
#	Immediate Operand
@	Indirect operand in which the address of operand is stored in pointer
C	Carry Flag
Rr	Working Register R0-R7
Rp	8-bit memory pointer in R0-R1
X	External memory access
C	Code memory access
A	A register
A	Absolute Branch Address
S	Short Branch
L	Long Branch
b	Bit Address
[A]	Content of A register
[(ADD}]	Content of memory where add is the address of that memory
[(Rp)]	Content of memory where the address of memory is stored in Rp
M	Machine Cycle
N	Flag in not affected
AF	Flag is affected

2.1.4 Data Transfer Instructions

- These instructions are used to copy contents of source into destination. In this case, the contents of source are not modified. These instructions do not affect flags except carry in bit manipulation. The instruction that contains 'X' letter in mnemonic is only used to access external data memory.

- Other instructions are never used to access external data memory. The instruction that contains 'C' in mnemonic is only used to access program memory. Other instructions are never used to access program memory. The stack pointer always point internal RAM.

Address Mode Register Addressing Mode	Flag – Affected are None
Instruction	**Operation/Symbol/Byte**
MOV A, Rr Rr = R0 – R7	Copy the content register Rr into Acc. [A] ← [Rr] 1Byte instruction
MOV Rr, A Rr = R0 – R7	Copy the content register Acc into Rr. [Rr] ← [A] 1 Byte Instruction.
XCH A, Rr Rr = R0 – R7	Exchange the content of Acc with the content of the specified register. [A]←→[Rr] 1 Byte Instruction.
Addressing Mode Immediate Addressing Mode	**Flag – Affected are None**
MOV A, #n n – 8-bit data	Load 8-bit number n into A register [A] ← n 1 Byte Instruction.

MOV Rr, #n
Rr = R0-R7
	Load 8-bit number n into Rr Register
	[Rr]← n 1 Byte Instruction.

MOV DPTR, #nn Nn – 16-bit data	Load 16-bit number nn into DPTR register [DPTR]←nn 1 Byte Instruction.
Addressing Mode Direct Addressing Mode	**Flag – Affected are None**
MOV A, add	Copy content of data memory into Acc. Where add is an 8-bit address of memory location [A]← [(add)] 2 Byte Instruction.
MOV add, A add = 8-bit address of data memory location	Copy content of Acc into data memory. Where add is an 8-bit address of memory location [(add)]←[A] 2 Byte Instruction.
MOV Rr, add	Copy content of data memory into Rr register. Where add is an 8-bit address of memory location. [Rr]←[(add)] 2 Byte Instruction.
MOV add, Rr Rr = R0-R7	Copy content of Rr into data memory. Where add is an 8-bit address of memory location. [(add)]←[Rr] 2 Byte Instruction.

MOV add1,add2	Copy content of source memory location into destination memory location. Where add1 is the address of the destination memory and add2 is the address of the source memory location. [(add1)]← [(add2)] 3 Byte Instruction.
XCH A, add	Exchange the content of A register with the content of data memory location. where add is the add of the data memory location [A] ←→[(add)] 2 Byte Instruction.

Addressing Mode **Immediate and Direct Address Mode**	**Flag – Affected are None**
MOV add, #n	Load 8-bit data n into memory location, whose add is an 8-bit address of memory location; this 8-bit address is part of instruction. [(add)]←n 2 Byte Instruction.

Addressing Mode – **Indirect Address Mode**	**Flag – Affected are None**
MOV A, @Rp Rp = R0, R1	Copy the content of data memory into register A, here register Rp specify 8-bit address of the data memory. (A)←[(Rp)] 1 Byte Instruction.
MOV @Rp, A	Copy the content of Acc into data memory, here register Rp specify 8-bit address of the data memory. [(Rp)]←(A) 1 Byte Instruction.
MOVX A, @Rp	Copy contents of external data memory into A register. The Address of external data memory is stored in Rp. (A)←[(Rp)] 1 Byte Instruction.
MOVX @Rp, A	Copy the content of Acc into data memory, here register Rp specify 8-bit address of the data memory. [(Rp)]←(A) 1 Byte Instruction.
MOVX A, @DPTR	Copy content of external data memory into A register, Address of external memory is stored in DPTR. [A]← [(DPTR)] 1 Byte Instruction.
MOVX @DPTR,A	Copy content of Register A into external data memory, Address of external memory is stored in DPTR. [(DPTR)]←[A] 1 Byte Instruction.

MOVC A, @A+DPTR	Copy content of code or program memory into Register A. Address of the code memory or program memory is content of DPTR + content of Register A. [A]←[(A+DPTR)] 1Byte Instruction.
XCH A, @Rp	[A] ←→[(Rp)] Exchange content of Register A with the content of data location, 1 Byte Instruction.
XCHD A, @Rp	Exchange lower nibble of A register with lower nibble of data location. Address of data memory is stored in Rp. [A$_{lower}$]←→[Rp$_{lower}$] 1 Byte Instruction.
Addressing Mode – Immediate and Indirect Address mode	**Flag – affected are None**
MOV @Rp, #n	Load data n into memory location, where the address of memory location is stored in Rp. [(Rp)]←n 1 Byte Instruction.
Addressing Mode – Indirect and Direct Address mode	**Flag – affected are None**
MOV add, @Rp	Copy content of source data memory location into destination data memory location, where the address of source data memory is stored in Rp, while add is the address of destination data memory location. [(add)]←[(Rp)] 1 Byte Instruction.
MOV @Rp, add	Copy content of source data memory location into destination data memory location, where the address of destination data memory is stored in Rp, while add is the address of source data memory location. [(Rp)]←[(add)] 1 Byte Instruction.
PUSH add	Increment Sp by 1 and then copy the content of data memory location 8-bit on current stack location, where add is an 8-bit address of the data memory while the address of the stack top is stored in Sp [(Sp)]←[(add)] [(Sp)]←[(Sp+1)] 1 Byte Instruction.

POP add	Copy the content of Stack top into data memory location and then decrement Sp by 1, where add is an 8-bit address of the data memory while the address of the stack top is stored in Sp. [(add)]←[(Sp)] [(Sp)]←[(Sp-1)] 1 Byte Instruction.
Addressing Mode – Bit Register	**Flag – Affected are None**
MOV C, b	Copy the content of memory bit into carry flag, where b is an 8-bit address of a memory bit. [C]←[b] 1 Byte Instruction.
MOC b, C	Copy the content of carry flag into memory bit, where b is an 8-bit address of a memory bit. [b]←[C] 1 Byte Instruction.

2.1.5 Arithmetic Instructions

- The 8051 provides arithmetic instructions for binary addition, subtraction, multiplication and division. It also provides a separate instruction to correct the result of BCD addition. These instructions affect flags. These instructions process only bytes not bits. There are two types of arithmetic instructions viz., single operand and two operands. These instructions do not perform arithmetic operation on external data memory.

2.1.5.1 Arithmetic Instruction – Single Operand

Addressing Mode – Register		Flags		
Instruction	**Operation Symbol Byte/Machine Cycle**	**C/OV/AC**		
INC A	Increment the content of register A by 1 and store the result in Register A [A] ← [A+1] 1 Byte Instruction.	N	N	N
INC Rr Rr =Ro- R7	Increment the content of register Rr by 1 and store the result in Register Rr [Rr]←[Rr+1] 1 Byte Instruction.	N	N	N
INC DPTR	Increment the content of register DPTR by 1 and store the result in Register DPTR. [DPTR] ←[DPTR+1] 1 Byte Instruction.	N	N	N
DEC A	Decrement the content of register A by 1 and store the result in Register A. [A] ← [A-1] 1Byte Instruction.	N	N	N

DEC Rr Rr = R0 – R7	Decrement the content of register Rr by 1 and store the result in Register Rr. [Rr]←[Rr-1] 1Byte Instruction.	N	N	N
DA A	Convert the Binary result into BCD, i.e. Decimal Adjust Accumulator. This instruction adds 06H, if AC flag is set or lower nibble result is greater than 09H. Also it adds 06H to higher nibble, if CY flag is set or higher nibble result is greater than 09H. [A] ←[A+06] 1 Byte Instruction.	Y	N	Y

Addressing Mode – Direct		Flags		
Instruction	**Operation/Symbol/Byte/Machine Cycle**	**C/OV/AC**		
INC add	Increment the content of data memory by 1, where add is 8-bit address of the data memory. [(add)] ← [(add)+1] 2 Byte Instruction.	N	N	N
DEC add	Decrement the content of data memory by 1, where add is 8-bit address of the data memory. [(add)] ← [(add)-1] 2 Byte Instruction.	N	N	N

Addressing Mode – Indirect		Flags		
Instruction	**Operation/Symbol/Byte/Machine Cycle**	**C/OV AC**		
INC @Rp Rp = R0, R1	Increment the content of data memory by 1, where 8-bit address of the data memory is stored in Register Rp. [(Rp)] ← [(Rp)+1] 1 Byte Instruction.	N	N	N
DEC @Rp Rp = R0, R1	Decrement the content of data memory by 1, where 8-bit address of the data memory is stored in register Rp. [(Rp)] ← [(Rp)-1] 1 Byte Instruction.	N	N	N

2.1.5.2 Arithmetic Instruction – Two Operand

Addressing Mode – Register		Flags		
Instruction	Symbol/Operation/Byte/Machine Cycle	C/OV/AC		
Add A, Rr Rr = R0-R7	Add content of Register Rr with the content of register A and store the result in A register. [A]← [A + Rr] 1Byte Instruction.	Y	Y	Y
ADDC A, Rr Rr = R0-R7	Add content of Register Rr and Content of carry flag with the content of register A and store the result in A register. [A]← [A + Rr + C] 1Byte Instruction.	Y	Y	Y
SUBB A, Rr Rr = R0-R7	Subtract content of Register Rr and Content of carry flag with the content of register A and store the result in A register. [A]← [A-Rr-C] 1Byte Instruction.	Y	Y	Y
MUL AB	Multiply content of register A (Multiplicand) with content of Register B(Multiplier) and Store the result in register B(Upper Byte) and Register A (Lower Byte). [B,A]← [A X B] 1Byte Instruction.	Y	Y	N
DIV AB	Divide content of register A(Dividend) with content of Register B(Divisor) and Store the result in register B(remainder) and Register A(Quotient). [B,A]←[A/B] 1Byte Instruction.	Y	Y	N

Addressing Mode – Immediate		Flags		
Instruction	Operation/Symbol/Byte/Machine Cycle	C/OV/AC		
Add A, #n	Add 8-bit number n with the content of register A and store the result in A register [A] ← [A + n] 2 Byte Instruction.	Y	Y	Y
ADDC A, #n	[Add 8-bit number n and Content of carry flag with the content of register A and store the result in A register A] ← [A + n + C] 2 Byte Instruction.	Y	Y	Y

SUBB A, #n	Subtract 8-bit number n and Content of carry flag with the content of register A and store the result in A register [A]← [A-n-C] 2 Byte Instruction.	Y	Y	Y

Addressing Mode – Direct		Flags		
Instruction	Operation/Symbol/Byte/Machine Cycle	C/OV/AC		
Add A, add	Add content of data memory with the content of register A and store the result in A register. The 8-bit address of data memory is added. [A]← [A+(add)] 2 Byte Instruction.	Y	Y	Y
ADDC A, add	Add content of data memory and Content of carry flag with the content of register A and store the result in A register. The 8-bit address of data memory is added. [A] ← [A+(add)+C] 1 Byte Instruction.	Y	Y	Y
SUBB A, add	Subtract content of data memory and Content of carry flag with the content of register A and store the result in A register. The 8-bit address of data memory is add. [A] ← [A-n-C] 2 Byte Instruction.	Y	Y	Y

Addressing Mode – Indirect		Flags		
Instruction	Symbol/Operation Byte/Machine Cycle	C/OV/AC		
Add A, @Rp Rp=R0,R1	Add content of data memory with the content of register A and store the result in A register. The 8-bit address of data memory is stored in Rp. [A] ← [A+(Rp)] 1 Byte Instruction.	Y	Y	Y
ADDC A, @Rp Rp=R0,R1	Add content of data memory and Content of carry flag with the content of register A and store the result in A register. The 8-bit address of data memory is stored in Rp. [A]← [A+(Rp)+C] 1 Byte Instruction.	Y	Y	Y

SUBB A, @Rp Rp=R0,R1	Subtract content of data memory and Content of carry flag with the content of register A and store the result in A register. The 8-bit address of data memory is stored in Rp. [A]← [A-(Rp)-C] 1 Byte Instruction.	Y	Y	Y

2.1.6 Logical Instruction

- 8051 provides logical instructions for AND, OR, EXOR, NOT, clear, set, rotate and swap logical operations.

- These instructions process bytes and bits. These instructions affect on only carry flag.

- The 8051 is powerful in logical operation as compared to other processor. There are two types of logical instructions viz. Single operand instruction and two operand instruction.

- These instructions do not perform logical operations on external data memory.

2.1.6.1 Logical Operator – Single Operand

Addressing Mode – Register		Flags		
Instruction	Operation/Symbol/Byte/Machine Cycle	C/OV/AC		
CLR A	Increment the content of register A by 1 and store the result in Register A. [A] ← [00] 1 Byte Instruction.	N	N	N
CPL A	Increment the content of register Rr by 1 and store the result in Register Rr [A]←[A] 1 Byte Instruction.	N	N	N
RLA	Rotate the content of Register A left by one bit position. For example A_7 bit is transferred to A_0 and so on. $A_0 \leftarrow A_7$ $A_7 \leftarrow A_6$ similarly $A_1 \leftarrow A_0$ 1 Byte Instruction.	N	N	N

RLCA	Rotate the content of Register A left by one bit position through carry. For example, A_7 bit is transferred to C and Carry content are transferred to A_0 and so on. $C \leftarrow A_7$ $A_0 \leftarrow A_7$ $A_7 \leftarrow A_6$ similarly $A_1 \leftarrow A_0$ 1 Byte Instruction.	Y	N	N
RRA	Rotate the content of register A right by one bit position. For example, A_0 bit is transferred to A_7 and so on. $A_7 \leftarrow A_0$ $A_6 \leftarrow A_7$ similarly $A_0 \leftarrow A_1$ 1 Byte Instruction.	N	N	N
RRCA	Rotate the content of register A right by one bit position through carry. For example, A_0 bit is transferred to C and carry content are transferred to A_7. and so on. $A_7 \leftarrow C$ $A_7 \leftarrow A_0$ $A_6 \leftarrow A_7$ similarly $A_0 \leftarrow A_1$ 1 Byte Instruction.	Y	N	N
SWAP A	Exchange the content of lower nibble with higher nibble of register A. This instruction is generally used in masking, packing, unpacking packed BCD numbers. $A_{Lower} \leftarrow \rightarrow A_{upper}$ 1 Byte Instruction.	N	N	N

2.1.6.2 Logical Bit Wise Instruction

Addressing Mode – Register		Flags		
Instruction	Operation/Symbol/Byte/Machine Cycle	C	OV	AC
CLR C	Clear Carry flag, i.e. make the content of carry flag as 0. [C] ← 0 1 Byte Instruction.	Y	N	N

| CPL C | Complement carry flag, i.e. make the content of carry flag as complement of previous data. [C] ← ~[C 1 Byte Instruction. | Y | N | N |
| SETB C | Set Carry flag, i.e. make the content of carry flag as 1. [C]←1 1 Byte Instruction. | Y | N | N |

Addressing Mode – Register		Flags		
Instruction	Operation/Symbol/Byte/Machine Cycle	C	OV	AC
CLR b	Clear the content of data bit, where b is 8-bit address of the data memory location. [b] ← 0 1 Byte Instruction.	N	N	N
CPL b	Complement the content of data bit, where b is 8-bit address of the data memory location. [b]←~[C] 1 Byte Instruction.	N	N	N
SETB b	Set the content of data bit, where b is 8-bit address of the data memory location. [b]←1 1 Byte Instruction.	N	N	N

2.1.6.3 Logical Instruction – Two Operand

Addressing Mode – Register		Flags		
Instruction	Symbol/Operation/Byte/Machine Cycle	C	OV	AC
ANL A, Rr ^ = AND	Logically AND the content of register Rr with content of register A and store the result in register A. [A] ← [A] ^ [Rr] 1 Byte Instruction.	N	N	N
ORL A, Rr V = OR	Logically OR the content of register Rr with content of register A and store the result in register A. [A] ← [A] V [Rr] 1 Byte Instruction.	N	N	N
XRL A, Rr V = XOR	Logically XOR the content of register Rr with content of Register A and Store the result in register A. [A] ← [A] ∀ [Rr] 1 Byte Instruction.	N	N	N

Addressing Mode – Immediate		Flags		
Instruction	Symbol/Operation/Byte/Machine Cycle	C	OV	AC
ANL A, #n ^ = AND n = 8-bit immediate data	Logically AND immediate data of 8-bit n with content of register A and store the result in register A. [A] ←[A] ^ [n] 2 Byte Instruction.	N	N	N

ORL A, #n
V = OR
	Logically OR immediate data of 8-bit n with content of register A and store the result in register A.
	
	[A] ← [A] V [n] 2 Byte Instruction.
		N	N	N

XRL A, #n
V = XOR
	Logically XOR immediate data of 8-bit n with content of register A and store the result in register A.
	
	[A] ← [A] ∀ [n] 2 Byte Instruction.
		N	N	N

Addressing Mode – Direct		Flags		
Instruction	Symbol/Operation/Byte/Machine Cycle	C	OV	AC
ANL A, add ^ = AND add = 8-bit address of the data memory	Logically AND content of 8-bit data memory with content of register A and store the result in register A, where add is an 8-bit address of data memory. [A] ← [A] ^ [(add)] 2 Byte Instruction.	N	N	N
ORL A, add V = OR	Logically OR content of 8-bit data memory with content of register A and store the result in register A, where add is an 8-bit address of data memory. [A] ← [A] V [(add)] 2 Byte Instruction.	N	N	N
XRL A, add V = XOR	Logically XOR content of 8-bit data memory with content of register A and store the result in register A, where add is an 8-bit address of data memory. [A] ← [A] ∀ [(add)] 2 Byte Instruction.	N	N	N

ANL add, A ^ = AND add = 8-bit address of the data memory	Logically AND content of 8-bit data memory with content of register A and store the result in data memory location, where add is an 8-bit address of data memory. [add] ← [A] ^ [(add)] 2 Byte Instruction.	N	N	N
ORL add, A V = OR	Logically OR content of 8-bit data memory with content of register A and store the result in data memory location, where add is an 8-bit address of data memory. [add] ← [A] V [(add)] 2 Byte Instruction.	N	N	N
XRL add, A V = XOR	Logically XOR content of 8-bit data memory with content of register A and store the result in data memory location, where add is an 8-bit address of data memory. [add] ← [A] ∀ [(add)] 2Byte instruction.	N	N	N

Addressing Mode – Immediate and Direct		Flags		
Instruction	**Symbol/Operation/Byte/Machine Cycle**	**C**	**OV**	**AC**
ANL add,#n ^ = AND add = 8-bit address of the data memory	Logically AND content of 8-bit data memory with immediate 8-bit data n and Store the result in data memory location. where add is an 8-bit address of data memory. [add] ← [A] ^[n] 3 Byte Instruction.	N	N	N

ORL add, #n
V = OR
	Logically OR content of 8-bit data memory with immediate 8-bit data n and store the result in data memory location, where add is an 8-bit address of data memory.
	[add] ← [A] V [n] 3 Byte Instruction.
		N	N	N

XRL add, #n
V = XOR
	Logically XOR content of 8-bit data memory with immediate 8-bit data n and store the result in data memory location, where add is an 8-bit address of data memory.
	[add] ← [A] ∀ [n] 3 Byte Instruction.
		N	N	N

Addressing Mode – Indirect		Flags		
Instruction	**Symbol/Operation/Byte/Machine Cycle**	**C**	**OV**	**AC**
ANL A, @Rp ∧ = AND Rp = store 8-bit address of the data memory	Logically AND content of 8-bit data memory with content of register A and store the result in register A, where Rp stores the address of 8-bit data memory. [A] ← [A] ∧ [(Rp)] 1 Byte Instruction.	N	N	N
ORL A, @Rp V = OR	Logically OR content of 8-bit data memory with content of register A and store the result in register A, where Rp stores the address of 8-bit data memory. [A] ← [A] V [(Rp)] 1 Byte Instruction.	N	N	N
XRL A, @Rp V = XOR	Logically XOR content of 8-bit data memory with content of register A and Store the result in register A, where Rp stores the address of 8-bit data memory. [A] ← [A] ∀ [(Rp)] 1 Byte Instruction.	N	N	N

2.1.6.4 Logical Instruction – Two Operand

Addressing Mode – Direct Bit		Flags		
Instruction	**Symbol/Operation/Byte/Machine Cycle**	**C**	**OV**	**AC**
ANL C, b ∧ = AND	Logically AND content of a data memory bit with content of carry flag and store the result in carry flag, where b is the 8-bit address of data memory bit. [C] ← [C ∧ b] 2 Byte Instruction.	N	N	N
ORL C, b V = OR	Logically OR content of a data memory bit with content of carry flag and store the result in carry flag, where b is the 8-bit address of data memory bit. [C] ← [C V b] 1 Byte Instruction.	N	N	N
XRL C, b V = XOR	Logically XOR content of a data memory bit with content of carry flag and store the result in carry flag, where b is the 8-bit address of data memory bit [C] ← [C ∀ b] 2 Byte Instruction.	N	N	N

ORL C, b V = OR	Complement content of data memory bit and logically OR content of a data memory bit with content of carry flag and store the result in carry flag, where b is the 8-bit address of data memory bit. [C] ← [C] V [b] 2 Byte Instruction.	N	N	N

2.1.6.5 Branch Group

- These instructions are used to change the program execution sequence.
- The 8051 provides powerful branch instructions. It provides branch instructions along with compare and decrement operations. Hence, it provides powerful instructions for looping.

Important Abbreviation Used :

S_{add}	S_{add} = 11 bit address of jump location.
Ladd	Ladd = 16 bit address of jump location.
R_{add}	r_{add} is 8-bit signed displacement represented in 2's complement form.
b	8-bit direct address of data memory bit → for bit wise operation.
n	8-bit immediate data.
Rr	Register R0-R7, to store 8-bit data, used in register addressing mode.
Rp	Register R0, R1, to store 8-bit address of data memory, used as indirect address.
add	8-bit direct address of data memory → for byte wise operation

Addressing Mode – Direct Bit	Flag Affected are None
Instruction	**Operation/Symbol/Byte/Machine Cycle**
AJMP S_{add} Unconditional absolute jump.	Jump to target program unconditionally, where s_{add} is 11-bit address of jump location. Upper 5 bits of jump remain constant. Upper 3 bits of 11-bit address are indicated by opcode bytes. [PC$_{11}$]←sadd$_{11}$ 2 Byte Instruction.

ACALL s_{add} Unconditional Call	Save the content of program counter PC at two stack location by incrementing SP twice and then jump to target program unconditionally, where s_{add} is 11-bit address of subprogram location. Upper 5 bits of subprogram location remain constant. Upper 3 bits of 11-bit address of subprogram are indicated by opcode byte. [Sp+1]←[PCL] [Sp+2]←[PCH] [SP]←[Sp+2] [PC$_{11}$]←sadd$_{11}$ 2 Byte Instruction.
LJMP l_{add} Unconditional long jump.	Jump to target program unconditionally, where L_{add} is 16-bit address of jump location. [PC]←[s_{add}] 3 Byte Instruction.
LCALL s_{add} Unconditional Call	Save the content of program counter PC at two stack location by incrementing SP twice and then jump to target program unconditionally, where Ladd is 16-bit address of sub program location. [Sp+1]←[PCL] [Sp+2]←[PCH] [SP]←[Sp+2] [PC]←Ladd 3 Byte Instruction.

Addressing Mode – Direct/Relative	Flag Affected are None
Instruction	**Operation/Symbol/Byte/Machine Cycle**
JC r_{add} Conditional Jump on Carry.	Jump to target program, if carry flag is set, where r_{add} is 8-bit signed displacement represented in 2's complement form; else execute next instruction of the current. [PC]←[PC + r_{add}] if CY = 1 else [PC]←[PC+1] 2 Byte Instruction.

JNC r_{add} Conditional Jump on no Carry.	Jump to target program, if carry flag is not set, where r_{add} is 8-bit signed displacement represented in 2's complement form; else execute next instruction of the current program. $[PC] \leftarrow [PC + r_{add}]$ if CY = 0 else $[PC] \leftarrow [PC+1]$ 2 Byte Instruction.
JZ r_{add} Conditional Jump on Zero.	Jump to target program, if data in A register is Zero, where r_{add} is 8-bit signed displacement represented in 2's complement form; else execute next instruction of the current program. $[PC] \leftarrow [PC + r_{add}]$ if A register = 0 else $[PC] \leftarrow [PC+1]$ 2 Byte Instruction.
JNZ r_{add} Conditional Jump on no Zero.	Jump to target program, if data in A register is not zero, where r_{add} is 8-bit signed displacement represented in 2's complement form; else execute next instruction of the current. $[PC] \leftarrow [PC + r_{add}]$ if A Register ≠ 0 else $[PC] \leftarrow [PC+1]$ 2 Byte Instruction.
JB b, r_{add}	Jump to target program, if memory bit is set; else it will execute next instruction of the current program, where b is 8-bit address of the memory bit. $[PC] \leftarrow [PC + r_{add}]$ if [(b)] = 1 else $[PC] \leftarrow [PC+1]$ 3 Byte Instruction.
JNB b, r_{add}	Jump to target program, if memory bit is not set (Reset); else it will execute next instruction of the current program, where b is 8-bit address of the memory bit. $[PC] \leftarrow [PC + r_{add}]$ if [(b)] = 0 else $[PC] \leftarrow [PC+1]$ 3 Byte Instruction.

JBC b, r_{add}	Jump to target program, if memory bit is set and also complement this particular a data memory bit; else it will execute next instruction of the current program but the bit not complemented now, where b is 8-bit address of the memory bit. $[PC] \leftarrow [PC + r_{add}]$ if $[(b)] = 1$ and $[(b)] \leftarrow 0$ else $[PC] \leftarrow [PC+1]$ 3 Byte Instruction.
CJNE A, #n, r_{add}	Compare the content of A register with the 8-bit data n and then jump to target program, if the content of register A and the 8-bit data n are not equal; else continue executing next instruction of the main/current program. $[PC] \leftarrow [PC + r_{add}]$ if $[A] \neq n$ and else $[PC] \leftarrow [PC+1]$ 3 Byte Instruction.
CJNE Rr, #n, r_{add}	Compare the content of Rr register with the 8-bit data n and then jump to target program if the content of register A and the 8-bit data n are not equal; else continue executing next instruction of the main/current program. $[PC] \leftarrow [PC + r_{add}]$ if $[Rr] \neq n$ and else $[PC] \leftarrow [PC+1]$ 3 Byte Instruction.
CJNE A, add, r_{add}	Compare the content of A register with content of data memory whose address is specified by add and then jump to target program, if the content of register A and the content of 8-bit data memory are not equal; else continue executing next instruction of the main/current program. $[PC] \leftarrow [PC + r_{add}]$ if $[(add)] \neq A$ and else $[PC] \leftarrow [PC+1]$ 3 Byte Instruction.
CJNE @Rp, #n, r_{add}	Compare the content of data memory whose address is specified register Rp with the 8-bit data n and then jump to target program, if the content of memory and the data n not equal; else continue executing next instruction of the main/current program. $[PC] \leftarrow [PC + r_{add}]$ if $[(Rp)] \neq n$ and else $[PC] \leftarrow [PC+1]$ 3 Byte Instruction.

DJNZ Rr, r$_{add}$	Decrement content of Register Rr and then jump to target program, if content of Rr are not zero; else execute next instruction of current/main program. [PC]←[PC + r$_{add}$] if [Rr] ≠ 0 and else [PC]←[PC+1] 2 Byte Instruction.
DJNZ add, radd	Decrement content of 8-bit data memory whose address is specified in add and then jump to target program, if content of Rr are not zero; else execute next instruction of current/main program. [PC]←[PC + r$_{add}$] if [(add)] ≠ 0 and else [PC]←[PC+1] 2 Byte Instruction.
JMP @A+DPTR	Jump unconditional to destination/target program, where address of destination/target program is content of DPTR and content of A register. This instruction adds content of DPTR and A to form Address of memory. [PC]←[A+DPTR] 1 Byte Instruction.
RET	Return to the main program from subroutine by transferring the content of the stack top two locations to cohere top byte from the stack is transferred to PCH and next byte after decrementing is transferred to PCL. [PCH]←[(Sp)] [PCL]←[(Sp-1)] [Sp]←[Sp-2] 1 Byte Instruction.
RETI	Return to the main program from Interrupt service subroutine by transferring the content of the stack top two locations to PC. ere Top byte from the stack is transferred to PCH and next byte after decrementing is transferred to PCL. Reset the interrupt logic. [PCH]←[(Sp)] [PCL]←[(Sp-1)] [Sp]←[Sp-2] 1 Byte Instruction.

2.1.7 Flow Charts

- A **flowchart** is a schematic representation of an algorithm or a stepwise process, showing the steps as boxes of various kinds, and their order by connecting these with arrows. Flowcharts are used in designing or documenting a process or program.

- It is not strictly necessary to use boxes, circles, diamonds or other such symbols to construct a flowchart, but these do help to describe the types of events in the chart more clearly.

- Described below are a set of standard symbols which are applicable to most situations without being overly complex.

- **Rounded box :** Use it to represent an event which occurs automatically. Such an event will trigger a subsequent action, for example `receive telephone call', or describe a new state of affairs.

- **Rectangle or box :-** Use it to represent an event which is controlled within the process. Typically this will be a step or action which is taken. In most flowcharts this will be the most frequently used symbol.

- **Diamond** : Use it to represent a decision point in the process. Typically, the statement in the symbol will require a `yes' or `no' response and branch to different parts of the flowchart accordingly.

- **Circle :** Use it to represent a point at which the flowchart connects with another process. The name or reference for the other process should appear within the symbol.

- **Arrows :** Showing what's called "flow of control". An arrow coming from one symbol and ending at another symbol represents that control passes to the symbol the arrow points to.

2.1.7.1 Steps in flow chart development

- Six steps which can be used as a guide for completing flowcharts.
    1. Describe the process to be charted (this is a one-line statement such as, "How to fill the car's petrol tank").
    2. Start with a 'trigger' event.

3. Note each successive action concisely and clearly.

4. Go with the main flow (put extra detail in other charts).

5. Make cross references to supporting information.

6. Follow the process through to a useful conclusion (end at a 'target' point).

2.1.7.2 Advantages of using flow charts

- The benefits of flow charts are as follows :

    1. **Communication** : Flowcharts are better way of communicating the logic of a system to all concerned.

    2. **Effective analysis** : With the help of flowchart, problem can be analysed in more effective way.

    3. Proper documentation : Program flowcharts serve as a good program documentation, which is needed for various purposes.

    4. **Efficient Coding** : The flowcharts act as a guide or blueprint during the systems analysis and program development phase.

    5. **Proper Debugging :** The flowchart helps in debugging process.

    6. **Efficient Program Maintenance :** The maintenance of operating program becomes easy with the help of flowchart. It helps the Programmer To Put Efforts More Efficiently On That Part

Limitations of using flow charts :

    1. **Complex logic :** Sometimes, the program logic is quite complicated. In that case, flowchart becomes complex and clumsy.

    2. **Alterations and Modifications :** If alterations are required the flowchart may require re-drawing completely.

    3. **Reproduction** : As the flowchart symbols cannot be typed, reproduction of flowchart becomes a problem.

- The essentials of what is done can easily be lost in the technical details of how it is done.

2.1.8 Program in C and Assembly Language 8051 Assembly Language Programming

Program No. 1 : Add 2 8-bit numbers.

- Write a program to add 2 8-bit numbers. Data in stored in registers R0, R1 and result to be stored in R2.

Algorithm	Flowchart
1. Load first number if Accumulator from register R0. 2. Add number from register R1 to content of accumulator. 3. Store the result in register R2. 4. End.	Start → Take first number in Accumulator from register R0 → Add content of register R1 and content of accumulator → Store the result in register R2 → Stop

Label	Program	Comment
	MOV A, R0	; Load the content of the register R0 in Register A
	ADD A, R1	; Add the content of Register A with the content of Register R1
	MOV R2, A	; Store the result of addition in Register R2
Here :	SJMP Here	; Stop

Program No. 2 : Add 2 8-bit Numbers

- Write a program to add 2 8-bit numbers. Data is stored in internal memory and store the result in register R2.

Label	Program	Comment
	MOV A, #44H	; Load the content 44H in Register A
	ADD A, #66H	; Add the content of Register A with the content 66H
	MOV R2, A	; Store the result of addition in Register R2

Program No. 3 : Add 2 8-bit Numbers

- Write a program to add 2 8-bit numbers. Data is stored in data memory location 51H, 52H and store the result in data memory location 53H.

Label	Program	Comment
	MOV A, 51H	; Load Register A with the content of memory location 55H
	ADD A, 52H	; Add the content of Register A with the content of data memory 52H
	MOV 53H, A	; Store the result of addition in data memory 53H
Here :	SJMP Here	; stop

Program No. 4 : Add 2 8-bit Numbers

- Write a program to add 2 8-bit numbers. Data is stored in data memory location whose address is stored in R1 and R2 register and store the result in data memory location 53H.

Label	Program	Comment
	MOV A, @R1	; Load Register A with the content of memory location pointer by register R1
	ADD A, @R2	; Add the content of Register A with the content of location pointer by register R2s
	MOV 53H, A	; Store the result of addition in data memory 53H
Here :	SJMP Here	

Program No. 5 : Subtract 2 8-bit Numbers

- Write a program to Subtract 2 8-bit numbers. Data in stored in Register R0, R1 and result to be stored in R2.

Label	Program	Comment
	MOV A, R0	; Load the content of the register R0 in Register A
	SUBB A, R1	; Subtract the content of Register A with the content of Register R1
	MOV R2,A	; Store the result of addition in Register R2
Here :	SJMP Here	; stop

Program No. 6 : Subtract 2 8-bit Numbers

- Write a program to Subtract 2 8-bit numbers. Data is stored in internal memory and store the result in register R2.

Label	Program	Comment
	MOV A, #44H	; Load the content 44H in Register A
	SUBB A, #66H	; Subtract the content of Register A with the content 66H
	MOV R2,A	; Store the result of addition in Register R2
Here :	SJMP Here	; stop

Program No. 7 : Subtract 2 8-bit Numbers

- Write a program to Subtract 2 8-bit numbers. Data is stored in data memory location 51H, 52H and store the result in data memory location 53H.

Label	Program	Comment
	MOV A, 51H	; Load Register A with the content of memory location 55H
	SUBB A, 52H	; Subtract the content of Register A with the content of data memory 52H
	MOV 53H, A	; Store the result of addition in data memory 53H
Here :	SJMP Here	; stop

Program No. 8 : Subtract 2 8-bit Number

- Write a program to Subtract 2 8-bit numbers. Data is stored in data memory location whose address is stored in R1 and R2 register and store the result in data memory location 53H.

Label	Program	Comment
	MOV A, @R1	; Load Register A with the content of memory location pointer by register R1
	SUBB A, @R2	; Subtract the content of Register A with the content of location pointer by register R2s
	MOV 53H, A	; Store the result of addition in data memory 53H
Here :	SJMP Here	; stop

Program No. 9 : Multiply 2 8-bit Numbers

- Write a program to multiply content of register R1 and register B and store the result in register 53 and 54 H memory.

Algorithm	Flowchart
1. Load first number if Accumulator from register R1. 2. Load Second number in register B. 3. Multiply the content of Accumulator and Register B. 4. Store the result memory location 53H and 54H. 5. End.	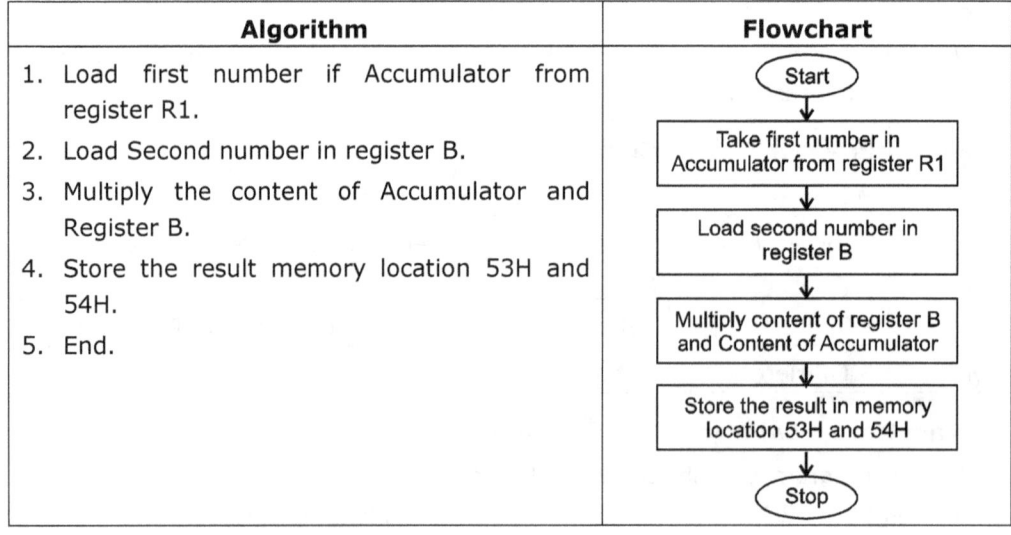

Label	Program	Comment
	MOV A, R1	; Load Register A with the content register R1
	MOV 0F0H, #66H	; Load the register B(0F0H) with 8-bit immediate data 66H
	MUL AB	; Multiply the content of register A and B and store the result in register A and B
	MOV 53H, A	; Store the Lower byte of product in data memory 53H
	MOV 54H, 0F0H	; Store the higher byte of product in data memory 54H
Here :	SJMP Here	; stop

Program No. 10 : Divide 2 8-bit Numbers

- Write a program to divide content of register R1 and register B and Store the result in register 53 and 54 H memory.

Label	Program	Comment
	MOV A, R1	; Load Register A with the content register R1
	MOV 0F0H, #66H	; Load the register B(0F0H) with 8-bit immediate data 66H
	DIV AB	; Divide the content of register A and B and store the result in register A and B
	MOV 53H, A	; Store the Quotient in data memory 53H
	MOV 54H, 0F0H	; Store the remainder in data memory 54H
Here :	SJMP Here	; stop

Program No. 11 : BCD Addition

- Write a program to perform BCD addition of 2 8-bit numbers. Data is stored in data memory location 51H, 52H and store the result in data memory location 53H.

Label	Program	Comment
	MOV A, 51H	; Load Register A with the content of memory location 55H
	ADD A, 52H	; Add the content of Register A with the content of data memory 52H
	DA A	; Convert the Binary result to BCD Format
	MOV 53H, A	; Store the result of addition in data memory 53H

Program No. 12 : BCD Addition

- Write a program to perform BCD addition of 2 8-bit numbers. Data is stored in data memory location 51H, 52H and store the result in data memory location 53H and carry in 54H

Algorithm	Flowchart
1. Load first number if Accumulator from 51H data memory location 2. Add content of accumulator with data of memory location 52H 3. Decimal adjust Accumulator 4. Store the result memory location 53H 5. Store Carry in 54H, memory location 6. End	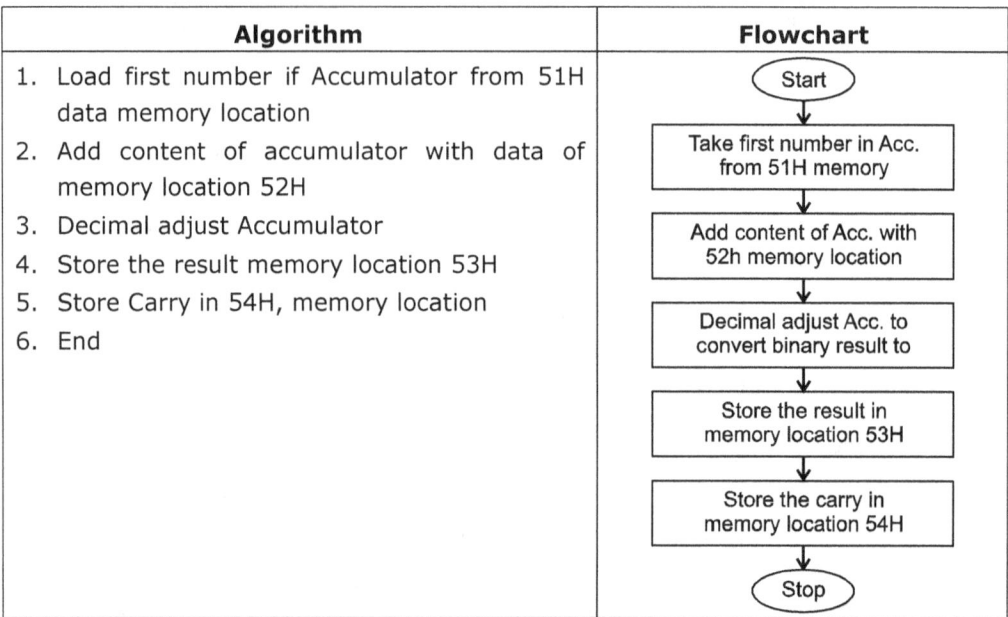

Label	Program	Comment
	MOV A, 51H	; Load Register A with the content of memory location 55H
	ADD A, 52H	; Add the content of Register A with the content of data memory 52H
	DA A	; Convert the Binary result to BCD Format
	MOV 53H, A	; Store the result of addition in data memory 53H
	MOV A, #00H	; Clear the content of accumulator
	RLC A	; bring carry in D0 Bit of Accumulator
	MOV 54H, |A	; Store in memory location 54H
Here :	SJMP Here	; stop

Program No. 13 : Add two 8-bit numbers

- Suppose the two data bytes are in Register R2 and R3 of the Bank 1. Perform addition on the data bytes stored in R2 and R3 register. If result is greater than 8-bit, then store LSB of result in R4 and MSB of result in R5.

Label	Mnemonic	Operands	Comment
	CLR	PSW.4	; Select Register Bank 1 of internal RAM
	SETB	PSW.3	
	MOV	R5, #00H	; Load MSB register R5 with 00H
	MOV	A, R2	; Load first number in Accumulator
	ADD	A, R3	; Add first number with second number
	JNC	Down	, If Result < 8-bit then go to Down
	INC	R5	; Increment MSB counter by 1
Down	MOV	R4, A	Store result in internal memory
Here :	SJMP	Here	;Stop

Program No. 14 : Sum of series

- Let the array of ten data bytes is stored in external RAM from memory location 5000H. Let sum be 16-bit. Store LSB of result in memory location 500AH and MSB of result in memory location 500BH. Write an Assembly Language Program.

Algorithm :

1. Select Register Bank 0
2. Initialize register to store Carry
3. Initialize register as counter
4. Initialize memory pointer for array
5. Clear Accumulator which is uses as sum register
6. Add number from array
7. If Result < 8-bit, then go to Step 9
8. Increment Carry counter by 1
9. Increment memory pointer by 1
10. Decrement byte counter by 1
11. If byte counter <> 0, then go to Step 6
12. Store LSB and MSB (Value of Carry Counter) of result in memory.
13. Stop.

Label	Mnemonic	Operands	Comment
	CLR	PSW.3	; Select Register Bank 0
	CLR	PSW.4	
	CLR	PSW.7	; Clear Carry Flag
	MOV	R1, #00H	; Initialize Carry Counter with 00

Label	Mnemonic	Operands	Comment
	MOV	R0, #0AH	; Initialize byte Counter
	MOV	DPTR, #5000H	; Initialize memory pointer
	MOV	R2, #00H	; Clear R2
UP :	MOVX	A, @DPTR	;Copy content of external memory to register A
	ADDC	A, R2	; Add R2 register with number from array in A with Cy
	MOV	R2, A	; Store Result to R2
	JNC	DN	; IF CY = 0, then go to Down
	INC	R1	;Increment register R1
Down	INC	DPTR	; Increment memory pointer
	DJNZ	R0, UP	; Decrement byte counter, if byte counter ≠ 0 Then go to up
	MOV	@DPTR, A	; Store LSB of result in internal memory
	INC	DPTR, A	; Increment memory pointer by1
	MOV	A, R1	;Copy content of register R4 to register A
	MOV	@DPTR, A	; Store MSB of the result in internal memory
Here :	AJMP	Here	; Stop

Program No. 15 : Multiply 2 8 numbers

- Let multiplicand is stored in external memory location 8000H and multiplier is stored in memory location 8001H. Store LSB and MSB of the result in external memory locations 8002H and 8003H respectively. Write an assembly language program.

Label	Mnemonic	Operands	Comment
	MOV	DPTR, #8000H	; Initialize memory pointer to point external memory location 8000H
	MOVX	A, @ DPTR	; Load Multiplicand in A
	MOV	0F0H, A	; Copy in to B register
	INC	DPTR	; Increment memory pointer i.e. DPTR
	MOVX	A, @DPTR	; Load Multiplier in A
	MUL	AB	; Multiply multiplicand with multiplier

	INC	DPTR	; Increment memory pointer
	MOVX	@ DPTR, A	; Store LSB of result in memory
	MOV	A, 0F0H	; Copy MSB of result in A
	INC	DPTR	; Increment memory pointer by 1
	MOVX	@ DPTR, A	; Store MSB of result in memory
Here :	SJMP	Here	; Stop

Program No. 16 : Smallest from an Array

- Let array of the ten bytes is stored in internal memory of 8051 from memory, location 60H and Store smallest number in memory location 70H. Write an assembly language program.

Label	Mnemonic	Operands	Comment
	MOV	R1, #0AH	; Initialize register R1 as counter
	MOV	R0, #5OH	; Initialize memory pointer
	DEC	R1	; Decrement counter by 1 i.e. R1 register
	MOV	70H, @R0	; Store number in memory location 70 H
UP :	INC	R0	; Increment memory pointer by 1
	MOV	A, @R0	; Read Next number
	CJNE	A, 70H, DN	; if number ≠ next number, then go to Down
	AJMP	NEXT	; else go to NEXT
Down :	JNC	NEXT	; If next number < number then go to NEXT
	MOV	70H, A	; Else replace next number with number
NEXT :	DJNZ	R1, UP	; Decrement byte counter by 1, if byte counter ≠ o then go to UP
Here :	SJMP	Here	; Stop

Program No. 17 : Arranging number in ascending order

- The block or array is stored in external memory from address 9000H. Write a program to arrange number in ascending order

Algorithm :

1. Initialize comparison/pass counter to count number of passes
2. Initialize memory pointer to
3. read data byte from array

4. Initialize counter equal to number of data bytes

5. Read numbers from the array

6. Compare two numbers

7. If number <= next number then go to step 8

8. Exchange or swap numbers

9. Increment memory pointer to

10. read next number from array

11. Decrement byte counter by one

12. If byte counter <> 0 then go

13. step 4

14. Decrement comparison counter

15. By one

16. If comparison counter <> 0 then go to step 2

17. Stop

Label	Mnemonic	Operands	Comment
	MOV	R0, #0AH	; Initialize pass counter
UP1 :	MOV	DPTR, #9000H	; Initialize memory pointer DPTR to 9000H
	MOV	R1, #0AH	; Initialize byte Counter
UP :	MOV	R2, DPL	; Save the lower byte address
	MOVX	A, @DPTR	; Read number from array
	MOV	0F0H, A	; Copy number to B register
	INC	DPTR	; Increment memory Pointer
	MOVX	A, @DPTR	; Read next number from array
	CJNE	A, 0F0, Down	; Compare number with next number
	SJMP	SKIP	; Jump to skip
Down :	JNC	SKIP	; If number > next number then skip
	MOV	DPL, R2	; Else exchange the number with next number
	MOVX	@ DPTR, A	; store data in memory
	INC	DPTR	;Increment memory pointer
	MOV	A, 0F0H	
	MOVX	@ DPTR, A	

SKIP :	DJNZ	R1 UP	; Decrement byte counter if not 0 go to UP
	DJNZ	RO UP1	; Decrement pass counter if not 0 go to UP1
Here :	SJMP	Here	; Stop

Note : To arrange numbers in array in descending order, the above both i.e. for byte and word program for ascending order can be executed by replacing JNC instruction with JC instruction.

Program No. 18 : Block Transfer

Let 15 bytes are stored in the internal memory from address 50H and the starting address of the destination block where we want to transfer these 15 bytes is 60H. Write an assembly language program.

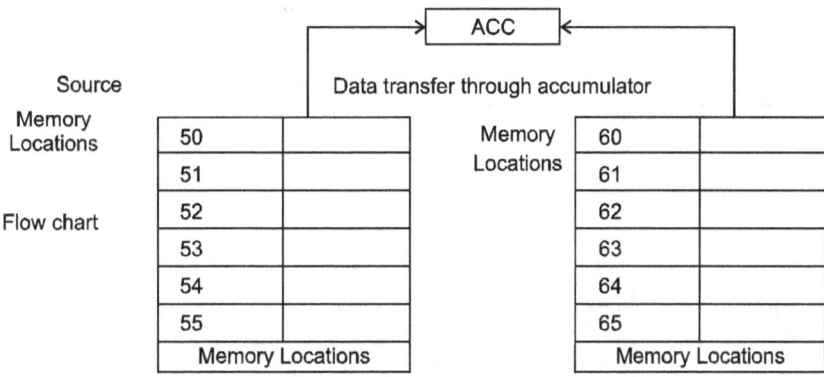

Fig. 2.4

Label	Mnemonic	Operands	Comment
	MOV	R3, #0AH	; Initialize byte counter
	MOV	RO, #50H	; Initialize memory pointer for source array
	MOV	R1, #60H	; Initialize memory pointer for destination array
UP :	MOV	A, @RO	; Read number from source array
	MOV	@R1, A	; Copy number to destination array
	INC	RO	; Increment source memory pointer by 1
	INC	R1	; Increment destination memory pointer by 1
	DJNZ	R3, UP	; Decrement byte counter by 1
Here :	SJMP	Here	; Stop

Program No. 19 : Count of ODD Numbers

- Write an assembly language program to count odd number in a block of N numbers stored in internal RAM starting from 40H. Count of numbers is 15 bytes.

Logic :

- Number is considered as odd number, if it's D0 i.e. LSB bit is 1. Hence, rotate the content of Accumulator towards right, bring D0 bit carry and check whether it is one or zero.

Label	Mnemonic	Operands	Comment
	MOV	R0, #0FH	; Initialize counter in register R0
	MOV	R2, #00H	; Initialize ODD counter to count ODD number
	MOV	R1, #40H	; Initialize memory pointer
UP :	MOV	A, @ R1	; Read number from array store in memory 40H
	RRC	A	; Rotate number to right by 1
	JNC	Next	; If number ≠ ODD, then jump to Next
	INC	R2	; Else increment ODD Counter by
Next :	INC	R1	; Increment memory pointer by 1
	DJNZ	R0,UP	; Decrement byte Counter by 1, If byte counter ≠0, then go to UP
Here :	SJMP	here	; Stop

Note : For Finding number of even numbers, change JNC instruction to JC instruction.

Program No. 20. : Count of negative numbers

- Write an assembly language program to count negative numbers in Block of N numbers stored in internal RAM starting from 40H. Count of number is 15 bytes.

Logic :

- Number is considered as negative number if its D7 i.e. MSB bit is 1. Hence, rotate the content of accumulator towards left, bring D7 bit carry and check whether it is one or zero.

Label	Mnemonic	Operands	Comment
	MOV	R0, #0FH	; Initialize counter in register R0
	MOV	R2, #00H	; Initialize ODD counter to count ODD number

Label	Mnemonic	Operands	Comment
	MOV	R1, #40H	; Initialize memory pointer
UP :	MOV	A, @ R1	; Read number from array store in memory 40H
	RRC	A	; Rotate number to right by 1
	JNC	Next	; If number ≠ ODD, then jump to Next
	INC	R2	; Else increment ODD Counter by
Next :	INC	R1	; Increment memory pointer by 1
	DJNZ	R0,UP	; Decrement byte Counter by 1, If byte counter ≠0, then go to UP
Here :	SJMP	here	; Stop
Label	Mnemonic	Operands	Comment

Note : For finding number of positive numbers, change JNC instruction to JC instruction.

Program No. 21 : 2's complement of a number

- Let the number is stored in R0 register of bank 0, then find out the 2's complement of the number and store result in R1 register of the same bank.

Label	Mnemonic	Operands	Comment
	CLR	PSW.4	; Clear RS1
	CLR	PSW.3	; Clear RS0, Select Bank 0
	MOV	A, R0	; Copy number to accumulator
	CPL	A	; Complement the accumulator
	ADD	A, #01H	; Find 2nd Complement
	MOV	R1, A	; Store result in R1

Program No. 22 : Packing two unpacked BCD bytes

- Packing two unpacked BCD bytes are stored in r0, r1. The program below packs these two unpacked bytes into a single byte and store in r2.
- **Unpacked BCD :** In unpacked BCD, the lower 4 bits of the number represent the BCD number, and rest of the bits are 0.

  Example : "0000 1001" and "0000 0101" are unpacked BCD for 9 and 5, respectively. Unpacked BCD requires 1 byte of memory or an 8-bit register to store it.
- **Packed BCD :** In packed BCD, a single byte has two BCD numbers in it; one in the lower 4 bits and one in upper 4 bits.

Example : "0101 1001" is packed BCD for 59H. It takes one byte of memory to store the packed BCD operands. Packed BCD is used since it is twice as efficient in storing data.

Label	Mnemonic	Comments
	MOV R1, #05H	; Move 05 into the register r1
	MOV R0, #09H	; Move 09 into the register r0
	MOV A, R1	; Move 1st number in accumulator
	ANL A, #0FH	; Masking upper nibble
	SWAP A	; Contents of lower and higher nibble of accumulator are exchanged
	MOV R2, A	; Contents of accumulator transferred to r2
	MOV A, R0	; Move 2nd number in accumulator
	ANL A, #0FH	; Masking upper nibble
	ADD A, R2	; The 2 bytes are packed
	MOV R2, A	; Packed result is stored in register R2
Here :	SJMP HERE	; Stay in this loop

Program No. 23 : Unpacking

- Write a program to unpack packed BCD number stored in 40H. Store the unpacked number in 41H and 42H respectively using direct addressing mode

Label	Mnemonic	Comments
	MOV A, 40H	; Move data from 40H memory to accumulator
	MOV R1, A	; copy content of accumulator to register R1
	ANL A, #0FH	; Masking upper nibble
	MOV 41H, A	; Copy content of register A to memory location 41H
	MOV A, R1	; Copy content of register R1 to register A
	SWAP A	; Contents of lower and higher nibble of accumulator are exchanged
	ANL A, #0FH	; Masking upper nibble
	MOV 42H, A	; Store the content of register A memory location 42H
Here :	SJMP HERE	; Stop

Program No. 24 : Unpacking

- Write a program to unpack packed BCD number stored in 50H. Store the unpacked number in 51H and 52H respectively using indirect addressing mode.

Label	Mnemonic	Comments
	MOV R0,#50H	; Initialize memory pointer Ro to 50H data memory location
	MOV A, @R0	; Move data from data memory to accumulator
	MOV R1, A	; Copy content of Accumulator to register R1
	ANL A,#0FH	; Masking upper nibble
	INC R0	; Increment memory pointer to point Next location
	MOV @R0, A	; Store content of register A to memory location pointer by R0 register
	MOV A,R1	; Copy content of register R1 to register A
	SWAP A	; Contents of lower and higher nibble of accumulator are exchanged
	ANL A,#0FH	; Masking upper nibble
	INC R0	; Increment memory pointer to point Next location
	MOV @R0, A	; Store content of register A to memory location pointer by R0 register
Here :	SJMP HERE	; Stop

Program No. 26 : Masking

- Write a program to mask the upper nibble of BCD number stored in 50H. Store the masked number in 51H and to mask lower nibble of number stored at 52H, store the result at 53H using indirect addressing mode.

Label	Mnemonic	Comments
	MOV R0,#50H	; Initialize memory pointer Ro to 50H data memory location
	MOV A, @R0	; Move data from data memory to accumulator
	MOV R1, A	; Copy content of Accumulator to register R1
	ANL A,#0FH	; Masking upper nibble
	INC R0	; Increment memory pointer to point Next location
	MOV @R0, A	; Store content of register A to memory location pointer by R0 register

	MOV A,R1	; Copy content of register R1 to register A
	ANL A,#0F0H	; Masking Lower nibble
	INC R0	; Increment memory pointer to point Next location
	MOV @R0, A	; Store content of register A to memory location pointer by R0 register
Here :	SJMP HERE	; Stop

Program No. 25 : Masking

- Write a program to mask the upper nibble of BCD number stored in 50H. Store the masked number in 51H and to mask lower nibble of number stored at 52H. Store the result at 53H using direct addressing mode.

Label	Mnemonic	Comments
	MOV A, 50H	; Move data from 40H memory to accumulator
	MOV R1, A	; Copy content of Accumulator to register R1
	ANL A,#0FH	; Masking upper nibble
	MOV 51H, A	; Copy content of register A to memory location 51H
	MOV A,R1	; Copy content of register R1 to register A
	ANL A,#0F0H	; Masking Lower nibble
	MOV 52H, A	; Store the content of Register A memory location 52H
Here :	SJMP HERE	; Stop

Program No. 27 : Largest from block of data

- Write a program to find largest from a block of 10 bytes stored from memory location 50H. Store the result at 60H.

Algorithm :

1. Initialize byte counter for number of bytes to be arranges
2. Initialize memory pointer to read numbers from data memory array
3. Read number from the memory
4. Increment memory pointer to read next number
5. Decrement counter
6. Compare Max Number with next number
7. If max > next number, then go to step 8

8. Make max next number which is largest

9. Increment memory pointer to read next number in the array

10. Decrement byte counter by 1

11. If byte counter <> 0 then go to step 5

12. Store result

13. Stop

Label	Mnemonic	Operands	Comment
	CLR	PSW.3	; Clear RS1
	CLR	PSW.4	;Clear RS0 so as to select register bank 0
	MOV	R1, 0AH	; Initialize byte pointer
	MOV	RO, #5OH	; Initialize memory pointer to point data memory
	DEC	R1	; Decrement byte counter by 1
	MOV	60H, @R0	; Store number in memory location 60 H
UP :	INC	RO	; Increment memory pointer by 1
	MOV	A, @R0	; Read Next number
	CJNE	A, 60H, Down	; if number ≠ next number, then go to Down
	SJMP	NEXT	; else go to NEXT
Down :	JC	NEXT	; If next number > number then go to NEXT
	MOV	60H, A	; Else replace next number with number
NEXT :	DJNZ	R1, UP	; Decrement byte counter by 1, if byte counter ≠ o then go to UP
LOOP :	SJMP	LOOP	; Stop

2.1.9 Programs in C Language

Program 1 : Write 'C' language program to add data of data memory locations from 00H to 0AH. Store the result in register R5 and register R6.

```
    #include <reg51.h>                //header file for 89C51
    void main (void)
{
    unsigned char idata *x _at_ 0x00;    //Memory Pointer to point 00h
```

```
        unsigned char sum = 0;
        unsigned char I;
        register data r7, r6;                    //declare Registers
        For (i=0; i<=9; i++)
            {

                                                 sum = sum + *x;
                                                 x++;

            }
        R6 = sum ;
        R7 = Sum ;
    }
```

Program 2 : Write 'C' language program for the operation R5 :R4 = R1/R2.

```
        #include <reg51.h>                       //header file for 89C51
        void main (void)
    {
        register data r1 = 0x40;                 //Initialize Register R1
        register data r2 = 0x04;                 //Initialize Register R2
        register data r4 = 0x00;                 //Initialize Register R4
        register data r5 = 0x00;                 //Initialize Register R5
        r4 = r1/r2;                              //Store Quotient
        r5 = r1%r2;                              //Store remainder
        while(1)
            { }                                  //Do Nothing loop
    }
```

Program 3 : Write 'algorithm for averaging ten-8-bit hex numbers in Microcontroller 8051.

```
        #include <reg51.h>                       //header file for 89C51
        void main (void)
    {
        unsigned char num[10] = { 01, 02,03, 04, 05, 06, 07, 08, 09, 10 };
        unsigned char idata *x _at_ 0x50;        //Data memory pointer
        unsigned char sum = 0;                   //Variable to Store Sum
        unsigned char I;
```

```
    for(i=0;i<=9;i++)                    //For Loop to add array
    {
        sum = sum + num[i];
    }                                    //End of For
    x = sum;                             //Store result at data memory location 50H
}
```

Program 4 : Write 'algorithm for comparing ten- 8-bit hex numbers to get maximum of them in Microcontroller 8051.

```
    #include <reg51.h>                   //header file for 89C51
    void main (void)
{
    unsigned char num[10] = {01, 02, 03, 04, 05, 06, 07, 08, 09, 10};
    unsigned char idata *x _at_ 0x50;    //Data memory pointer
    unsigned char max = 0;               //Variable to Store Sum
    unsigned char i;
    max = num[0];                        //Take first data in max
    for(i=1;i<=9;i++)                    //For Loop to Find maximum
    {
        if (max < num[i])
    {
        max = num[i];
    }                                    //End of IF
    }                                    //End of For
        x = max;                         //Store result at data memory location 50H
}
```

Program 5 : Write an 8051 C program to convert 11111101 (FD hex) to decimal and display the digits on P0, P1 and P2.

```
    #include <reg51.h>                   //header file for 89C51
    void main(void)
{
    unsigned char x,binbyte,d1,d2,d3;
    bin byte=0xFD;                       //Store Data FD in variable
    x=binbyte/10;
```

```
d1=binbyte%10;
d2=x%10;
d3=x/10;
P0=d1;                                    //Output on port P0
P1=d2;                                    //Output on port P1
P2=d3;                                    //Output on port P2
}
```

Program 6 : Write an 8051 C program to calculate the checksum byte for the data 25H, 62H, 3FH, and 52H.

```
#include <reg51.h>                     //header file for 89C51
void main(void)
{
unsigned char mydata[]={0x25,0x62,0x3F,0x52};
unsigned char sum=0;
unsigned char x;
unsigned char chksumbyte;
for (x=0;x<4;x++)                       //For loop to calculate CheckSum
{
    P2=mydata[x];
    sum=sum+mydata[x];
    P1=sum;
}
    chksumbyte=~sum+1;
    P1=chksumbyte;
}
```

Program 7 : Write an 8051 C program to perform the checksum operation to ensure data integrity. If data is good, send ASCII character 'G' to P0.

Otherwise send 'B' to P0.

```
#include <reg51.h>
void main(void)
{
    unsigned char mydata[] ={0x25,0x62,0x3F,0x52,0xE8};
    unsigned char chksum=0;
```

```
        unsigned char x;
        for (x=0;x<5;x++)                    //For loop to find CheckSum
        {
        chksum=chksum+mydata[x];
        }
        if (chksum==0)                       //Decide for Good data
        P0='G';
        else
        P0='B';
}
```

Program 8 : Write a program to demonstrate Logical Operations.

```
    #include <reg51.h>
    void main(void)
    {
        P0=0x35 & 0x0F;                  //ANDing
        P1=0x04 | 0x68;                  //ORing
        P2=0x54 ^ 0x78;                  //XORing
        P0=~0x55;                        //inversing
        P1=0x9A >> 3;                    //shifting right 3
        P2=0x77 >> 4;                    //shifting right 4
        P0=0x6 << 4;                     //shifting left 4
    }
```

Program 9 : Write an 8051 C program to toggle all the bits of P0 and P2 continuously with a 250 ms delay using the inverting and Ex-OR operators, respectively.

```
    #include <reg51.h>
    void MSDelay(unsigned int);
    void main(void)
    {
        P0=0x55;
        P2=0x55;
        while (1)
```

```
    {
    P0=~P0;                          //Complement Po
    P2=P2^0xFF;                      //Exor P2 content with 0xFFh
    MSDelay(250);
    }                                //End of While Loop
}
```

Program 10 : Write an 8051 C program to get bit P1.0 and send it to P2.7 after inverting it.

```
    #include <reg51.h>
    sbit inbit=P1^0;
    sbit outbit=P2^7;                //SFR Single Bit
    bit membit;                      //Bit data to store 1 bit
    void main(void)
    {
        while (1)
        {
            membit=inbit;            //get a bit from P1.0
            outbit=~membit;          //invert it and send it to P2.7
        }                            //End of While
    }
```

Program 11 : Write an 8051 C program to convert packed BCD 0x29 to ASCII and display the bytes on P1 and P2.

```
    #include <reg51.h>
    void main(void)
    {
        unsigned char x, y, z;
        unsigned char mybyte=0x29;
        x=mybyte&0x0F;
            P1=x|0x30;               //Bitwise Oring
            y=mybyte&0xF0;           //Bitwise Anding
            y=y>>4;                  //Shift Right by 4 bit
            P2=y|0x30;               //Bitwise Oring
    }
```

Program 12 : Write an 8051 C program to convert ASCII digits of '4' and '7' to packed BCD and display them on P1.

```
#include <reg51.h>
    void main(void)
{
    unsigned char bcdbyte;
    unsigned char w='4';
    unsigned char z='7';
    w=w&0x0F;
    w=w<<4;
    z=z&0x0F;
    bcdbyte=w|z;
    P1=bcdbyte;
}
```

Program 13 : Write an 8051 C program to send hex values for ASCII characters of 0, 1, 2, 3, 4, 5, A, B, C and D to port P1.

```
#include <reg51.h>
Void main (void)
{
    unsigned char mynum [ ]="012345ABCD";
    unsigned char z;
    for (z=0; z<=10; z++)
    P1=mynum [z];
}
```

Run the above program on your simulator to see how P1 displays the values 30H, 31H, 32H, 33H, 34H, 35H, 41H, 42H, 43H and 44H, the hex values for ASCII 0, 1, 2 and so on.

Program 14 : Write an 8051 C program to send values of –4 to +4 to port P1.

```
//sign numbers
#include <reg51.h>
Void main (void)
```

```
    {
        char my num [ ]={+1, −1, +2, −2, +3, −3, +4, −4};
        unsigned char z;
        for (z=0; z<=8; z++)
        P1=my num [z];
    }
```

Program 15 : Write a C program in 8051 to toggle all bits of P1 continuously every 500 ms. Using timer 1, mode 1. The XTAL frequency = 11.0592 MHz.

```
    #include <reg51.h>
    void TOG Delay (void);
    void main (void)
        {
        unsigned char z
        P2=0x55;
        while (1)
        {
        P2=~P2;                         //toggle all bits of port 2
        for (z=0; z<10; z++)
        Tog Delay ( );
        }
        void TOG Delay (void);
        {
            TMOD=0x10                   //Timer 1, mode 1
            TL1=0xFF;                   //load TL1
            THL=0x27;                   //load TH1
            TR1=1                       //turn on T1
            While (TF1=0);              //wait for TF1 to roll over
            TR1=0;                      //turn off T1
            TF1=0;                      //clear TF1
        }
```

2.1.10 Execution of Program using Cross Compiler like Keil IDE, SPJ, RIDE Keil C Compiler

2.1.10.1 Keil C Compiler

- The Keil C51 C Compiler for the 8051 microcontroller is the most popular 8051 C compiler in the world. It provides more features than any other 8051 C compiler available today.

- The C51 Compiler allows you to write 8051 microcontroller applications in C that, once compiled, have the efficiency and speed of assembly language. Language extensions in the C51 Compiler give you full access to all resources of the 8051.

- The C51 Compiler translates C source files into relocatable object modules which contain full symbolic information for debugging with the μVision Debugger or an in-circuit emulator. In addition to the object file, the compiler generates a listing file which may optionally include symbol table and cross reference information.

2.1.10.2 Features of Keil C Compiler

- Nine basic data types, including 32-bit IEEE floating-point,
- Flexible variable allocation with **bit**, **data**, **bdata**, **idata**, **xdata**, and **pdata** memory types,
- Interrupt functions may be written in C,
- Full use of the 8051 register banks,
- Complete symbol and type information for source-level debugging,
- Use of **AJMP** and **ACALL** instructions,
- Bit-addressable data objects,
- Built-in interface for the RTX51 Real-Time Kernel,
- Support for dual data pointers on Atmel, AMD, Cypress, Dallas Semiconductor, Infineon, Philips, and Triscend microcontrollers,
- Support for the Philips 8xC750, 8xC751, and 8xC752 limited instruction sets,
- Support for the Infineon 80C517 arithmetic unit.

2.1.10.3 Keil C Cross Compiler

- Keil is a German based Software development company. It provides several development tools like
  - ➢ IDE (Integrated Development environment)
  - ➢ Project Manager

➢ Simulator

➢ Debugger

➢ C Cross Compiler, Cross Assembler, Locator/Linker

- Keil Software provides you with software development tools for the 8051 family of microcontrollers. With these tools, you can generate embedded applications for the multitude of 8051 derivatives. Keil provides following tools for 8051 development

1. C51 Optimizing C Cross Compiler,

2. A51 Macro Assembler,

3. 8051 Utilities (linker, object file converter, library manager),

4. Source-Level Debugger/Simulator,

5. µVision for Windows Integrated Development Environment.

➢ The Keil 8051 tool kit includes three main tools, assembler, compiler and linker.

➢ An **assembler** is used to assemble your 8051 assembly program

➢ A **compiler** is used to compile your C source code into an object file

➢ A **linker** is used to create an absolute object module suitable for your in-circuit emulator.

2.1.10.4 8051 Project Development Cycle

These are the steps to develop 8051 project using Keil

- Create source files in C or assembly.

- Compile or assemble source files.

- Correct errors in source files.

- Link object files from compiler and assembler.

- Test linked application.

How to work with Keil

- Keil is a cross compiler. So first we have to understand the concept of compilers and cross compilers. After then we shall learn how to work with Keil.

Working with Keil

- To open Keil software click on start menu then program and then select keil2 (or any other version keil3 etc. here the discussion is on keil2 only). Following window will appear on your screen.

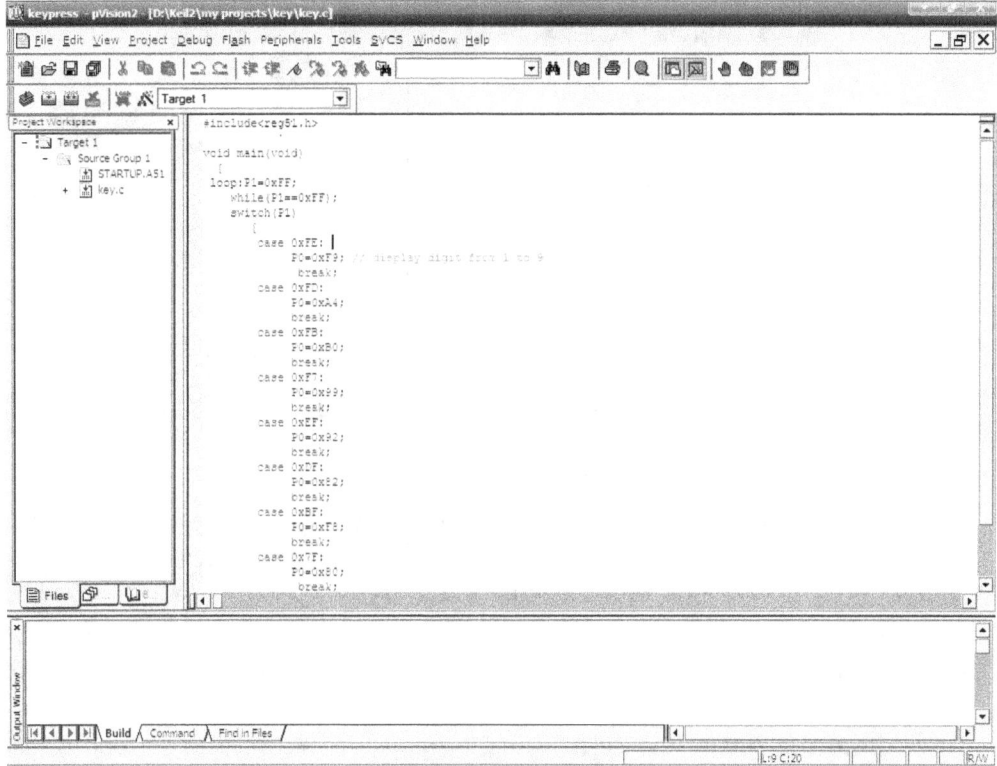

Fig. 2.5 : KEIL IDE

- There are three different windows in this screen.

  1. project work space window

  2. editing window

  3. output window.

- **Project workspace window** is for showing all the related files connected with your project.

- **Editing window** is the place where you will edit the code

- **Output window** will show the output when you compile or build or run your project.

Now to start with new project follow the steps :

- click on project menu and select new project

- you will be asked to create new project in specific directory.

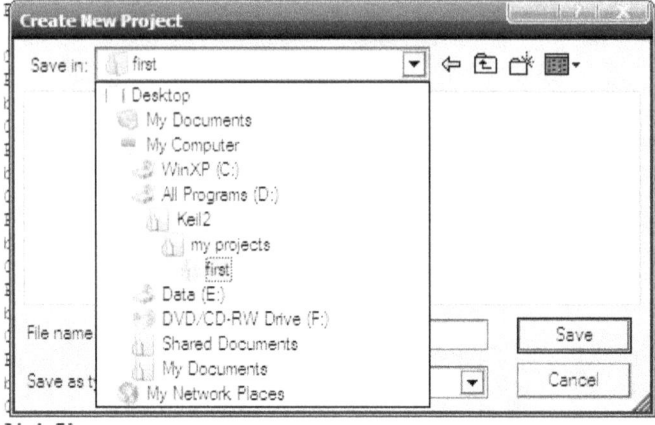

Fig. 2.6 : Create Project Window

- Just move to your desired directory and there create a new folder for your project named "first". Here I am creating new project in d :\keil2\myprojects\first as shown in Fig. 2.6 give the name of project as "test". By default it will be saved as *.v2 extension.

- Now you will be asked to choose your target device for which you want to write the program.

- Scroll down the cursor and select generic from list. expand the list and select 8051 (all variants).

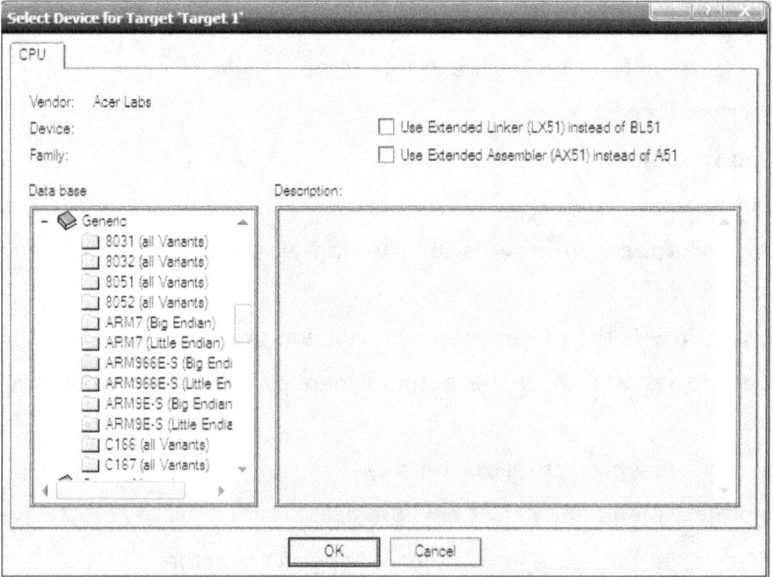

Fig. 2.7 : Target Selection Window

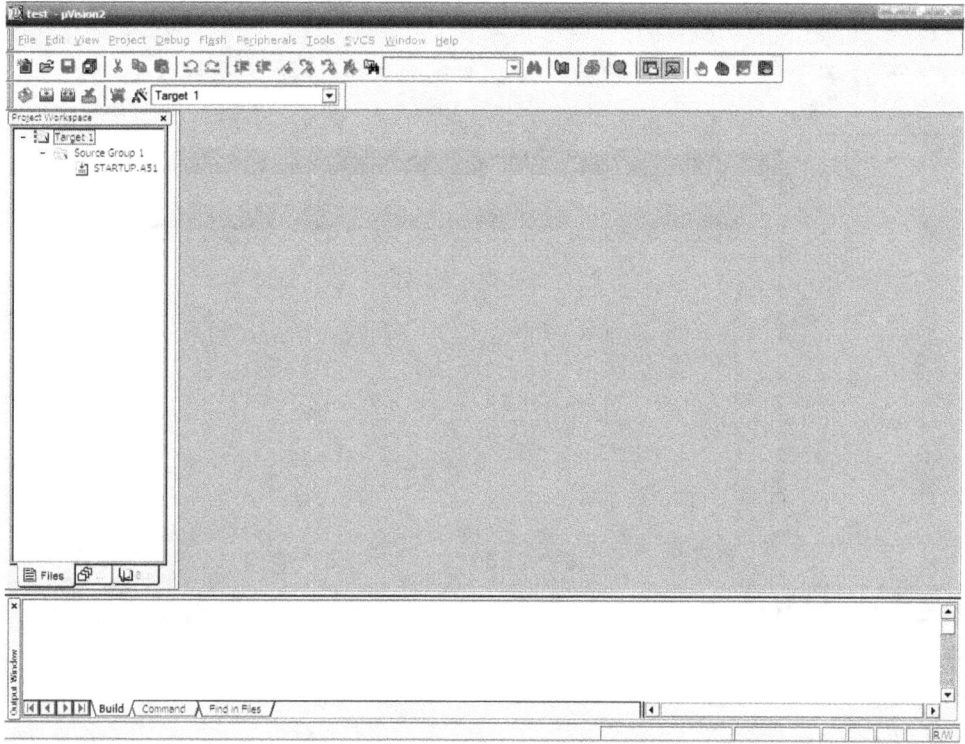

Fig. 2.8 : Code Window

- When you click OK, you will be asked to add startup code and file to your project folder. click yes. Now on your screen expand target1 list fully. You will see following window.

- now click on file menu and select new file. editor window will open. Now you can start writing your code.

- As you start writing program in C, same way here also you have to first include the header file. Because our target is 8051 our header file will be "reg51.h".

- After including this file. just right click on the file and select open document <reg51.h>. The following window will appear :

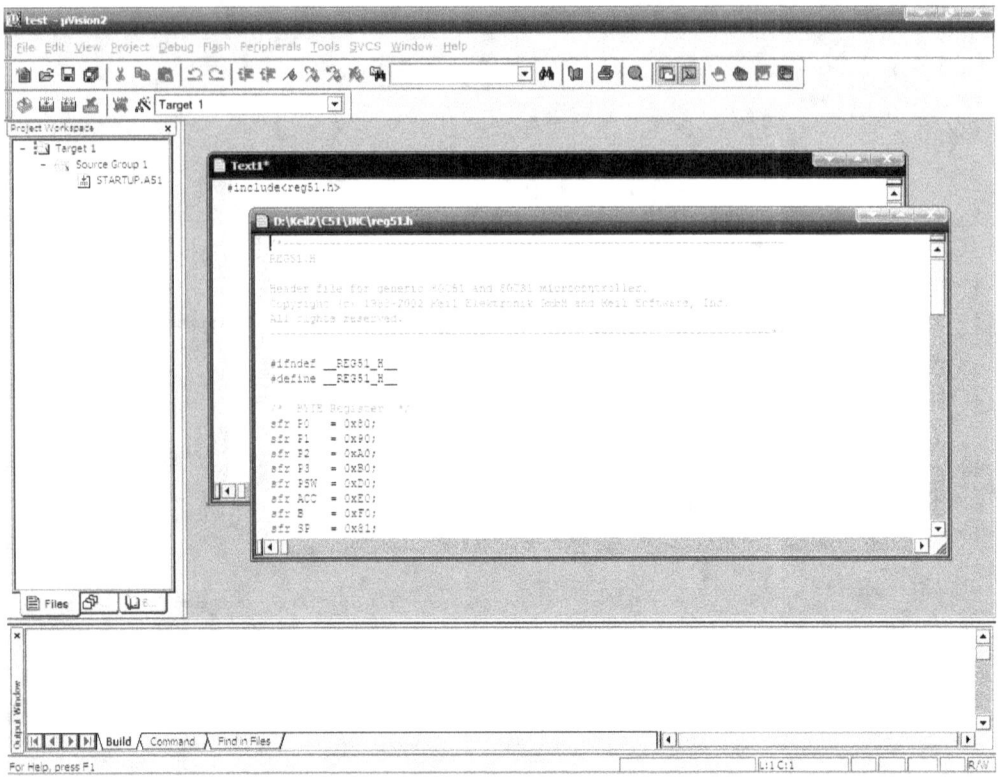

Fig. 2.9 : Include Reg51 Header File

- If you scroll down cursor you will see that all the SFRs like P0-P3, TCON, TMOD, ACC, bit registers and byte registers are already defined in this header file. so one can directly use these register names in coding.

- Now you can write your program same as c language starting with void main()

- After completing the code save the file in project folder with ".c" extension.

- Now right click on "source group 1" in project workspace window. select "add files to source group 1"

- Select the C file you have created and click add button.

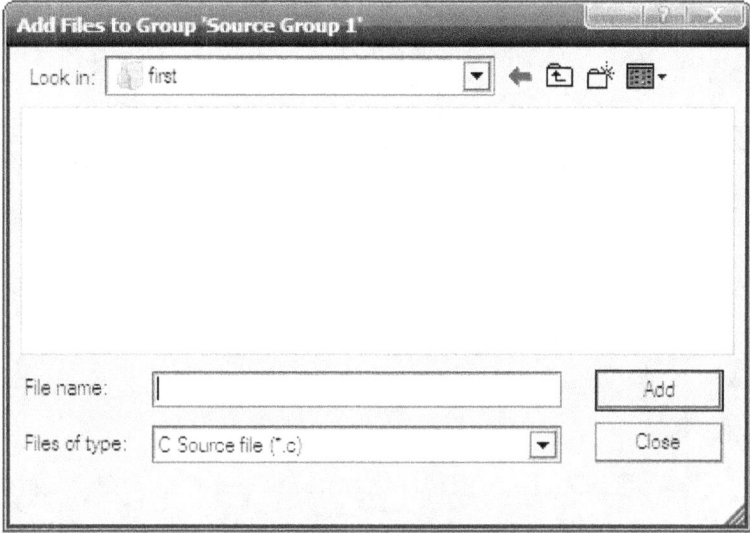

Fig. 2.10 : Source Grouping

- You will see that the c file has been added in source group.

- Now to compile the program from project menu select "build target". In the output window you will see the progress

- If there is any compilation error then target will not be created. Remove all the errors and again build the target till you find "0 Error(s)"

- Now you are ready to run your program. from debug menu select "start/stop debug session"

- You will see your project workspace window now shows most of the SFRs as well as GPRs(General Purpose Registers) r0-r7. also one more window is now opened named "watches". in this window you can see different variable values.

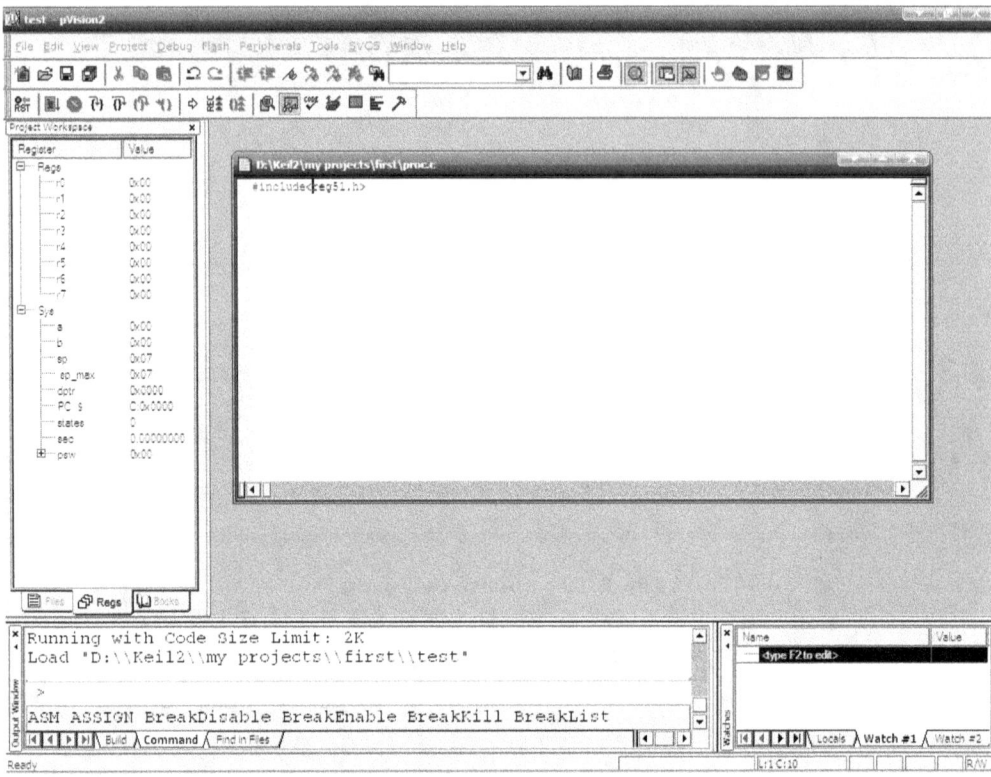

Fig. 2.11 : Watch Window

- To add variable in watch window go to "watch#1" tab. then type F2 to edit and type the name of your variable

- If you want to see the output on ports go to peripheral menu and select I/O ports. Select the desire port. you can give input to port pins by checking or unchecking any check box. here the check mark means digit 1 and no check mark means 0. the output on the pin will be shown in same manner.

- To run the program you can use any of the option provided "go", "step by step", "step forward", "step move" etc.

- Now after testing your program you need to down load this program on your target board that is 8051. for this you have to create hex file

- To create hex file first stop debug session. Again you will be diverted to project workspace window.

- Right click on "target 1" and select "option for target 1". Following window will appear.

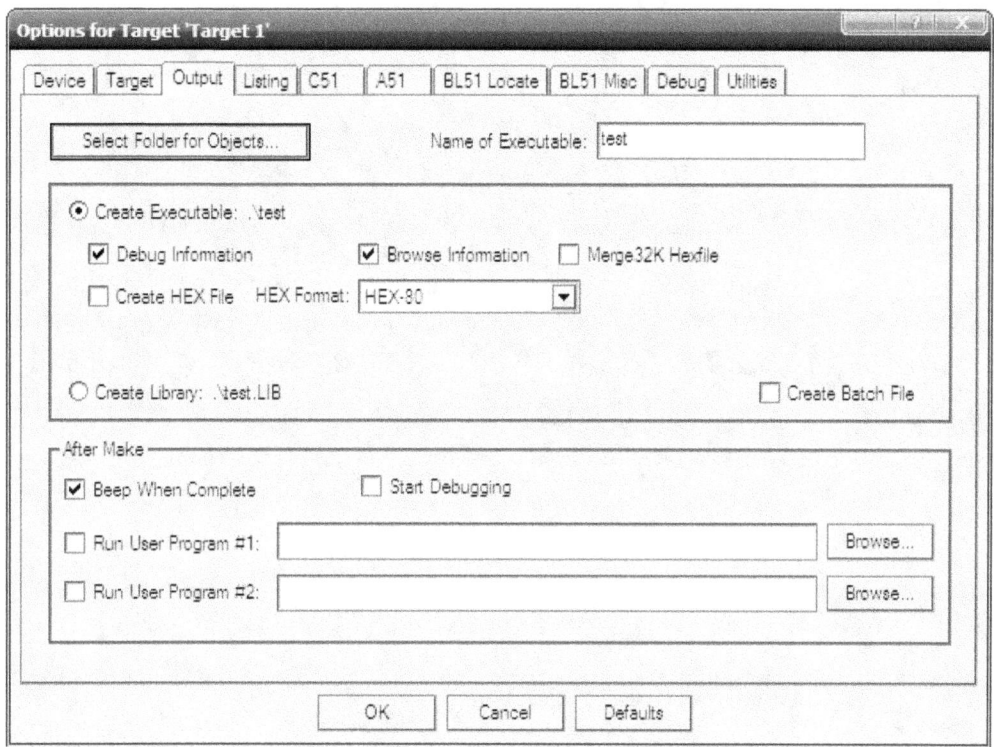

Fig. 2.12 : Option for Target Window

- Select output tag and check "create hex file" box.

- Now when you again build your program you will see the message in output window "hex file is created".

- In your project folder you can see the hex file with same name of your project as "test.hex".

- This file you can directly load in 8051 target board and run the application on actual environment.

SPJ-System Side-51 :

Starting the IDE

- Click on START button and select Programs/SPJ Systems' SC51/SIDE51. The screen should look something like this.

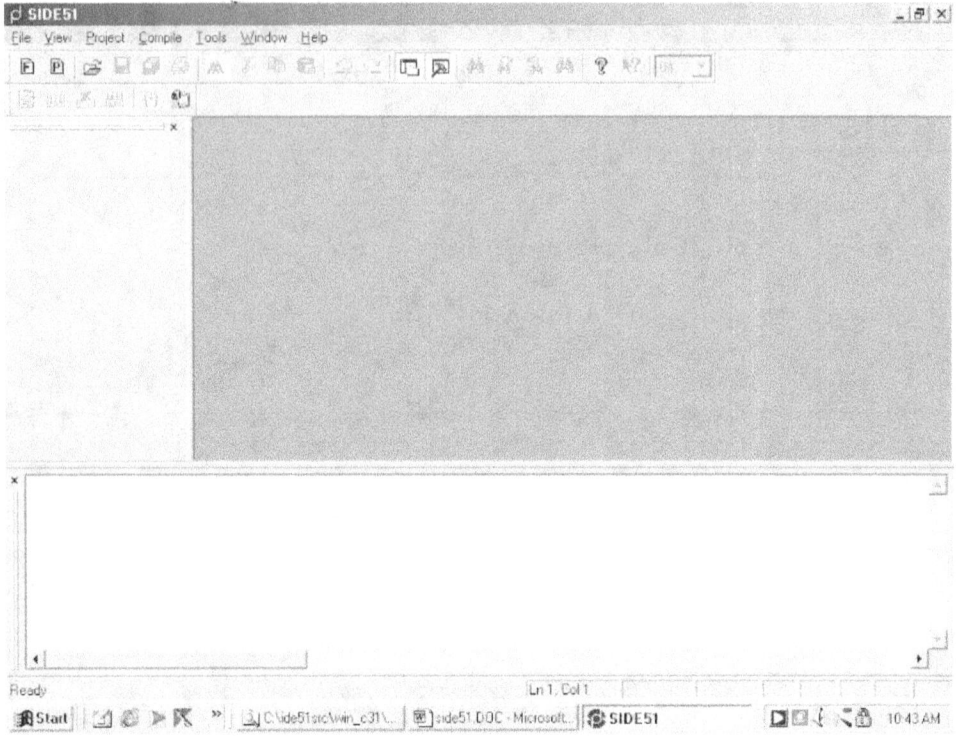

Fig. 2.13 : Side-51 IDE

Opening a project :

- Now select **Project/Open Project** from the menu. Select the path where you installed SC51 and select the EXAMPLES folder. You will see a list of project files (extention.P51). From the list, select hello.p51. Click Ok. Doing that will open the project HELLO.P51. This will also automatically open the file HELLO.C in the editor.

- This is simple program which outputs the character string "Hello World !\n" on the standard output device (i.e. the on-chip serial port of 8051). If the HELLO.C file is not automatically opened, you can select File/Open from the menu and then double-click

  Hello.C from the list of files.

Compiling the program :

- To compile the program, select **Compile/Build** or **Compile/Re-build All** from the menu.

- Doing this may invoke one or more these applications : C compiler, Assembler, Linker. If there are no errors, then Intel HEX format file (.HEX) and optionally

.BIN file will be produced. The error and warning messages produced by compiler, assembler, linker will be displayed in the error window. If there are any errors, you may correct them and repeat the process until all errors are gone.

Running the program :

- To run (i.e. debug) the program, select **Tools/Simulator** from the menu. Doing this will invoke the Simulator program. The screen should look something like this :

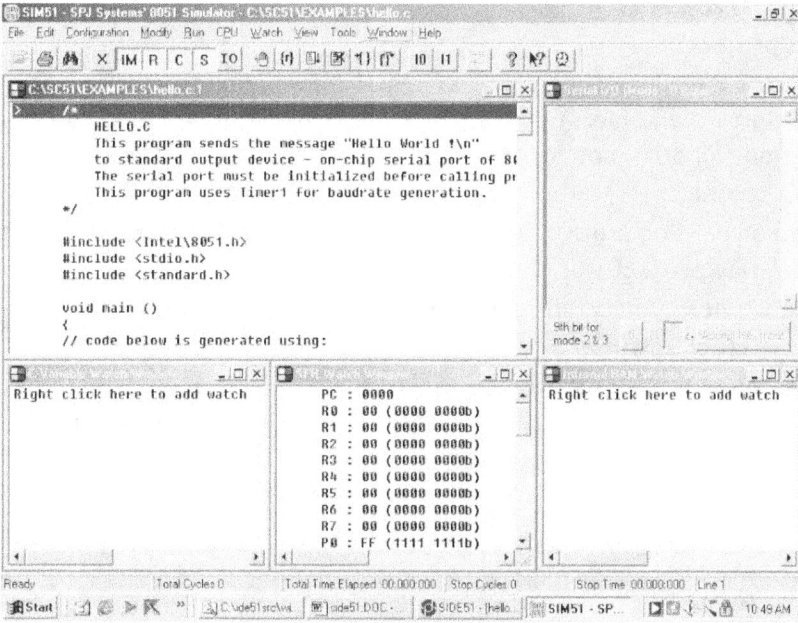

Fig. 2.14 : Side051 Simulator

- Please note that the program window is already open. In our example, the program simply sends a message "Hello World !\n" to the serial port. In order to debug the program, we must monitor the serial port output. It can be monitored in the Serial Port Window – which is already visible. To view/hide the Serial Port Window, select View/Serial window from the menu.

- Similarly, you can show or hide other windows visible as per your need. To monitor memory locations in the external RAM, select View/External RAM watch. To monitor memory locations in the internal RAM, select View/Internal RAM watch.

- To monitor the status of connected peripheral devices, select View/I/O watch from the menu. To monitor the internal registers/SFRs of 8051, select View/SFR watch from the menu. To monitor 'C' program variables, select View/C variable watch from the menu.

- Once you have made the required windows visible, you can run the program either in continuous mode or in single step mode. To single step through your program, select Run/Single step from the menu or press F7.

- Doing this will execute on 'C' language statement at a time. On the contrary, if you select Run/Run from the menu (or press Ctrl.F7), the program will run in continuous mode.

- To stop the program execution, select Run/Terminate program, or press Ctrl.F2.

More about "Project" :

What is a project :

- A project is a file in which SIDE51 stores all information related to an application. e.g. it stores the name(s) of 'C' and/or Assembler source file(s), memory model to be used and other options for compiler, assembler and linker.

Opening a project :

- To open an existing project file, select **Project/Open Project** from the menu.

Creating a new project :

- To create a new project, select **Project/New Project** from the menu.

Changing project settings :

- To change the project settings (such as adding or removing 'C' and/or Assembler source file(s), changing memory model etc.), select Project/Settings from the menu. The screen should now look like this :

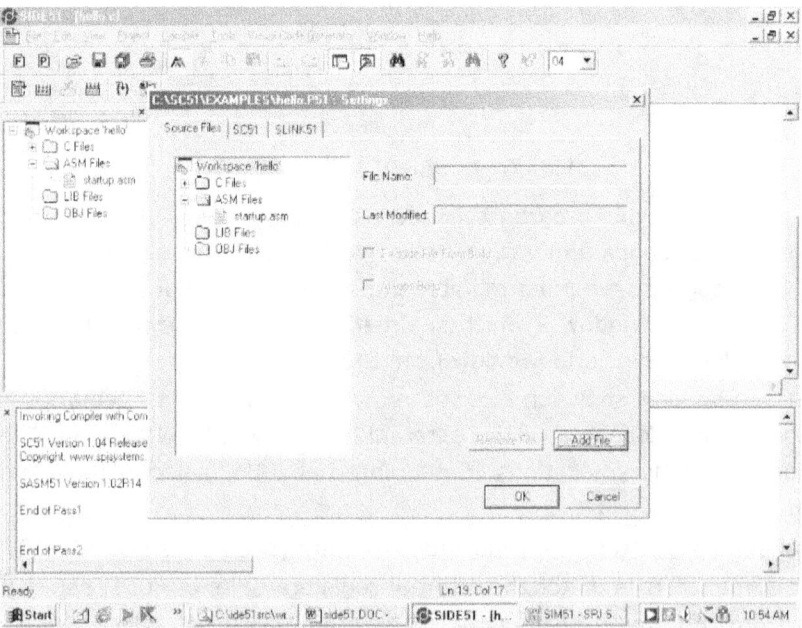

Fig. 2.15 : Side-51 Work Space

There are 3 tabs in the project settings window.

1. **Source Files :** This tab is automatically selected when you open the Project Settings window. When this tab is selected, you can see the list of files that are part of this project. This list is divided into groups of C files, ASM files, OBJ files and LIB files.

   To remove a file from the project, select the filename by clicking on it and then press the "Remove File" button. To add a file to project, press the "Add File" button, select desired file and then press Open button. The SIDE51 allows adding upto 16 C files, 16 ASM files, 16 OBJ files and 16 LIB files in a project.

2. **SC51 :** This tab lists some options for the SC51 compiler. You can select the "Target micro-controller" by selecting desired manufacturer name from the list and then selecting the desired 8051 derivative name from the list of micro-controllers.

   Depending on the processor selected, the amount of internal data memory (128 or 256bytes) is usually automatically set appropriately, however, you may change it if you need so. You can also enter the crystal frequency used in the target (this information maybe later used by the Simulator). You may check the "Generate debug info" option if you wish to use the simulator. Check the "Include C source lines in generated ASM file" option if you desire so.

3. **SLINK51 :** This tab lists some options for SLINK51 linker. You may enter the start and end address of xdata memory. If you need the ROM image file (.BIN) file, you should check the option "Generate BIN file". If you are going to use an In-Circuit-Emulator which requires Intel AOMF file for debugging, you may check the option "Generate Absolute OMF file". If this option is checked, then the absolute OMF file will be created; it will have the same name as project filename but extension will be .AOM.

   Set the necessary options in all the 3 tabs and when done, press Ok button. This will save the changed settings in the project file. To discard the changes made, press Cancel button.

Using SPJ Terminal and the Flash ISP programming tool :

• To start the SPJ Terminal program, select **Tools/SPJ Terminal** from the menu. This will start the SPJ Terminal application and the screen will look like this :

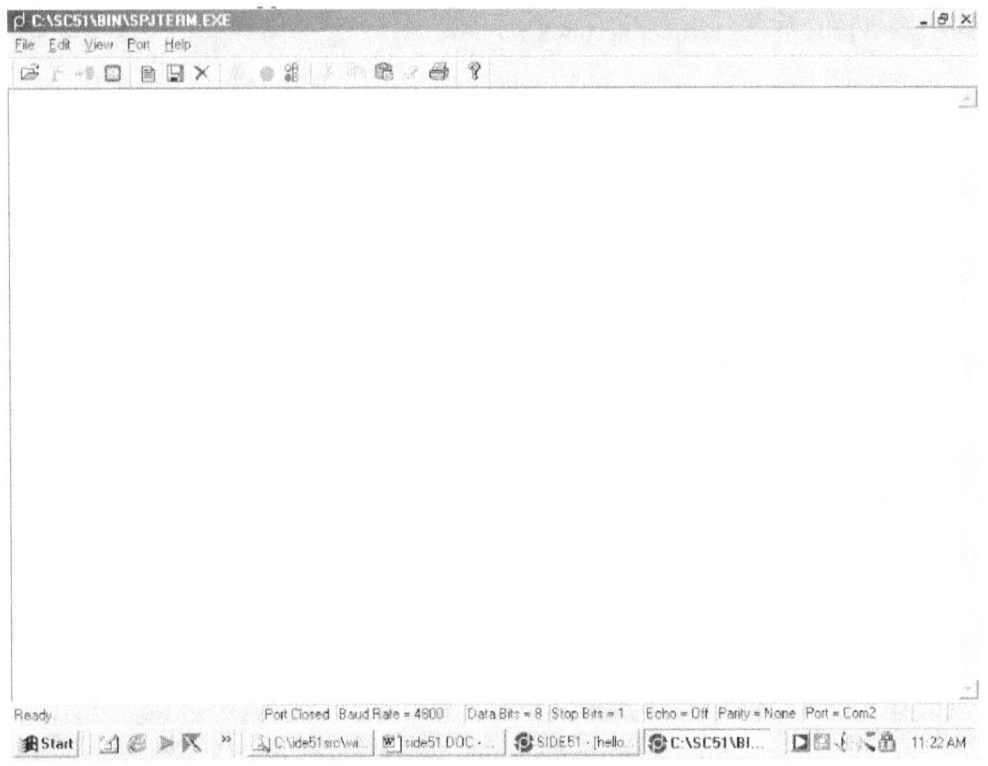

Fig. 2.16 : Sputter for ISP

- This application emulates some features of a "Terminal" and it also includes the flash ISP programming tool. The SPJ Terminal program can communicate with the target processor via a serial port (COM1, COM2 etc) of the computer. In order to establish this communication, it is necessary to set the COM port parameters correctly. To do so, select **Port/Settings** from the menu. Now you can select the desired COM port, desired baud rate and other parameters related to COM port. When done, press Ok button. Once the COM port parameters are set correctly, you may open the port by selecting **Port/Open** from the menu. As long as the port is open :

- All characters received on the selected COM port will be displayed in the SPJ Terminal window (and also saved in a file named spjterm.log, in the folder where the SPJTerm.EXE application is located). If the serial port of target 8051 hardware is connected to the selected COM port, then all characters output to serial port by the target 8051 will be displayed in SPJ Terminal window. For example, if the target hardware is running the "hello" example program, then the characters "Hello World!" should be displayed in SPJ Terminal window.

- (If focus is in SPJ Terminal window, then) all keystrokes typed will result in sending the corresponding ASCII character to the selected COM port. This way, input can be supplied to the target 8051 via its serial port. For example, if you use the scanf function for receiving input via serial port, such input can be supplied to the target 8051 using SPJ Terminal program.

- To close the port, select **Port/Close** from the menu.

- To start the flash ISP programming tool, select **File/In System Programming** from the menu. This ISP tool can be used for Philips processors, Dallas processors or for programming the external flash code memory of SBC51. Select appropriate tab as desired. Appropriate settings options are displayed according to the tab selected. For example, when Philips tab is selected, you can select desired processor from the list of chips. All the tabs include some common buttons like :

  ➢ Browse button allows you to select the .HEX file to be used for programming.

  ➢ Erase button allows you to erase the selected flash code memory.

  ➢ Program button allows you to program the flash with the selected .HEX file.

  ➢ Test communication button to verify whether communication between the SPJ Terminal program and target processor is established correctly.

  ➢ When done, you may press the Close button to close the flash ISP programming tool.

Important Points

Arithmetic Instructions :

Mnemonic	Description	Byte	Cycle
ADD A, Rn	Adds the register to the accumulator	1	1
ADD A, direct	Adds the direct byte to the accumulator	2	2
ADD A, @Ri	Adds the indirect RAM to the accumulator	1	2
ADD A, #data	Adds the immediate data to the accumulator	2	2
ADDC A, Rn	Adds the register to the accumulator with a carry flag	1	1
ADDC A, direct	Adds the direct byte to the accumulator with a carry flag	2	2
ADDC A, @Ri	Adds the indirect RAM to the accumulator with a carry flag	1	2
ADDC A, #data	Adds the immediate data to the accumulator with a carry flag	2	2

SUBB A, Rn	Subtracts the register from the accumulator with a borrow	1	1
SUBB A, direct	Subtracts the direct byte from the accumulator with a borrow	2	2
SUBB A, @Ri	Subtracts the indirect RAM from the accumulator with a borrow	1	2
SUBB A, #data	Subtracts the immediate data from the accumulator with a borrow	2	2
INC A	Increments the accumulator by 1	1	1
INC Rn	Increments the register by 1	1	2
INC Rx	Increments the direct byte by 1	2	3
INC @Ri	Increments the indirect RAM by 1	1	3
DEC A	Decrements the accumulator by 1	1	1
DEC Rn	Decrements the register by 1	1	1
DEC Rx	Decrements the direct byte by 1	1	2
DEC @Ri	Decrements the indirect RAM by 1	2	3
INC DPTR	Increments the Data Pointer by 1	1	3
MUL AB	Multiplies A and B	1	5
DIV AB	Divides A by B	1	5
DA A	Decimal adjustment of the accumulator according to BCD code	1	1

Branch Instructions :

Mnemonic	Description	Byte	Cycle
ACALL addr11	Absolute subroutine call	2	6
LCALL addr16	Long subroutine call	3	6
RET	Returns from subroutine	1	4
RETI	Returns from interrupt subroutine	1	4
AJMP addr11	Absolute jump	2	3
LJMP addr16	Long jump	3	4
SJMP rel	Short jump (from −128 to +127 locations relative to the following instruction)	2	3
JC rel	Jump if carry flag is set. Short jump.	2	3
JNC rel	Jump if carry flag is not set. Short jump.	2	3
JB bit, rel	Jump if direct bit is set. Short jump.	3	4

Mnemonic	Description	Byte	Cycle
JBC bit, rel	Jump if direct bit is set and clears bit. Short jump.	3	4
JMP @A+DPTR	Jump indirect relative to the DPTR	1	2
JZ rel	Jump if the accumulator is zero. Short jump.	2	3
JNZ rel	Jump if the accumulator is not zero. Short jump.	2	3
CJNE A, direct, rel	Compares direct byte to the accumulator and jumps if not equal. Short jump.	3	4
CJNE A, #data, rel	Compares immediate data to the accumulator and jumps if not equal. Short jump.	3	4
CJNE Rn, #data, rel	Compares immediate data to the register and jumps if not equal. Short jump.	3	4
CJNE @Ri, #data, rel	Compares immediate data to indirect register and jumps if not equal. Short jump.	3	4
DJNZ Rn, rel	Decrement registers and jumps, if not 0. Short jump.	2	3
DJNZ Rx, rel	Decrements direct byte and jump if not 0. Short jump.	3	4
NOP	No operation	1	1

Data Transfer Instructions :

Mnemonic	Description	Byte	Cycle
MOV A, Rn	Moves the register to the accumulator	1	1
MOV A, direct	Moves the direct byte to the accumulator	2	2
MOV A, @Ri	Moves the indirect RAM to the accumulator	1	2
MOV A, #data	Moves the immediate data to the accumulator	2	2
MOV Rn, A	Moves the accumulator to the register	1	2
MOV Rn, direct	Moves the direct byte to the register	2	4
MOV Rn, #data	Moves the immediate data to the register	2	2
MOV direct, A	Moves the accumulator to the direct byte	2	3
MOV direct, Rn	Moves the register to the direct byte	2	3
MOV direct, direct	Moves the direct byte to the direct byte	3	4
MOV direct, @Ri	Moves the indirect RAM to the direct byte	2	4
MOV direct, #data	Moves the immediate data to the direct byte	3	3
MOV @Ri, A	Moves the accumulator to the indirect RAM	1	3
MOV @Ri, direct	Moves the direct byte to the indirect RAM	2	5
MOV @Ri, #data	Moves the immediate data to the indirect RAM	2	3

MOV DPTR, #data	Moves a 16-bit data to the data pointer	3	3
MOVC A,@A+DPTR	Moves the code byte relative to the DPTR to the accumulator (address=A+DPTR)	1	3
MOVC A,@A+PC	Moves the code byte relative to the PC to the accumulator (address=A+PC)	1	3
MOVX A, @Ri	Moves the external RAM (8-bit address) to the accumulator	1	3-10
MOVX A,@DPTR	Moves the external RAM (16-bit address) to the accumulator	1	3-10
MOVX @Ri, A	Moves the accumulator to the external RAM (8-bit address)	1	4-11
MOVX @DPTR,A	Moves the accumulator to the external RAM (16-bit address)	1	4-11
PUSH direct	Pushes the direct byte onto the stack	2	4
POP direct	Pops the direct byte from the stack/td>	2	3
XCH A, Rn	Exchanges the register with the accumulator	1	2
XCH A, direct	Exchanges the direct byte with the accumulator	2	3
XCH A, @Ri	Exchanges the indirect RAM with the accumulator	1	3
XCHD A, @Ri	Exchanges the low-order nibble indirect RAM with the accumulator	1	3

Logic Instructions :

Mnemonic	Description	Byte	Cycle
ANL A, Rn	AND register to accumulator	1	1
ANL A, direct	AND direct byte to accumulator	2	2
ANL A, @Ri	AND indirect RAM to accumulator	1	2
ANL A, #data	AND immediate data to accumulator	2	2
ANL direct, A	AND accumulator to direct byte	2	3
ANL direct, #data	AND immediate data to direct register	3	4
ORL A, Rn	OR register to accumulator	1	1
ORL A, direct	OR direct byte to accumulator	2	2
ORL A, @Ri	OR indirect RAM to accumulator	1	2
ORL direct, A	OR accumulator to direct byte	2	3
ORL direct, #data	OR immediate data to direct byte	3	4
XRL A, Rn	Exclusive OR register to accumulator	1	1

XRL A, direct	Exclusive OR direct byte to accumulator	2	2
XRL A, @Ri	Exclusive OR indirect RAM to accumulator	1	2
XRL A, #data	Exclusive OR immediate data to accumulator	2	2
XRL direct, A	Exclusive OR accumulator to direct byte	2	3
XORL direct, #data	Exclusive OR immediate data to direct byte	3	4
CLR A	Clears the accumulator	1	1
CPL A	Complements the accumulator (1=0, 0=1)	1	1
SWAP A	Swaps nibbles within the accumulator	1	1
RL A	Rotates bits in the accumulator left	1	1
RLC A	Rotates bits in the accumulator left through carry	1	1
RR A	Rotates bits in the accumulator right	1	1
RRC A	Rotates bits in the accumulator right through carry	1	1

Bit-oriented Instructions :

Mnemonic	Description	Byte	Cycle
CLR C	Clears the carry flag	1	1
CLR bit	Clears the direct bit	2	3
SETB C	Sets the carry flag	1	1
SETB bit	Sets the direct bit	2	3
CPL C	Complements the carry flag	1	1
CPL bit	Complements the direct bit	2	3
ANL C, bit	AND direct bit to the carry flag	2	2
ANL C,/bit	AND complements of direct bit to the carry flag	2	2
ORL C, bit	OR direct bit to the carry flag	2	2
ORL C,/bit	OR complements of direct bit to the carry flag	2	2
MOV C, bit	Moves the direct bit to the carry flag	2	2
MOV bit, C	Moves the carry flag to the direct bit	2	3

Practice Questions

1. State function of IDE and its features.
2. Describe function of assembles complier, interpreter.

3. Explain linker and loader.

4. List the different extension and full form of same which are generated while using embedded 'C' simulator.

5. Write short note on cross complier, emulator and Flash/OTP programmer.

6. Differentiate between simulator and emulator.

7. State difference between complier and interpreter.

8. Write short note on ICE and JTAG port.

9. Compare 'C' and embedded C.

10. Compare assembly language and embedded C language.

11. List 5 simulator along with their programming language used for programming 8051.

12. State features of Keil and SPJ side S1, simulator.

13. State purpose of using Keil, side S1, flash magic software.

14. Write short note of ISP/IAP.

15. List arithmetic, relational, logical and conditional operator used in embedded C with example.

16. Describe TMOD and TCON SFR bit pattern.

17. Describe SMOD and SCON SPR bit pattern.

18. Describe PCON and PSW bit pattern.

19. Describe IP and IE SFR bit pattern.

20. Write a program to generate delay of 1 second using for loop and show calculation for same.

21. Describe operation of counters of 8051 and demonstrate same with C code.

22. State advantages of using assembly code in C language i.e. mixed programming.

23. Write C program to perform R3 = R2 | R1 and R4 and ~ R5.

24. Write C program to perform A = R1 | R2 and R3 and ~ R4.

25. Write C program to perform :
    (a) A = R1 AND R2 OR R3 AND R4 OR R5 AND R6
    (b) R7 = R1 EXOR R2 EXOR R3.

26. Write C program to implement full adder and full subtractor using 8051.

27. Write C program to glow LED in binary bit pattern on lower nibble of 8051. (i.e. 0000 to 1111)

28. Write C program to implement count to count following steps : 1, 3, 5, 7, 9, 11, 13, 15.

29. Write C program to read data form port 0, port 1 add both data and display sum on port 2 and carry on port 3.

30. State difference between logical and bitwise operators and state their functions.

MSBTE Questions

Summer 2012

1. Divide the data in RAM location 13H by the data in RAM location 14H, then restore the original data in 13H by multiplying the answer by the data in 14H. Use assembly language for 8051 microcontroller.

2. Write 'C' or assembly language program for 8051 to transfer letter "M" serially at 4800 baud rate.

3. Describe any four bit handling instructions of 8051.

4. Write assembly on 'C' language program to generate a square wave of 50Hz frequency on Pin PI-2. Use interrupts for timer. Assume crystal frequency 11.0592 MHz.

Winter 2012

1. Write assembly language program to transfer a block of data.

2. Write a program in C to generate a square wave of 50% duty cycle on bit 0 of Port 1.

3. Write the steps in programming 8051 to receive character byte serially.

Summer 2013

1. Identify the addressing mode used in following instruction Four instructions
   (a) MOV A, #55H,
   (b) ADD B,
   (c) MOV @Ri, 35H,
   (d) MOVC A, @A+DPTR.

2. Write assembly language program to exchange contents of the RAM locations from 30H in microcontroller 8051.

3. Write an assembly language program to toggle all the bits of port P1 every 200ms. Assume crystal frequency of 12MHz.

Winter 2013

1. Write a program in 'c' to transfer the message 'WELCOME' serially at 9600 baud, 8 bit data 1 stop bit continuously.

2. Explain the following instructions :
   (a) MOVDPTR, # F018H,
   (b) MOVA, # 22H,
   (c) MOVA, @ R0,
   (d) MOVX @ DPTR, A

3. Write a program in 'C' to get data AA from port O and sent it to port 1 of 8051.

4. State the types of instructions available in 8051 and explain any two Boolean instructions.

5. Identify the addressing modes of the following instruction :
   (a) MOVA, # 20H,
   (b) MOV 80H, A,
   (c) MOV@R1, # 35H,
   (d) MOVA, RO.

6. Write a program in 'C' to generate square wave on p1.2 bit use interrupt for timer.

Summer 2014

1. Write 'C' or assembly language program for 8051 to transfer letter "M" serially at 4800 baud rate.

2. List the addressing mode of 8051 and give example of each.

3. Write assembly language program to add m. subtract, multiply, divide two numbers.

Winter 2014

1. Write an assembly or C language program to send 'YES' on TXD LINE OF 8051. Assume BR=9600 bps and crystal frequency 11.0592 MHz.

2. Enlist any four addressing modes with suitable examples.

3. Write any four instructions to read/write data from/to external RAM.

4. Describe function of following instruction with examples :

   (a) SWAP A,   (b) RRC A,

   (c) CJNE A, #25h, NEXT,   (d) DJNZ Rz, NEXT.

5. Write an ALP or C language program to generate square wave of 1kHz frequency on P1-0.

6. Write an assembly/C language program to generate ASCII code for 4 using lookup table.

7. Write an assembly/C language program to generate ASCII code for 4 using lookup table.

Chapter 3...

I/O Ports, Timers/Counters, Interrupts and Serial Communication Programming

Weightage of Marks = 16, Teaching Hours = 10

Specific Objectives

➢ Students will be able to
  ❖ Configure the different ports as input or output
  ❖ Use of timer/counter in different modes
  ❖ Understand interrupts handling

3.1 PORT STRUCTURE AND SIMPLE PORT PROGRAMMING

3.1.1 Input/Output Ports

- The 8051 microcontroller provides I/O ports for external device interfacing. They are used to interface sensors, control valves, keyboards, displays, relays and lamp monitors etc.
- To save pins of chips, the 8051 provides multifunctional ports. These ports can be used as data bus or add address bus. Each I/O port is byte or bit addressable. The 8051 provides quasi bidirectional ports.

3.1.2 Features of Input/Output Port

1. 8051 provides four 8bit I/O ports.
2. All four ports are bidirectional.

3. Each port consists of a D-latch, an output driver, and an input buffer.

4. Each port line will input or output data under software control.

5. Each port can be accessed in byte or bit mode.

6. The port latches should not be confused with the port pins; the data on the latches does not have to be the same as that on the pins.

   ➢ All ports operate in various modes. However, some ports are used for special functions, port 0 functions as a multiplexed address/data bus, i.e. 8051 places lower byte of external memory address on the port 0. Port 2 is used to provide higher byte of external memory address. All port 3 pins are multifunctional, i.e. each line of port 3 pins has a special function.

   ➢ The alternate function can only be activated if the corresponding bit in latch or SFR contains logic 1. If the alternate function is not in use then port 3 can be used as a simple I/O port.

   ➢ Each line of the port 1, 2 and 3 is individually programmable as input or output. Let us study details of structure and operation of each port.

   ➢ The SFR (Special Function Register) for each port is made up of these eight latches, which can be addressed at the SFR address for that port. For example, the eight latches for port 0 are addressed at location 80h port 0 pin 3 is bit 2 of the Port0 SFR.

   ➢ The two data paths are shown in Fig. 3.1 by the circuits that read the latch or pin data using two entirely separate buffers. The upper buffer is enabled when latch data is read, and the lower buffer, when the pin state is read.

   ➢ The status of each latch may be read from a latch buffer, while an input buffer is connected directly to each pin so that the pin status may be read independently of the latch state.

3.1.2.1 Port 0 (8bit, bit/byte Addressable – 80H)

* Fig. 3.1 shows the details of the port 0 architecture.

* Each port consists of latch, an output driver and an input buffer. The bit latch is shown as a D flip-flop, which clocks in a value from the internal data bus in response to the Write to Latch signal from the CPU. The Q-output from the flip-flop can be read onto the internal data bus in response to a Read Latch signal from the CPU.

* Read pin is a different operation from reading a Latch. The port pin status can be read onto the internal data bus when CPU gives a 'read pin' command.

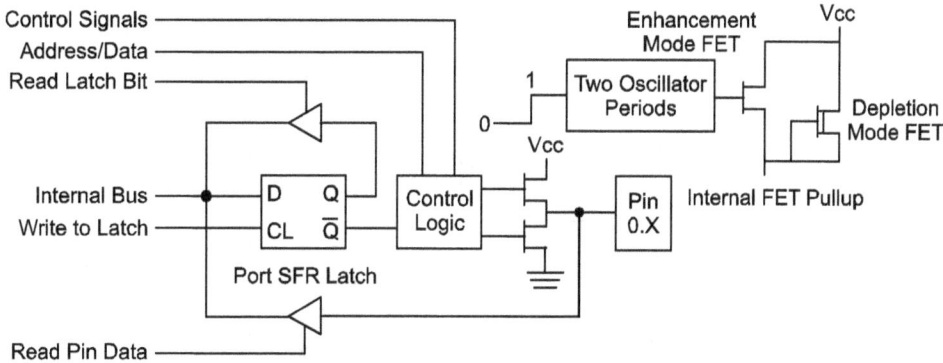

Fig. 3.1 : Port 0 Structure of 8051

- Port 0 occupies a total of 8 pins (pins 32 - 39).Each bit of the SFR corresponds to one bit of the port pin for example bit 0 of port 0 is P0.0 and bit 7 is P0.7. It can be used for input or output. To use the pins of port 0 as both input and output ports, each pin must be connected externally to a 10 K ohm pull-up resistor.

- This is due to the fact that P0 is an open drain. Open drain is a term used for MOS (Metal Oxide Semiconductor) chips in the same way that open collector is used for TTL (Transistor Transistor Logic) chips. In any system normally connect P0 to pull-up resistors.

- With external pull-up resistors connected upon reset, port 0 is configured as an output port.

- Address Port 0 is 80H. Port can be addressed as P0 complete 8 bit port and P0.0 to P0.7 as bit addressable port.

      MOV A, P0   ; Read Data port from Port 0 and store in Acc.
      SETB P0.1   ; Set the port0's bit 1

3.1.2.2 Functions of Port 0

1. Simple 8-bit input port.
2. Simple 8-bit output port.
3. Bidirectional Multiplexed Address/Data Bus.

Port 0–Input :

- With resistors connected to port 0, in order to make it an input, the port must be programmed by writing 1 to all the bits. In the following code, port 0 is configured first as an input port by writing 1's to it, and then data is received from the port and sent to P1.

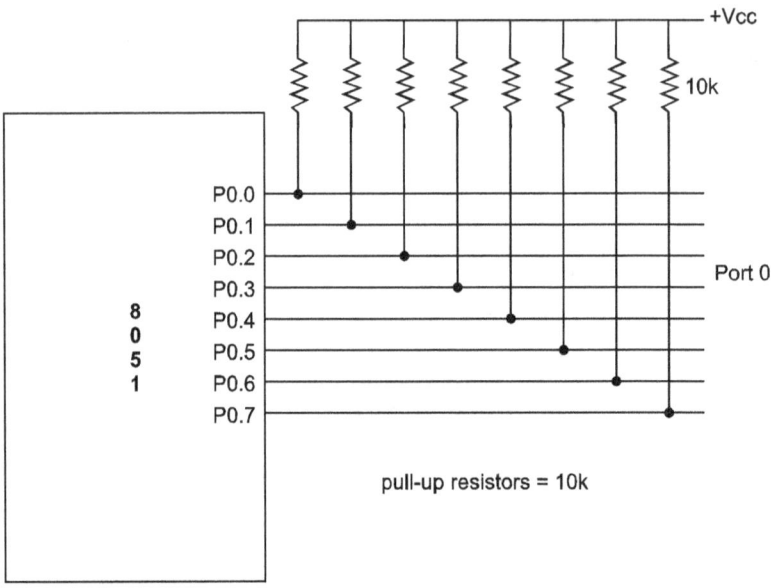

Fig. 3.2 : Port 0 with pull up resistor

MOVA, #0FFH	; A = FF hex
MOV P0, A	; make P0 an input port by writing port with data 1.
BACK: MOV A,P0	; get data from P0 i.e. read
MOV P1, A	; send it to port 1 i.e. write
SJMP BACK	

Read Pin :

- During this operation the 8051 activates an internal read signal to read level of port pin. In this case, it does not read contents of SFR latch.

Read Latch :

- In this operation, the 8051 activates an internal read latch signal to read contents of latch. In- this case, the processor reads contents of latch. It does not read contents of port pin. For read modify operation, the processor performs this operation.

- The instruction that read the latch are the ones that read a value of latch, processes this value and then rewrites this result into the same latch. Some instructions read byte from the port, modify the selected bit, and then write the new byte into the port (e.g. Clear a particular bit of port).

- These instructions are called read, modify, and write instructions. These instructions do not read port lines.

Output Mode :

- When used as an output, the pin latches that are programmed to a 0 will turn on the lower FET, grounding the pin. All latches that are programmed to a 1 still float; thus, external pull-up resistors will be needed to supply logic high when using port 0 as an output.

Alternate Function of Port 0- Multiplexed Bidirectional Address/Data Bus :

- When port 0 is used as an address bus to external memory, internal control signals switch the address lines to the gates of the Field Effect Transistors (FETs). Logic 1 on an address bit will turn the upper FET (T1) on and the lower FET (T2) off to provide logic high at the pin. When the address bit is a zero, the lower FET (T2) (Field Effect Transistor) is on and the upper FET (T1) off to provide a logic low at the pin.

- After the address has been formed and latched into external circuits by the Address Latch Enable (ALE) pulse, the bus is turned around to become a data bus. Port 0 now reads data from the external memory and must be configured as an input, so logic 1 is automatically written by internal control logic to all port 0 latches.

Port1-(Bit/Byte Addressable – 90H)

- Port 1 occupies a total of 8 pins (pins 1 - 9).Each bit of the SFR corresponds to one bit of the port pin, for example bit 0 of port 1 is P1.0 and bit 7 is P1.7. It can be used for input or output.

- In contrast to port 0, this port does not need any pull-up resistors since it already has pull-up resistors internally made up of FET also called as active pull up. Upon reset, port 1 is configured as an output port. Fig. 3.3 shows the architecture of Port 1.

Port 1-Input :

- To use port as an input, a 1 is written to the latch, turning the lower FET (T2) off; the pin and the input to the pin buffer are pulled high by the FET load. An external circuit can overcome the high-impedance pull-up and drive the pin low to input a 0 or leave the input high for a 1.

Port 1-Output :

- To use port as an output, the latches containing a 1 can drive the input of an external circuit high through the pull-up. If a 0 is written to the latch, the lower FET is on, the pull-up is off, and the pin can drive the input of the external circuit low.

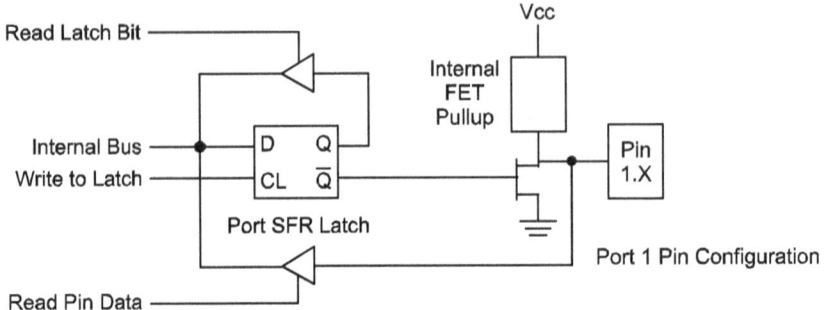

Fig. 3.3 : Port 1 Structure of 8051

Usage of Port :

- Address Port 1 is 90H. Port can be addressed as P1 complete 8 bit port and P1.0 to P1.7 as bit addressable port.

  Mov A, P1   ; Read Data port from Port 1 and store in Acc

  CLR P1.1   ; Set the port1's bit 0

Port 2-(Bit/Byte Addressable–0A0H) :

- Port 2 occupies a total of 8 pins (pins 21 - 29).Each bit of the SFR corresponds to one bit of the port pin, for example bit 0 of port 2 is P2.0 and bit 7 is P2.7.

Functions of Port 2 :

- ➢ Simple 8-bit input port.

- ➢ Simple 8-bit output port.

- ➢ Functions as high order Address Bus.

- Port 2 does not need any pull-up resistors since it already has pull-up resistors internally. Upon reset, port 2 is configured as an output port.

- Writing 1 in the port latch will make the port to function as input port.

Usage of Port :

- Address Port 2 is 0A0H. Port can be addressed as P2 complete 8 bit port and P2.0 to P2.7 as bit addressable port.

  CLR P2.1   ; Set the port 2's bit 0

  SetB P2.3   ; set the port 2's bit 3 to High

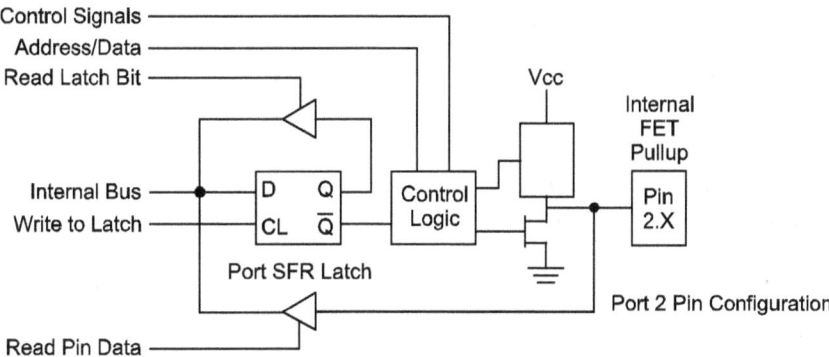

Fig. 3.4 : Port 2 Structure of 8051

Port 2 as Address Bus :

- During external memory access, these lines are used to transfer higher byte of external memory address. During external memory access, the 8051 places higher byte of address on port 2 lines. In this mode, the 'control' signal goes to logic 1.

- This signal connects inverter to the address line. The 'control' signal goes to logic 1 during address time. If address bit is logic 0, it turns OFF the transistor T1 and ON the transistor T2.

- But the impedance of the transistor T2 is less than that of internal pull-up, hence the port pin is held at logic 0. When ALE is high, it provides strong pull up for two crystal clock periods.

Port3 (Bit/Byte Addressable-0B0H) :

- Port 3 occupies a total of 8 pins (pins 10 - 17).Each bit of the SFR corresponds to one bit of the port pin, for example bit 0 of port 3 is P3.0 and bit 7 is P3.7.

Functions of Port 2 :

> Simple 8-bit input port

> Simple 8-bit output port

> Alternate Function for Serial I/O. Read/Write, Timer, External Interrupt

- Port 3 does not need any pull-up resistors since it already has pull-up resistors internally. Upon reset, port 2 is configured as an output port. Writing 1 in the port latch will make the port to function as input port.

Port3-Input/Output :

- Port 3 is an input/output port similar to port 1. The input and output functions can be programmed under the control of the Port 3 latches or under the control of various other special function registers.

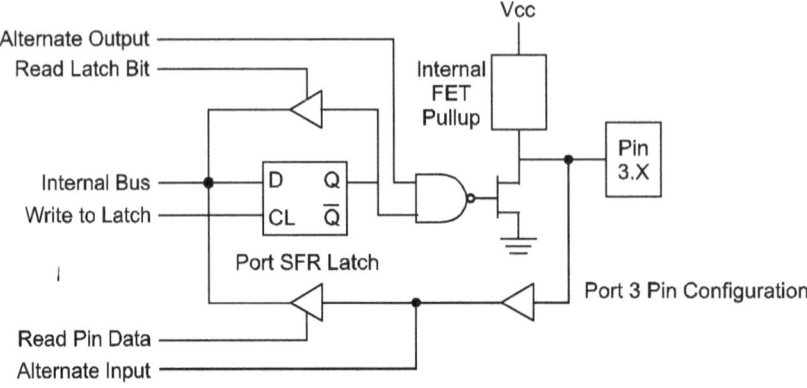

Fig. 3.5 : Port 3 Structure of 8051

Port3 – Alternate Function :

- The port 3 alternate uses are shown in the following table :

Pin	Label	Usage	SFR Needed
P3.0	RXD	Serial Data Input	SBUF
P3.1	TXD	Serial Data Output	SBUF
P3.2	INT0	External Interrupt 0	TCON.1
P3.3	INT1	External Interrupt 1	TCON.3
P3.4	T0	External Timer 0	TMOD
P3.5	T1	External Timer 1	TMOD
P3.6	WR	External Memory Write Pulse	-------
P3.7	RD	External Memory Read Pulse	-------

- Unlike ports 0 and 2, which can have external addressing functions and change all eight port bits when in alternate use, each pin of port 3 may be individually programmed to be used either as I/O or as one of the alternate functions.

- Even though all pins on this port can be used as universal I/O port, they also have an alternative function. Since each of these functions use inputs, then the appropriate pins have to be configured like that. In other words, prior to using some of reserve port functions, a logical one (1) must be written to the appropriate bit in the P3 register.

Usage of Port

- Address Port 3 is 0B0H. Port can be addressed as P3 complete 8 bit port and P3.0 to P3.7 as bit addressable port.

```
Mov A, P3                ; Read Data port from Port 3 and store in Acc
CLR P3.2                 ; Set the port3's bit 0
Set B P3.3               ; set the port3's bit 3 to High
```

Read, Modify Write Feature :

- The ports in the 8051 can be accessed by the read-modify-write technique. This feature saves many lines of code by combining in a single instruction all three actions of (1) reading the port, (2) modifying it, and (3) writing to the port.

- The following code first places 01010101 (binary) into port 1. Next, the instruction "XLR P1, #0FFH" performs an XOR logic operation on P1 with 1111 1111 (binary), and then writes the result back into P1.

```
MOV P1, #55H             ; P1=01010101
AGAIN: XLR P1, #0FFH     ; EX-OR P1 with 1111 1111
ACALL DELAY
SJMP AGAIN
```

- Note that XOR of 55H and FFH gives AAH. Likewise, the XOR of AAH and FFH gives 55H

Bit Addressing of Port :

- There are times that we need to access only 1 or 2 bits of the port instead of the entire 8 bits. A powerful feature of 8051 I/O ports is their capability to access individual bits of the port without altering the rest of the bits in that port. For example, the following code toggles the bit p1.2 continuously.

```
BACK: CPL P1.2           ; complement p1.2 only
ACALL DELAY
SJMP BACK
```

- Note that P1.2 is the third bit of P1, since the first bit is P1.0, the second bit is P1.1, and so on. Notices in example of those unused portions of port1 are undisturbed. Table bellow shows the bits of 8051 I/O ports. This single bit addressability of I/O ports is one of the features of the 8051 microcontroller.

Note :

1. The state of a port bit, besides being reflected in the pin, determines at the same time whether it will be configured as input or output.

2. If a bit is cleared (0), the pin will be configured as output. In the same manner, if a bit is set to 1 the pin will be configured as input.

3. After reset, as well as when turning the microcontroller on, all bits on these ports are set to one (1). This means that the appropriate pins will be configured as inputs.

4. Status of the Port pins of all the ports after reset

Port	Bit7	Bit6	Bit5	Bit4	Bit3	Bit2	Bit1	Bit0	Address
P0	1	1	1	1	1	1	1	1	80H
P1	1	1	1	1	1	1	1	1	90H
P2	1	1	1	1	1	1	1	1	0A0H
P3	1	1	1	1	1	1	1	1	0B0H

3.2 TIMER/COUNTER

- There are many such applications which require the counting of external events, such as the frequency of a pulse train, or the generation of precise internal time delays between computer actions, baud rate generation, pulse width and frequency generation.

- All these tasks can be accomplished using software techniques, but software loops for counting or timing keep the processor occupied so that other, perhaps more important, functions are not done.

- Hence, disadvantages of Software Technique are :

  1. Delays are not accurate.

  2. Microprocessor cannot perform its task.

  3. System Performance is degraded.

  4. Limitation on minimum delay.

  5. More delay events cannot be handled simultaneously.

  6. It is expensive because costly processor is evolved.

- Hence hardware technique is used. Like using timer IC 555, 566, micro-processor in support with 8155, 8253, 8254 and even microcontroller 8051.

3.2.1 Microcontroller Timer/Counter

- The difference between a timer and a counter.

3.2.1.1 Timer

- Timer counts machine cycles and provides a reference time delay or a clock. A machine cycle of 8051 consists of 12 oscillator periods or the counting rate is 1/12 of the oscillator frequency. At 12 MHz, the clocking period will be equal to 1 μs.

3.2.1.2 Counter

- Counter of 8051 is incremented in response to a transition from '1' to '0' at its corresponding external pin (either T0 or TI). Thus, the counter output will be a count or a number representing the occurrence of such '1' to '0' transitions at the external pin.

- For counting function, 8051 takes 2 cycles or 24 oscillator periods to detect a '1' to '0' transition at Pin T0 or T1.

- When a timer or counter overflows from FFFFH to 0000H, it sets a flag and generates an interrupt.

3.2.1.3 8051 Timer/Counter

- To relieve the processor of this burden, two 16bit up counters, named T0 and T1, are provided for the general use of the programmer. Each counter may be programmed to count internal clock pulses, acting as a timer, or programmed to count external pulses as a counter

- The counters are divided into two 8-bit registers called the timer low (TL0, TL1) and high (TH0, TH1) bytes. All counter action is controlled by bit states in the timer mode control register (TMOD), the timer/counter control register (TCON), and certain program instruction.

- TMOD is totally used for the two timers and can be considered to be two duplicate 4-bit registers, each of which controls the action of one of the timers. TCON has control bits and flags for the timers in the upper nibble, and control bits and flags for the external interrupts in the lower nibble. Figure shows the bit assignments for TMOD and TCON.

3.2.1.4 SFR related to Timer/Counter

Timer 0 Register(T0) – TL0/TH0 – 8AH/8CH

- The 16-bit register of timer 0 can be used low byte and high byte. The low byte register is called TL0 (timer 0 low byte) and the high byte register is referred to as TH0 (timer 0 high byte). These registers can be accessed like any other register, such as A, B, R0, RI, R2, etc.

- For example

  MOV TL0, #4FH   ; Load 4FH into TL0,

  MOV R4, TH0   ; Store TH0 (high byte of timer 0) in R4.

D15	D14	D13	D12	D11	D10	D9	D8
Timer High Register TH0							

D7	D6	D5	D4	D3	D2	D1	D0
			Timer Low Register TL0				

Timer 1 registers(T1) – TL1/TH1 – 8BH/8DH

* Timer 1 is also 16 bits, and its 16-bit register is spitted into two bytes, referred to as TL1 (timer 1 low byte) and TH1 (timer 1 high byte). These registers are accessible in the same way as the registers of timer 0.

D15	D14	D13	D12	D11	D10	D9	D8
			Timer High Register TH1				

D7	D6	D5	D4	D3	D2	D1	D0
			Timer Low Register TL1				

Note : On reset, the value for both TLx and THx is equal to 0(zero).Maximum value loaded will be 65535 (FFFFH)

TMOD – Timer Mode Register – 89H :

D7	D6	D5	D4	D3	D2	D1	D0
Gate	C/T	M1	M0	Gate	C/T	M1	M0
Timer 1				Timer 0			

Bits	Symbol	Functions
D7, D3	Gate	Gating control when set. Timer/counter is enabled only while the INTx pin is high and the TRx control pin is set. When cleared, the timer is enabled whenever the TRx control bit is set.
D6, D2	C/T	Timer or counter selected cleared for timer operation (input from internal system clock). Set for counter operation (input from TRx input pin).
D5, D1	M1	Mode Bit 1.Set and cleared by the program.
D4, D0	M0	Mode Bit 0. Set and cleared by the program.
M1	M0	Modes of Timer/Counter
0	0	13 bit timer mode 8 bit timer/counter THx and 5bit timer/counter TLx
0	1	16 bit timer mode 8 bit timer/counter THx and 8bit timer/counter TLx

1	0	8-bit auto load 8-bit reload timer/counter; THx holds a value which is to be reloaded into TLx each time it overflows
1	1	Spilt timer mode

Details of the bits :

- **Gate :** OR gate enable bit which controls RUN/STOP of timer 1/0. Set to 1 by program to enable timer to run, if bit TR1/0 in TCON is set and signal on external interrupt INT1/0(P3.2, P3.0)pin is high. Cleared to 0 by program to enable timer to run if bit TR1/0 in TCON is set.

- SETB and CLR can be used to set and reset the Gate bit. Hence this bit can be used to RUN or STOP the timer.

- **C/T :** Set to 1 by program to make timer 1/0 act as a counter by counting pulses from external input pins 3.5 (T1) or 3.4 (T0) i.e. event counter. Cleared to 0 by program to make timer act as a timer by counting internal frequency or delay generator.

Examples :

1. MOV TMOD, #01H

0000000**1** => Mode 1 of timer 0 is selected.

2. MOV TMOD, #20H

00**1**00000 => Mode 2 of timer 1 is selected.

3. MOV TMOD, #12H

000**1**00**10** => Mode 2 of timer 0 is selected and mode1 of timer 1 is selected.

TCON – Timer Control Register Address – 88H- Bit Addressable " :

D7	D6	D5	D4	D3	D2	D1	D0
TF1	**TR1**	**TF0**	**TR0**	**IE1**	**IT1**	**IE0**	**IT0**
Timer1		Timer0		Interrupt 1		Interrupt 0	

Bit		Symbol	Function
7,5	TCON.7,TCON.5	TFx	Timer x (0,1) overflow flag, set when timer(0,1) overflow from FFFFH to 0000H
6,4	TCON.6,TCON.4	TRx	Timer (0,1) run control bit.
3,1	TCON.3,TCON.1	IEx	External Interrupt for interrupt 0,1
2,0	TCON.2,TCON.0	ITx	Timer interrupt for TI 0,1

- **TFx – Timer Overflow (0, 1) :** This bit can be set through software. This bit is set when timer overflows from FFFFH to 0000H. This bit is cleared or reset as soon as timer jump to its service routine whose vector address is 001BH(Timer 1) or 000BH(Timer 0)

- **TRx – Timer Run bit (0, 1) :** This bit is used to Turn Timer On/OFF. When set to 1, timer is enabled to count.

  ➢ When reset or cleared to 0 by program, timer is halted or stops counting. It does not reset the timer.

- IEx – External Interrupt Edge Flag set (0, 1 – Pin 3.2 (INT0) Pin3.3 (INT1)) : This bit indicates whether external interrupt is activated or not.

  ➢ In **edge triggered mode**, it is set at the falling (High to Low) mode of the external interrupt signal.

  ➢ In **level triggered mode**, this bit set at the low level of the external interrupt signal. When this bit is set, it activate external signal and cleared automatically when jump to ISR at location 0013(IE1) and 0003(IE0). It can be set through software. These bits are not related to timer operation.

- ITx – External Interrupt Signal Type control bit (0,1) :

  ➢ This bit is used triggering type of the external internal pins INT0 and INT1. Each interrupt input can be initialized in either edge or level triggered mode.

  ➢ When this bit 1, it operates in edge triggered mode.

  ➢ When this bit is 0, it operates in level triggered mode.

Example :

SETB TCON.0　　; Set the TCON.0 (IT0) bit, i.e. make interrupt level triggered

CLR TCON.7　　; Reset the TCON.7 bit i.e. clear the timer overflow flag

SETB TR1　　　; Start timer 0

CLR TR0　　　; Stop Timer 0

Note : TCON value is set to 00000000(00)H after reset i.e. TCON register is cleared.

Mode of Timer operations :

Timer is operated in 4 modes by setting TMODs M1, M0 bits :

Four modes of Timer operation are :

Mode 0 : M1 = 0, M0 = 0 → 13 bit timer counter mode

Mode 1 : M1 = 0, M0 = 1 → 16 bit timer counter mode

Mode 2 : M1 = 1, M0 = 0 → 8 bit auto reload mode

Mode 3 : M1 = 1, M0 = 1 → 2- 8 bit timer using timer 0

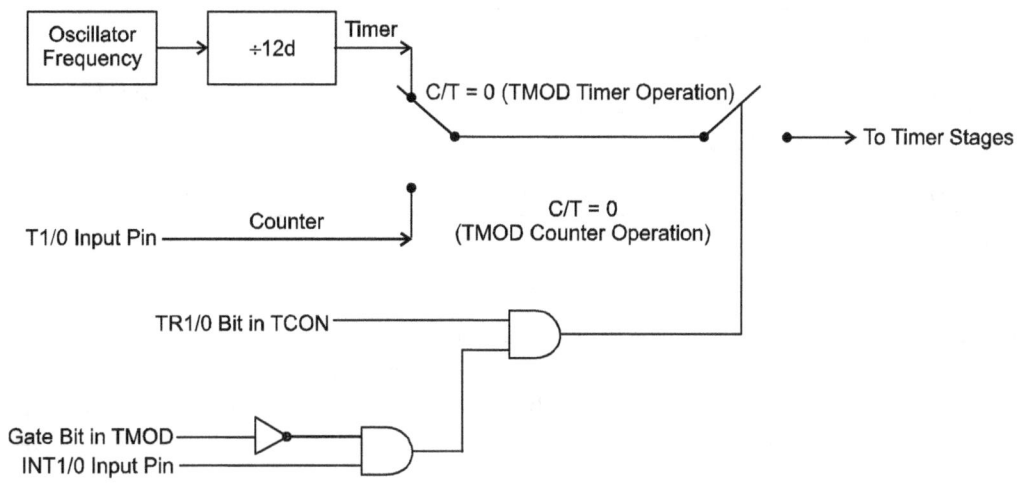

Fig. 3.6 : Timer/counter Control Logic

Timer Mode 0

- Set M1 = 0, M0 = 0 → 13 bit timer counter mode register results in using the THX register as an 8-bit counter and TLX as a 5bit counter. The pulse input is divided by 32d in TL so that TH counts the original oscillator frequency reduced by a total 384d.

- When the count overflows, it sets the timer interrupt flag (TF1 for timer 1 and TF0 for timer 0). To start timer 0, TR0 bit in TCON is to be set. This 13-bit operation is just to have compatible timer function as that of 8048 family. Using the upper byte TH0 (TH1) and the lower 5 bits of TL0 (or TL1) form the 13 bits. This is shown in Fig. 3.7.

Fig. 3.7 : Timer in mode 0 – 13bit Timer/Counter

Timer Mode 0 - 13 bit Timer/Counter

- As an example, the 6 megahertz oscillator frequency would result in a final frequency to T1 of 15625 hertz The Timer flag is set whenever THX goes from FFh to 00h, or in 0.0164 seconds for a 6 megahertz crystal if THX starts at 00h.

Timer TH Register								Timer TL register							
D15	D14	D15	D14	D15	D14	D15	D14	D15	D14	D15	D14	D15	D14	D15	D14
Upper 8 bits TH								X							
	D12		D12		D12		D12		D12		D12		D12		D12

Initialization in Mode 0 :

    Mov TMOD, #80H   ; 10 00 00 00b

- It initializes timer 1 in mode 0. In the above code, timer 1 is configured as a timer in mode 0. Observe that bit TMOD.7 in TMOD is set to 1. This is the GATE bit. If this is set to 1 and TR1 is 1, then the timer 1 is controlled by the external input at Pin 13 (INT1). When GATE is 0, then, it is only TR1 which enables the timer.

    SETB TR0   ; Set bit of TCON.4 = 1
    CLR TF0   ; Clear TF0 i.e. TCON.5 = 0

Timer Mode 1 :

- Mode 1 is same as mode 0, except the timers are 16 bits wide. Mode 1 is again the same for timer 0 and timer 1. The maximum count in this mode is FFFFH. There is always a natural tendency to use mode 1 than mode 0, since the 13-bit operation in mode 0 has no specific advantage.

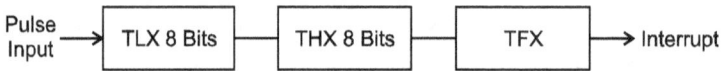

Fig. 3.8 Timer Mode 1 – 16 bit timer/counter

- Mode 1 is similar to mode 0 except TLX is configured as a full 8-bit counter when the mode bits are set to 01 b in TMOD. The Timer flag would be set in 0.1311 seconds using a 6 megahertz crystal.

Initialization in Mode 1 :

        Mov TMOD, #01H   ; 00000001b

                          ; Set the Timer 0 in Mode 1

        SETB TR0   ; Set gate bit to zero (0), and Start Timer 0

Timer Mode 2 :

- Setting the made bits to 10b in TMOD configures the timer to use only the TLX counter as an 8-bit counter. THX is used to hold a value that is loaded into TLX every time TLX overflows from FFh to 00h. The Timer flag is also set when TLX overflows. Fig. 3.9. shows auto reload mechanism.

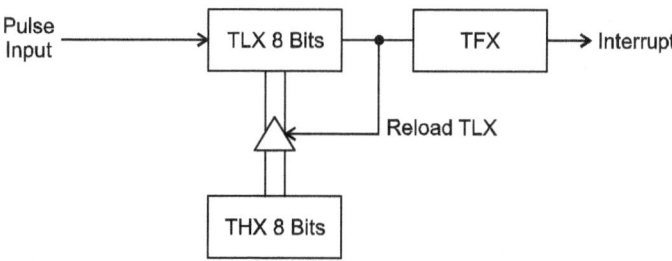

Fig. 3.9 : Timer Mode2 Auto Reloaded of TL from TH

- This mode exhibits an auto-reload feature
  1. TLX will count up from the number in THX,
  2. It overflow when count run from FFH to 00H, set TFx flag and
  3. Initialized again with the contents of THX.
- For example, placing 9Ch in THX will result in a delay of exactly 0.0002 seconds before, the Overflow flag is set if a 6 megahertz crystal is used.

Initialization in Mode 2 :

```
Mov TMOD, #0000 0010b      ; Load TMOD, making Timer 0 in mode 2
Mov THO, #66H              ; Load THO with data 66H, which will be reloaded
Mov TLO, #66H              ; Load TLO with data 66H
SETB TR0                   ; Start timer 0, timer with generate Square wave
```

- Mode 2 is mostly used for baud rate generation for serial Port. It is also used when square wave output is needed whose frequency is constant. The program load TMOD and then the auto-reload value must be written in the timer high byte THO.
- The starting count will also be the same as that of the reload value in general i.e. 66h, value should selected such that it count up to FFH and then overflow.
- However, it is very essential to load the timer high byte with the auto-reload value, otherwise the timer after each overflow will start from 00H, which can cause error in timings or delays generated using this timer.

Timer Mode 3 – Two 8 bit Timer using Timer 0 – split Timer mode :

- Timers 0 and 1 may be programmed to be in mode 0, 1, or 2 independently of a similar mode for the other timer. But in mode 3, both the timers do not operate independently. Setting timer 1 in mode 3 causes it to stop counting. The control bit TR1 and the timer 1 flag TF1 are then used by timer 0.
- Timer 0 in mode 3 acts two completely separate 8-bit counters. TL0 is controlled by the gate arrangement of Fig. 3.10. and sets timer flag TF0 whenever it

overflows from FFh to 00h. TH0 receives the timer clock (the oscillator divided by 12) under the control of TR1 only and sets the TF 1 flag when it overflows.

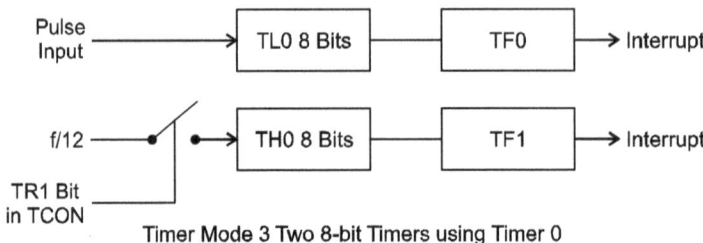

Timer Mode 3 Two 8-bit Timers using Timer 0

Fig. 3.10 : Timer mode 3 Two 8-bit times using Timer 0

- Timer 1 still is used in modes 0, 1, and 2, while timer 0 is in mode 3 with one important exception that No interrupts will be generated by timer 1 while timer 0 is using the TF1 overflow flag. Switching timer 1 to mode 3 will stop it (and hold whatever count is in timer 1).

- Timer 1 can be used for baud rate generation for the serial port, or any other mode 0, 1, or 2 functions that does not depend on an interrupt (or any other use of the TF1 flag) for proper operation.

Timer/Counter related Programs :

Example 1 : Generate square wave on pin2.0 of port 2 of 8051.

Label	Mnemonics	Comments
	MOV SP, #64H	; Initialize Stack Pointer
	MOV TMOD, #00000010B	; Set timer 0 in mode 2 (Auto-reload)
	MOV TH0, #06H	; Set TH0 to 66h for 2khz square wave
	MOV TL0, #06H	; set TL0 to 66h for 2khz square wave, i.e. starting value of the timer
	SETB TR0	; Start timer0
LOOP:	JB TF0, COMPL	
	SJMP LOOP	
COMPL	CPL P2.0	; Toggle bit P2.0
	SJMP LOOP	

Example 2 : Generate square wave on pin2.0 of port 2 of 8051 on interrupt.

Label	Mnemonics	Comments
	ORG 0000H	
	AJMP STRT	; Main Program start
	ORG 000BH	
	AJMP INT_FO	; ISR is at INT_TFO
	MOV SP, #64H	; Initialize Stack Pointer
	SETB ET0	
	SETB EA	
	MOV TMOD, #00000010B	; Set timer 0 in mode 2 (Auto-reload)
	MOV TH0, #06H	; Set TH0 to 66h for 2khz square wave
	MOV TL0, #06H	; Set TL0 to 66h for 2khz square wave, i.e. starting value of the timer
	SETB TR0	; Start timer0
	SJMP $	; Infinite the stack pointer
COMPL	CPL P2.0	; Toggle bit P2.0
	RETI	
	END	

Example 3 : A clock pulse is fed to TI input, write the program to count the pulses in mode 2 by counter 1 and display the status of TL1 count out pin2.

Label	Mnemonics	Comments
	MOV SP, #64H	; Initialize Stack Pointer
	MOV TMOD, #0C06H	; Counter 1, mode 2, C/T=1 i.e. count external pulse
	MOV TH1, #0H	; Clear the timer high register
	MOV TMOD, #00000010B	; Set timer 0 in mode 2 (Auto-reload)
	SETB P3.5	; Make TI input High
Here :	SETB TR1	; Start timer counter
BACK :	MOV A, TL1	; Copy the content of TL1 in Acc.
	MOV P2, A	; Display count on port2

	JNB TF1, NEXT	; Repeat till TFx is not TF = 0
	CLR TF1	; Stop the Counter/Timer 1
	CLR TF1	; Make timer overflow flag = 0
	SJMP here	; Repeat the process

Example 4 : Write a program to generate continuous square wave on pin P1.3 using timer 1 and mode1 for a time delay generated by count 7634 loaded in Timer register. Find the frequency of the square wave, if XTAL is used is of 11.0592 MHz.

Solution :

Calculation of frequency of square wave :

$$\text{Clock Count} = (\text{Max Count} - \text{Given Count}) + 1$$

$$\text{Max Count} = \text{FFFFH}$$

$$\text{Given Count} = 7634$$

$$\text{Clock Count} = (\text{FFFF} - 7634) + 1$$

$$= \text{89CC H}$$

$$= 35276D$$

XTAL frequency = 11.0592 MHz, XTAL Time Period is

$$T_{xtal} = 1/\text{XTAL} = 1/11.0592 * 10^6$$

$$= 1.085 \ \mu sec$$

$$T_{on} = \text{Clock Count} * T_{xtal}$$

$$= 35276 * 1.085 * 10^{-6}$$

$$= 38.275 \ \mu Sec$$

$$T_{square} = T_{on} * 2$$

$$= 38.275 \ \mu Sec * 2$$

$$= 76.55 \ \mu Sec$$

Frequency of aquare wave is = $1/T_{square}$

$$= 1/76.55 \ \mu Sec$$

$$= 13.05 \ Hz$$

Algorithm for the Program :

Step 1 : Set the 16 bit timer mode for timer 1 by loading TMOD register

    MOV TMOD, #0000 0001b

Step 2 : Load 16bit count in TH and TL register

    MOV TL0, #34H
    MOV TH0, #76H

Step 3 : Start timer by Setting TRO bit in TCON register

SETB TR0

Step 4 : Check Timer Register <> 0 then go to step4

JNB TF0, step4

Step 5 : Stop Timer by resetting TR0 bit in TCON register

CLR TR0

Step 6 : Complement Port P1.3 make it High or Low

CPL P1.5

Step 7 : Clear Timer Flag of Timer 1

CLR TF0

Step 8 : Repeat from step 2.

- The only and main difference between counting and timing is the source of the clock pulses to the counters. When used as a timer, the clock pulses are sourced from the oscillator through the divide -by- 12d circuit. When used as a counter, pin T0 (P3.4) supplies pulses to counter 0, and pin T1 (P3.5) to counter 1.

- The C/T bit in TMOD must be set to 1 to enable pulses from the TX pin to reach the control circuit.

3.3 SERIAL COMMUNICATION

- Computers transfer data in two ways:
  1. Parallel and
  2. Serial.

3.3.1 Parallel Data Transfer

- In this type of transfer often 8 or more lines (wire conductors) are used to transfer data to a device that is only a few feet away. Since microprocessor communicates with the outside world, it provides the data in byte-sized chunks.

- Examples of parallel transfers are printers and hard disks, each uses cables with many wire strips. Although in such cases a lot of data can be transferred in a short amount of time by using many wires in parallel, the distance cannot be great. In printers, the information is simply grabbed from the 8-bit data bus and presented to the 8-bit data bus of the printer.

- Because parallel data transfer work only if the cable is not too long, since long cables diminish and even distort signals.

- To transfer to a device located many meters away, the serial method is used.

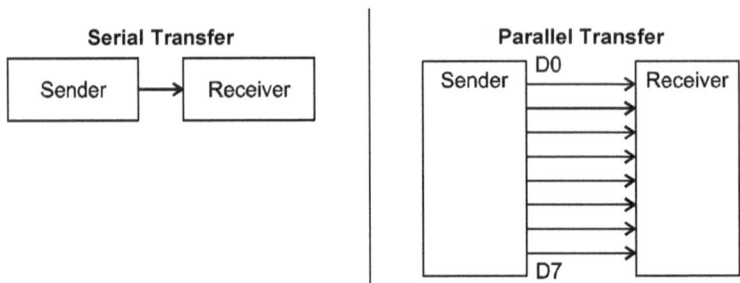

Fig. 3.11 : Type of data transfer

3.3.2 Serial Data Transfer

- In serial communication, the data is sent one bit at a time, in contrast to parallel communication, in which the data is sent a byte or more at a time. Furthermore, 8-bit data is expensive due to these reasons; serial communication is used for transferring data between two systems located at distances of hundreds of feet to millions of miles apart.

- But in serial communication a single data line is used instead of the 8-bit data line of parallel communication which makes it cheaper and also makes it possible for two computers located in two different cities to communicate over the telephone. In serial communication the byte of parallel data must be converted to serial bits using a parallel-in-serial-out shift register, and then it can be transmitted over a single data line.

- At the receivers end there must be a serial-in-parallel-out shift register to receive the serial data and pack them into a byte.

3.3.3 Modulator and Demodulator

- If data is to he transferred on the telephone line, it must be converted from 0s and 1s to audio tones, which are sinusoidal-shaped signals. This conversion is performed by a peripheral device called a modem, which stands for "modulator/demodulator".

3.3.4 Transmission Format

- A transmission format is concerned with issues such as synchronization, direction of data flow, speed, errors, and medium of transmission (telephone lines, for example).

3.3.2 Synchronous Vs. Asynchronous Transmission

- There are two formats in which Serial communication can occur those are
  1. Asynchronous format.
  2. Synchronous format.

3.3.5.1 Synchronous Data Transmission

- In the synchronous format, a receiver and a transmitter are synchronized; a block of characters is transmitted along with the synchronization information, as in Fig. 3.12. This format is generally used for high-speed transmission (more than 20 k bits/second).

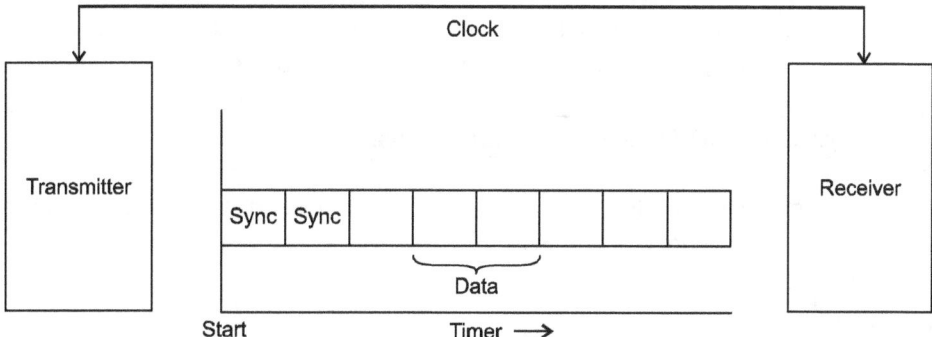

Fig. 3.12 : Synchronous data transmission

3.3.5.2 Asynchronous Data Transmission

- The asynchronous format is character-oriented. Each character carries the information of the Start and the Stop bits, shown in Fig. 3.13. When no data are being transmitted, a receiver stays high at logic 1, called Mark, logic 0 is called Space.

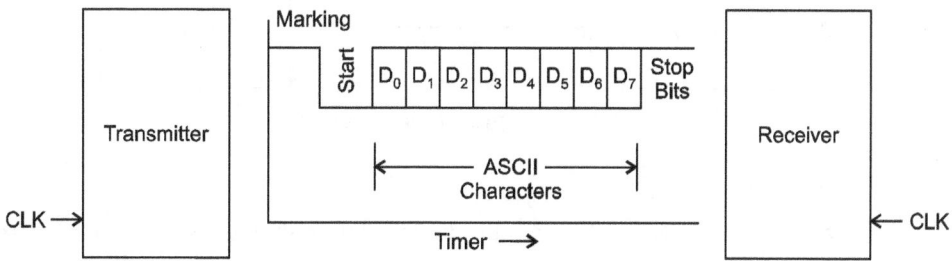

Fig. 3.13 : Asynchronous data transmission

- Transmission begins with one Start bit (low), followed by a character and one or two Stop bits (high). This is also known as framing. Fig. 3.13 shows the transmission of 11 bits for an ASCII character in the asynchronous format :
  - ➢ one Start bit,
  - ➢ eight character bits, and
  - ➢ two Stop bits.
- The format shown in Fig. 3.13 is similar to Morse code, but the dots and dashes are replaced by logic 0's and 1's. The asynchronous format is generally used in low-speed transmission (less than 20 k bits/second).
- It is possible to write software to use either of these methods, but the programs can be tedious, cumbersome and long. For this reason, there are special IC chips made by many manufacturers for serial data communications. These chips are commonly referred to as UART (universal asynchronous receiver-transmitter) and USART (universal synchronous-asynchronous receiver-transmitter).

3.3.6 Simplex and Duplex Transmission

- Serial communication also can be classified according to the direction and simultaneity of data flow as follows :
  1. Simplex transmission.
  2. Duplex transmission.
- The Duplex transmission is further classified into :
  1. Half Duplex transmission.
  2. Full Duplex transmission.

3.3.6.1 Simplex Transmission

- In simplex transmission, data are transmitted in only one direction. A typical example is transmission from a microcomputer to a printer.

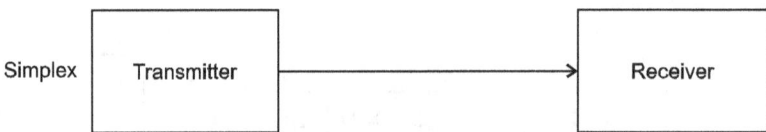

Fig. 3.14 : Simplex Transmission

3.3.6.2 Duplex Transmission

- Duplex transmissions can be half or full duplex depending on whether or not the data transfer can be simultaneous. In duplex transmission, data flow in both directions.

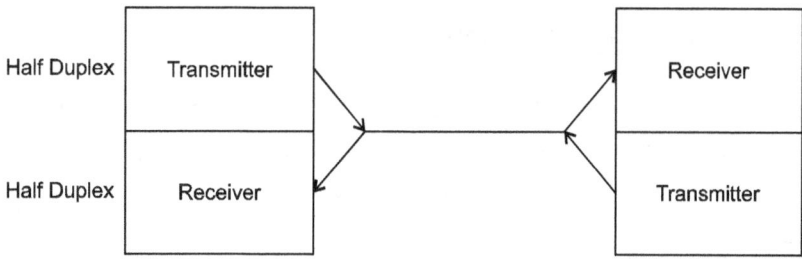

Fig. 3.15 : Half duplex transmission

- However, if the transmission goes one way at a time, it is called half duplex, if it goes both ways simultaneously, it is called full duplex. Generally, transmission between two computers or between a computer and a terminal is full duplex.

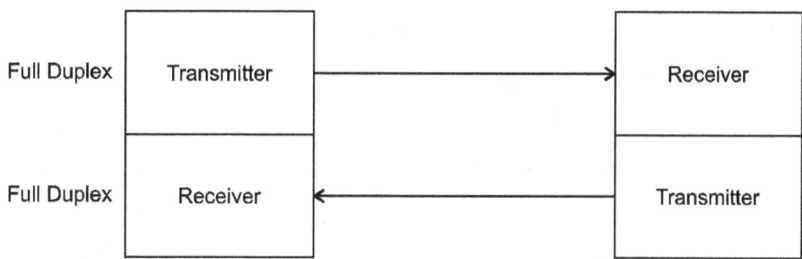

Fig. 3.16 : Full duplex transmission

3.4 SERIAL COMMUNICATION IN 8051

- 8051 supports a full duplex serial port. Full duplex means, it can transmit and receive a byte simultaneously. 8051 has TXD and RXD pins for transmission and reception of serial data respectively. The 8051 serial communication is supported by RS232 standard. The term "RS" stands for Recommended Standard.

- Communication between two microcontrollers and multiprocessors is also possible. In serial transmission, baud rate is one important factor.

- The baud rate is the reciprocal of the time to send 1 bit. Baud rate need not equal to number of bits per second. This is because; each byte is preceded by a start bit and followed by one stop bit. The start and stop bits are used to synchronize the serial receivers.

- The data byte is always transmitted with least-significant-bit first. For error checking purpose. It is also possible to add parity bit before transmitting stop bit.

3.4.1 Error Free Transmission

- For error free transmission it is necessary that the baud rate, the number of data bits, number of stop bit and presence or absence of parity bit along with its status be the same at both transmitter and receiver ends.

3.4.2 Serial Communication in 8051

- 8051 supports full duplex serial communication with the help of following :
  1. PIN RXD (P3.0).
  2. PIN TXD (P3.1) connects to the serial data network.
  3. SFR SBUF to hold data.
  4. SFR SCON controls data communication.
  5. SFR PCON controls data rates.
  6. Timer to generate Baud Rate.

RxD (Pin 10 - P3.0 & Pin 11-P3.1) and TxD pins in the 8051 :

- The 8051 has two pins that are used specifically for transferring and receiving data serially. These two pins are called TxD and RxD and are part of the port 3 group (P3.0 and P3.1). Pin 11 of the 8051 (P3.1) is assigned to TxD and pin 10 (P3.0) is designated as RxD. These pins are TTL compatible and therefore, they require a line driver to make them RS232 compatible. One such line driver is the MAX232 chip.

3.4.3 Special Function Registers

3.4.3.1 SBUF (Serial Port Data Buffer - Address – 99H)

- SBUF is an 8-bit register used only or fully for serial communication in the 8051. SBUF is physically two register,
  1. One for a byte of data to be transferred via the TxD line, it must be placed in the SBUF register.
  2. Similarly, another SBUF holds the byte of data when it is received by the 8051's RxD line.
- SBUF can be accessed like any other register in the 8051.Both SBUF are accessible via address 99H single address.

	D7	D6	D5	D4	D3	D2	D1	D0
SBUF								
Value after reset								
	X	X	X	X	X	X	X	X

Format of SBUF Used for Serial communication

3.4.3.2 Programming SBUF

- As soon as Data is written into SBUF, the data is added with the start and stop bits and transferred serially via the TxD pin. Similarly, when the bits are received serially via RxD, the 8051 the stop and start bits are removed to recover the data back, making a byte out of the data received, and then placing it in the SBUF.

  MOV SBUF, # 'M'   ; Load data 'M' is SBUF, 'M' is loaded in ASCII

  MOV SBUF,A   ; Load content of Acc in SBUF

  MOV 99H, '44'   ; Load data 44H is SBUF For transmission

  MOV A, SBUF   ; Read content of SBUF received, Load it in Acc

  MOV A, 99H   ; Read content of SBUF received, Load it in Acc

SCON (Serial Port Control register - Address – 98H, Bit/Byte addressable) :

- Serial port is to be configured prior to being used in the application. This is done by writing word in SCON register. The SCON register is an 8-bit register used to program the start bit, stop bit, and data bits of data framing, among other things.

- SCON Determines how many bits one serial word should contain, what should be the baud rate and of course the synchronization pulse source (Timer). Fig. shows the Format of SCON register.

	D7	D6	D5	D4	D3	D2	D1	D0
SCON	SM0	SM1	SM2	REN	TB8	RB8	TI	RI
After Reset	0	0	0	0	0	0	0	0

Symbol	Bit Address	Bit Symbol	Function
SM0	9FH	SCON.7	Serial Port Mode Specifier
SM1	9EH	SCON.6	Serial Port Mode Specifier
SM2	9DH	SCON.5	Used for Multiprocessor Communication

REN	9CH	SCON.4	Receive enable bit
TB8	9BH	SCON.3	Transmitted bit 8
RB8	9AH	SCON.2	Received bit 8
TI	99H	SCON.1	Transmit Interrupt Flag
RI	98H	SCON.0	Receive Interrupt Flag

Description :

SM0, SM1 (D7 and D6 bit of SCON) :

- These two bits determine the framing of data by specifying the number of bits per character, and the start and stop bits. Combination of bits are :

SM0	SM1	Function
0	0	Serial Mode 0, Serial Shift Register, Baud = F/2
0	1	Serial Mode 1, 8 bit UART, With Variable Baud Rate
1	0	Serial Mode 2, 9 bit UART, Baud rate = f/32, f/64
1	1	Serial Mode 3, 9 bit UART, With Variable Baud Rate

Note :

- Mostly Mode 1 is used because mode 1 has the data framing of 8 bits, 1 stop bit, and 1 start bit which makes it compatible with the COM port of IBM PCs. Also, serial mode 1 allows the, baud rate to be variable and is set by timer 1 of 805. Hence, mode 1 serial frame consist of 10 bit (10bit data = 8 data + 1start bit +1stop bit).

SM2 (D5 bit of SCON)

- SM2 is the D5 bit of the SCON register. This bit enables the multiprocessing capability of the 8051. This bit used in the system which share the same interface. This bit SM2 = 0 when programmer us not using the 8051 in a multi processor environment.

- Set/cleared by program to enable multiprocessor communications in modes 2 and 3.

- When set to 1 an interrupt is generated if bit of data 9 of the received data is a 1; no interrupt is generated when bit 9 of data is received as 0.

- When this bit is set to 1 for mode 1 no interrupt will be generated unless a valid stop bit is received. Clear to 0 if mode 0 is in use.

REN (D4 bit of SCON) :

- Receive enable bit. Set to 1 to enable reception; cleared to 0 to disable reception. When the REN bit is high, it allows the 8051 to receive data on the RxD pin of the 8051, by making REN=0 the receiver is disabled or blocked.

- By using Boolean instruction this bit can be set or resetted so receiver can be enabled or disabled

  For example :

  SETB SCON.4   ; Enable the receiver by setting REN bit

  CLR SCON.4   ; Disable the receiver by resetting REN bit

TB8 and RB8 (bit D3 and D2 of SCON) :

TB8 (Transmitted bit 8) :

- It is set/cleared by program in modes 2 and 3. TB8 (transfer bit 8) is bit b3 of SCON. It is used for serial modes 2 and 3. We make TB8 = 0 since it is not used in our applications. This bits content is sent as 9th bit during transmission.

RB8 (Received bit 8) :

- This bit has different use in different modes.
  - ➢ Bit 8 of received data in modes 2 and 3.
  - ➢ Stop bit in mode 1.
  - ➢ Not used in mode 0.
- In serial mode 1, this bit gets a copy of the stop bit when an 8-bit data is received. This bit (as is the case for TB8).This bit is the 9th bit of the received data. After that stop bit will be received.

TI and RI (Bit D1 and Bit D0 of SCON) :

TI (Transmit Interrupt) :

- Transmit Interrupt flag is Set to one at the end of bit 7 times in mode 0, and at the beginning of the stop bit for other modes. Must be cleared by the program.
- This is an extremely important flag bit in the SCON register. When the 8051 finishes the transfer of the 8-bit character, it raises the TI flag to indicate that it is ready to transfer another byte. The TI bit is raised the beginning of the stop bit.

RI (Receive Interrupt) :

- Receive Interrupt flag is set to one at the end of bit 7 time in mode 0, and halfway through the stop bit for other modes. Must be cleared by the program.
- This is another extremely important flag bit in the SCON register. When the 8051 receives data serially via RxD, it gets rid of the start and stop bits and places the byte in the SBUF register. Then it raises the RI flag bit to indicate that a byte has been received and should be picked up before it is lost. RI is raised halfway through the stop bit.

Note : TI and RI indicates the Completion of data transfer from SBUF on Txd line and Reception of data from RxD Line into the SBUF. This flag can be set or reset by the program.

PCON (Power Mode Control Register –Address 87H) :

- There are two ways to increase the baud rate of the data transfer
  - ➢ To use a higher frequency crystal :
  - ➢ It is not feasible in many situations since the system crystal is fixed. More importantly, it is not feasible because the new crystal may not be compatible with the IBM PC serial COM ports baud rate.
  - ➢ To change a bit in the PCON register :
  - ➢ This is a software way to double the baud rate of the 8051 while the crystal frequency is fixed. This is done with the register called PCON (power control). The PCON register is an 8-bit register. Of the 8 bits, some are unused, and some are used for the power control capability of the 8051. The bit which is used for the serial communication is D7, the SMOD (serial mode) bit. When the 8051 is powered up, D7 (SMOD bit) of the PCON register is zero. We can set it to high by soft ware and thereby double the baud rate.

	D7	D6	D5	D4	D3	D2	D1	D0
PCON	SMOD	----	---	---	GF1	GF0	PD	IDL
After Reset	0	0	0	0	0	0	0	0

Symbol	Bit	Function
SMOD	7	Serial baud rate modify bit. Set to 1 by program to double baud rate using timer 1 for modes 1, 2, and 3. Cleared to 0 by program to use timer 1 baud rate.
----	6-4	Not Implemented
GF1	3	General purpose user flag bit 1. Set/cleared by program.
GF0	2	General purpose user flag bit 0. Set/cleared by program.
PD	1	Power down bit. Set to 1 by program to enter power down configuration for CHMOS processors.
IDL	0	Idle mode bit. Set to 1 by program to enter idle mode configuration for CHMOS processors. PCON is not bit addressable.

Doubling the Baud Rate :

- Since PCON is not bit addressable, first the D7 bit is to be set in Acc and then data is to be copied into the PCON register.

```
MOV A,PCON      ; Copy content of PCON in Acc
SETB Acc.7      ; Make it D7 = 1 i.e. set D7 bit
MOV PCON, A     ; Modify content of PCON without effecting other bit
```

3.4.3.3 Serial Data Transmission, Reception and Interrupts

Transmission :

- Transmission of serial data bits begins anytime data is written to SBUF. TI is set to a 1 when the data has-been transmitted and indicates that SBUF is empty (for transmission purposes) and that another data byte can be sent. If the program fails to wait for the TI flag and overwrites SBUF while a previous data byte is in the process of being-transmitted, the results will be unpredictable ("garbage out").

Reception :

- Reception of serial data will begin if the receiver enable bit (REN) in SCON is set to 1 for all modes. In addition, for mode 0 only, RI must be cleared to 0. Receiver Interrupt-flag RI is set after data has been received in all modes. Setting REN is the only direct program control that limits the reception of unexpected data; the requirement that RI also be 0 for mode 0 prevents the reception of new data until- the program has dealt with the old data and reset RI.

Interrupt :

- The serial data flags in SCON, TI and RI, are set whenever a data byte is transmitted (TI) or received (RI). These flags are ORed together to produce an interrupt to the program. The program must read these flags to determine which caused the interrupt and then clear the flag. This is unlike the timer flags that are cleared automatically; it is the responsibility of the programmer to write routines that handle the serial data flags.

3.4.3.4 Modes of Serial Communication

- There are four modes in which 8051 serial port can be configured.

Mode 0 – Shift Register Mode (SM0 = 0, SM1= 0 of SCON)

- Set SBUF to receive or transmit eight data bits using pin RXD for both functions. Pin TXD is connected to the internal shift frequency pulse source to supply shift pulses to external circuits. The shift frequency or baud rate is fixed at 1/12 of the oscillator frequency, the same rate used by the timers when in the timer configuration.

- After transmitting 8 bit TI flag is set.. For reception of data REN=1 and RI=0 condition are to satisfied. Upon receiving 8 bit in SBUF RI flag is set.

- Since there are no start and stop bit, this particular mode is used for short distance communication. Mode 0 is intended not for data communication-between computers, but arts a high-speed serial data-collection method using discreet logic to achieve high data rates. The baud rate used in mode 0 will be much higher than standard for any reasonable oscillator frequency) for a 6 megahertz crystal, the shift rate will be 500 kHz.

- When transmitting, data is shifted out of the data changes on the falling edge, i.e. one clock pulse after the rising edge of the output TXD shift clock.

- Received data comes in on pin- RXD and should be synchronized with the shift clock produced at TXD. Data is sampled on the falling edge and shifted in to SBUF on the rising edge of the shift clock.

Example : Serial transmission in mode 0 :

    MOV SCON, #00H   ; Set mode 0

    MOV SBUF, # 'M'   ; Load SBUF with data to be transmitted

    Over JNB TI, over   ; Wait till TI flag is set, indicating that 8 bits are transmitted

    CLR TI   ; Clear TI flag so that next data can be transmitted

Mode 1 - Standard UART (SM0=0, SM1 =1 of SCON) :

- In mode 1, 10 bits are transmitted through TXD pin or received through RXD pin It is Full Duplex mode of Transmission i.e. it will transmit and receive the data simultaneously. There is a start bit (0), then 8 data bits (LSB first) and a stop bit (1). This is shown in Fig.

Data transmission :

- The Data to be transmitted is loaded in SBUF. Transmitted data is sent as a start bit, eight data bits (least significant bit, LSB, first), and a stop bit. Interrupt flag TI is set once all ten bits have been sent. Each bit interval is the inverse of the baud rate frequency, and each bit is maintained high or low over that interval. -

Data reception :

- Received data is obtained in the same order; reception is triggered by the falling edge of the start bit and continues if the stop-bit is true (0 level) halfway through the start bit interval. For Reception to be started REN=1 and RI = 0 in SCON.RI is automatically set after receiving the complete data.

Note : If RI is found to be set at the end of the reception, indicating that the previously received data byte has not been read by the program, or if the other conditions listed are not true, the new data will not be loaded and will be lost.

Baud rate in mode1 :

• For setting baud in mode 1, timer 1 is used in mode 2, i.e. 8 bit auto reload mode (For more details, refer timer section). For this mode :

1. Timer TH1 is loaded with the count which is loaded in TL1 on overflow.

2. TMOD High Nibble is set to 02H (0010b) to select Timer 1 in mode 2.

3. Crystal of 12 MHz is used so that each pulse is of 1µsec.

   (a) When Timer is running in mode 2

$$F_{baud} = \frac{2^{smod}}{32} \times \frac{\text{Ocillator Frequency}}{12d \times (256d - TH1)}$$

   (b) When Timer is not running in mode 2

$$F_{baud} = \frac{2^{smod} \times (\text{Timer Overflow Frequency})}{32d}$$

• SMOD bit of PCON is used to Double the baud rate, i.e. when SMOD =1.

• Baud rate is double of the actual calculated.

• The oscillator frequency is chosen to help generate both standard and non standard baud rates. If standard baud rates are desired, then an 11.0592 megahertz crystal could be selected.

• If SMOD is cleared to 0, then the frequency generated by the timer is 16 (SMOD = 0) or 32 (SMOD = 1) times the actual serial data communication rate. The UART must be fed a clock frequency that is much higher than the serial baud rate in order to be able to sample close to the center of each received bit. Hence, it is clear that a UART clock rate equal to the baud rate would not be "fine" enough to slice each serial bit into pieces.

Example Serial Transmission in mode 1

```
MOV SP, #60H        ; Initialize stack at memory location 60H

MOV SCON, #00H      ; Set serial port in mode 1

MOV TMOD, #20H      ; Set timer in mode 2, auto reload mode

MOV Th1, E6H        ; Set count for baud rate 1200 at frequency 12 MHz

SETB TR1            ; Set TR1 bit to start transmission

MOV SBUF, #56h      ; Load SBUF data for transmission

JNB TI, $           ; Wait till transmission is over

CLR TI              ; Clear TI bit which is set, after Transmission
```

Count and Comparison of standard Baud rate :

TH1 Decimal	TH1 HEX	SMOD =0	SMOD=1
−3	FD	9,600	19,200
−6	FA	4,800	9,600
−12	F4	2,400	4,800
24	E8	1,200	2,400

Mode 2 – Multi Processor (SM0=1, SM1 =0 of SCON)

- In Mode 2, 11 bits are sent through TXD or received through RXD a START bit (always 0), 8 data bits (LSB first), additional 9th data bit and a STOP bit (always 1) last. On transmission, the 9th data bit is actually the TB8 bit from the SCON register. This bit commonly has the purpose of parity bit. Upon transmission, the 9th data bit is copied to the RB8 bit in the same register (SCON). The baud rate is either 1/32 or 1/64 the quartz oscillator frequency. After transmission TI and after reception RI bit is automatically set. Also For reception to be initiated REN =1 and RI = 0 condition is to be full filled.

Baud rate can be set by the formula :

$$\text{Baud rate} = \frac{2^{smod} \times \text{Ocillator Frequency}}{64d}$$

Mode 3 - Serial Data Mode (SM0=1, SM1 = 1 of SCON) :

- Mode 3 is the same as Mode 2 except the baud rate which is defined by the timer 1 overflow rate. In Mode 3, baud rate is variable and can be selected using Timer 1.

3.4.3.4 Multiprocessor Communication

- In modes 2 and 3 enable the additional 9th data bit to be part of message. It can be used for checking data via parity bit.

- Another useful application of this bit is in communication between two microcontrollers, i.e. multiprocessor communication.

- By setting SM2 bit in SCON register this communication can be initiated. The multiprocessor communication is supported in modes 2 and 3 only.

- Again 9 bits are transmitted or received. The 9 bit goes to RB8. The configuration of multiprocessor system assumes the transmitting processor as a master and all others as slaves.

- When the master wants to transmit a block of data, it sends first the address byte of the slave. How this address byte is distinguished from the data byte? The 9 bit, while transmitting the address byte, does this. The 9 bit is '1' in case of address byte and '0' in case of data byte transmission.

- SM2 bit of all the slaves is 1 after initialization in the multiprocessor mode. With SM2 = I the slave will be interrupted with the address byte only and no data byte can do so. The addressed slave will clear its SM2 bit, and start receiving the data bytes. Other slaves who are not addressed will continue their own operations.

- In short, the 9th bit does the work of Talk- Listen protocol in multiprocessor communication. It differentiates between address and data, Master and Slave.

3.4.3.5 Importance of RI bit In Serial Transmission

- In receiving bits via its RxD pin, the 8051 goes through the following step

  1. It receives the start bit indicating that the next bit is the first bit of the character byte it is about to receive.

  2. The 8-bit character is received one bit at time. When the last bit is received, a byte is formed and placed in SBUF.

  3. The stop bit is received. It is during receiving the stop bit that the 8051 makes RI = 1, indicating that an entire character byte has been received and must be picked up before it gets overwritten by an incoming character.

  4. By checking the RI flag bit when it is raised, we know that a character has been received and is sitting in the SBUF register. We copy the SBUF contents to a safe place in some other register or memory before it is lost.

  5. After the SBUF contents are copied into a safe place, the RI flag bit must be forced to 0 by the "CLR RI" instruction in order to allow the next received character byte to be placed in SBUF. Failure to do this causes loss of the received character.

- Hence it is understood that by checking the RI flag bit we know whether or not the 8051 has received a character byte. If we fail to copy SBUF into a safe place, we risk the loss of the received byte. More importantly, it must be noted that the RI flag bit is raised by the 8051, but it must be cleared by the programmer with an instruction such as "CLR TI". It also must be noted that if we copy SBUF into a safe place before the RI flag bit is raised, we risk copying garbage. The RI flag bit can be checked by the instruction "JNB RI, xx"

3.4.3.6 Count for Different Baud Rate at 11.0592 and 12 MHz Clock

| | Value to be loaded in TH1 timer register (Timer 1 Mode 2) | | | |
Baud Rate	11.0592 MHz	Baud Rate	11.0592 MHz	Baud Rate
150	40	150	40	150
300	A0	300	A0	300
600	D0	600	D0	600
1200	E8	1200	E8	1200
2400	F4	2400	F4	2400
4800		4800		4800
4800	FA	4800	FA	4800
9600	FD	9600	FD	9600
9600		9600		9600
19200	FD	19200	FD	19200
38400		38400		38400
76800		76800		76800

Example : Find he baud rate, if TH1 = −2, SMOD =1 and Xtal = 11.0592 MHz.

Solution :

Xtal = 11.0592, SMOD=1

Timer1 Frequency = 57,600 Hz

Baud rate = 57,600/2 = 28,800

Note : Calculation is to be done by the user.

3.5 INTERRUPT

- The process of data transfer between the micro processor and the peripherals is controlled either by the microcontroller or by the peripherals. Data transfer is generally implemented under the microcontroller control when the peripheral response is slow relative to that of the microprocessor.

- Most peripherals respond slowly in comparison with the speed of the microcontroller. Therefore, it is necessary to set up conditions for data transfer so that data will not be lost during the transfer. Microcontroller or-controlled data transfer can take place under five different conditions: unconditional, polling (also known as status check), interrupt, with READY signal, and with handshake signals.

- **Data Transfer with Polling (Status Check):** In this form of data transfer, the microcontroller is kept in a loop to check whether data are available; this is called polling. For example, to read data from an input keyboard in a single-chip microcomputer, the microcontroller can keep polling the port until a key is pressed.

- **Data Transfer with Interrupt :** In this condition, when a peripheral is ready to transfer data, it sends an interrupt signal to the microcontroller. The microcontroller stops the execution of the program, accepts the data from the peripheral, and then returns to the program. In the interrupt technique, the controller is free to perform other tasks rather than held in a polling loop.

3.5.1 Interrupts in 8051

- Interrupts may be generated by internal chip operations or provided by external sources. Any interrupt can cause the 8051 to perform a hardware call to an interrupt-handling subroutine that is located at a predetermined vector address in program memory.

- In 8051 total Five interrupts are provided.

  1. Three of these are generated automatically by internal operations :
     - Timer flag 0,
     - Timer flag 1, and
     - the serial port interrupt (RI or TI).

  2. Two interrupts are triggered by external signals provided by circuitry that is connected to pins

     INT0 (port pin P3.2)

     INT1 (port pins P3.3)

- All interrupt functions are under the control of the program. The programmer is able to change control bits in the Interrupt Enable register the Interrupt Priority register (IP), and the Timer Control register (TCON). The program can block all or any combination of the interrupts from acting on the program by suitably setting or clearing bits in these registers.

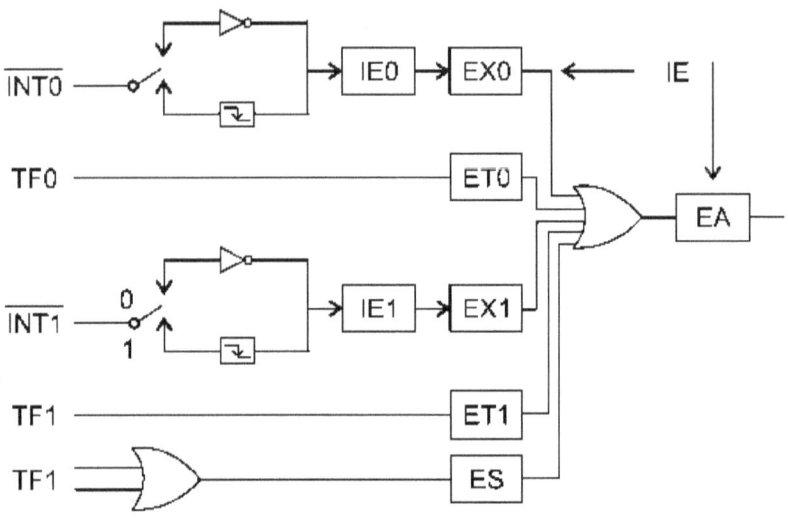

Fig. 3.17 : Interrupt structure

SFR used for interrupt programming :

In interrupt programming, two SFR are used as given below :

1. Interrupt priority (IP).
2. Interrupt Enable (IE).

SFR – Interrupt Enable IE (Address – 0A8 – Bit/Byte Addressable)

	D7	D6	D5	D4	D3	D2	D1	D0
IE	EA	----	ET2	ES	ET1	EX1	ET0	EX0
After Reset	0	X	0	0	0	0	0	0

Symbol	Bit Address	Bit Symbol	Function
EA	0AFH	IE.7	Enable Interrupt Bit 0-Disable the interrupt system, 1-Enable the interrupt system
------	-----	----	Unspecified
ET2	0ADH	IE.5	Reserved for Future use
ES	0AC H	IE.4	Enable Serial Port Interrupt 0-Disable the Serial interrupt, 1-Enable the Serial interrupt

ET1	0A BH	IE.3	Enable Timer overflow interrupt 1 0-Disable the timer 1 interrupt, 1-Enable the Timer interrupt 1
EX1	0A AH	IE.2	Enable External Interrupt 1 0-Disable the External interrupt 1, 1-Enable the External interrupt 1
ET0	0A9 H	IE.1	Enable Timer overflow interrupt 0 0-Disable the timer 0 interrupt, 1-Enable the Timer interrupt 0
EX0	0A8H	IE.0	Enable External Interrupt 0 0-Disable the External interrupt 0, 1-Enable the External interrupt 0.
Symbol	Bit Address	Bit Symbol	Function
EA	0AFH	IE.7	Enable Interrupt Bit 0-Disable the interrupt system, 1-Enable the interrupt system
------	-----	----	Unspecified
ET2	0ADH	IE.5	Reserved for Future use
ES	0AC H	IE.4	Enable Serial Port Interrupt 0-Disable the Serial interrupt, 1-Enable the Serial interrupt

SFR – Interrupt Priority IP (Address – 0B8 – Bit/Byte Addressable)

	D7	D6	D5	D4	D3	D2	D1	D0
IP	----	----	PT2	PS	PT1	PX1	PT0	PX0
After Reset	X	X	0	0	0	0	0	0

Symbol	Bit Address	Bit Symbol	Function
----	-----	-----	Not implemented
------	-----	----	Not implemented
PT2	0BDH	IP.5	Reserved for Future use

PS	0BC H	IP.4	Priority bit for Serial Port Interrupt 0- Low Priority, 1-High Priority
PT1	0BBH	IP.3	Priority bit for Timer overflow interrupt 1 0- Low Priority, 1 High Priority
PX1	0BAH	IP.2	Priority bit for External Interrupt 1 0- Low Priority, 1-High Priority
PT0	0B9 H	IP.1	Priority bit for Timer overflow interrupt 0 0- Low Priority, 1-High Priority
PX0	0B89H	IP.0	Priority bit for External Interrupt 0 0- Low Priority, 1-High Priority

Instruction to Enable/disable interrupt

MOV IE, #8CH	; Enable Interrupt EX1 and Et1
SETB PT1	; Timer Interrupt is set to highest priority
SETB PX0	; External interrupt 0 to highest priority
CLR IE.1	; Disable Timer 0 Interrupt
CLR IE.7	; Disable all Interrupts
CLR IE.7	; Disable all Interrupts

Interrupt Vector Address, Priority :

Interrupt Identity	Symbol	Priority	Vector Address	Port Pin
Reset	RST	Highest	0000H	9
External Interrupt 0	IE0	1	0003H	P3.2
Timer Interrupt 0	TF0	2	000BH	Internal
External Interrupt 1	IE1	3	0013H	P3.3
Timer Interrupt 0	TF1	4	001BH	Internal
Serial Interrupt	TI or RI	5	0023H	Internal

Activation of all interrupts at the same time :

- Register IP bits determine if any interrupt is to have a high or low priority bits set to 1 give the accompanying interrupt a high priority, a 0 assigns a low priority.
  - ➢ Interrupts with a high priority can interrupt another interrupt with a lower priority, the lower priority interrupt continues after the higher is finished.

> ➢ If two interrupts with the same priority occur at the same time, then they have the following ranking:
>   1. IE0
>   2. TF0
>   3. IE1
>   4. IT1
>   5. Serial Interrupt
> ➢ Interrupt request is ignored if an interrupt of the same priority level is being in progress.
> ➢ Upon interrupt routine has been executed, a new interrupt is not executed until at least one instruction from the main program is executed.

- To set the respective interrupt at highest priority set that Interrupt bit in IP = 1. For example, the serial interrupt could be given the highest priority by setting the PS bit in IP to 1, and all others to 0.
- Instruction SETB IP.4 will set Serial interrupt to High Priority.
- Instruction CLR IP.2 will set External Interrupt to Low Priority.

3.5.2 Different Interrupt Flags

- **Serial Port :** When a timer/counter overflows, the corresponding Timer flag, TF0 or TF1, is set to 1. The flag is cleared to 0 when the resulting interrupt generates a program call to the appropriate timer subroutine in memory.
- **Timer Interrupt :** When a data byte is received; an interrupt bit, RI, is set to 1 in the SCON register. When a data byte has been transmitted an interrupt bit, TI, is set in SCON.
- **External Interrupt :** Pins INTO and INT1 are used by external circuitry or peripheral Device. Inputs on these pins can set the Interrupt flags IE0 and IE1 in the TCON_register to 1 by two different methods :
  1. The IEX flags may be set when the INTX pin signal reaches a low level or the flags may be set when a high to low transition takes place on the INTX pin.
  2. Bits ITX in TCON program the INTX pins for low-level interrupt when set to 0 and program the INTX pins for transition interrupt when set to 1.
- Flags IEX will be reset when a transition-generated interrupt is accepted by the processor and the interrupt subroutine is accessed. It is the responsibility of the system designer and programmer to reset any level generated external interrupts when they are serviced by the program. The external circuit must remove the low

level before an RETI is executed. Failure to remove the low will result in an immediate interrupt after RETI, from the same source.

3.5.3 Condition of Register on Reset

- A reset can be considered as an interrupt because the program disable block the action of the voltage on the RST pin. Such interrupts are often called non-maskable, because no combination of bits in any register can stop, or mask, the reset action.

- Here, the PC is not stored for later program use a reset is an absolute command to jump to program address 0000h and execution start from there.

- Whenever a high level is applied to the RST pin, the 8051 enters a reset condition. After the RST pin is brought low, the internal registers will have the values shown in the following list:

Register Status	Value in Hex
PC	0000
DPTR	0000
A	00
B	00
PSW	00
P0-3	FF
IP	XXX00000b
IE	0XX00000b
TCON	00
TMOD	00
TH0	00
TL0	00
TH1	00
TL1	00
SCON	00
SBUF	XX
PCON	0XXXXXXXb
SP	07

Note : Internal RAM contents may change during reset; also, the states of the internal RAM bytes when power is first applied to the 8051 are random. Register bank 0 is selected on reset as all bits in PSW are 0.

3.5.4 Software Interrupts

- When any Interrupt flag is set to 1 by any means, an interrupt is generated unless disabled. This means that the program itself can cause interrupts of any kind to be generated simply by setting the desired Interrupt flag to 1 using a program instruction. Refer the code in the above section.

- When an interrupt is activated, the microcontroller goes through the perform steps.

  1. Microcontroller finishes the instruction it is executing and saves the address of the next instruction (PC) on the stack.

  2. Microcontroller also saves the current status of all the interrupts internally (i.e., not on the stack).

  3. Microcontroller jumps to a fixed location in memory called the **I**nterrupt **V**ector **T**able (IVT) that holds the address of the interrupt service routine.

- The microcontroller gets the address of the ISR (**I**nterrupt **S**ervice **R**outine) from the interrupt vector table and jumps to it. It starts to execute the interrupt service subroutine till it reaches the last instruction of the subroutine which is RETI (return from interrupt).

- The Last instruction RETI when executed, the microcontroller returns to the program location where it was interrupted. Following are the steps

  1. It gets the program counter (PC) address from the stack by popping the top two bytes of the stack into the PC.

  2. Then it starts to execute from that address.

Program based on IO port programming

Program 1 : (a) Write a program to toggle all bits of port 1.

```
#include <Intel\8051.h>        // header file for 89C51
#include <standard.h>          // For delay routine
#define period 100             // 100 ms
void main ( )
{
    while (1)                  // Always perform
```

```
    {
        P1=0XFF;                    // To send 1's to port 1
        delay_ms (period);
        P1=0X00;                    // To send 0's to port 1
         delay_ms (period);
    }                               // End of while
}
```

(b) Write a program to toggle MSB bit of port 0.

```
    //C program to toggle MSb bit of port 1.
    #include <intel\8051.h>         // header file for 89C51
    #include<standard.h>            // For delay routine
    #define period 100              // 100 ms
    Bit displ P0.7                  // Identity port P0.7 as displ
    void main ( )
    {
        while (1)                   // Always perform
        {
            displ = 1               // send 1 to port P0.7
            delay_ms (period);
            displ_0;                // send 0 to port P0.7
            delay_ms (period);
        }
    }
```

Program 2 : Write C program for 8051 microcontroller to right shift the data at port 1.

```
    #include<intel\8051.h>          // header file for 89C51
    #include<standard.h>            // For delay routine
    #define period 100              // 100 ms
    void main ( )
    {
        unsigned char X;
        P1=0X01;                    // Send a number to port 1
        while (1)                   // Always perform
```

```
    {
        for (x=0; x<8; x++)
    {
        P1=P1>>1;                    // shift data at port 1 to right by one bit
        delay_ms (period);
    }                                // End of For Loop
    }                                // End of While Loop
}
```

Program 3 : Write C Read input port and send hex data to output port.

```
    #include<intel\8051.h>          // header file for 89C51
    unsigned char a;
    unsigned char b=0x00;           // Declare variable b=00H
    void main ( )
    {
        a=p1;                        // Read port P1 to 9
        P2=b;                        // Send 00H to port P3
    }
```

Program 4 : (a) Write an 8051 C program to toggle bits of P0 continuously.

```
    #include <reg51.h>              //header file for 89C51
    void main (void)
    {
        unsigned int x;
        for (;;)                     // repeat forever
        {
            P1=0x55;
            for (x=0; x<40000; x++);  // delay size unknown
            P1=0XAA;
            for (x=0; x<40000; x++);
        }                            // End of For Loop
    }
```

(b) Repeat Forever loop using while

```
#include <reg51.h>                    //header file for 89C51
void main (void)
{
    unsigned int x;
    while(1)                          // repeat forever
    {
        P1=0x55;
        for (x=0; x<40000; x++);      // delay size unknown
        P1=0XAA;
        for (x=0; x<40000; x++);
    }                                 // End of while Loop
}
```

Program 5 : Write a C program for 8051 to toggle bits of P2 ports continuously with a 500 ms delay.

```
#include <reg51.h>                    // header file for 89C51
void delay (unsigned int);
void main (void)
{
    while (1)                         // Repeat forever
    {
        P2=0x55;
        Delay (500);
        P2=0XAA;
        Delay (500);
    }
    void delay (unsigned int dtime)
    {
        unsigned int i, j;
        for (i=0; i<dtime; i++)
        for (j=0; j<275; j++);
    }
}
```

Program 6 : Write an C program for 8051 that displays the count from 0 to FFH on the LED's connected to port 0 (P0).

```
#include <reg51.h>                    // header file for 89C51
void main (void)
{
    P0=00;                            // clear P2
    for (i=0; i<=255; i++)
    {
        P0++;
    }                                 // End of For Loop
}
```

Program 7 : Write a C program for 8051 to read a byte of data from P1, wait for half second and then send it to P2.

```
#include <reg51.h>                    // header file for 89C51
void t_delay (unsigned int);
void main (void)
{
    unsigned char num_byte;
    P1=0xFF;                          // make P1 as input port
    while (1)
    {
    num_byte=P1;                      // read data byte from port 1
    t_delay (500);                    // delay of half Second
    P2=num_byte;                      // send it to port 2
    }
    void t_delay (unsigned int dtime)
    {
    unsigned int i, j;
    for (i=0; i<dtime; i++)
    for (j=0; j<275; j++);
    }
}
```

Program 8 : Write a C program for 8051 to read a byte of data from P0. If it is greater than 100, send it to P1, otherwise send it to P2.

```c
#include <reg51.h>              // header file for 89C51
void main (void)
{
    unsigned char input1;
    P0=0xFF;                    // set P0 as input port
    while (1)
    {
    input1=P0;                  // read data byte from port 0
    it (input 1<100)
        P1=input1;              // send it to port 1
    else
        P2=input1;              // or else send it to port 2
    }
}
```

Program 9 : Write a program in C for 8051 to check bit P1.2. If it is high, send 55H to P0; otherwise send AAH to P2.

```c
#include <reg51.h>              // header file for 89C51
sbit mybit=P1^2                 // declare bit P1.2 as mybit
void main (void)
{
    mybit=1;                    // set bit P1.2 as an input
    while (1)
    {
    if (mybit==1)
        P0=0x55;                // if 1 send 55H to port 0
    else
        P2=0xAA;                // if 0 then send AAH to port 2
    }                           // End of For Loop
}
```

Program 10 : Write a C program for 8051 to read 10 bytes of data from P1 and store them into array and add these data bytes.

```
#include <reg51.h>              // header file for 89C51
void main (void)
{
    unsigned char mybyte[10], i, sum=0;
    P0=0xFF;                    // set P0 as in input
    for (i=0; i<=10; i++)
    {
        mybyte[i]=P0;            // read data byte from port 0
    }
    for (i=1; i<=10; i++)
    {
        sum=sum+mybyte [i];     // Performing Addition
    }
}
```

Program based on Timer and Counter

Delay calculation :

- While designing delay programs in 8051, calculating the initial value that has to be loaded into TH and TL registers forms a very important thing. Let us see how it is done.

  ➢ Assume the processor is clocked by a 12 MHz crystal.

  ➢ That means, the timer clock input will be 12 MHz/12 = 1 MHz

  ➢ That means, the time taken for the timer to make one increment = 1/1 MHz = 1 µs.

  ➢ For a time delay of "X" µS the timer has to make "X" increments.

  ➢ 2^{16} = 65536 is the maximum number of counts possible for a 16 bit timer.

  ➢ Let TH be the value that has to be loaded to TH register and TL be the value that has to be loaded to TL register.

  ➢ Then, THTL = Hexadecimal equivalent of (65536-X) where (65536-X) is considered in decimal.

Example :

  ➢ Let the required delay be 1000 µs (i.e. 1 ms).

  ➢ That means X = 1000

> ➢ 65536 – X = 65536 – 1000 = 64536.
> ➢ 64536 is considered in decimal and converting it to hexadecimal gives FC18
> ➢ That means THTL = FC18
> ➢ Therefore, TH = FC and TL = 18

To generate Time delay using timer registers :

- Load the TMOD value register indicating which timer (timer 0 or timer 1) is to be used and which timer mode (0 or is selected

   1. Load registers TL and TH with initial count value

   2. Start the timer

   3. Keep monitoring the timer flag (TF) until it rolls over from FFFFH to 0000.

   4. After the timer reaches its limit and rolls over, in order to repeat the process - TH and TL must be reloaded with the original value, and TR is turned off by setting value to 0 and TF must be reloaded to 0.

Program 1 : Write C program to demonstrate how to write delay.

```
#include <REG51.h>
void T0Delay(void);
void main(void)
{
    while (1)
    {
        P1=0x55;
        T0 Delay();
        P1=0xAA;
        T0 Delay();
    }
}
void T0 Delay()
{
    TMOD=0x01;          // timer 0, mode 1
    TL0=0x00;           // load TL0
    TH0=0x35;           // load TH0
    TR0=1;              // turn on Timer0
    while (TF0==0);     // wait for TF0 to roll over
    TR0=0;              // turn off timer
    TF0=0;              // clear TF0
}
```

Another way to generate delay :

Code to generate 250 ms delay on Port P1 of 8051.

```c
#include "REG52.h"
void MSDelay (unsigned int);
void main (void)
    {
        while (1)                      // repeat forever
        {
            P1 = 0x55;
            MSDelay (250);
            P1=0xAA;
            MSDelay(250);
        }
    }


    void MSDelay (unsigned int itime)
        {
            unsigned int i, j;
            for (i=0;i<itime; i++)   // this is For(); loop delay used to
                                     // define delay value in Embedded C
        {
            for (j=0;j<1275;j++);
        }
        }
```

Program 2 : Write an 8051 C program to toggle only bit P1.5 continuously every 50 ms. Use Timer 0, mode 1 (16-bit) to create the delay. Test the program on the AT89C51. Crystal = 11.0592 MHz.

```c
#include <reg51.h>
void T0M1Delay(void);
sbit mybit=P1^5;                // Declare Port Bit
void main(void)
    {
        while (1)
```

```
                    {
                                        mybit=~mybit;
                                        T0M1Delay();
            }                           // End of while
    }
void T0M1Delay(void)          // delay Routine
    {
        TMOD=0x01;
        TL0=0xFD;
        TH0=0x4B;
        TR0=1;
        while (TF0==0);           // Waiting for Count to get Over
        TR0=0;                    //Clear Timer Run Flag
        TF0=0;                    // Clear Timer Over Flow Flag
    }
```

Calculation :

Timer count   = FFFFH – 4BFDH = B402H

Timer Count   = 46082 + 1 = 46083

Delay   = Count * Timer per Clock

              = 46083 × 1.085 µs

              = 50 ms

Program 3 : Write an 8051 C program to toggle all bits of P2 continuously every 500 ms. Use Timer 1, mode 1 to create the delay.

```
#include <reg51.h>
void T1M1Delay(void);
void main(void)
    {
        unsigned char x;
        P2=0x55;
        while (1)
            {
                P2=~P2;
                for (x=0;x<20;x++)
```

```
                T1M1Delay();
            }
        }

    void T1M1Delay(void)
        {
            TMOD=0x10;
            TL1=0xFE;
            TH1=0xA5;
            TR1=1;
            while (TF1==0);
            TR1=0;
            TF1=0;
        }
```

Calculation :

Loaded Count = A5FEH = 42494 in decimal

Timer Count   = 65536 – 42494

              = 23042

Delay   = 23042 × 1.085 µs = 25 ms

This 25ms loop is executed 20 times using for loop

              = 20 × 25 ms = 500 ms

Program 4 : A switch is connected to pin P1.2. Write an 8051 C program to monitor SW and create the following frequencies on pin P1.7: SW0 = 500Hz, SW1 = 750 Hz, use Timer 0, mode 1 for both of them.

```
    #include <reg51.h>
    sbit mybit=P1^5;
    sbit SW=P1^7;
    void T0M1Delay(unsigned char);
    void main(void)
        {
            SW=1;
            while (1)
```

```
            {
                Mybit = mybit;
                if (SW==0)
                T0M1Delay(0);
                else
                T0M1Delay(1);
            }
        }
    void T0M1Delay (unsigned char c)
        {
            TMOD=0x01;
            if (c==0)
            {
                TL0=0x67;
                TH0=0xFC;
            }
            else
            {
                TL0=0x9A;
                TH0=0xFD;
            }
            TR0=1;
            while (TF0==0);
            TR0=0;
            TF0=0;
        }
```

Calculations :

Loaded Count = FC67H = 64615

Timer count = 65536 − 64615 = 921

Time Delay = Count * Time for one clock

      = 921×1.085 μs

      = 999.285 μs

Frequency = 1/time delay

      = $1/(999.285$ μs $\times 2)$

      = 500 Hz

Note : Same way Do calculation for 750Hz

Program 5 : Write an 8051 C program to toggle only pin P1.5 continuously every 250 ms. Use Timer 0, mode 2 (8-bit auto-reload) to create the delay.

```c
#include <reg51.h>
void T0M2Delay(void);
sbit mybit=P1^5;
void main(void)
    {
        unsigned char x, y;
        while (1)
        {
            mybit=~mybit;
            for (x=0;x<250;x++)
            for (y=0;y<36;y++)       //we put 36, not 40
            T0M2Delay();
        }
    }
void T0M2Delay(void)
    {
        TMOD=0x02;
        TH0=-23;
        TR0=1;
        while (TF0==0);
        TR0=0;
        TF0=0;
    }
```

Calculation :

Timer Count = 256 – 23 = 233

Time Delay   = Count × time per clock

                = 23 × 1.085 µs

                = 25 µs

Loop goes for 250 times, Inner Loop 40 times

Total Delay = 25 µs × 250 × 40 = 250 ms

Program 6 : Write an 8051 C program to create a frequency of 2500 Hz on pin P2.7. Use Timer 1, mode 2 to create delay.

```c
#include <reg51.h>
void T1M2Delay(void);
sbit mybit=P2^7;
void main(void)
    {
        unsigned char x;
        while (1)
        {
            mybit=~mybit;
            T1M2Delay();
        }
    }
void T1M2Delay(void)
    {
        TMOD=0x20;
        TH1=-184;
        TR1=1;
        while (TF1==0);
        TR1=0;
        TF1=0;
    }
```

Calculation :

Time period   = 1/2500 Hz
                      = 400 µs
Time for one Pulse   = 400 µs/2
                      = 200 µs
Count   = 200 µs/1.085 µs
                      = 184

Program 7 : Assume that a 1 Hz external clock is being fed into pin T1 (P3.5). Write a C program for counter 1 in mode 2 (8-bit auto reload) to count up and display the state of the TL1 count on P1. Start the count at 0H.

```c
#include <reg51.h>
sbit T1=P3^5;
void main(void)
```

```
            {
                T1=1;
                TMOD=0x60;
                TH1=0;
                while (1)
                {
                do
                    {
                        TR1=1;
                        P1=TL1;
                    }
                while (TF1==0);
                TR1=0;
                TF1=0;
                }
            }
```

Program 8 : Assume that a 1 Hz external clock is being fed into pin T0 (P3.4). Write a C program for counter 0 in mode 1 (16-bit) to count the pulses and display the state of the TH0 and TL0 registers on P2 and P1, respectively.

```
    #include <reg51.h>
    void main(void)
        {
            T0=1;
            TMOD=0x05;
            TL0=0
            TH0=0;
            while (1)
            {
                do
                {
                    TR0=1;
                    P1=TL0;
                    P2=TH0;
                }
```

```
          while (TF0==0);
       TR0=0;
       TF0=0;
          }
       }
```

Serial port Programming :

Baud rate generation :

Example : With XTAL = 11.0592 MHz, find the TH1 value needed to have the following baud rates. (a) 9600 (b) 2400 (c) 1200

Solution :

The machine cycle frequency of 8051 = 11.0592/12 = 921.6 kHz, and 921.6 kHz/32 = 28,800 Hz is frequency by UART to timer 1 to set baud rate.

   (a) 28,800/3 = 9600 where -3 = FD (hex) is loaded into TH1.

   (b) 28,800/12 = 2400 where -12 = F4 (hex) is loaded into TH1.

   (c) 28,800/24 = 1200 where -24 = E8 (hex) is loaded into TH1.

Note that dividing 1/12 of the crystal frequency by 32 is the default value upon activation of the 8051 RESET pin.

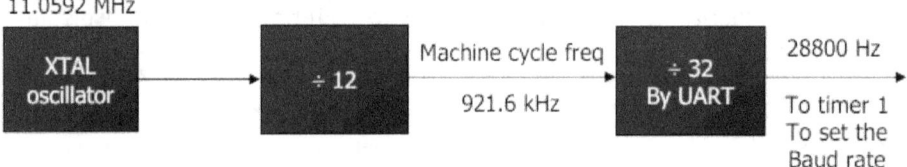

Count for Different Baud Rate :

Sr. No.	Baud Rate	Th1 Decimal Count	TH1 – Hex Count
1	9600	-3	FD
2	4800	-6	FA
3	2400	-12	FE
4	1200	-24	E8
5	600	-48	D0
6	300	-96	A0

In programming the 8051 to transfer character bytes serially :

1. TMOD register is loaded with the value 20H, indicating the use of timer 1 in mode 2 (8-bit auto-reload) to set baud rate.

2. The TH1 is loaded with one of the values to set baud rate for serial data transfer.

3. The SCON register is loaded with the value 50H, indicating serial mode 1, where an 8- bit data is framed with start and stop bits.

4. TR1 is set to 1 to start timer 1.

5. TI is cleared by CLR TI instruction.

6. The character byte to be transferred serially is written into SBUF register.

7. The TI flag bit is monitored with the use of instruction JNB TI, xx or while (T1!=1)to see if the character has been transferred completely.

8. To transfer the next byte, go to step 5

The steps that 8051 goes through in transmitting a character via TxD :

1. The byte character to be transmitted is written into the SBUF register.

2. The start bit is transferred.

3. The 8-bit character is transferred on bit at a time.

4. The stop bit is transferred.

   ➢ It is during the transfer of the stop bit that 8051 raises the TI flag, indicating that the last character was transmitted.

5. By monitoring the TI flag, we make sure that we are not overloading the SBUF.

   ➢ If we write another byte into the SBUF before TI is raised, the untransmitted portion of the previous byte will be lost.

6. After SBUF is loaded with a new byte, the TI flag bit must be forced to 0 by CLR TI in order for this new byte to be transferred0 By checking the TI flag bit, we know whether or not the 8051 is ready to transfer another byte.

   ➢ It must be noted that TI flag bit is raised by 8051 itself when it finishes data transfer.

   ➢ It must be cleared by the programmer with instruction CLR TI

   ➢ If we write a byte into SBUF before the TI flag bit is raised, we risk the loss of a portion of the byte being transferred

   ➢ The TI bit can be checked by

• The instruction JNB TI, xx or while(TI!=1)

• Using an interrupt

In programming the 8051 to receive character bytes serially :

1. TMOD register is loaded with the value 20H, indicating the use of timer 1 in mode 2 (8-bit auto-reload) to set baud rate

2. TH1 is loaded to set baud rate

3. The SCON register is loaded with the value 50H, indicating serial mode 1, where an 8- bit data is framed with start and stop bits

4. TR1 is set to 1 to start timer 1

5. RI is cleared by CLR RI instruction

6. The RI flag bit is monitored with the use of instruction JNB RI, xx to see if an entire character has been received yet

7. When RI is raised, SBUF has the byte, its contents are moved into a safe place

8. To receive the next character, go to step 5

In receiving bit via its RxD pin, 8051 goes through the following steps

1. It receives the start bit

   ➢ Indicating that the next bit is the first bit of the character byte it is about to receive.

2. The 8-bit character is received one bit at time

3. The stop bit is received

- When receiving the stop bit 8051 makes RI = 1,indicating that an entire character byte has been received and must be picked up before it gets overwritten by an incoming character by checking the RI flag bit when it is raised, we know that a character has been received and is sitting in the SBUF register

- We copy the SBUF contents to a safe place in some other register or memory before it is lost 5. After the SBUF contents are copied into a safe place, the RI flag bit must be forced to 0 by CLR RI in order to allow the next received character byte to be placed in SBUF.

- Failure to do this causes loss of the received character. By checking the RI flag bit, we know whether or not the 8051 received a character byte.

- If we failed to copy SBUF into a safe place, we risk the loss of the received byte.

- It must be noted that RI flag bit is raised by 8051 when it finish receive data.

- It must be cleared by the programmer with instruction CLR RI.

- If we copy SBUF into a safe place before the RI flag bit is raised, we risk copying garbage.

- The RI bit can be checked by

   ➢ The instruction JNB RI, xx

   ➢ Using an interrupt.

Program 1 : Write a C program for 8051 to transfer the letter "A" serially at 4800 baud continuously. Use 8-bit data and 1 stop bit.

```c
#include <reg51.h>
void main(void)
    {
        TMOD=0x20;                  // Use Timer 1, mode 2
        TH1=0xFA;                   // 4800 baud rate
        SCON=0x50;                  // 01010000 Serial mode1
        TR1=1;                      // Start Timer
        while (1)
        {
            SBUF='A';               // Place value in buffer
            while (TI==0);          // Wait Till Transmission over
            TI=0;                   // Clear Transmission Intr
        }                           // End of While
    }
```

Program 2 : Write an 8051 C program to transfer the message "SIR" serially at 9600 baud, 8-bit data, and 1 stop bit. Do this continuously.

```c
#include <reg51.h>
void SerTx(unsigned char);
void main(void)
    {
        TMOD=0x20;                  // Use Timer 1, mode 2
        TH1=0xFD;                   // 9600 baud rate
        SCON=0x50;                  // 01010000 Serial mode1
        TR1=1;                      // Start timer
        while (1)
        {
            SerTx('S');
            SerTx('I');
            SerTx('R');
        }                           // End of While
    }
```

```
void SerTx(unsigned char x)
    {
        SBUF=x;                     // Place value in buffer
        while (TI==0);              // Wait until transmitted
        TI=0;                       // Clear TI Flag
    }
```

Program 3 : Program the 8051 in C to receive bytes of data serially and put them in P1. Set the baud rate at 4800, 8-bit data, and 1 stop bit.

```
#include <reg51.h>
void main(void)
    {
        unsigned char mybyte;
        TMOD=0x20;                  // Use Timer 1, mode 2
        TH1=0xFA;                   // 4800 baud rate
        SCON=0x50;
        TR1=1;                      // Start timer
        while (1)
        {                           // Repeat forever
            while (RI==0);          // Wait to receive
            mybyte=SBUF;            // Store Value from SBUF
            P1=mybyte;             // Write value to port
            RI=0;                  // Clear RI Flag
        }                           // End of While repeat Forever
    }
```

Program 4 : Write an 8051 C Program to send the two messages "Normal Speed" and "High Speed" to the serial port. Assuming that SW is connected to pin P2.0, monitor its status and set the baud rate as follows:

SW = 0, 28,800 baud rate

SW = 1, 56K baud rate

Assume that XTAL = 11.0592 MHz for both cases.

```
#include <reg51.h>
sbit MYSW=P2^0;                     //input switch
```

```
void main(void)
    {
        unsigned char z;
        unsigned char Mess1[]="Normal Speed";
        unsigned char Mess2[]="High Speed";
        TMOD=0x20;                      // Use Timer 1, mode 2
        TH1=0xFF;                       // 28800 for normal
        SCON=0x50;
        TR1=1;                          // Start timer
        If (MYSW==0)
        {
            for (z=0;z<12;z++)
            {
                SBUF=Mess1[z];          // Place value in buffer
                while(TI==0);           // Wait for transmit
                TI=0;                   // Clear TI Flag
            }                           // End of For Z
        }                               // End of IF
        Else
        {
            PCON=PCON|0x80;             // For high speed of 56 K
            for (z=0;z<10;z++)
            {
                SBUF=Mess2[z];          // Place value in buffer
while(TI==0);                           // Wait for transmit
TI=0;                                   // Clear TI Flag
            }                           // End of Else
        }                               // End of While
    }
```

Program 5 : Write a C program for the 89C51 to transfer the letter "A" serially at 4800 baud continuously. Use the second serial port with 8-bit data and 1 stop bit. We can only use Timer 1 to set the baud rate.

```
#include <reg51.h>
sfr SBUF1=0xC1;
```

```c
sfr SCON1=0xC0;
sbit TI1=0xC1;
void main(void)
    {
        TMOD=0x20;                  // Use Timer 1, mode 2
        TH1=0xFA;                   // 4800 baud rate
        SCON=0x50;
        TR1=1;                      // Start timer
    while (1)
        {
            SBUF='A';               // Load SBUF with 'A
            while (TI1==0);         // Wait for transmit
            TI1=0;                  // Clear TI flag
        }                           // End of While
    }                               // End of Main
```

Program-7 : Program the 89C51 in C to receive bytes of data serially via the second serial port and put them in P1. Set the baud rate at 9600, 8-bit data and 1 stop bit. Use Timer 1 for baud rate generation.

```c
#include <reg51.h>
sfr SBUF1=0xC1;
sfr SCON1=0xC0;
sbit RI1=0xC0;
void main(void)
    {
        unsigned char mybyte;
        TMOD=0x20;                  // Use Timer 1, mode 2
        TH1=0xFD;                   // 9600 baud rate
        SCON=0x50;
        TR1=1;                      // Start timer
    while (1)
        {
            while (RI1==0);         // Monitor RI1
            mybyte=SBUF1;           // Use SBUF1
```

```
        P2=mybyte;              // Place value on port
        RI1=0;                  // Clear RI Flag
    }                           // End of Repeat For everwhile Loop
}
```

Interrupt Programming :

Program 1 : Write a C program that continuously gets a single bit of data from P1.7 and sends it to P1.0, while simultaneously creating a square wave of 200 μs period on pin P2.5. Use Timer 0 to create the square wave. Assume that XTAL = 11.0592 MHz.

We will use timer 0 mode 2 (auto-reload). One half of the period is 100 μs.

= 100/1.085 μs

= 92, and TH0 = 256 – 92

= 164 or A4H

```
#include <reg51.h>
sbit SW =P1^7;                  // Declare P1.7 as Sw
sbit IND =P1^0;                 // Declare P1.0 as IND
sbit WAVE =P2^5;                // Declare P2.5 as Wave
void timer0(void) interrupt 1
    {
        WAVE=~WAVE;             // Toggle pin
    }
void main()
    {
        SW=1;                   // Make switch input
        TMOD=0x02;
        TH0=0xA4;               // TH0=-92
        IE=0x82;                // Enable interrupt for timer 0
while (1)
        {
            IND=SW;             // Send switch to LED
        }                       // End of While
    }
```

Program 2 : Write a C program using interrupts to do the following :

(a) Receive data serially and send it to P0.

(b) Read port P1, transmit data serially, and give a copy to P2.

(c) Make timer 0 generate a square wave of 5 kHz frequency on P0.1.

Assume that XTAL = 11.0592 MHz. Set the baud rate at 4800.

```c
#include <reg51.h>
sbit WAVE =P0^1;
void timer0() interrupt 1
    {
        WAVE=~WAVE;                  // Toggle pin
    }
void serial0() interrupt 4
    {
        if (TI==1)
        {
            TI=0;                    // Clear interrupt
        }
    else
        {
            P0=SBUF;                 // Put value on pins
            RI=0;                    // Clear interrupt
        }
    }
void main()
    {
        unsigned char x;
        P1=0xFF;                     // Make P1 an input
        TMOD=0x22;
        TH1=0xF6;                    // 4800 baud rate
        SCON=0x50;
        TH0=0xA4;                    // 5 kHz has T=200 µs
        IE=0x92;                     // Enable interrupts
        TR1=1;                       // Start timer 1
        TR0=1;                       // Start timer 0
        while (1)
```

```c
    {
        x=P1;                   // Read value from pins
        SBUF=x;                 // Put value in buffer
        P2=x;                   // Write value to pins
    }                           // End of while Loop
}
```

Program 3 : Write a C program using interrupts to do the following :

(a) Generate a 10 KHz frequency on P2.1 using T0 8-bit auto-reload.

(b) Use timer 1 as an event counter to count up a 1-Hz pulse and display it on P0. The pulse is connected to EX1.

Assume that XTAL = 11.0592 MHz. Set the baud rate at 9600.

```c
#include <reg51.h>
sbit WAVE =P2^1;
Unsigned char cnt;
void timer0() interrupt 1
    {
        WAVE=~WAVE;             // Toggle pin
    }
void timer1() interrupt 3
    {
        cnt++;                  // Increment counter
        P0=cnt;                 // Display value on pins
    }
void main()
        {
            cnt=0;              // Set counter to 0
            TMOD=0x42;
            TH0=0x-46;          // 10 kHz
            IE=0x86;            // Enable interrupts
            TR0=1;              // Start timer 0
    while (1); // Wait until interrupted
        }
```

Important Points

- 8051 provides four 8bit I/O ports.

- All four ports are bidirectional.

- Each port consists of a D-latch, an output driver, and an input buffer.

- Each port line will input or output data under software control.

- Each port can be accessed in byte or bit mode.

- The port latches should not be confused with the port pins; the data on the latches does not have to be the same as that on the pins.

- **Functions of Port 0 are it can be used as** simple 8-bit input port, simple 8-bit output port and Bidirectional Multiplexed Address/Data Bus.

- Functions of Port 1 are it can be used as simple 8-bit input port.

- **Functions of Port 2 are it can be used as** simple 8-bit input port, simple 8-bit output port, Functions as high order Address Bus.

- **Functions of Port 3 are it can be used as** simple 8-bit input port, simple 8-bit output port, alternate function for Serial I/O. Read/Write, Timer, External Interrupt.

The difference between a timer and a counter :

- **Timer :** Timer counts machine cycles and provides a reference time delay or a clock. A machine cycle of 8051 consists of 12 oscillator periods or the counting rate is 1/12 of the oscillator frequency. At 12 MHz, the clocking period will be equal to 1μs.

- **Counter :** Counter of 8051 is incremented in response to a transition from '1' to '0' at its corresponding external pin (either T0 or TI). Thus, the counter output will be a count or a number representing the occurrence of such '1' to '0' transitions at the external pin.

- For counting function, 8051 takes 2 cycles or 24 oscillator periods to detect a '1' to '0' transition at Pin T0 or T1.

- When a timer or counter overflows from FFFFH to 0000H, it sets a flag and generates an interrupt 8051 has two independent 16 bit timer.

- Timer is operated in 4 mode by setting TMODs M1, M0 bits.

- Mode 0 : M1= 0, M0= 0 → 13 bit timer counter mode.

- Mode 1 : M1= 0, M0= 1 → 16 bit timer counter mode.

- Mode 2 : M1= 1, M0= 0 → 8 bit auto reload mode.

- Mode 3 : M1= 1, M0= 1 → 2- 8 bit timer using timer 0.

- 8051 supports a full duplex serial port. Full duplex means, it can transmit and receive a byte simultaneously. 8051 has TXD and RXD pins for transmission and reception of serial data respectively. The 8051 serial communication is supported by RS232 standard. The term "RS" stands for Recommended Standard.

- The oscillator frequency is chosen to help generate both standard and non standard baud rates. If standard baud rates are desired, then an 11.0592 megahertz crystal could be selected.

- In 8051 total Five interrupts are provided.
- Three of these are generated automatically by internal operations
  - ➢ Timer flag 0,
  - ➢ Timer flag 1, and
  - ➢ the serial port interrupt (RI or TI).
- Two interrupts are triggered by external signals provided by circuitry that is connected to pins
  - ➢ INT0 (port pin P3.2)
  - ➢ INT1 (port pins P3.3).

Practice Questions

Port Programming :

1. What bit addresses are assigned to P0, P1, P2, P3?
2. What bit addresses are assigned to register A, register B, register PSW, Register DPTR.
3. Write instructions to save the CY flag bit in bit location 4.
4. Write instructions to save the AC flag bit in bit location I6H.
5. Write instructions to save the P flag bit in bit location 12H.
6. Show how would you check whether the OV flag is low.
7. Show how would you check whether the CY flag is high.
8. Show how would you check whether the P flag is high.
9. Show how would you check whether the A flag is high.
10. Write a program to generate a square wave with 75% duty cycle on bit P1.5.
11. Write a program to generate a square wave with 80% duty cycle on bit P2.7
12. Write a program to monitor P1.4. When it goes high, the program will generate a sound (square wave of 50% duty cycle) on P2.7.
13. Write a program to monitor P2.1. When it goes low, the program will send the value 55H to P0.
14. Describe Port 0 structure of 8051 and State its different function.
15. Describe Port 1 structure of 8051 and State its different function.
16. Describe Port 2 structure of 8051 and State its different function.
17. Describe Port 3 structure of 8051 and State its alternate function and there user.
18. Describe the Demultiplexing of Address data used for memory interfacing.
19. How to make Port as Input or output describe with example?

Timer/Counter :

1. Explain Timer/counter section of 8051. Explain use of SFR for this operation.
2. Explain the mode 0 of timer of 8051 with its internal logic diagram.
3. Explain the mode 1 of timer of 8051 with its internal logic diagram.

4. Explain the mode 2 of timer of 8051 with its internal logic diagram.

5. State the application of mode 1 and mode 2 of timer of 8051.

6. Draw and describe the format of TMOD SFR of 8051.

7. Draw and describe the format of TCON SFR of 8051.

8. What should be the count loaded into TH register of timer 1 using Mode 2 to get 100usec delay? Assume XTAL = 11.0592 Hz.

9. Describe the function of TMOD and TCON SFR's of timer section of 8051.

10. Write an assembly language program to generate continuous square wave of 1 kHz using timer 1 and mode. Assume XTAL = 11.0592 MHz.

11. Write an assembly language program to generate time delay of lms using any timer you wish. Assume XTAL = 11.0592 MHz.

12. Describe operating modes of 8051 timer.

13. Discuss the various timer modes supported by 8051. What is special about the auto_ reload mode? Write a program to initialize timer 1 in auto-reload mode, so that it overflows 10,000 times in a second.

14. In which timer mode, timer 1 does not set its own overflow flag TF1 and will no generate its own interrupt? (Assume that all care has been taken to initialize interrupts a this timer mode correctly.) If this is true, then what is the use of this timer/counter?

15. Assuming XTAL = 11.0592 MHz, indicate when the TFO flag is raised for the following program :
    MOV TMOD, #01H
    MOV TL0, #12H
    MOV TH0, #1CH
    SETB TR0.

16. Assume that XTAL = 16 MHz. find the TH1, TL1 value to generate a time delay of 5 ms. Timer 1 is programmed in mode 1.

17. Assuming that XTAL = 11.0592 MHz, program timer 1 to generate a time delay of 0.2 ms.

18. Assuming that XTAL = 20 MHz, program timer 1 to generate a time delay of lOOus.

19. Assuming that XTAL = 11.0592 MHz, and we are generating a square wave on pin P1.2, find the lowest square wave frequency that we can generate using mode 1.

20. Assuming that XTAL = 11.0592 MHz, and we are generating a square wave on pin P1.2, find the highest square wave frequency that we can generate using mode 1.

21. In mode 2 assuming that TH1 F1H, indicate which states timer 2 goes through until TF1 is raised. How many states is that?

22. Program timer 1 to generate a square wave of 1 kHz. Assume that XTAL =11.0592 MHz.

23. Program timer 0 to generate a square wave of 3 kHz. Assume that XTAL =11.0592 MHz.

24. Program timer 1 to generate a square wave of 10 kHz. Assume that XTAL = 20 MHz.

25. Assuming that XTAL = 11.0592 MHz, show a program t generate a 1-second time delay. Use any timer you want.

26. Assuming that XTAL = 16 MHz, show a program to generate a 0.25-second time delay. Use any timer you want.

27. Assuming that XTAL = 11.0592 MHz and that we are generating a square wave on pin P1.3, find the lowest square wave frequency that we can generate using mode 2.

Serial Communication :

1. Explain the operating modes of serial port of 8051.

2. Describe the data transmission and reception in mode 0 of serial port in 8051. Describe the data transmission and reception in mode 1 of serial port in 8051.

3. Describe the data transmission and reception in mode 2 of serial port in 8051.

4. Describe the data transmission and reception in mode 3 of serial port in 8051.

5. How will you read and write serial port?

6. Explain mul1iprocessor communication in multiple 8051 system.

7. Draw and describe the format of SCON SFR in serial communication of 8051.

8. Explain how PCON SFR is used to doubled the baud rate in serial communication?

9. What is serial interface? Explain interrupts presents in microcontroller 8051 with example.

10. Which is more expensive, parallel or serial data transfer?

11. Which timer of- the 8051 is used for baud rate programming?

12. Which mode of the timer is used for baud rate programming?

13. What is the role of the SBUF register in serial data transfer?

14. What is the role of the SCON register in serial data transfer?

15. For XTAL 11.0592 MHz, find the TH value (in both decimal and hex) for each of the following baud rates. (a) 9,600; (b) 4,800; (c) 1,200; (d) 300; (e) 150.

16. What is the baud rate if we use "MOV TH1,#-1" to program the baud rate?

17. Write an 8051 program to transfer serially the letter "Z" continuously at 1,200 baud rate.

18. When is the TI and RI flag bit raised? To which register do RI and TI belong? Is that register bit-addressable?

19. What is the role of the REN bit in SCON register?

20. In a given situation we cannot accept reception of any serial data. How do you block such a reception with a single instruction?

21. To which register does the SMOD bit belong? State its role in rate of data transfer.

22. Is SMOD bit high or low when the 8051 is powered up?

23. Find the baud rate for the following if XTAL=16 MHz. and SMOD=0 :
   (a) MOV TH1,#-10   (b) MOV TH1,#-25
   (c) MOV TH1,#-200   (d) MOV TH1,#-18O.

24. Find the baud rate for the following if XTAL=24 MHz. and SMOD=0 :
   (a) MOV TH1,#-15   (b) MOV TH1,#-24
   (c) MOV TH1,#-100   (d) MOV TH1,#-150.

25. Find the baud rate for the following if XTAL=16 MHz. and SMOD=1 :

   (a) MOV TH1,#-10   (b) MOV TH1,#-25

   (c) MOV TH1,#-200   (d) MOV TH1,#-18O.

26. Find the baud rate for the following if XTAL=24 MHz. and SMOD=1 :

   (a) MOV TH1,#-15   (b) MOV TH1,#-24

   (c) MOV TH1,#-100   (d) MOV TH1,#-150.

Interrupt Programming :

1. Draw and describe the format of IE SFR of 8051.

2. Draw and describe the format of IP SFR of 8051.

3. Explain the interrupt operation of 8051.

4. Explain the interrupt system of 8051 microcontroller. List the functions of IE, IP and TCON SFR.

5. How do you decide the edge- and level-triggered configurations of external interrupt INTO and INT1?

6. If two requests of interrupt are received simultaneously, how those are handled in 8051?As a programmer, how will you take care of this while writing an 8051 program?

7. It is required to generate baud rate of 2.4K in mode 3 of the 8051 serial port. Calculate the required count for timer 1, settings in various SFRs and write an initialization program to transmit and receive the same data byte again and again.

8. Which technique, interrupt or polling, avoids tying down the microcontroller?

9. Including reset, how many interrupts do we have in the 8051?

10. In the 8051 what memory area is assigned to the interrupt vector table?

11. True or false. The 8051 programmer cannot change the memory space assigned to the interrupt vector table.

12. What memory address in the interrupt vector table is assigned to INTO, INTI?

13. What memory address in the interrupt vector table is assigned to timer 0, Timer1, Serial Communication interrupt.

14. What are the contents of the IE register upon reset, and what do these values mean?

15. Show the instruction to enable the EX and timer I interrupts.

16. Show the instruction to enable every interrupt of the 8051.

17. Which pin of the 8051 is assigned to the external hardware interrupts INTO and INT1?

18. How many bytes of address space in the interrupt vector table are assigned to the INTO and TNT I interrupts?

19. How many bytes of address space in the interrupt vector table are assigned to the timer 0 and timer I interrupts?

20. True or false. The IE register is not a bit-addressable register.

21. With a single instruction, show how to disable all the interrupts.

22. With a single instruction, show how to disable the EX interrupt.

23. True or false. Upon reset, all interrupts are enabled by the 8051.

24. Which bit of IE belongs to the timer 0 interrupt? Show how it is enabled.

25. Which bit of IE belongs to the timer I interrupt? Show how it is enabled.

26. Assume that timer 1 is programmed for mode I, THO = FFH, TL1 F8H, and the IE bit for timer 1 is enabled. Explain how the interrupt is activated.

27. If timer 1 is programmed for interrupts in mode 2, explain when the interrupt is activated.

28. Write a program to create a square wave of T = 160 ms on pin P2.2 while at the same time the 8051 is sending out 55H and AAH to P1 continuously.

29. Write a program in which every 2 seconds, the LED connected to P2.7 is turned on and off four times, while at the same time the 8051 is getting data from P1 and sending it to P0 continuously. Make sure the on and off states are 50 ms in duration.

30. Explain the role of TCON.O and TCON.2 in the execution of external interrupt 0.

31. Explain the role of TCON.1 and TCON.3 in the execution of external interrupt 1.

32. Explain the difference between the low-level and edge-triggered interrupts.

33. How do we make the hardware interrupt edge-triggered?

34. Which interrupts are latched, low-level, or edge-triggered?

35. Which register keeps the latched interrupt for INTO and INT1?

36. Write a program using interrupts to get data from P1 and send it to P2 while timer 0 is generating a square wave of 3 kHz.

37. Write a program using interrupts to get data from P1 and send it to P2 while timer 1 is turning on and off the LED connected to P0.4 every second.

MSBTE Questions

Summer 2012

1. Draw the port '3' structure of 8051 with neat label. Also list any two alternate functions of port 3.

2. Draw the format of SCON and describe its bits functionality How many timer/counters are available in 8051? When they are used? Write its initialization instruction if any.

3. Enlist the various interrupts of 8051 with their priorities, vector locations and cause of interrupts.

4. Compare serial and parallel communication.

Winter 2012

1. State the interrupts in 8051 microcontroller. At what part pins are external interrupts located? State the role of the two bits of TCON.0 and TCON.2 play in execution of the external interrupts.

2. Differentiate between Microcontroller and Microprocessor.

3. Draw the formats of SFRs TCON and SCON in 8051 Microcontroller. What are the functions of bits TR0 and TR1

4. What are the various SFRs needed while programming a serial port in 8051? Write a program to initialize the serial port of 8051 in mode 1?

5. Enlist any eight special function registers of 8051 microcontroller.

6. Write the steps in programming 8051 to receive character byte serially.

Summer 2013

1. Draw pin diagram of RS232 DB9 connector and describe all pins.

2. Describe the operation of Mode 0 and Mode 1 of timer in 8051 microcontroller.

3. State the 8051 interrupts with priorities, vector location and cause.

4. Describe why mode 3 of 8051 microcontroller is called split timer mode. Write an assembly language program to generate a square wave of 4KHz. Assume clock frequency of 12 MHz. Show calculations of count to be loaded in timer.

Winter 2013

1. List the sequence of events that take place while executing an interrupt.

2. Draw the formats of TCON and TMOD registers and explain the bits.

3. Explain interrupt handing mechanism with the help of an example.

Summer 2014

1. Draw the format of SFR TCON and SCON of 8051 microcontroller.

2. Draw the format of TMOD SFR and state mode of timer in 8051 microcontroller.

3. Describe different ways of Handling Interrupts.

4. Describe serial port communication in 8051 microcontroller.

5. Compare Serial and Parallel Communication.

Winter 2014

1. Write formula to generate variable baud rate. Which timer is used in which mode for it?

2. Draw format of TCON register. What is the function of TR0 and TRI bits?

3. Name vector addresses for any four interrupts.

4. Which steps are executed by µC while handling interrupt?

✍ ✍ ✍

Chapter **4**...

8051 Interfacing Application

Weightage of Marks = 16,   Teaching Hours = 08

Specific Objectives

➤ Students will be able to
   ❖ Understand the interfacing of display
   ❖ Learn the function of ADC and DAC
   ❖ Know the application of Stepper motor

4.1 INTRODUCTION

- Microcontrollers are useful to the extent that they communicate with other devices, such as sensors, motors, switches, keypads, displays, memory and even other microcontrollers as shown in Fig. 4.1.

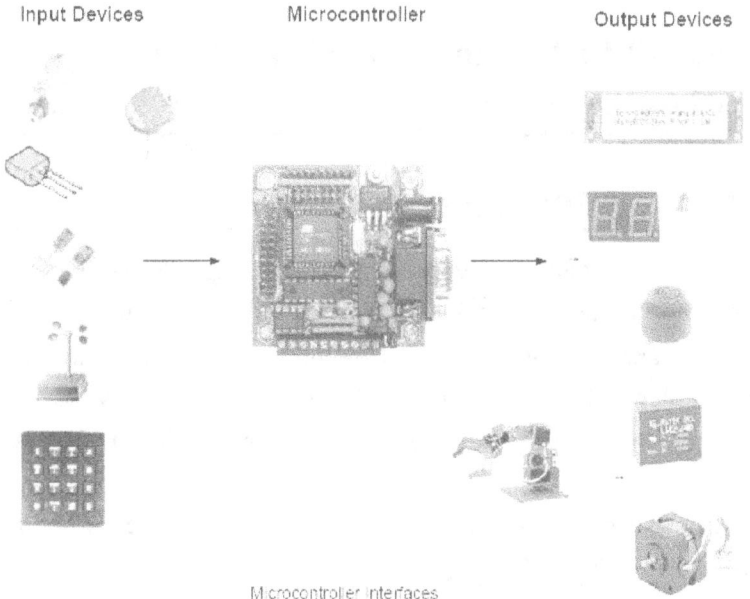

Input Devices   Microcontroller   Output Devices

Microcontroller Interfaces

Fig. 4.1 : Interfacing devices and Microcontroller Interfaces

- Many interface methods have been developed over the years to solve the complex problem of balancing circuit design criteria such as features, cost, size, weight, power consumption, reliability, availability, manufacturability.

- Many microcontroller designs typically mix multiple interfacing methods. In a very simplistic form, a microcontroller system can be viewed as a system that reads from (monitors) inputs, performs processing and writes to (controls) outputs.

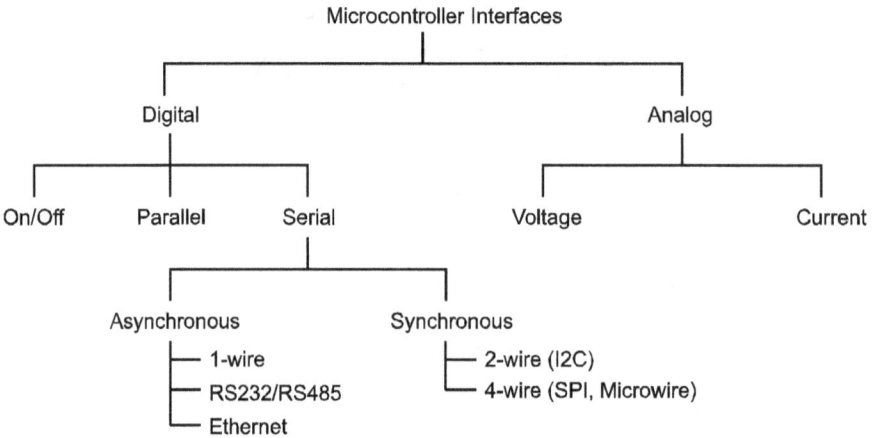

4.2 INTERFACING 7-SEGMENT DISPLAY AND ITS PROGRAMMING WITH 'C'

4.2.1 Seven Segment Display

- Seven segment LED display is very popular and it can display digits from 0 to 9 and quite a few characters like A, b, C, ., H, E, e, F, n, o, t, u, y, etc.

- A seven segment display consists of seven LEDs arranged in the form of a squarish **'8'** slightly inclined to the right and a single LED as the dot character. Different characters can be displayed by selectively glowing the required LED segments.

- Seven segment displays are of two types, ***common cathode and common anode*** as shown in Fig. 4.2.

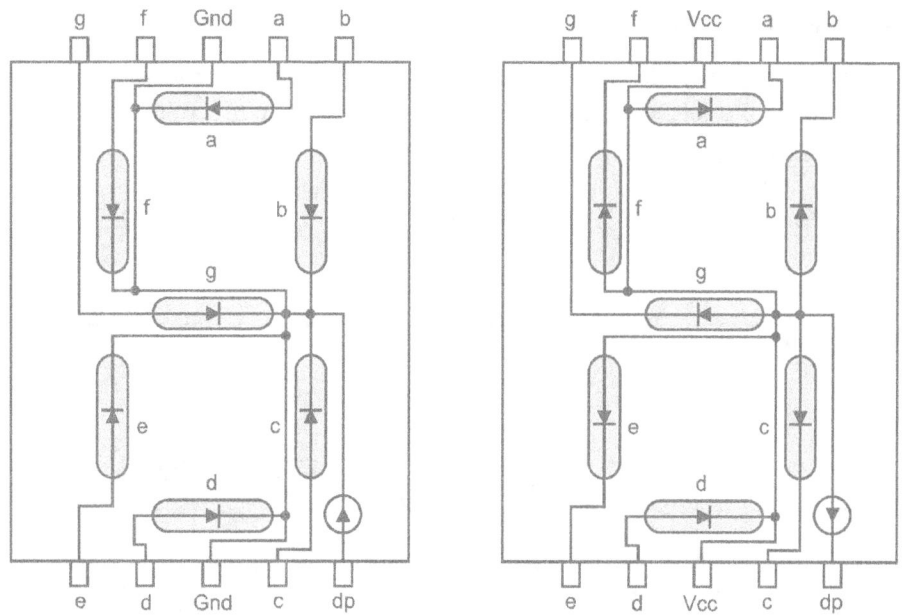

Fig. 4.2 : Seven Segment Display (SSD)

4.2.1.1 Common Cathode

- In common cathode type, the cathode of all LEDs are tied together to a single terminal which is usually labeled as '**com**' and the anode of all LEDs are left alone as individual pins labeled as a, b, c, d, e, f, g and h (or dot). To glow Common Cathode Segment LED Logic 1 is needed on port pin. And common terminal is grounded.

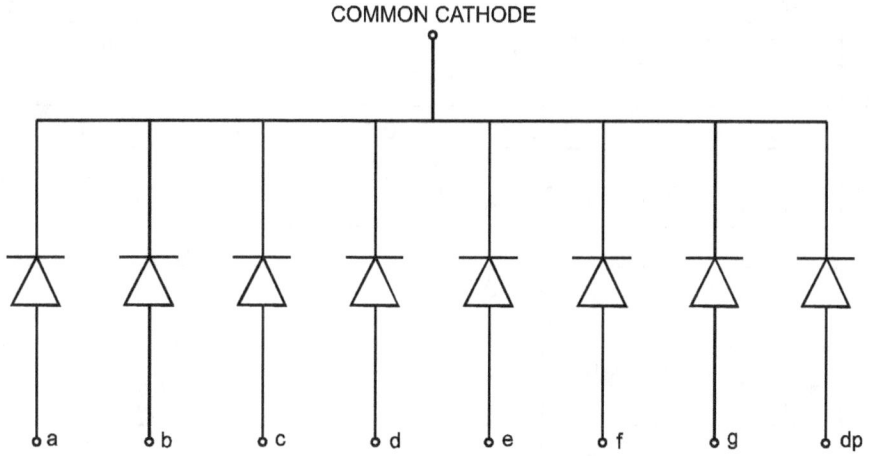

Fig. 4.3 : Common Cathode

4.2.1.2 Common Anode

- In common anode type, the anode of all LEDs is tied together as a single terminal and cathodes are left alone as individual pins. The pin out scheme and picture of a typical 7 segment LED display is shown in the image. In Common Anode is tied to logic 1 and to glow segment LED logic 0 is applied on port pin.

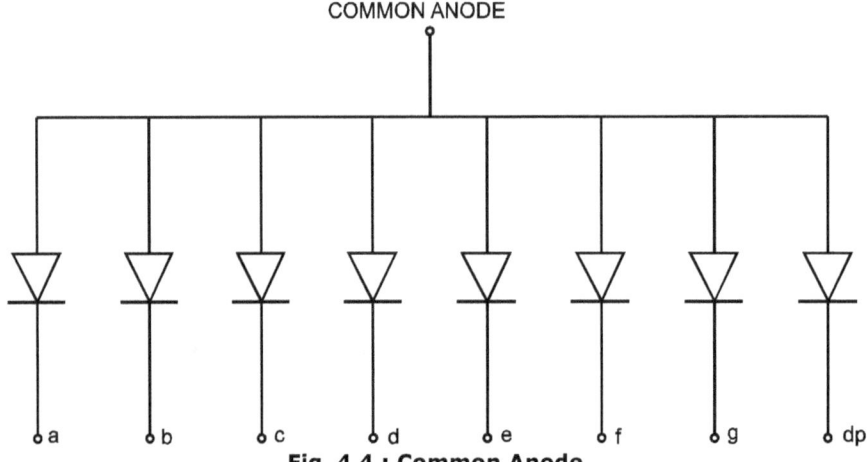

Fig. 4.4 : Common Anode

4.2.1.3 Driving Pattern for Digit

- Digit drive pattern of a seven segment LED display is simply the different logic combinations of its terminals **'a' to 'h'** in order to display different digits and characters. The common digit drive patterns (0 to 9) of a seven segment display are shown in the table below. This pattern s for Common Cathode segment.

Digit	Dp	g	f	e	d	c	b	a	Data
Port	P1.7	P1.6	P1.5	P1.4	P1.3	P1.2	P1.1	P1.0	
0	0	0	1	1	1	1	1	1	3F H
1	0	0	0	0	0	1	1	0	06H
2	0	1	0	1	1	0	1	1	5BH
3	0	1	0	0	1	1	1	1	4FH
4	0	1	1	0	0	1	1	0	66H
5	0	1	1	0	1	1	0	1	6DH
6	0	1	1	1	1	1	0	1	7DH
7	0	0	0	0	0	1	1	1	07H
8	0	1	1	1	1	1	1	1	7FH
9	0	1	1	0	1	1	1	1	6FH

Note : Pattern will be reversed for Common Anode type of segment.

4.2.2 Interfacing with SSD with 8051/8951

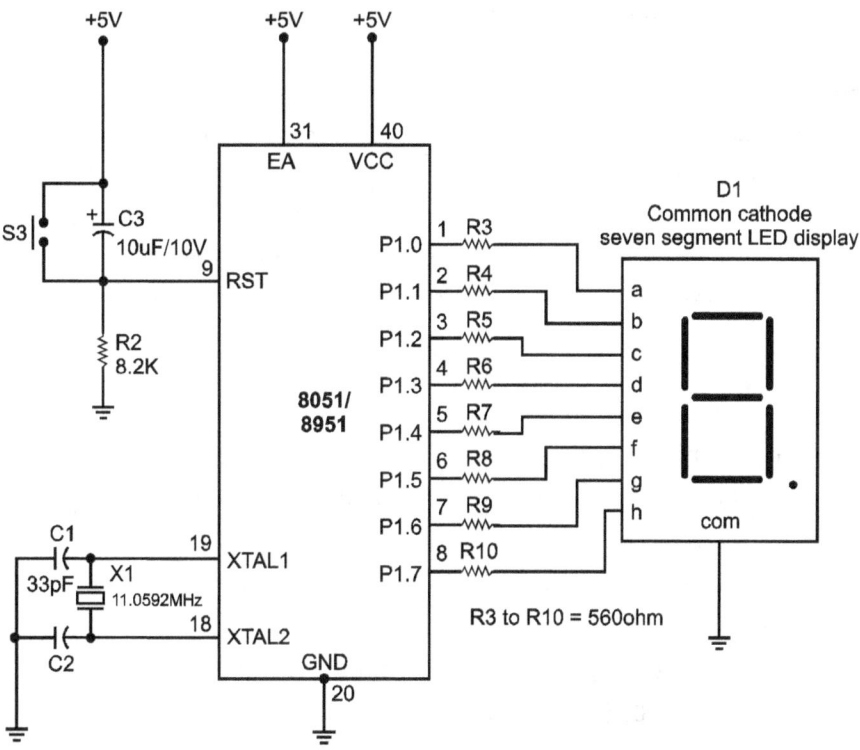

Fig. 4.5 : Interfacing SSD with 8051/8951

Circuit Description :

- The circuit diagram shown in Fig. 4.5 is of an 89C51 microcontroller based 0 to 9 counter which has a 7 segment LED display interfaced to it in order to display the count. This simple circuit illustrates two things. How to setup simple 0 to 9 up counter using 8051 and more importantly how to interface a seven segment LED display to 8051 in order to display a particular result.

- The common cathode seven segment display D1 is connected to the Port 1 of the microcontroller (AT89S51) as shown in the circuit diagram. R3 to R10 are current limiting resistors. S3 is the reset switch and R2, C3 forms a debouncing circuitry. C1, C2 and X1 are related to the clock circuit. The software part of the project has to do the following tasks.

  ➢ Form a 0 to 9 counter with a predetermined delay (around 1/2 second here).
  ➢ Convert the current count into digit drive pattern.
  ➢ Put the current digit drive pattern into a port for displaying.

- All the above said tasks are accomplished by the program given below.

4.2.3 C Language Programs for Seven Segment Display Interfacing

Program 1 : Program to display from 0 to 9 on 7 segment display, with some delay in between.

Solution :

```
#include <reg51.h>                    // Define 8051 Registers
#define SevenSegment P1

                                       // Array store the 7 segment code for
                                       // each digit to be displayed
unsigned char ssd[10] = { 0x3F, 0x06, 0x5B, 0x4F, 0x66, 0x6D,0x7DH, 0x07,
0x7F, 0x6F };
void main()
    {
        unsigned int i = 0, j;
        while(1)                       // Infinite while loop
        {
            if (i<=9)
            {
                P1 = ssd[i];           // Output 7 segment on port1
                For (j=0; j<3000; j++); // Delay Loop
                i++;
            }
            else                       // End of IF statement
            {
                i=0;                   // Reset i, if it is more than 9
            }
        }                              // End of While loop
    }
```

Program 2 : Program to display from 0 to 9 on 7 segment display, with some delay in between without using array.

Solution :

```
#include <reg51.h>                    // Define 8051 Registers
#define SevenSegment P1               // Array store the 7 segment code for
                                       // each digit to be displayed
```

```c
unsigned char ssd[10] = {0x06, 0x5B, 0x4F, 0x66, 0x6D, 0x7DH, 0x07,0x7F, 0x6F} ;
void main()
    {
        unsigned int j;
while(1)                            // Infinite while loop
        {
            SevenSegment = 0x3F         // Display 0 on 7segment
            for (j=0; j<3000; j++);     // Delay Loop
            SevenSegment = 0x06         // Display 1 on 7segment
            for (j=0; j<3000; j++);     // Delay Loop
            SevenSegment = 0x5B         // Display 2 on 7segment
            for (j=0; j<3000; j++);     // Delay Loop
            SevenSegment = 0x4F         // Display 3 on 7segment
            for (j=0; j<3000; j++);     //Delay Loop
            SevenSegment = 0x66         // Display 4 on 7segment
            for (j=0; j<3000; j++);     // Delay Loop
            SevenSegment = 0x6D         // Display 5 on 7segment
            for (j=0; j<3000; j++);     // Delay Loop
            SevenSegment = 0x7D         // Display 6 on 7segment
            for (j=0; j<3000; j++);     // Delay Loop
            SevenSegment = 0x07         // Display 7 on 7segment
            for (j=0; j<3000; j++);     // Delay Loop
            SevenSegment = 0x7F         // Display 8 on 7segment
            for (j=0; j<3000; j++);     //Delay Loop
            SevenSegment = 0x6F         // Display 9 on 7segment
            for (j=0; j<3000; j++);     // Delay Loop
        }                               // End of While loop
    }
```

Program 3 : Write a C to display 0 to 7 on 7 segment display when switch connected to port2 pins are pressed. On Port1 7-segment is connected.

Solution :

```c
#include<reg51.h>              // Define 8051 Registers
#define SevenSegment P1        // Define 7 segment port
sbit sw0 = P2^0;               // Defining Switch PIN P2.0
```

```
sbit sw1 = P2^1;                    // Defining Switch PIN P2.1
sbit sw2 = P2^2;                    // Defining Switch PIN P2.2
sbit sw3 = P2^3;                    // Defining Switch PIN P2.3
sbit sw4 = P2^4;                    // Defining Switch PIN P2.4
sbit sw5 = P2^4;                    // Defining Switch PIN P2.5
sbit sw6 = P2^4;                    // Defining Switch PIN P2.6
sbit sw7 = P2^4;                    // Defining Switch PIN P2.7

void Delay(int);                    // Function prototype declaration
void main (void)
{
    LED = 0x00;                     // Turn off all the LEDS
    while(1)                        // Infinite loop
    {
        if (sw0 == 0)               // If switch 0 pressed
        {
            SevenSegment = 0x3F     // Display 0 on 7segment
            for (j=0;j<3000;j++);   // Delay Loop
        }
            if (sw1 == 0)           // If switch 1 pressed
        {
            SevenSegment = 0x06     // Display 1 on 7segment
            For (j=0; j<3000; j++); // Delay Loop
        }
            if (sw2 == 0)           // If switch 2 pressed
        {
            SevenSegment = 0x5B     // Display 2 on 7segment
            for (j=0; j<3000; j++); // Delay Loop
        }
            if (sw3 == 0)           // If switch 3 pressed
        {
            SevenSegment = 0x4F     // Display 3 on 7segment
            for (j=0; j<3000; j++); // Delay Loop
        }
            if (sw4 == 0)           // If switch 4 pressed
```

```
        {
            SevenSegment = 0x66          // Display 4 on 7segment
            for(j=0;j<3000;j++);         // Delay Loop
        }
            if (sw5 == 0)                // If switch 5 pressed
        {
            SevenSegment = 0x6D          // Display 5 on 7segment
            for (j=0; j<3000; j++);      // Delay Loop
        }
            if (sw6 == 0)                // If switch 6 pressed
        {
            SevenSegment = 0x7D          // Display 6 on 7segment
            for (j=0; j<3000; j++);      // Delay Loop
        }
            if (sw7 == 0)                // If switch 7 pressed
        {
            SevenSegment = 0x07          // Display 7 on 7segment
            for (j=0; j<3000; j++);      // Delay Loop
        }
        }                                // End of While Loop
    }
    void Delay (int k)                   // Delay Loop
    {
    int j;
    int i;
    for (i=0; i<k; i++)
    {
    for (j=0; j<100; j++)
        {
        }
    }
    }
}
```

Program 4 : Write a C to display 0 to 7 on 7 segment display when switch connected to port2 pins are pressed. On Port1 7-segment is connected.

Solution :

```
    #include <reg51.h>                   // Define 8051 Registers
```

```
#define Key Switch P2              // Define Key Switch Port
#define SevenSegment P1            // Define Seven Segment Port
    //Array store the 7 segment code for each digit to be displayed unsigned char
ssd [10] = {0x3F, 0x06, 0x5B, 0x4F, 0x66, 0x6D,0x7DH, 0x07};
void main()
    {
        unsigned int j;
        unsigned char data;
        while (1)                  // Infinite while loop
        {
            data = ~KeySwitch;
            P1 = ssd [data];       // Output 7 segment on port1
            for (j=0; j<3000; j++); // Delay Loop
        }                          // End of While loop
    }
}
```

Explanation :

• When key switch 0 is pressed, port 2 state will 1111 1110, complement of these data will be 0000 0001, i.e. 0x01, in these location of array 7 segment code for 0 is stored and so on.

4.2.4 Interfacing of Multiplexed 7-Segment Display

Multiplexing of 7 segment display :

• If one need more than one segment then Multiplexing of display is to be done. Each 7 segment display have 8 pins and so a total amount of 24 pins are to the connected to the microcontroller and there will be only 8 pins left with the microcontroller for other input output applications. Also the maximum number of displays that can be connected to the 8051 is limited to 4 because 8051 has only 4 ports.

• More over three (3) displays will be ON always and this consumes a considerable amount of power. All these problems associated with the straight forward method can be solved by multiplexing.

• In multiplexing, all displays are connected in parallel to one port and only one display is allowed to turn ON at a time, for a short period. This cycle is repeated for at a fast rate and due to the persistence of vision of human eye, all digits seems to glow. The main advantages of this method are :

  ➢ Fewer number of port pins are required.

  ➢ Consumes less power.

➢ More number of display units can be interfaced (maximum 24 – One port for data and other three ports for control lines for turning on and off segment.).

• The circuit diagram for multiplexing 2 seven segment displays to the 8051 is shown below.

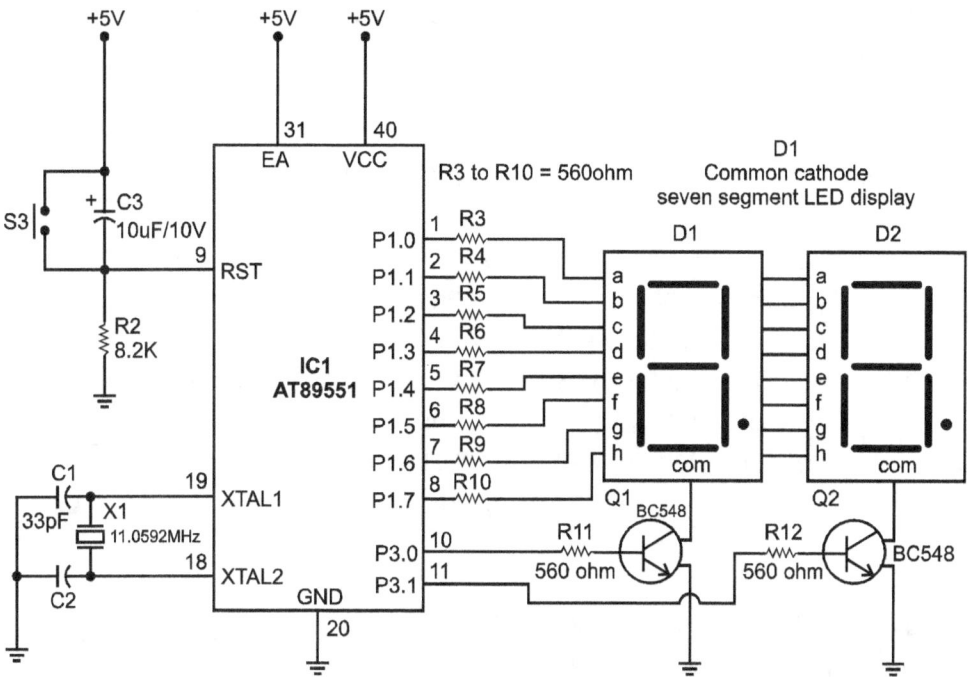

Fig. 4.6 : Multiplexed 7 segment Display interfacing with 8051

• When assembled and powered on, the circuit will display the number '43' and let us see how it is done. Initially the first display is activated by making P3.0 high and then digit drive pattern for "4" is loaded to the Port 1. This will make the first display to show "4".

• In the mean time, P3.1 will be low and so do the second display will be OFF. This condition is maintained for around 1ms and then P3.0 is made low. Now both displays will be OFF.

• Then the second display is activated by making P3.1 high and then the digit drive pattern for "3" is loaded to the port 1. This will make the second display to show "3". In the mean time P3.0 will be low and so the second display will be OFF.

• This condition is maintained for another 1ms and then port 3.1 is made low. This cycle is repeated and due to the persistence of vision you will feel it as "43".

• Transistor Q1 drives the first display (D1) and transistor Q2 drives the second display (D2). R11 and R12 are the base current limiting resistors of Q1 and Q2.

Program 1 : Write a C to display 43 on seven segment display.

Solution :

```
#include <REGX51.H>              // Define 8051 registers
#define Control P3               // Define control port
#define SevenSegment P1          // Define Seven Segment port
void main()
    {
        unsigned int j;
        while(1)                      // Infinite while loop
        {
            SevenSegment = 0x4FH;     // Sent code for 3 on port1
            Control = 0x01;           // Enable port 3 to display
            for (j=0; j<3000; j++);   // Delay Loop
            SevenSegment = 0x66H;     // Sent code for 4 on port1
            Control = 0x02;           // Enable port 3 to display
            for (j=0; j<3000; j++);   // Delay Loop
        }                             // End of While loop
    }
```

Program 2 : Write a C to display 66 on seven segment display.

Solution :

```
#include <regs51.H>              // Define 8051 registers
#define SevenSegment P1          // Define SevenSegment port
sbit Cntl0 = P3^0;               // Defining Switch PIN P3.0
sbit Cntl1 = P3^1;               // Defining Switch PIN P3.1

void main()
    {
        unsigned int j;
        while(1)                      // Infinite while loop
        {
            SevenSegment = 0x7DH;     // Sent code for 6 on port1
            Cntl0 = 1;                // Enable segment 1
            Cntl1 = 0;                // Disable Segment 2
            for (j=0; j<3000; j++);   // Delay Loop
```

```
        SevenSegment = 0x7DH;      // Sent code for 6 on port1
        Cntl0=0;                   // Disable Segment 1
        Cntl1=;                    // Enable segment 2
        for (j=0; j<3000; j++);    // Delay Loop
    }                              // End of While loop
}
```

Explanation :

- A login 1 on port pin3.0 or P3.1 will turn on the transistor, turning on the transistor will connect common pin of segment to ground and that respective 7 segment will glow.

- A login 0 on port pin3.0 or P3.1 will turn OFF the transistor, turning OFF the transistor will disconnect common pin of segment from ground and that respective 7 segment will OFF.

4.3 INTERFACING LCD ITS PROGRAMMING WITH 'C'

4.3.1 LCD Background (Liquid Crystal Display)

- Any program must interact with the outside world using input and output devices that communicate directly with a human being.

- LEDs (lights), interfaced with 8051 microcontroller, can be used to display binary numbers or on/off states while Seven Segment Displays (SSD) can display digits but that's not enough. What if you wanted to display a proper message consisting of **numbers, letters, characters, symbols,** etc.? That's where **LCD Screens** jump in. LCDs make it convenient to display anything to the user. Fig. 4.7 shows LCD display.

- One of the most common devices attached to an 8051 is an LCD display. Another is 7segment display. Some of the most common LCDs connected to the 8051 are 16x2 and 20x2 displays. This means 16 characters per line by 2 lines and 20 characters per line by 2 lines, respectively.

- Fortunately, a very popular standard exists which allows us to communicate with the vast majority of LCDs regardless of their manufacturer. The standard is referred to as HD44780U, which refers to the controller chip which receives data from an external source (in this case, the 8051) and communicates directly with the LCD.

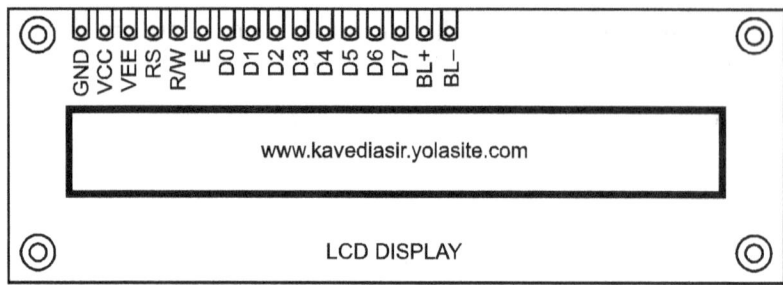

Fig. 4.7 : LCD Display

4.3.2 LCD Signals for Interfacing

Pin No.	Name	Function
1.	VSS	Ground pin
2.	VCC	Power supply pin of 5V
3.	VEE	Used for adjusting the contrast commonly attached to the potentiometer.
4.	RS	RS is the register select pin used to write display data to the LCD (characters), this pin has to be high when writing the data to the LCD. During the initializing sequence and other commands this pin should low.
5.	R/W	Reading and writing data to the LCD for reading the data R/W pin should be high (R/W=1) to write the data to LCD R/W pin should be low (R/W=0)
6.	E	Enable pin is for starting or enabling the module. A high to low pulse of about 450ns pulse is given to this pin.
7.	DB0	
8.	DB1	
9.	DB2	
10.	DB3	
11.	DB4	DB0-DB7 Data pins for giving data(normal data like numbers characters or command data) which is meant to be displayed
12.	DB5	
13.	DB6	
14.	DB7	
15.	LED+	Back light of the LCD which should be connected to Vcc
16.	LED-	Back light of LCD which should be connected to ground.

4.3.3 Interfacing Circuit LCD in 8-bit Mode

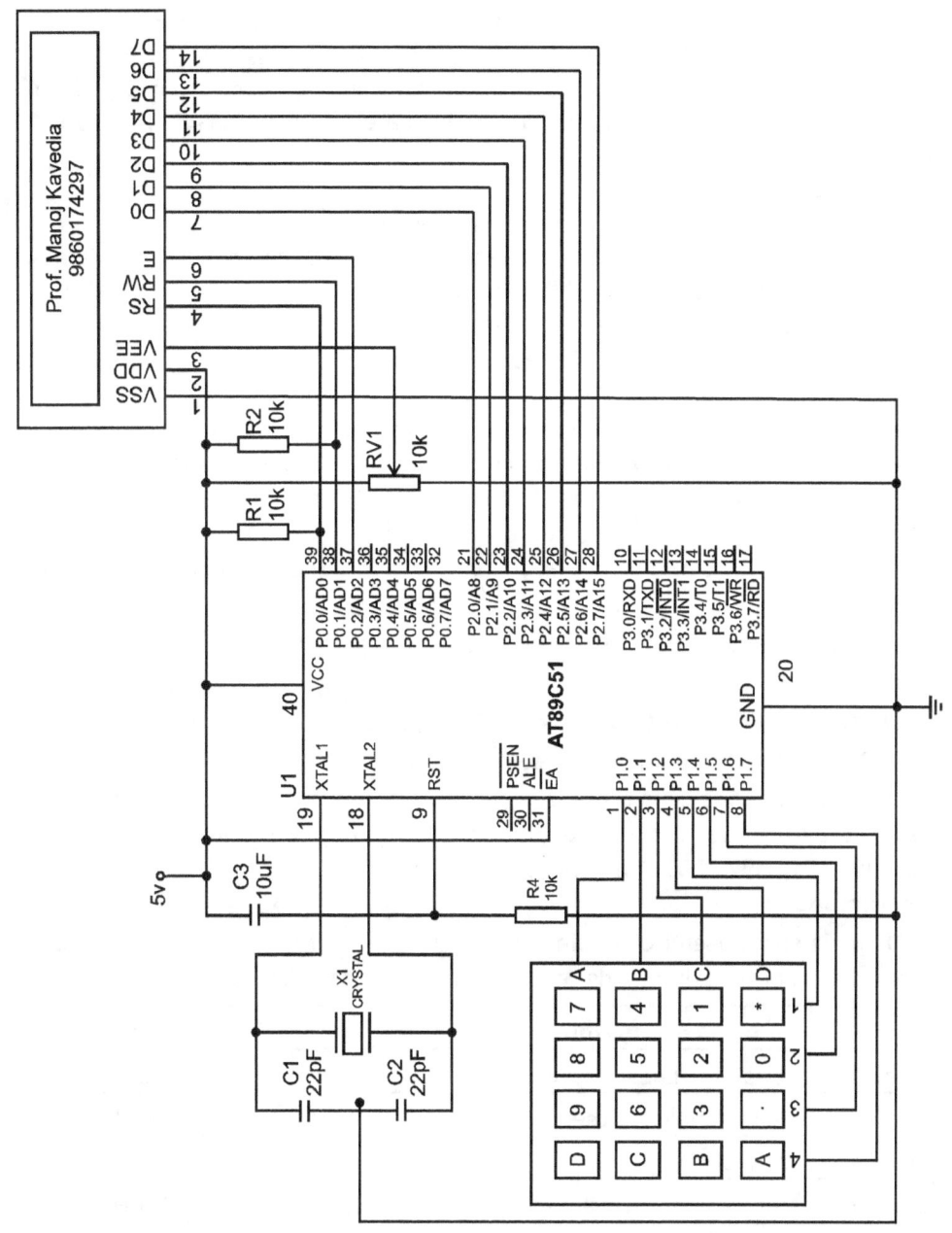

Fig. 4.8 : Interfacing of LCD 16x2 in 4-bit mode

Interfacing signal of LCD :

- The 44780 standard requires 3 control lines as well as either 4 or 8 I/O lines for the data bus. The user may select whether the LCD is to operate with a 4-bit data bus or an 8-bit data bus. If a 4-bit data bus is used the LCD will require a total of 7 data lines (3 control lines plus the 4 lines for the data bus). If an 8-bit data bus is used the LCD will require a total of 11 data lines (3 control lines plus the 8 lines for the data bus). The three control lines are referred to as **EN**, **RS**, and **RW** as shown in Fig. 4.8.

RS – Register Select :

- The **RS** (Register Select) control pin is used to select either command or data register as described in the pin configuration table. Once selected, all data sent on the 8-bit data lines will be latched to that register.
    - ➢ RS = 0, Command Register is selected.
    - ➢ RS = 1, Data Register is Selected

RW – Read/Write select :

- The **R/W** (Read/Write) control pin is used to determine the flow of data. You have to select **write mode,** when one is sending something **to** the LCD (data or command) and **read mode** when one is reading **from** the LCD.

E – Enable LCD

- The **E** (Enable) control pin acts as a guard to allow exchange of data. This pin is very important in this whole process and must be handled precisely. The following animation explains its function. It must be used in the following manner:
    - ➢ **HIGH** to **LOW** transition for **Write** Operation.
    - ➢ **LOW** to **HIGH** transition for **Read** Operation.
- Finally, the data bus consists of 4 or 8 lines (depending on the mode of operation selected by the user). In the case of an 8-bit data bus, the lines are referred to as DB0, DB1, DB2, DB3, DB4, DB5, DB6, and DB7.

LCD commands :

- LCDs have some useful commands that you can use for different operations. For more details of the commands refer to Data sheet of LCD.

Instruction	Hexadecimal
Enable 8-bit interface, 2 lines, 5*7 Pixels	0x38
making LCD on and initializing the cursor	0xFH
Display ON, Cursor Blinking	0x0E
Incrementing the cursor which will help to display another character in the LCD	0X6H
Clear Screen	0x01

Program 1 : Write a C to Interface LCD with 8051 in 8-bit mode

Solution :

Step-1 : Define the Pins :

```
#define lcdport P2
#define rs P0_0              // Set P0.0 as Register Selected Signal
#define rw P0_2              // Set P0.2 as Read Write signal
#define en P0_1              // Set P0.1 as Enable Signal
```

Step-2 : Code to send Command to Port pins

```
void lcdcmd(unsigned char value)
    {
        lcdport = value;
        rw = 0;              // Set rw pin low
        rs = 0;              // Set rs pin low to select command Register
        en=1;                // Set en pin high to enable LCD
        delay(1);            // Cal delay routine
        en=0;                // Set en pin to low
    }
```

Step-3 : Code to send Data to Port pins

```
void lcdcmd (unsigned char value)
    {
        lcdport = value;
        rw = 0;              // Set rw pin low
        rs = 1;              // Set rs pin high to select data Register
        en=1;                // Set en pin high to enable LCD
        delay(1);            // Cal delay routine
        en=0;                // Set en pin to low
    }
```

Step-4 : Code for Delay routine

```
void delay(unsigned int msec)   // Function to provide time delay in msec.
    {
        int i, j;
        for(i=0; i<msec; i++)
        for(j=0;j<1275;j++);
    }
```

Step-5 : Main Program

```
void main()
    {
                                    // Initialize LCD
        lcdcmd(0x38);               // For using 8-bit double row mode of LCD
        lcdcmd(0x0E);               // Turn display ON for cursor blinking
        lcdcmd(0x01);               // Clear screen
                                    // PRINT M CHARACTER
        lcddata('M');
        while(1);                   // Do nothing Loop
    }
```

Program 2 : Complete C code to interface LCD in 8-bit mode display.

Solution :

```
#include <regs51.h>
#define lcdport P2
#define rs              P0_0
#define rw              P0_2
#define e               P0_1
void lcdcmd (unsigned char);
void lcddata(unsigned char);
void delay (unsigned int);
void main()
    {
                                    // INITIALIZE LCD
        lcdcmd(0x38);               // For using 8-bit double row mode of LCD
        lcdcmd(0x0E);               // Turn display ON for cursor blinking
        lcdcmd(0x01);               // Clear screen
                                    // PRINT K CHARACTER
        lcddata('K');
        while(1);
    }
                                    // Function to send command to LCD
```

```c
void lcdcmd(unsigned char value)
    {
        lcdport = value;
        rw = 0;
        rs = 0;
        e=1;
        delay(1);
        e=0;
    }
                                    // Function to send data to LCD
void lcddata(unsigned char value)
    {
        lcdport = value;
        rw = 0;
        rs = 1;
        e=1;
        delay(1);
        e=0;
    }
                                    // Function to provide time delay in msec.
void delay(unsigned int msec)
    {
        int i, j;
        for (i=0; i<msec; i++)
        for (j=0;j<1275;j++);
    }
```

4.3.4 Interfacing Circuit LCD in 4-bit Mode

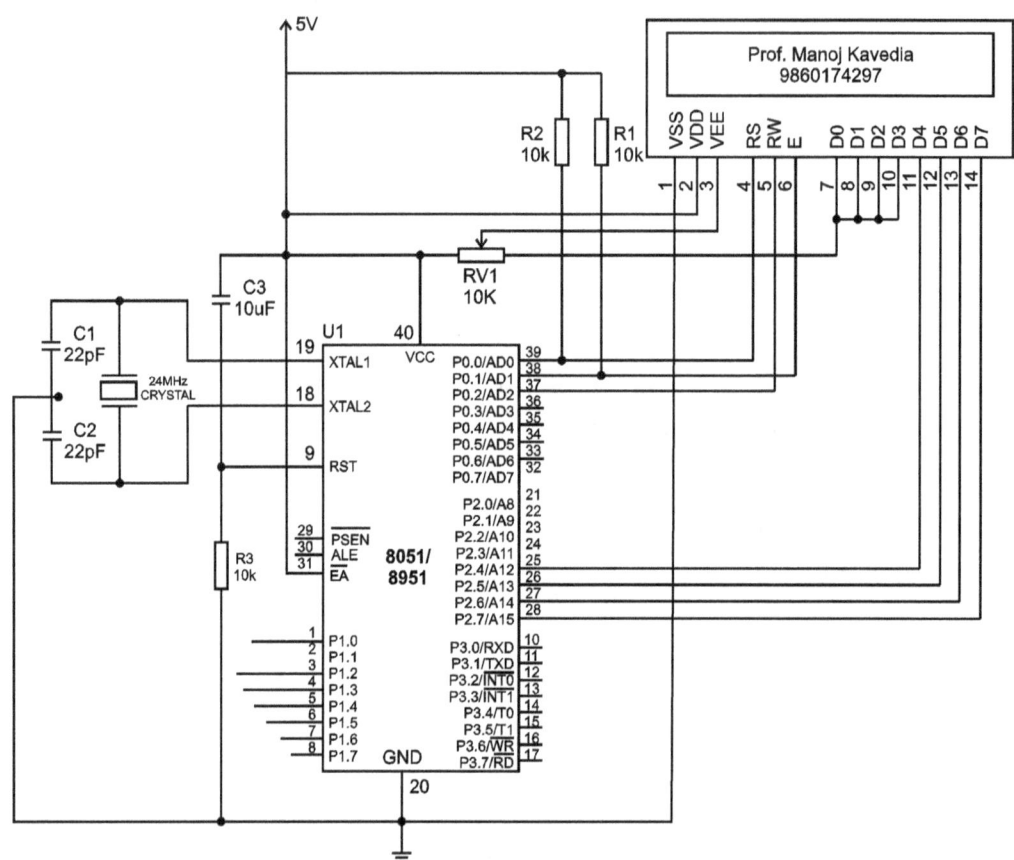

Fig. 4.9 : Interfacing LCD in 4-bit mode with 8051

About circuit :

- In the Fig. 4.9, the port 2 upper four lines of the 8051 microcontroller are connected to data lines (D4-D7) of the LCD. In 8051 microcontroller, the port 0 doesn't have the internal pull-up resistors and all these port0 pins are open drain configuration.

- So, we need to connect an external pull-up resistor to each port pin to improve the driving capability of the port0. The pull-up resistor values should be between 4.7 k ohms to 10 k ohms as recommended in the data sheet of the microcontroller.

Explanation :

- The data can be sent to LCD in two different 4-bit transfers. Hence, two enable pulses are shown for each byte transfer.

- During the data or command transfer to LCD, the higher nibble (D7-D4) of a byte should be transferred first.

- After the command or data byte is transferred, the LCD will take some time to process it.

- A time delay N milliseconds should be provided to LCD for internal processing. 100 milliseconds as time delay between each byte transfer (check out the source code below). If delay is not provided between each byte transfers, the LCD will not accept the second byte until the first byte is completed. Therefore, the LCD will not show desire output to user.

- The main disadvantage of this procedure is unnecessary wastage of CPU or MCU time, because there is no exact time provided in the data sheet that an LCD will take to process the command or data. This can be solved by using busy status.

LCD Commands :

Sr. No.	Command	Description
1.	0x01	Clear Display Screen
2.	0x28	Configuring LCD as 2 line 5x7 matrix in 4-bit mode
3.	0x0E	Display on, cursor blinking
4.	0x06	Increment cursor right side
5.	0x80	Force cursor to beginning of 1st line, if the number is 0x85 then force the cursor to 5th position
6.	0xC0	Force cursor to beginning of 2nd line
7.	0x1C	Shift the display to right side
8.	0x02	Return Home
9.	0x30	Configure LCD as 1-line 5x7 matrix

Description about the LCD functions used:

- There are five functions are implemented in embedded C (Keil c). In each function, the data byte is divided into two parts (nibbles) by using logical masking, and then transferred. The higher nibble is transferred first and then lower nibble.

  1. LCD_cmd() : Microcontroller sends command to LCD using "LCD_cmd()" function, in which the RD and R/W signals both are at logic low.

  2. LCD_string() : Data string can be sent to LCD using this "LCD_string()" function, in which the RS should be at logic high and R/W should be at logic low. When the number of characters in a string is greater than display size (> 16 characters), then the function "LCD_string()" will automatically shift the display to right side.

3. **LCD_char()** : Using this function, we can send single char at a time.

4. **delayms(1)** : This function generates 1 ms delay approximately and it is tested in Keil software. It uses a new function _nop_(), which generates 1 μs time delay and it available in intrins.h header file.

5. **LCD_Init()** : By using this function, LCD is configured as 2 line with 5x7 matrix. This function makes the LCD display ON with cursor blinking and also has automatic cursor increment to right side. The commands used in this function are 0x83, 0x01, 0xc0, 0x80. Refer table for description about the commands.

Program : Write a C program to interface LCD in 4-bit mode.

Solution :

```
#include <reg51.h>
                              // LCD control signals declaration
        sbit RS = P0^0;       // Register Select line
        sbit RW = P0^2;       // Read/write line
        sbit Enable = P0^1;   // Enable line


#define LCD_PORT P2
                              // LCD function prototypes
void LCD_cmd(unsigned char);
void LCD_string(unsigned char*);
void delayms(unsigned int);
void LCD_Char(unsigned char);
void LCD_Init(void);
                              // Main function declaration
void main()
    {
        P0 = 0x00;
        P2 = 0x00;
                                     // LCD reset process sequence as per datasheet
        delayms(15);        // Wait for more than 15 ms after supply rises to 4.5V
        LCD_cmd(0x30);
        delayms(4);             // Wait more than 4.1 ms
        LCD _cmd(0x30);
        delayms(1);     // Wait more than 100us, but delayms(1) will provide 1 ms
```

```c
        LCD _cmd(0x30);
        delayms(1);
        LCD_cmd(0x02);          // Return to home
        delayms(1);
        LCD_Init();
    while(1)
        {
        LCD_cmd(0x80);      // Move cursor to beginning of 1st line, if the number
                            // is 0x85, then force the cursor to 5th position
        delayms(1);
        LCD_string("Prof. Manoj Kavedia");
        delayms(50);
        LCD_cmd(0xC0);      // Move cursor to beginning of 2nd line
delayms(1);
        LCD_string("http:     // Displays at first line
        delayms(20);
        LCD_cmd(0x01);      // Move cursor to beginning of 2nd line
        }
    }
void LCD_Init()
        {
        LCD_cmd(0x28);      // Configuring LCD as 2 line 5x7 matrix in 4-bit mode
        delayms(1);
        LCD_cmd(0x0C);          // Display on, cursor blinking
        delayms(1);
        LCD _cmd(0x01);         // Clear display screen
        delayms(1);
        LCD _cmd(0x06);         // Increment cursor (right side)
        delayms(1);
        }
                                // LCD command sending function
void LCD_cmd(unsigned char command)
        {
        unsigned char ch=0;
        LCD_PORT &= 0x00;   // Make upper bits of port as zero
        LCD_PORT =(Command);        // Mask lower nibble and send upper nibble
        RS = 0;                 // Select command register
```

```
        RW = 0;                    // Write operation
        Enable = 1;                // High to Low pulse provided on the enable pin with
                                   // nearly 1 ms (> 450 ns)
        delayms(1);
        enable = 0;
        delayms(1);
        LCD_PORT &= 0x00;          // Make upper bits of port as zero
        LCD_PORT =(Command<<4);    // Upper nibble
        RS = 0;                    // Select Data Register
        RW = 0;                    // Write operation
        Enable = 1;                // High to Low pulse provided on the enable pin with
                                   // nearly 1 ms (> 450 ns)
        delayms(1);
        Enable = 0;
        delayms(1);
        }
                                   // LCD data sending function declaration
    void LCD_string(unsigned char *String)
        {
        unsigned char i=0, ch=0, temp=0;
        while(String[i]!='\0')
        {
        temp = String[i++];
        LCD_PORT &= 0x00;          // Make upper bits of port as zero
        LCD_PORT = (temp);         // Mask lower nibble and send upper nibble
        RS = 1;                    // Select data register
        RW = 0;                    // Write operation
        Enable = 1;                // High to Low pulse provided on the enable pin with
                                   // nearly 1 ms (> 450 ns)
        delayms(1);
        Enable = 0;
        delayms(1);
        LCD_PORT &= 0x00;          // Make upper bits of port as zero
        LCD_PORT = ((temp<<4));    // Lower nibble
        RS = 1;                    // Select data register
        RW = 0;                    // Write operation
        Enable = 1;                // High to Low pulse provided on the enable pin with
                                   // nearly 1 ms (> 450 ns)
```

```
delayms(1);
Enable = 0;
delayms(1);
 if (i > = 16)
LCD_cmd(0x1C);
delayms(100);
}
return;                      // LCD single character sending function declaration
void send_Char(unsigned char character)
{
unsigned char ch=0;
LCD_PORT &= 0x00;            // Make upper bits of port as zero
LCD_PORT = (character);      // Mask lower nibble and send upper nibble
RS = 1;                      // Select command register
RW = 0;                      // Write operation
Enable = 1;                  // High to Low pulse provided on the enable pin with
                             // nearly 1 ms (> 450 ns)
delayms(1);
Enable = 0;
delayms(1);
LCD_PORT &= 0x00;            // Make upper bits of port as zero
LCD_PORT = ((character<<4)); // Lower nibble
RS = 1;                      // Select data register
RW = 0;                      // Write operation
Enable = 1;                  // High to Low pulse provided on the enable pin with
                             // nearly 1 ms (> 450 ns)
delayms(1);
Enable = 0;
delayms(1);
delayms(100);
}
                             // Delayms function declaration
void delayms(unsigned int value)
{
unsigned int i, j;
for (i=0; i<=value; i++)
```

```
{
For (j=0; j<100; j++)
_nop_();              // No operation produce 1 µs time delay
}
}
```

4.4 INTERFACING ADC (ANALOG TO DIGITAL CONVERTOR) AND IT'S PROGRAMMING WITH 'C'

4.4.1 ADC0804 (Analog to Digital Conversion)

- ADC0804 is an 8-bit successive approximation analog to digital converter from National Semiconductors. The features of ADC0804 are :
  - Differential analog voltage inputs, 0-5V input voltage range.
  - No zero adjustment.
  - Built-in clock generator.
  - Reference voltage can be externally adjusted to convert smaller analog voltage span to 8-bit resolution etc.
- The pin out diagram of ADC0804 is shown in the Fig. 4.10 below.

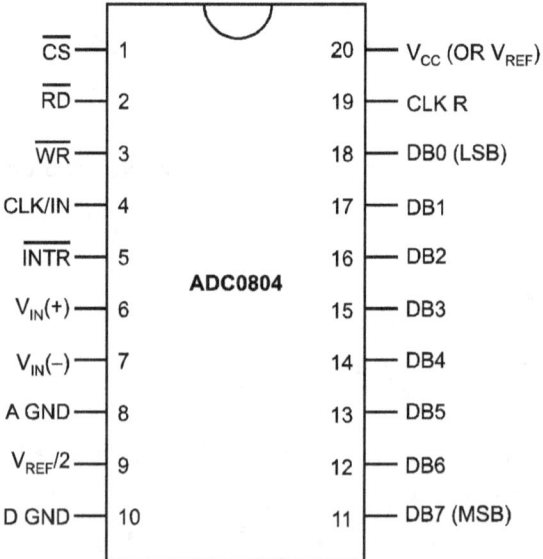

Fig. 4.10 : ADC0804 pin out Diagram

- The voltage at $V_{ref}/2$ (pin 9) of ADC0804 can be externally adjusted to convert smaller input voltage spans to full 8-bit resolution. $V_{ref}/2$ (pin 9) left open means input voltage span is 0-5 V and step size is 5/255 = 19.6 mV. Table below shows different $V_{ref}/2$ voltages and corresponding analogue input voltage spans.

Vref/2 (pin 9) (volts)	Input voltage span (volts)	Step size (mV)
Left open	0 – 5	5/255 = 19.6
2	0 – 4	4/255 = 15.69
1.5	0 – 3	3/255 = 11.76
1.28	0 – 2.56	2.56/255 = 10.04
1.0	0 – 2	2/255 = 7.84
0.5	0 – 1	1/255 = 3.92

4.4.2 Circuit Diagram

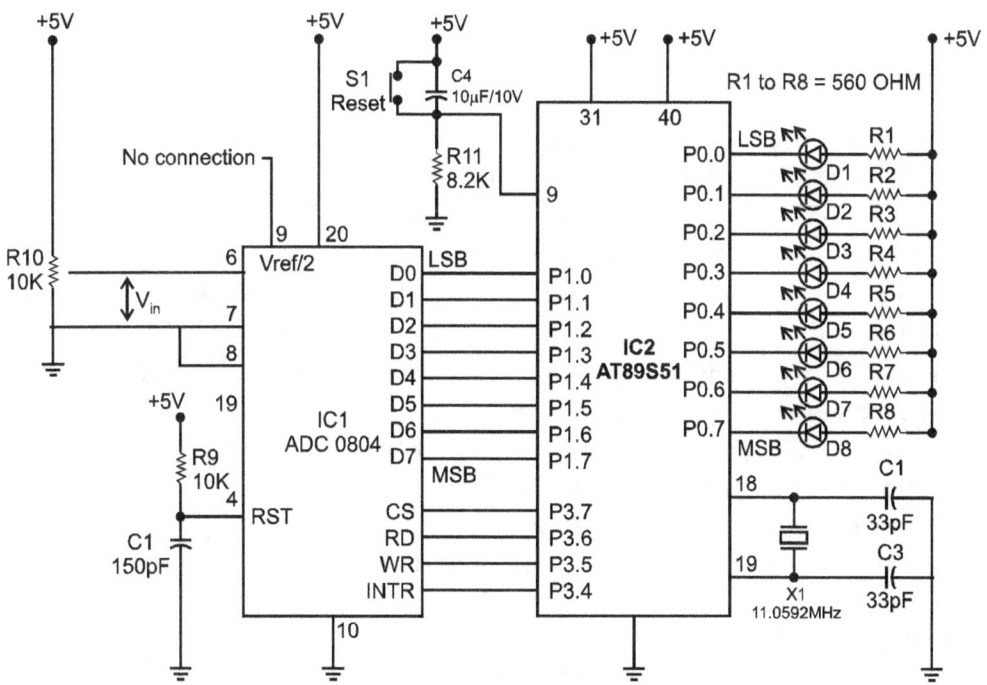

Fig. 4.11 : Interfacing ADC0804 to 8051/8951

- The Fig. 4.11 shows the schematic for interfacing ADC0804 to 8051. The circuit initiates the ADC to convert a given analog input, then accepts the corresponding digital data and displays it on the LED array connected at P0.

- For example, if the analogue input voltage V_{in} is 5V, then all LEDs will glow indicating 11111111 in binary which is the equivalent of 255 in decimal. AT89C51 is the microcontroller used here. Data out pins (D0 to D7) of the ADC0804 are connected to the port pins P1.0 to P1.7 respectively. LEDs D1 to D8 are connected to the port pins P0.0 to P0.7 respectively. Resistors R1 to R8 are current limiting resistors.

- In simple words, P1 of the microcontroller is the input port and P0 is the output port. Control signals for the ADC (INTR, WR, RD and CS) are available at port pins P3.4 to P3.7 respectively. Resistor R9 and capacitor C1 are associated with the internal clock circuitry of the ADC. Preset resistor R10 forms a voltage divider which can be used to apply a particular input analogue voltage to the ADC.

- Push button S1, resistor R11 and capacitor C4 forms a debouncing reset mechanism. Crystal X1 and capacitors C2, C3 are associated with the clock circuitry of the microcontroller.

Steps for converting the analogue input and reading the output from ADC0804 :

- Make CS = 0 (low) and send a low to high pulse to WR pin to start the conversion.

- Now keep checking the INTR pin. INTR will be 1(High) if conversion is not finished and INTR will be 0 if conversion is finished.

- If conversion is not finished (INTR=1), poll until it is finished.

- If conversion is finished (INTR=0), go to the next step.

- Make CS=0 and send a high to low pulse to RD (High) pin to read the data from the ADC.

Program : Write aC code to interface ADC 0804 to port P1, LED for display on port P0 and control signals are generated from Port 3.

```
#include <reg51.h>
#define adc_port P1          // ADC Port P1
#define rd P3_6              // Read signal P3.6
#define wr P3_5              // Write signal P3.5
#define cs P3_7              // Chip Select P3.7
#define intr P3_4            // INTR signal P3.4
void conv();                 // Start of conversion function
void read();                 // Read ADC function
unsigned char adc_val;
```

```
void main()
    {
while (1)
        {                       // Forever loop
        conv();                 // Start conversion
        read();                 // Read ADC
        P3 = adc_val;           // Send the read value to P3
        }
    }
void conv()
        {
        cs = 0;                 // Make CS low
        wr = 0;                 // Make WR low
        wr = 1;                 // Make WR high
        cs = 1;                 // Make CS high
        while (intr);           // Wait for INTR to go low
        }
void read()
        {
        cs = 0;                 // Make CS low
        rd = 0;                 // Make RD low
        adc_val = ~adc_port;    // Read ADC port
        rd = 1;                 // Make RD high
        cs = 1;                 // Make CS high
    }
```

Note : In above circuit, all anodes are connected together. Hence, to glow LED, logic 0 is needed on the port. If all cathodes are connected together, then Logic 1 is to be given on port pins.

4.4.3 Interfacing ADC (Analog to Digital Converter) and its Programming with 'C'

ADC0808 :

- ADC0808 is such a parallel ADC with 8-bit resolution. ADC0808 has 8 input channels, i.e., it can take eight analog signals. To select these input channels, three select pins are to be configured. In this circuit, the microcontroller is used to send the control and enabling signals to ADC.

- In ADC V_{ref} (+) (pin12) and V_{ref} (−) (pin16) are used to set the reference voltage. If V_{ref} (−) is GND and V_{ref} (+) = 5 V, the step size is 5V/256 = 19.53 mV. ADC0808 has 8 input pins IN0-IN7 (pins 1-5 and 26-28). To select an input pin, there are three selector pins A, B and C (pin 25, 24 and 23, respectively). ALE (Address Latch Enable, pin 22) is given a low to high pulse to latch in the address. SC (Start Conversion, pin 6) instructs the ADC to start the conversion.

- When a low to high pulse is given to this pin, ADC starts converting the data. EOC (End Of Conversion, pin 7) is an output pin and goes low, when the conversion is complete and ready to be picked up, and OE (output enable, pin 9) is given a low to high pulse to bring the converted data from the internal register of ADC to the output pins. Pin11 is V_{cc} and pin13 is GND.

- Here, we are using external clock for clock input (pin 10). Analog-to-Digital converters are among the most widely used devices for data acquisition. Digital computers use binary values; but in physical world, everything is analog. Therefore, we need an analog-to-digital converter to translate these analog signals to digital signals.

Pin Diagram:

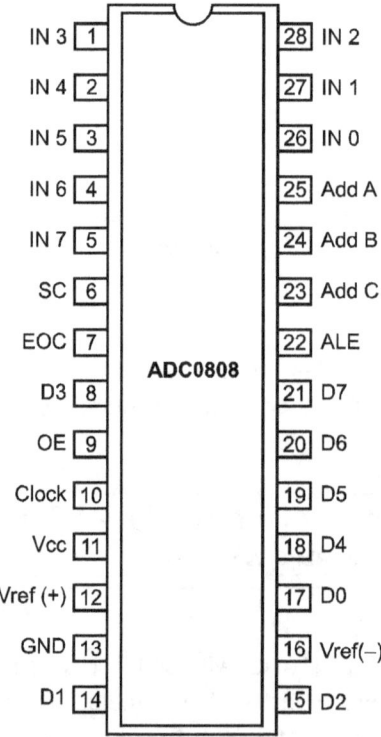

Fig. 4.12 : Pin description diagram of 0808

Pin No.	Function	Name
1	Analog input pins	IN3
2		IN4
3		IN5
4		IN6
5		IN7
6	Start conversion; input pin; a low to high pulse is given	SC
7	End of conversion; output pin; goes low when the conversion is over	EOC
8	Digital output bit 4	D3
9	Input pin; a low to high pulse brings data to output pins from the internal registers at end of conversion	Output enable
10	Clock input; to provide external clock	Clock input
11	Supply voltage; 5V	Vcc
12	Positive reference voltage	Vref(+)
13	Ground ()v)	GND
14	Digital output bit	D1
15		D2
16	Negative reference voltage	Vref(-)
17	Digital output bits	D0
18		D4
19		D5
20		D6
21		D7
22	Address latch enable; Input pin; low to high pulse is required to latch in the address	ALE
23	Address lines	AddressC
24		AddressB
25		AddressA
26	Analog inputs	IN0
27		IN1
28		IN2

- ADC 0808 has 8 different channels. For proper channel selection, logic as per table is provided to pin no. 23, 24, and 25.

Selected Analog Channel	Address Line		
	C	B	A
IN0	L	L	L
IN1	L	L	H
IN2	L	H	L
IN3	L	H	H
IN4	H	L	L
IN5	H	L	H
IN6	H	H	L
IN7	H	H	H

Circuit diagram :

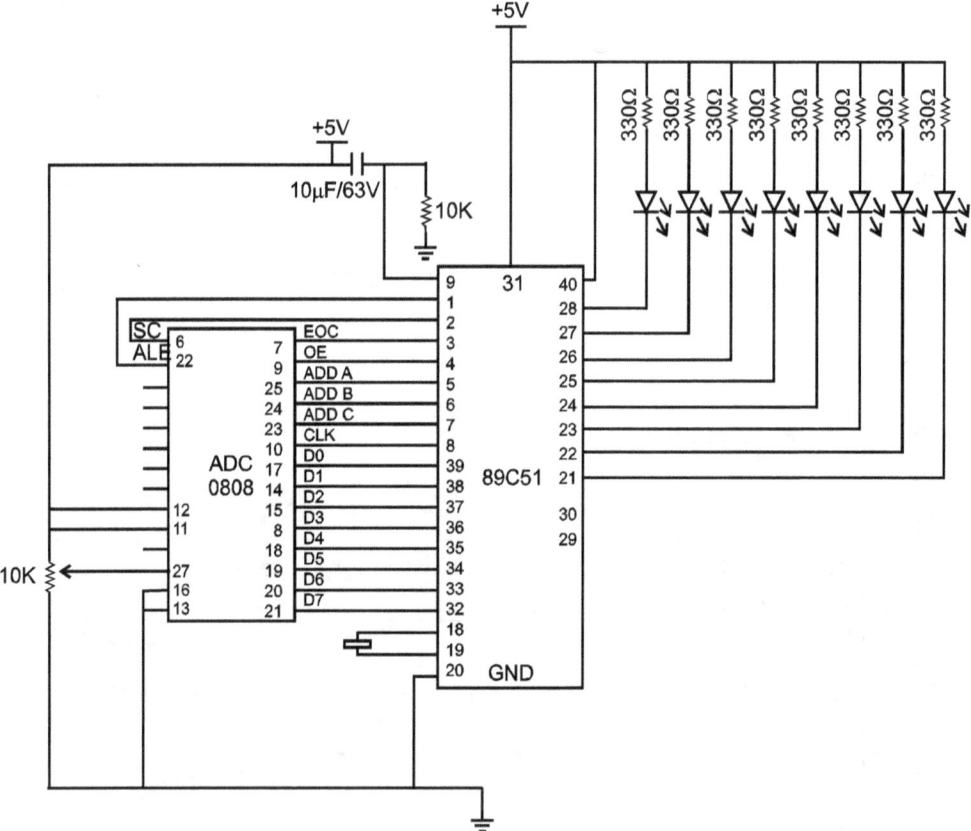

Fig. 4.13 : Interfacing ADC0808 with 89C51/80C51

Circuit explanation :

- The connection of the ADC with the microcontroller can be seen on the circuit diagram in Fig. 4.13.

- ALE (pin 22) of ADC is connected to P1.0 of controller AT89C51. Selector pins A, B and C (pins 25, 24 and 23) of ADC are connected to P1.4, P1.5 and P1.6 pins of microcontroller, respectively.

- SC (pin 6) of ADC is connected to P1.1 of controller. EOC (pin 7) of ADC is connected to P1.2 of microcontroller and OE (pin 9) of ADC is connected to P1.3 of microcontroller. Output of ADC goes to port P0 (pins 32-39) of controller AT89C51. The output is sent to the port P2 (pins 21-28) of controller which is connected to eight LEDs.

- The program continuously scans the input of ADC and displays the output on the output port P2. By varying the input of ADC, output of ADC changes and the change is reflected in the glowing pattern of LEDs connected to the port.

- To provide clock input to the ADC, Timer 0 is used in interrupt enabled mode to generate a clock of frequency 500 kHz. To enable the Timer0 in interrupt enable mode, the register IE is loaded with the value 0×82. Every time the Timer completes the counting, pin P1.7 toggles its state.

Algorithm For Programming ADC :

- An analog channel is selected by giving bits to A, B, C addresses.

- ALE(Address Latch Enable) is activated by a low to high pulse in order to latch in the address.

- SC(Start Conversion) is activated by a low to high pulse in order to start the conversion.

- If a high to low output is obtained at EOC(End of Conversion), it indicates that the data conversion is finished and the data is ready.

- OE(Output Enable) is activated to read output data from the ADC chip.

- In order to bring the digital data out of the chip a low to high pulse is given to the OE pin.

Program : Write a C program to demonstrate interfacing of ADC0808 with 89c51. The output pins are connected to LED's. Controller interrupt is used to generate the clock for driving the ADC 0808.

Solution :

```
#include<reg51.h>
sbit ale=P1^0;            // Address latch enable
sbit oe=P1^3;             // Output enable
sbit sc=P1^1;             // Start conversion
```

```
sbit eoc=P1^2;                    // End of conversion
sbit clk=P1^7;                    // Clock
sbit ADD_A=P1^4;                  // Address pins for selecting input channels.
sbit ADD_B=P1^5;
sbit ADD_C=P1^6;
sfr input_port=0×80;
sfr output_port=0xA0;

void timer0() interrupt 1         // Function to generate clock of frequency 500 kHZ
//using Timer 0 interrupt.
    {
        clk=~clk;
        }
        void delay(unsigned int count) // Function to provide time delay in msec.
        {
        int i, j;
        for (i=0; i<count; i++)
        for (j=0; j<1275; j++);
        }
        void main()
        {
        eoc=1;
        input_port=0xFF;
        ale=0;
        oe=0;
        sc=0;
        TMOD=0×22;                // Timer0 setting for generating clock of 500 kHz
                                  // using interrupt enable mode.
        TH0=0xFD;
        IE=0×82;
        TR0=1;
        while(1)
        {
        ADD_C=0;                  // Selecting input channel 2 using address lines
        ADD_B=0;
        ADD_A=1;
```

```
            delay(2);
            ale=1;
            delay(2);
            sc=1;
            delay(1);
            ale=0;
            delay(1);
            sc=0;
            while(eoc==1);
            while(eoc==0);
            oe=1;
            output_port=input_port;
            delay(2);
            oe=0;
            }
    }
```

Note : in Above interfacing clock for ADC is generated from Timer output of Microcontroller. In some Design Oscillator is used for Clock generation in that case the timer code written in above program can be eliminated

4.5 INTERFACING DAC (DIGITAL TO ANALOG CONVERTER) AND IT'S PROGRAMMING WITH 'C'

4.5.1 DAC 0808

- The digital to analog converter is a device widely used to convert digital pulses to analog signals. The two methods of creating DAC are binary weighted and R-2R ladder.

- DAC 0808 uses the R-2R method since it can achieve a high degree of precision. The first criterion for judging a DAC is its resolution, which is the function of the number of binary inputs. The common ones are 8, 10 and 12 bits. The number of data bit inputs decides the resolution of the DAC since the number of analog output levels is equal to 2n, where n is the number of data inputs.

- DAC 0808 provides 256 discrete voltage or current levels of output. In DAC 0808, the digital inputs are converted into current Iout and by connecting a resistor to I_{out} pin, we convert the result to voltage. The total current provided by IOUT pin is a function of binary numbers at the D0-D7 pins inputs to DAC 0808 and reference current (I_{ref}) is as follows:

$$I_{out} = I_{ref}\left(\frac{D7}{2} + \frac{D6}{4} + \frac{D5}{8} + \frac{D4}{16} + \frac{D3}{32} + \frac{D3}{64} + ... + \frac{D0}{256}\right)$$

where D0 is the LSB, D7 is the MSB for the inputs and Iref is the input current that must be applied.

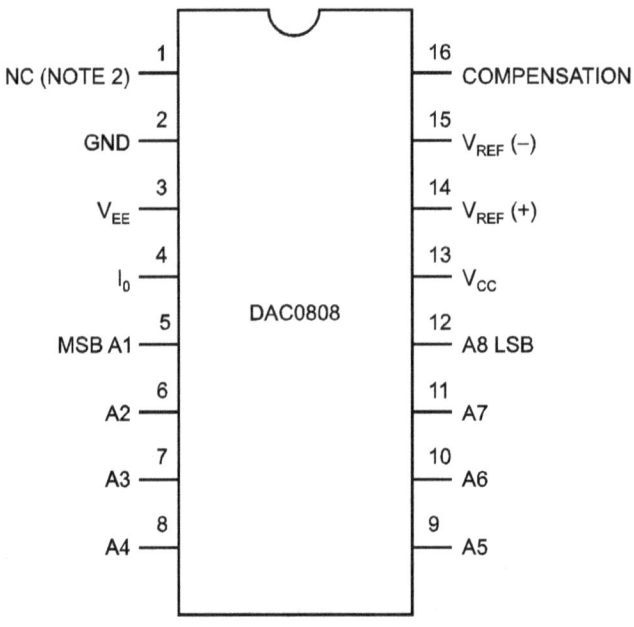

Fig. 4.14 (a) : Pin Diagram of DAC0808

4.5.2 Circuit Diagram

Explanation :

*   The pins are labeled A1 through A8, but note that A8 is the Most Significant Bit, and A1 is the Least Significant Bit (the opposite of the normal convention). Ground the two least significant bits. The D/A converter has an output current, instead of an output voltage.

*   The output current from pin 4 ranges between 0 (when the inputs are all 0) to Imax*255/256 when all the inputs are 1. The current, Imax, is determined by the current into pin 14 (which is at 0 volts). Note: Since we are using 8-bits, the maximum value is Imax*255/256.

Waveform Generation – Triangular Wave :

Logic :

- To generate triangular wave, Go on increasing the count up to FFH from 00H and then decrease it from FFH to 00H.

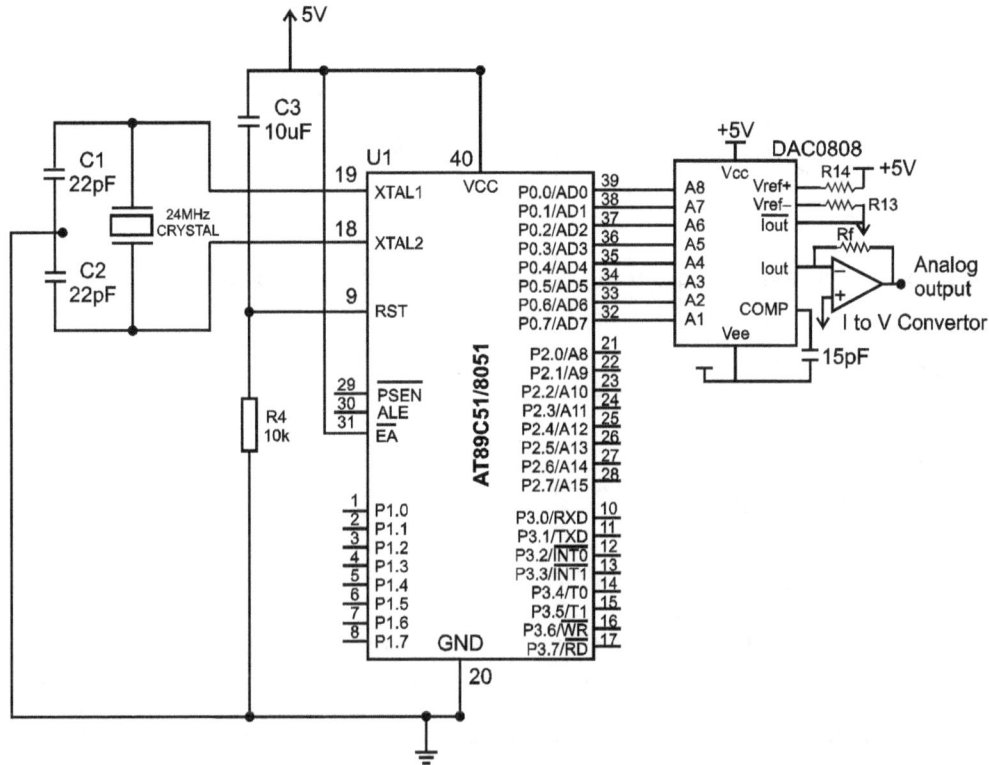

Fig. 4.14 (b) : Interfacing DAC 0808 with 8051/8951

Program 1 : Write a C program to generate triangular wave using DAC 0808.

Solution :

```c
void main()
#include <reg51.h>
    {
        unsigned char data;
        while(1)
        {
            for (data=0x00; data<0xFF; data++)        // Send values 00 to FF
        {
            P2 = data;        // Increment D for positive ramp
        }
```

```
        for (data = 0xFF; data<0x00; data--)          // Send values FF to 00
    {
    P2=data;                        // Decrement D for negative ramp
    }
}
```

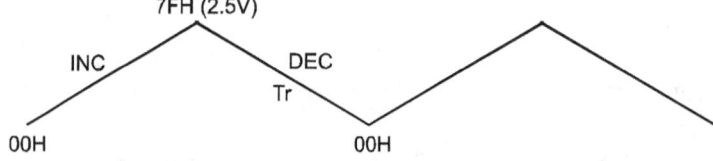

Program 2 : Write a C program to generate triangular wave using DAC 0808.

Solution :

```
#include <reg51.h>
void main()
    {
        unsigned char data;
        while(1)
        {
        for (data=0x00;data<0x7F;data++) // send values 00 to FF
        {
        P2=data;                        // increment D for positive ramp
        }
        for(data=0x7F;data<0x00;data--) // send values FF to 00
        {
        P2=data;                        // Decrement D for negative ramp
        }
    }
```

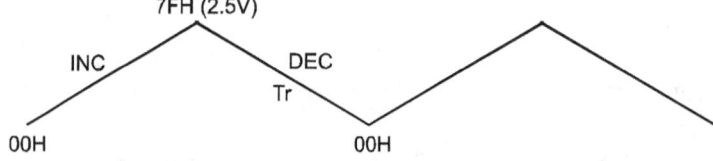

Fig. 4.15 : Triangular wave with 2.5 V as peak amplitude

Waveform Generation – Saw Tooth Wave – Ramp waveform.

Logic :

• To generate sawtooth wave, Go on increasing the count up to FFH from 00H and then reset the count to 00H and repeat the process. Or vice versa.

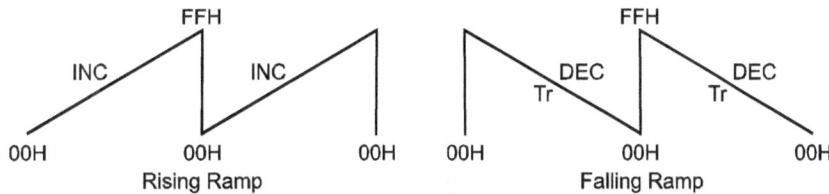

Fig. 4.16 : Rising and Falling ramp wave

Note : Once Acc content reach FFH, an increment from this count make the content off Acc as 00H,Hence, no need to compare the content of Acc with FFH.

Program-1 : Write a C program to generate rising ramp using DAC 0808.

Solution :

```
#include <reg51.h>
void main()
    {
        unsigned char data;
        while(1)
        {
        for (data=0x00; data<0xFF; data++) // send values 00 to FF
            {
            P2=data;                    // increment D for positive ramp
            }
        }
    }
```

Program 2 : Write a C program to generate falling ramp using DAC 0808.

Solution :

```
#include <reg51.h>
void main()
    {
        unsigned char data;
```

```
while(1)
{
for (data=0xFF; data<0x00; data--) // send values FF to 00
    {
    P2=data;                        // Decrement D for negative ramp
    }
}
}
```

4.5.3 Waveform Generation – Square Wave

Logic : To generate square wave, first data 00H is given to DAC which will give output as 0 V and then data FFH is given to DAC which will give output as 5 V. Between these two data, a delay is provided. Depending on delay :

➤ If delay is same in between both data the square wave is the output with 50% duty cycle, as shown in the Fig. 4.17.

➤ If delay is not same in between both data the pulse is the output with more or less than 50% duty cycle, as shown in the Fig. 4.17.

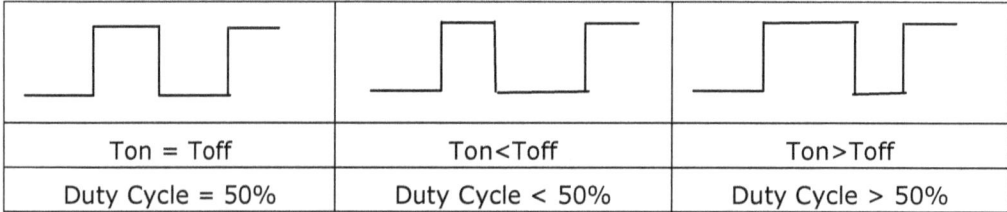

Ton = Toff	Ton<Toff	Ton>Toff
Duty Cycle = 50%	Duty Cycle < 50%	Duty Cycle > 50%

Fig. 4.17 : Square wave with different duty cycle

Program 1 : Write a C program to generate square wave with DAC0808 with 50% duty cycle.

Solution :

```
#include<reg51.h>
void delay1();              // Delay for frequency
void delay1()               // Approx. 100 ms delay
    {
        int a, b;
        for (a = 0; a<100; a++)
        for (b=0; b<1000; b++);
    }
```

```
void main()
    {
        while(1)                // Infinite loop
    {
    P2=0xFF;                    // First send all high to P2
    Delay1();                   // Delay
    P2=0x00;                    // Then send all low to P2
    Delay1();                   // Delay
    }
    }
```

Program 2 : Write a C program to generate square wave with DAC0808 different duty cycle more ON time and less OFF time.

Solution :

```
#include<reg51.h>
void main()
    {
        while(1)                // Infinite loop
        {
            P2=0xFF;            // First send all high to P2
            Delay1();           // Delay
            P2=0x00;            // Then send all low to P2
        Delay2();               // Delay
        }
    }
```

Program 3 : Write a C program to generate Square wave with DAC0808 different duty cycle. 0 More Off time and Less On Time

Solution :

```
#include<reg51.h>
void main()
    {
        while(1)                // Infinite loop
        {
            P2=0xFF;            // First send all high to P2
            Delay2();           // Delay
```

```
        P2=0x00;              // Then send all low to P2
        Delay1();             // Delay
    }
}
```

4.5.4 Waveform Generation – Stair Case Wave

Logic :

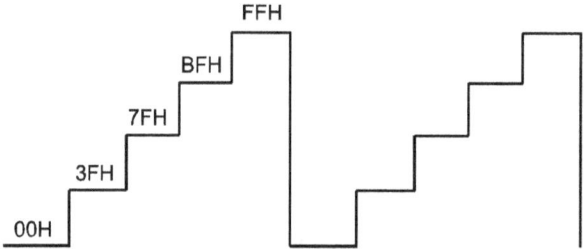

Fig. 4.18 : Stair case Wave form

- To generate stair case wave, First output data 00H, and goon adding 3FH to Existing data before sending on Port A, Then call delay in between the successive Data output.

  00H + 3Fh = 3FH

  3FH+01H = 40H

  40H + 3FH = 7FH

  7FH+01H=80H and so on

Program 1 : Write a program to generate square wave using DAC 0808.

Solution :

```
#include<reg51.h>
void main()
    {
        while(1)
        {
            P2=0x00;              // Step by step increment
            Delay2();
            P2=0x33;              // Values sent to P2
            Delay2();
            P2=0x66;
```

```
            Delay2();
            P2=0x99;
            Delay2();
            P2=0xcc;
            Delay2();
            P2=0xff;
        }
    }
```

Program 2 : Write a program to generate square wave using DAC 0808 using arrays.

Solution :

```
    #include<reg51.h>
    void main()
        {
            unsigned char stair[] = {0x00,0x33,0x66,0x99,0xcc,0xff };
            int i;
            while(1)
        {
            for (i=0; i<=5; i++)
            {
                P2 = stair[i];        // Sent value to port 2 for conversion
                Delay2();             // Delay
            }
        }
        }
```

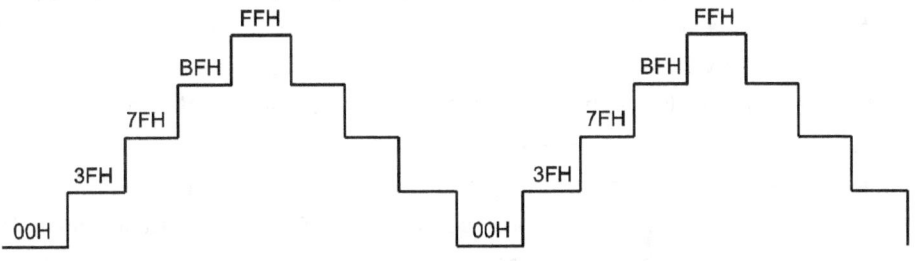

Fig. 4.19 : Stair case wave form

Solution :

```c
#include<reg51.h>
void main()
    {
        unsigned char stair[] = {0x00,0x33,0x66,0x99,0xcc,0xff}
        int i;
        while(1)
    {
        for (i=0; i<=5; i++)
        {
            P2 = stair[i];
            Delay2();
        }
            for (i=4; i>=1; i--)
        {
            P2 = stair[i];
            Delay2();
        }
    }
    }
```

4.6 INTERFACING STEPPER MOTOR AND ITS PROGRAMMING WITH 'C'

4.6.1 About Stepper Motor

- A unipolar stepper motor is rotated by energizing the stator coils in a sequence. In unipolar stepper motoer, the direction of current in stator coils is not required to be controlled by the driving circuit. Just applying the voltage signals across the motor coils or motor leads in a sequence is sufficient to drive the motor.

- A two phase unipolar stepper motor has a total of six wires/leads of which four are end wires (connected to coils) and two are common wires. The color of common wires in the stepper motor used here is Green. Each common wire is connected to two end leads thus forming two phases. The end leads corresponding to each phase have to be identified.

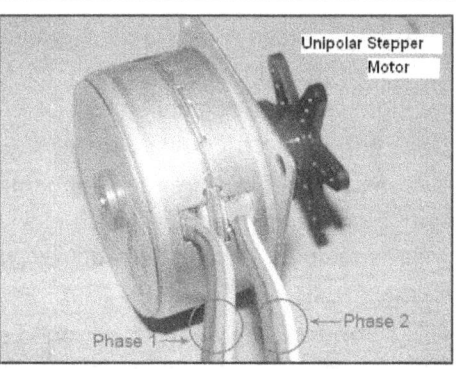

Fig. 4.20 : Stepper motor

- In some cases, when the leads cannot be directly identified in the motor, the identification of endpoints and common points can be done by measuring the resistance between the leads. The leads of different phase will show open circuited condition with respect to each other. This way the leads corresponding to different phase can be separated. The resistance between any two end points of same phase will be twice the resistance between a common point and an end point. This way the common and end points of both the phases can be identified. Shown in Fig. 4.21.

- Stepper motors can be easily interfaced with a microcontroller using driver ICs such as L293D or ULN2003 or transistorized Driver using SL100, 2N2222 or TIP122 etc.

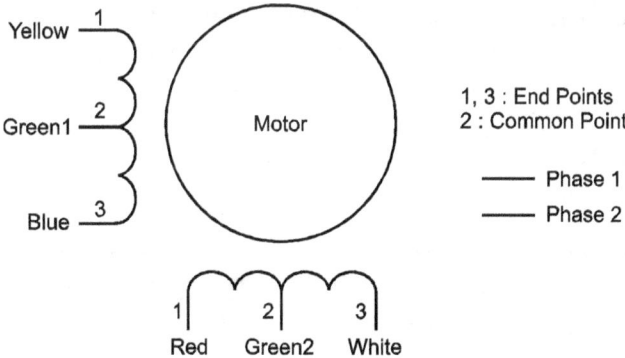

Fig. 4.21 : Six lead unipolar stepper motor

- To work with the unipolar stepper motor, the common points are connected to either Ground or V_{cc} and the end points of both the phases are usually connected through the port pins of a microcontroller. In present case, the common (Green) wires are connected to V_{cc}. The end points receive the control signals as per the controller's output in a particular sequence to drive the motor.

- Since the coils related to each phase are arranged in alternate manner, the end points of two phases are energized in alternate fashion to rotate the motor. This means that the voltage signal should be applied to first end point of Phase 1 and then to the first end point of the Phase 2 and so on.

- Unipolar stepper motors can be used in three modes namely the Wave Drive, Full Drive and Half Drive mode. Each drive have its own advantages and disadvantages, thus we should choose the required drive according to the application and power consumption.

  1. **Wave drive stepping mode :** The above mentioned sequence is repeated to rotate the motor in wave drive stepping mode. The direction of rotation can be clockwise or anti-clockwise depending upon the selection of end points.

Signal sequence for wave drive stepping mode				
Step	Yellow lead (End point 1 of Phase1)	Blue lead (End point 2 of Phase1)	Red lead (End point 1 of Phase2)	White lead (End point 2 of Phase2)
1.	1	0	0	0
2.	0	0	1	0
3.	0	1	0	0
4.	0	0	0	1

  2. **Full drive stepping mode :** The Full Drive Stepping can be achieved by energizing two endpoints of different phases simultaneously.

  In this mode, two electromagnets are energized at a time, so the torque generated will be larger when compared to wave drive. This drive is commonly used than others. Power consumption will be higher than other modes.

Signal sequence for full drive stepping mode				
Step	Yellow lead (End point 1 of Phase1)	Blue lead (End point 2 of Phase1)	Red lead (End point 1 of Phase2)	White lead (End point 2 of Phase2)
1.	1	0	1	0
2.	0	1	1	0
3.	0	1	0	1
4.	1	0	0	1

3. **Half drive stepping mode :** The Half Drive Stepping is achieved by combining the steps of wave and full drive stepping modes. This divides the stepping angle by half.

In this mode, alternatively one and two electromagnets are energized, so it is a combination of wave and full drives. This mode is commonly used to increase the angular resolution of the motor but the torque will be less, about 70% at its half step position. We can see that the angular resolution doubles when using half drive.

Signal sequence for Half Drive Stepping Mode			
Step	**Yellow lead** (End point 1 of Phase1)	**Blue lead** (End point 2 of Phase1)	**Red lead** (End point 1 of Phase2)	**White lead** (End point 2 of Phase2)
1.	1	0	0	0
2.	1	0	1	0
3.	0	0	1	0
4.	0	1	1	0
5.	0	1	0	0
6.	0	1	0	1
7.	0	0	0	1
8.	1	0	0	1

Note: The stepping angle depends upon the resolution of the stepper motor. The direction of rotation and size of steps is directly related to the order and number of input sequence. The shaft rotation speed depends on the frequency of the input sequence. The torque is proportional to the number of magnets magnetized at a time.

4.6.2 Circuit Description

- In the circuit, Port P2 is defined as output port to provide the input sequence for the stepper motor. Four transistors (TIP122) are used as switches to drive the motor. The motor leads are not directly interfaced with the microcontroller pins because stepper motor requires 60 mA current while AT89C51 has the maximum current rating of 50 mA. So, the transistors switches are used to transfer signals from the microcontroller to the stepper wires.

- The sequence of signals mentioned in the tables above rotates the motor in clockwise direction. Reversing these input sequences would rotate the motor in counter clockwise direction.

Circuit diagram :

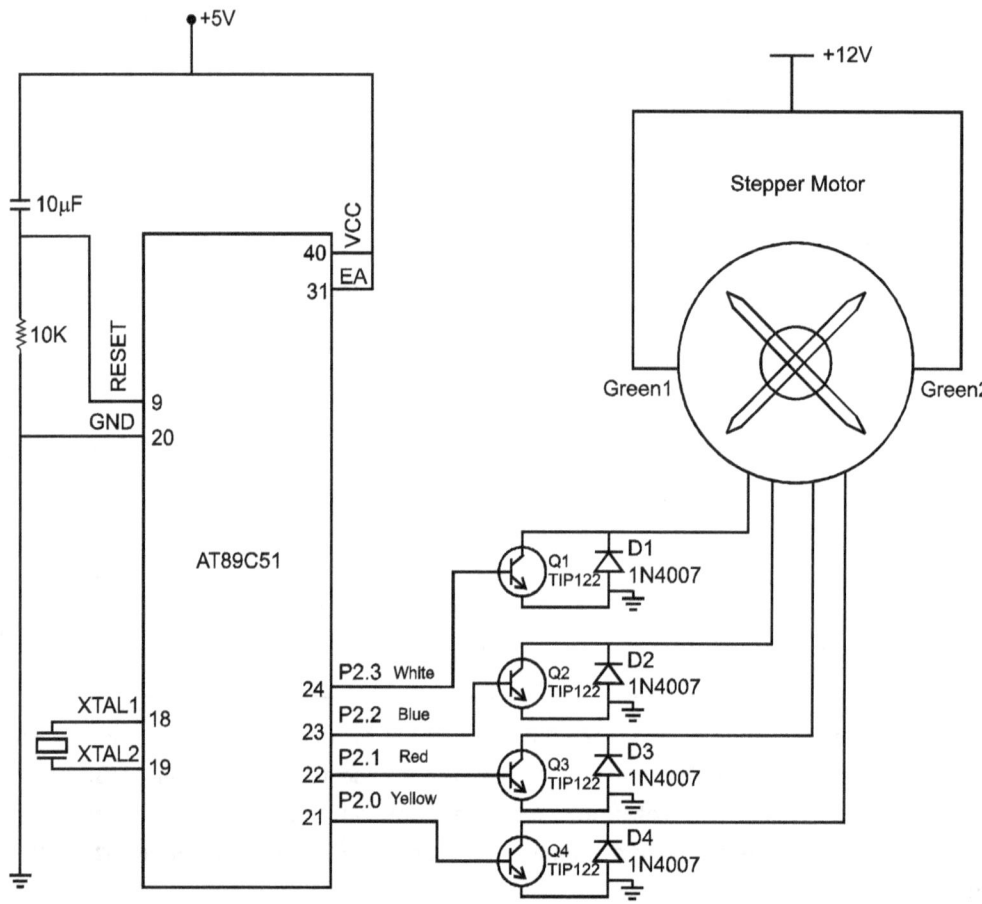

Fig. 4.22 : Interfacing of stepper motor to 8051 using transistorized driver

Program : Write a program to demonstrate stepper motor interfacing with 8051.

Solution :

```
#include <reg51.h>
void delay(unsigned int y);
void rotate()
```

```
    {
        P2 = 0x03;              // 0011
        delay(30);
        P2 = 0x06;              // 0110
        delay(30);
        P2 = 0x0C;              // 1100
        delay(30);
        P2 = 0x09;              // 1001
        delay(30);
    }
void delay(unsigned int y)
    {
        int i, j;               // Delay subroutine
        for (i=0; i<=y; i++)
        for (j=0;j<=498;j++);
    }
        void main()
        {
            while(1)
        {
            rotate();
        }
    }
```

Note : Reversing the bit sequence will reverse the direction of rotation. Speed of rotation can be increased or decreased by adjusting delay.

4.6.3 Stepper Motor Interfacing with 8051 Using L293D

L293D Description :

*   L293D is a typical Motor driver or Motor Driver IC which allows DC motor to drive on either direction. L293D is a 16-pin IC which can control a set of two DC motors simultaneously in any direction. It means that you can control two DC motor with a single L293D IC. Dual H-bridge Motor Driver integrated circuit (IC).

Concept :

- It works on the concept of H-bridge. H-bridge is a circuit which allows the voltage to be flown in either direction. As you know voltage need to change its direction for being able to rotate the motor in clockwise or anticlockwise direction, Hence, H-bridge IC are ideal for driving a DC motor.

- In a single l293d chip, there are two h-Bridge circuits inside the IC which can rotate two DC motor independently. Due its size, it is very much used in robotic applications for controlling DC motors. Given below is the pin diagram of a L293D motor controller.

- There are two Enable pins on l293d. Pin 1 and pin 9, for being able to drive the motor, the pin 1 and 9 need to be high. For driving the motor with left H-bridge you need to enable pin 1 to high. And for right H-Bridge you need to make the pin 9 to high. If anyone of the either pin1 or pin9 goes low then the motor in the corresponding section will suspend working. It's like a switch.

Note: You can simply connect the pin16 VCC (5v) to pin 1 and pin 9 to make them high.

L293D pin diagram :

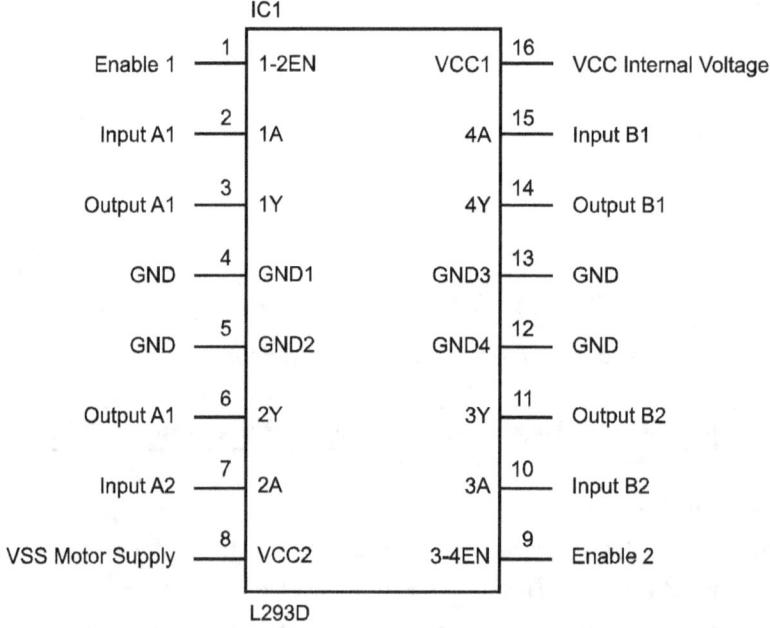

Fig. 4.23 : Pin diagram of L293D motor driver

4.6.4 Circuit Diagram

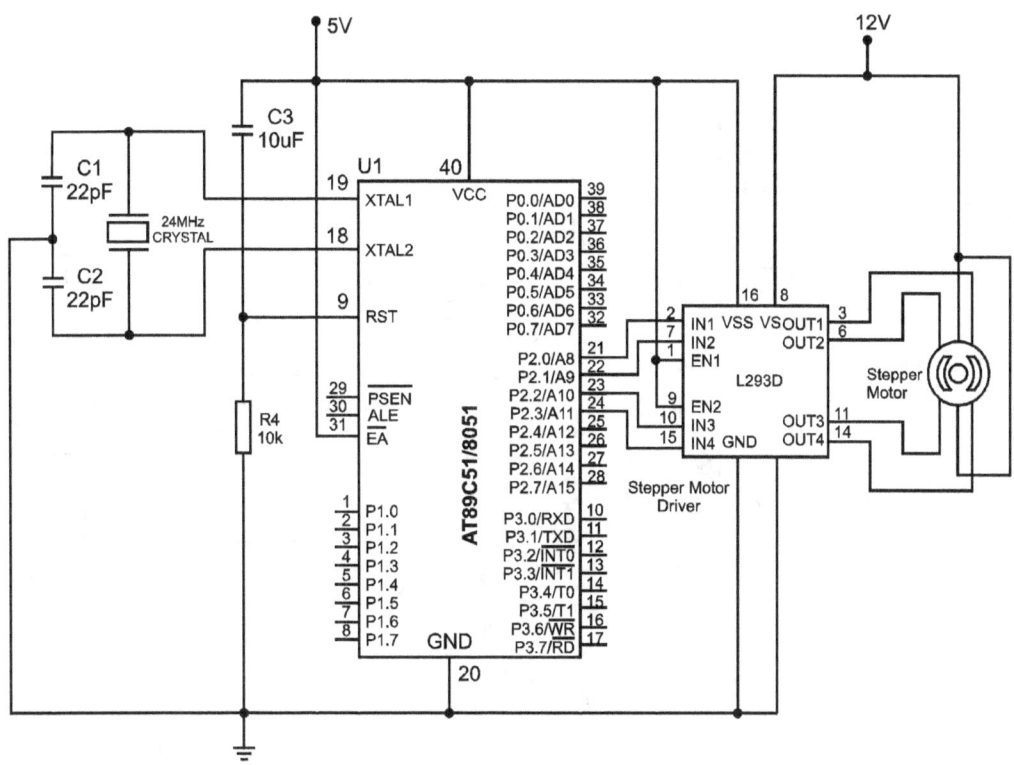

Fig. 4.24 : Interfacing of stepper motor using L293D to 8051/89C51

Explanation :

- Above Fig. 4.24 is the circuit diagram of driving a stepper motor using 8051 microcontroller using L293D. 12 MHz crystal is connected to provide the required clock for the microcontroller. 10µF capacitor and 10 kΩ is used to provide Power On Reset (POR) for the 8051 microcontroller.

- L293D is connected to pins P2.0, P2.1, P2.2, P2.3 of the microcontroller and two pairs of L293D are enabled by connecting EN1, EN2 to 5V.

- Logic Voltage (5 V) is connected to V_{ss} pin and motor supply (12 V) is connected to the V_s pin of L293D.

- Center tap of each windings of stepper motor is shorted and connected to the motor supply. Now we can energize each winding of the motor by making corresponding pin of L293D LOW.

4.6.5 Stepper Motor Interfacing with 8051 Using ULN2003

Circuit diagram :

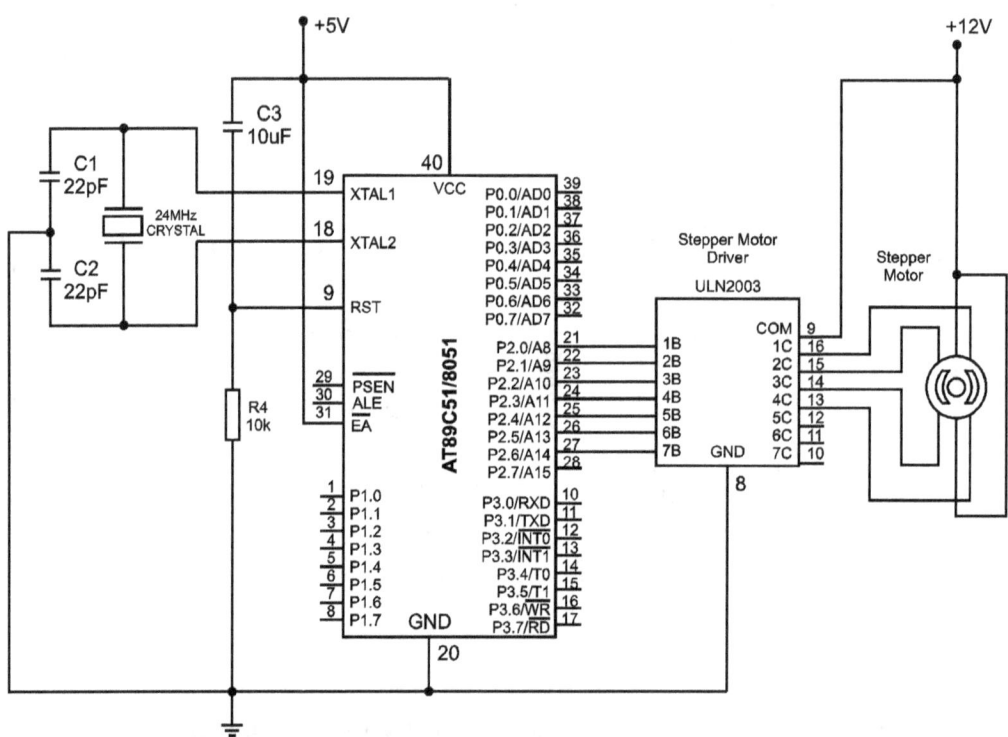

Fig. 4.25 : Interfacing of stepper motor using ULN2003 to 8051/89C51

Program 1 : Write a C program demonstrate wave drive movement of stepper motor.

Solution :

```
#include<reg51.h>
void delay(int);
void main()
    {
        while(1)
        {
            P2=0x01;            // 0001
```

```
            delay(1000);
            P2=0x02;                // 0010
            delay(1000);
            P2=0x04;                // 0100
            delay(1000);
            P2=0x08;                // 1000
            delay(1000);
        }
    }
void delay(int k)
    {
        int i, j;
        for (i=0; i<k; i++)
        {
        for (j=0; j<100; j++)
        {
        }
        }
    }
```

Program 2 : Write a program to demonstrate full drive movement of stepper motor.

Solution :

```
    #include<reg51.h>
    void delay(int);
    void main()
        {
            while(1)
            {
                P2 = 0x03;                // 0011
                delay(1000);
                P2 = 0x06;                // 0110
                delay(1000);
```

```
            P2 = 0x0C;              // 1100
            delay(1000);
            P2 = 0x09;              // 1001
            delay(1000);
        }
    }
void delay(int k)
    {
        int i, j;
        for (i=0; i<k; i++)
        {
            for(j=0;j<100;j++)
        {
        }
        }
```

Program 3 : Write a C program to demonstrate half drive movement of stepper motor.

Solution :

```
    #include<reg51.h>
    void delay(int);
    void main()
        {
        while(1)
        {
            P2=0x01;            // 0001
            delay(1000);
            P2=0x03;            // 0011
            delay(1000);
            P2=0x02;            // 0010
            delay(1000);
```

```
                P2=0x06;              // 0110
                delay(1000);
                P2=0x04;              // 0100
                delay(1000);
                P2=0x0C;              // 1100
                delay(1000);
                P2=0x08;              // 1000
                delay(1000);
                P2=0x09;              // 1001
                delay(1000);
            }
        }
    void delay(int k)
        {
            int i, j;
            for (i=0; i<k; i++)
            {
                for (j=0; j<100; j++)
            {
            }
            }
        }
```

Program 4 : Rotate stepper motor with angle of 45°.

Solution :

Minimum angle of rotation is 1.8°

$$\text{Count} = \frac{\text{Total Angle needed}}{\text{Minimum Angle of rotation}}$$

$$= \frac{45°}{1.8°}$$

$$= 25 \text{ decimal}$$

$$= 19H$$

Sr. No.	Angle	Decimal	Hexadecimal
1	45	25	19
2	90	50	32
3	180	100	64
4	270	150	96

Program :

```c
#include <reg51.h>
void delay(unsigned int y);
void rotate()
    {
        P2 = 0x03;              // 0011
        delay(30);
        P2 = 0x06;              // 0110
        delay(30);
        P2 = 0x0C;              // 1100
        delay(30);
        P2 = 0x09;              // 1001
        delay(30);
    }
void delay(unsigned int y)
    {
        int i, j;               // Delay subroutine
        for (i=0; i<=y; i++)
        for (j=0; j<=498; j++);
    }
void main()
    {
        for (i=0; i<=25; i++)       // For loop for count of 25 i.e. 25*1.8 = 90°
    {
        rotate();
    }
    }
```

Note :

1. Just by changing count stepping angle can be changed.

2. Reversing the sequence stepper motor can be rotated anticlockwise (0x09, 0x0c, 0x06, 0x03 for reverse rotation).

Practice Questions

1. Draw interfacing diagram to interface LED to port pin 2.0 and port pin 2.1 and switch to pin of port 3.1 and port 3.2. Write a program to turn ON the LEDs when switch on P3.1 is pressed and turn OFF the LED when switch on P3.2 is pressed.

2. Write a C program to scroll single LED on port 2. The port 2 is interfaced with 8 LEDs.

3. Write a C program to display "HELLO" on 7 segment display. Draw interfacing diagram for the same.

4. State advantages and disadvantages of Multiplexed 7 segment display.

5. List different techniques to interface 7 segment displays.

6. How many 7 segment displays can be directly interfaced with one 8051?

7. How many multiplexed 7 segment displays can be interfaced with one 8051?

8. How many keys can be interfaced to one port of 8051 in matrix method of interfacing?

9. How many keys in a matrix keyboard can be interfaced to two ports of 8051?

10. How many 7 segment displays can be interfaced to two ports of 8051 in multiplexed mode?

11. What is bouncing and debouncing related to matrix keyboard mean? Explain.

12. Draw a flow chart to generate scan code when a key is pressed in matrix keyboard of 4 × 4 matrix.

13. Write a C program to set upper nibble of accumulator and send data on port 0.

14. Write a C program to set lower nibble of accumulator and send data on port 1.

15. Write a C program to find one's and two's complement of data in accumulator.

16. Write a C program for 8051 to generate pulse with ON time = 10 msec and OFF time = 5 msec.

17. Write a C program for 8051 to generate a square wave of 10 kHz.

18. Write a C program for 8051 to generate a square wave of with 60% duty cycle and frequency = 5 kHz.

19. What is stepper motor? List different type of stepper motors.

20. State applications of stepper motors.

21. State applications of Analog to Digital Converter.

22. State applications of Digital to Analog Converter.

23. Describe the terms Sensor and Actuator with an example.

24. Write a C program to generate a baud rate of 9600 baud on timer of 8051.

25. Write a C program to receive data serially and output the same data on port 0 for microcontroller 8051.

26. Compare LCD and 7 segment interfacing with 8051.

27. Draw interfacing diagram to interface three switches to port 0 and one DC motor to port.

28. One switch will rotate motor in forward direction, second switch will rotate the motor in reverse direction and the third switch will, when pressed, stops the motor from rotating.

✑ ✑ ✑

Chapter 5...

Embedded Systems

Weightage of Marks = 18, Teaching Hours = 08

Specific Objectives

➢ Students will be able to

   ❖ Know the embedded system.

   ❖ Learn different software and hardware development tools.

   ❖ Understand embedded software development cycle.

5.1 INTRODUCTION TO EMBEDDED SYSTEM AND GENERAL PURPOSE SYSTEM

- An embedded system is some combination of computer hardware and software, either fixed in capability or programmable, that is specifically designed for a particular function.

- Industrial machines, automobiles, medical equipment, cameras, household appliances, airplanes, vending machines and toys (as well as the more obvious cellular phone and PDA) are among the myriad possible hosts of an embedded system.

- **Embedded systems are more limited in hardware and/or Software functionality than a personal computer (PC).**

- A general-purpose computer, such as a personal computer can do different tasks depending on programming.

- Embedded systems control many of the common devices in use today.

- Since the embedded system is dedicated to specific tasks, design engineers can optimize it, reducing the size and cost of the product, or increasing the reliability and performance.

- Some embedded systems are mass-produced, benefiting from economies of scale.

- The general purpose computer systems such as desktop PC or a laptop PC or a server PC, uses a general purpose processor like Intel Pentium Dual core/Quad core or AMD Athlon Processor and is designed to support the multiple peripheral like USO ports, parallel ports, AGP, Ethernet, MMC external interfaces, Bluetooth etc. and with additional interfaces for CD R/Writer, Hard Disk Drive, Floppy Disk Drive, Semiconductor memories such as RAM, EEPROM etc.

- Every desktop PC requires the operating system, so you can load any operating system available in market on the hard Disk of your PC such as Windows XP/Vista/7.

- Also you can buy the application software for your PC and you can run multiple applications as required by you.

5.1.1 Comparison of Embedded System and General Purpose Computer Systems

Sr. No.	Embedded System	General Purpose Computer
1.	It is a combination of specific purpose hardware and embedded real time OS for execution of specific programs and applications.	It is a combination of generic hardware and general purpose operating system for execution of variety of program and applications.
2.	May or may not be requires the operating system for the operations.	Requires general purpose operating system such as Window XP/Vista/windows 7.
3.	It is non changeable by the end user as they are pre-programmed.	Operating system and applications are changeable means user can add or remove the OS or applications.
4.	Response time is critical.	Response time is not critical.

5.1.2 History of Embedded System

- In the earliest years of computers in the 1930—40s, computers were sometimes dedicated to a single task, but were far too large and expensive for most kinds of tasks performed by embedded computers of today.

- Over time however, the concept of programmable controllers evolved from traditional electromechanical sequencers, via solid state devices, to the use of computer technology.

- One of the first recognizably modem embedded systems was the Apollo Guidance Computer, developed by Charles Stark Draper at the MIT Instrumentation Laboratory.

- At the project's inception, the Apollo guidance computer was considered the riskiest item in the Apollo project as it employed the then newly developed monolithic integrated circuits to reduce the size and weight.

- An early mass produce embedded system was the Automatics D-17 guidance computer for the Minuteman missile, released in 1961. It was built from transistor logic and had a hard disk for math memory.

- When the Minuteman I went into production in 1966, the 0-17 was replaced with a new computer that was the first high-volume use of integrated circuits.

- This program alone reduced prices on quad NAND gate ICs from $1000/each to $3/each, permitting their use in commercial products.

- Since these early applications in the 1960s, embedded systems have come down m price and there has been a dramatic rise in processing power and functionality.

- The first microprocessor for example, the Intel 4004, was designed for calculators and other small systems but still required many external memory and support chips.

- In 1978 National Engineering Manufacturers Association released a "standard" for programmable microcontrollers, including almost any computer-based controllers, such as single board computers, numerical, and event-based controllers.

- As the cost of microprocessors and microcontrollers fell it became feasible to replace expensive knob-based analog components such as potentiometers and variable capacitors with up/down buttons or knobs read out by a microprocessor even in some consumer products.

- By the mid-1980s, most of the common previously external system components had been integrated into the same chip as the processor and this modem form of the microcontroller allowed an even more widespread use, which by the end of the decade were the norm rather than the exception for almost all electronics devices.

- The integration of microcontrollers has further increased the applications for which embedded systems are used into areas where traditionally a computer would not have been considered.

- A general purpose and comparatively low-cost microcontroller may often be programmed to fulfill the same role as a large number of separate components.

- Although in this context an embedded system is usually more complex than a traditional solution, most of the complexity is contained within the microcontroller itself.

- Very few additional components may be needed and most of the design effort is in the software.
- The intangible nature of software makes it much easier to prototype and test new revisions compared with the design and construction of a new circuit not using an embedded processor.

5.1.3 Features of Microcontroller

The common critical features and design requirements of an embedded hardware include :

- **Processing power :** Selection of the processor is based on the amount of processing power to get the job done and also the basis of register width required.
- **Throughput :** The system may need to handle a lot of data in a short period of time.
- **Response :** The system has to react to events quickly.
- **Memory:** Hardware designer must make his best estimate of the memory requirement and must make provision for expansion.
- **Power consumption :** Systems generally work on battery and design of both software and hardware must take care of power saving techniques.
- **Number of units :** The no. of units expected to be produced and sold will dictate the Trade-off between production cost and development cost.
- **Expected lifetime** Design decisions like selection of components to system development cost will depend on how long the system is expected to run.
- **Program Installation :** Installation of the software on to the embedded system needs special tools.
- **Testability and Debug ability**: Setting up test conditions and equipment will be difficult and finding out what is wrong with the software will become a difficult task without a keyboard and the usual display screen.
- **Reliability:** It is critical if it is a space shuttle or a car but in case of a toy it doesn't always have to work right.

5.1.4 Applications of Embedded Systems

- Embedded systems span all aspects of modem life and there are many examples of their use.
- Telecommunications systems employ numerous embedded systems from telephone switches for the network to mobile phones at the end-user.

- Computer networking uses dedicated routers and network bridges to route data, Consumer electronics include personal digital assistants (PDAs), mp3 players, mobile phones, videogame consoles, digital cameras, DVD players, GPS receivers, and printers.

- Household appliances, such as microwave ovens, washing machines and dishwashers, are including embedded systems to provide flexibility, efficiency and features.

- Advanced HVAC systems use networked thermostats to more accurately and efficiently control temperature that can change by time of day and season.

- Home automation uses wired- and wireless-networking that can be used to control lights, climate, security, audio/visual, surveillance, etc., all of which use embedded devices for sensing and controlling.

- Transportation systems from flight to automobiles increasingly use embedded systems. New airplanes contain advanced avionics such as inertial guidance systems and OPS receivers that also have considerable safety requirements.

- Various electric motors i.e. brushless DC motors, induction motors and DC motors - are using electric/electronic motor controllers.

- Automobiles, electric vehicles, and hybrid vehicles are increasingly using embedded systems to maximize efficiency and reduce pollution.

- Other automotive safety systems such as Anti-lock Braking System (ABS), Electronic Stability Control (ESC/ESP), Traction Control (TCS) and automatic four-wheel drive.

- Medical equipment is continuing to advance with more embedded systems for vital signs monitoring, electronic stethoscopes for amplifying sounds, and various medical imaging (PET, SPECT, CT, MB) for non-invasive internal inspections.

5.1.5 Purpose of Embedded System

- Embedded systems are designed to do some specific task, rather than be a general-purpose computer for multiple tasks.

- Some also have real-time performance constraints that must be met, for reasons such as safety and usability; others may have low or no performance requirements, allowing the system hardware to be simplified to reduce costs.

- Embedded systems are not always standalone devices. Many embedded systems consist of small, computerized parts within a larger device that serves a more general purpose. For example the Gibson Robot Guitar features an embedded system for tuning the strings tuning but the overall purpose of the Robot Guitar is, of course, to play music.

- Similarly, an embedded system in all automobile provides a specific function as a subsystem of the car itself.

- The program instructions written for embedded systems are referred to as firmware, and are stored in read-only memory or Flash memory chips. They run with limited computer hardware resources little memory, small or nonexistent keyboard and/or screen.

5.1.6 Classification of Embedded System

- An embedded system is a system which consists of computer hardware with software embedded in it as one of its most important component.

- So, we can classify embedded system into three categories w.r.t. size and real time requirement as given below:
  - ➢ Small scale embedded system
  - ➢ Medium scale embedded system
  - ➢ Large scale or Sophisticated embedded system

5.1.6.1 Small Scale Embedded System

- Normally these systems are designed using with an 8 bit or 16 bit microcontroller based system.

- They have very small hardware and software complexities and involved board level design and may be battery operated.

- While developing embedded software for these system, an editor, assembler or cross assembler are used for specific microcontroller or processor used.

- Usually, 'C' language is used for the development of the system as C language support machine level programming and C programs compilation is done in assembly.

- Executable codes are then appropriately located into system memory, so software must has to fit into memory available and also keep in mind the need to limit power consumption when system is continuously running.

5.1.6.2 Medium Scale Embedded System

- These systems are usually design using single or multiple 16 bit or 32 bit microcontrollers or Digital Signal Processors (DSP or Reduced instruction Set Computers (RISC's).

- They have hardware and software complexities, so no board level design is possible.

- For such complex software design system, the development tools like it real Time Operating System (RTOS), Source code engineering tools, Simulator Debugger and Integrated Development Tools are required.

- These software tools also provide the solution for the hardware comp so assembler is rarely used.

- Such type of system may also use readily available Application Specific System Processor (ASSP) that is dedicated to specific task alone provide faster solution and Such type of system may also use readily available Intellectual Property (IP) gives a solution for synthesizing a higher level components that possess gal level sophistication in circuit above that of the counter, registers, floating point operation unit and ALU by configuring FPGA core or VLSI core.

5.1.6.3 Large Scale or Sophisticated Embedded System

- These types of embedded systems have large quantity of hardware a software co and may be required scalable processors configurable processors and programmable logic arrays (PLA's).

- Such systems are used for cutting edge application s that required hardwar4 and software co-design and integration in the final system.

- They are constrained by the processing speeds available in their hardwar4 units.

- Some software's functions as encryption and deciphering algorithms, discrete cosine transformation and inverse transformation algorithms, TCPIIP protocol stacking and network driver functions are implemented in the hardware to obtain additional speed by saving time.

- For these systems, the development tools may not be readily available at th4 reasonable cost or may be available at all.

- Sometime, a compiler or re-targetable compiler might have to be developed for these systems.

5.1.7 Different hardware Units of Embedded Systems

- The Embedded system consists of different components embedded into it as given below and shown in Fig. 5.1

  ➢ Embedded Processor

  ➢ Program and data Memory

  ➢ System Turners

  ➢ Serial Communication Port

  ➢ Interrupt Controller

- ➢ Parallel Ports
- ➢ Output interfacing/Driver Circuits
- ➢ Input interfacing/Driver Circuits
- ➢ Power Supply, reset and Oscillator circuits
- ➢ System Application specific circuits.

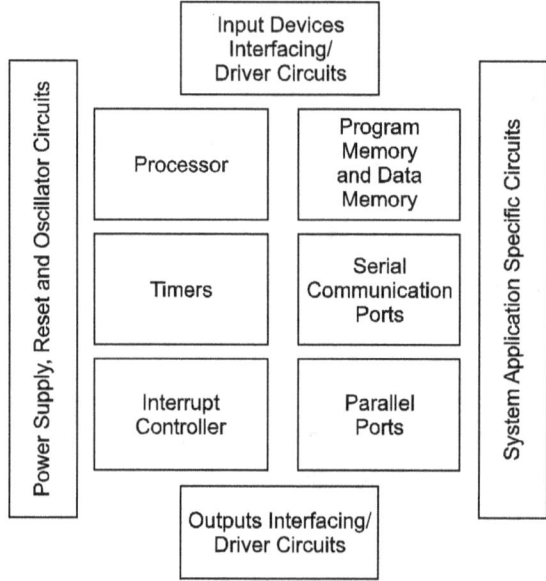

Fig. 5.1 : Components of Embedded Hardware

- **Embedded Processor :** It consists of Control Unit (CU) to perform instruction fetching operation from memory unit (EU) performs execution of the instruction for a program control task.

- **Program and data memory :** The most of processor i.e. microprocessor or microcontroller have inbuilt memory to store data and program such as RAM, ROM, Flash memory etc. Also, we can interface external memories for program and data.

- **System Timers :** Timer circuit is normally configured as the system clock used to generate system interrupts periodically and also configured a real time clock (RTC) to generate system interrupts periodically for the schedulers, real time programs and saving time and date in the systems.

- **Serial Communication Ports :** The purpose of having serial communication ports to interface serial devices with the systems. The most of the microcontroller have serial communication ports inbuilt.

- **Interrupt controller :** The interrupt controller must exists in the system to handle interrupt from various processes, handling multiple interrupt pending for services. So, the prime function of interrupt controller is to receive interrupt and resolve the priority and finally provides the service that interrupts.

- **Parallel Port :** The parallel ports are required for parallel communication. Most of the microcontroller provides more than one parallel ports to performing parallel communication between processor and parallel devices.

- **Input and Output Driver circuits :** As we know the behavior of input/output devices may be different those of processor, so input driver circuits are required to drive input or output devices.

- **Power Supply, Reset and Oscillator :** Most of the systems have their own power supply such as Network Interface Card (NIC), but system that do not have their own power supply and used processor power supply. The Various units in embedded system operate on different voltages. Reset means that the processor begins execution from the starting address which is set default by Program Counter in processor on power ON. From that address in memory, instructions are fetched following the reset of the processor. The Clock controls the time for execution an instruction. After the power supply, the clock is the basic unit of system. For the processing unit, a highly stable oscillator is required and the processor clock out signal provides the clock for synchronizing all the system units with the processor in the systems.

- **System Application Specific Circuits:** These circuits can used to control specific target circuits consists of ADC, DAC, Stepper motor, Sensors, Relays, etc.

5.1.8 Advantages of Embedded System

- Embedded systems refer to computer systems that are created to perform a set number of duties or functions.

- They are embedded in the sense that the computer system is embedded within a device alongside necessary hardware.

  - ➢ **Design and Efficiency:** The central processing core in embedded systems is generally less complicated, making it easier to maintain. The limited function required of embedded systems allows them to be designed to most efficiently perform their functions.

  - ➢ **Cost:** The streamlined make-up of most embedded systems allows their parts to be smaller less expensive to produce.

  - ➢ **Accessibility :** Embedded systems are difficult to service because they are inside another machine, so a greater effort is made to carefully develop them.

However, if something does go wrong with certain embedded systems they can be too inaccessible to repair. This concern is sometimes addressed in the design stage, such as by programming an embedded system so that it will not affect related systems negatively when malfunctioning.

➢ **Maintenance:** Embedded systems are easier to maintain because the supplied power is embedded in the system and does not require remote maintenance.

➢ **Redundancies:** Embedded systems do not involve the redundant programming and maintenance involved in other system models.

5.1.9 Core of the Embedded Systems

5.1.9.1 Microprocessors

- A microprocessor incorporates the functions of a computer's central processing unit (CPU) on a single integrated circuit, or at most a few integrated circuits.

- It is a multipurpose, programmable device that accepts digital data as input, processes it according to instructions stored in its memory, and provides results as output.

- It is an example of sequential digital logic, as it has internal memory.

- Microprocessors operate on numbers and symbols represented in the binary numeral system.

- The advent of low-cost computers on integrated circuits has transformed modem society.

- Many more microprocessors are part of embedded systems, providing digital control of a myriad of objects from appliances to automobiles to cellular phones and industrial process control.

- The integration of a whole CPU onto a single chip or on a few chips greatly reduced the cost of processing power.

- The integrated circuit processor was produced in large numbers by highly automated processes, so unit cost was low. Single-chip processors increase reliability as there were many fewer electrical connections to fail.

- As microprocessor designs get faster, the cost of manufacturing a chip (with smaller components built on a semiconductor chip the same size) generally stays the same, Microprocessors integrated into one or a few large-scale ICs the architectures that had previously been implemented using many medium-and small-scale integrated circuits.

- Continued increases in microprocessor capacity have rendered other forms of computers almost completely obsolete (see history of computing hardware),with one or more microprocessors used in everything from the smallest embedded systems and handheld devices to the largest mainframes and supercomputers.

- The first microprocessors emerged in the early 1970s and were used for electronic calculators, using binary-coded decimal (BCD) arithmetic on 4-bit words.

- Other embedded uses of 4-bit and 8-bit microprocessors, such as terminals, printers, various kinds of automation etc., followed soon after.

- Affordable 8-bit microprocessors with 16-bit addressing also led to the first general-purpose microcomputers from the mid- 1970s on.

- Since the early 1970s, the increase in capacity of microprocessors has followed Moore's law, which suggests that the number of transistors that can be fitted onto a chip doubles every two years.

- Although originally calculated as a doubling every year, Moore later refined the period to two years. It is often incorrectly quoted as a doubling of transistors every 18 months.

- The Intel 4004 was followed in 1972 by the Intel 8008, the world's first 8-bit microprocessor.

- The 8008 was not, however, an extension of the 4004 design, but instead the culmination of a separate design project at Intel, arising from a contract with Computer Terminals Corporation, of San Antonio TX, for a chip for a terminal they were designing, the Data point 2200- fundamental aspects of the design came not from Intel but from CTC.

- Intel marketed it as the 8008 in April, 1972, as the world's first 8-bit microprocessor. It was the basis for the famous "Mark-8" computer kit advertised in the magazine Radio-Electronics in 1974.

- The 8008 was the precursor to the very successful Intel 8080 (1974) which offered much improved performance over the 8008 and required fewer support chips, Zilog ZS0 (1976), and derivative Intel 8-bit processors.

- The competing Motorola 6800 was released August 1974 and the similar

- MOS Technology 6502 in 1975 (designed largely by the same people). The 6502 rivaled the Z80 in popularity during the 1980s.

- A low overall cost, small packaging, simple computer bus requirements, and sometimes the integration of extra circuitry (e.g. the Z80's built-in memory refresh circuitry) allowed the home computer 'revolution" to accelerate sharply in the early 1980s. This delivered such inexpensive machines as the Sinclair ZX-81, which sold for US$99.

Application Specific Instruction Set Processor (ASIP) :

- An application-specific instruction-set processor (ASIP) is a component used in system-on-a-chip design.

- The instruction set of an ASIP is tailored to benefit a specific application.

- This specialization of the core provides a tradeoff between the flexibility of a general purpose CPU and the performance of an ASIC.

- Some ASIPs have a configurable instruction set. Usually, these cores are divided into two parts: static logic which defines a minimum ISA and configurable logic which can be used to design new instructions.

- The configurable logic can be programmed either in the field in a similar fashion to an FPGA or during the chip synthesis.

5.1.9.2 Microcontroller

- A microcontroller is a small and low-cost computer built for the purpose of dealing with specific tasks, such as displaying information in a microwave LED or receiving information from a television's remote control.

- Microcontrollers are mainly used in products that require a degree of control to be exerted by the user.

Microcontroller V/S Microprocessor :

- Microprocessors are used to execute big and generic applications, while a microcontroller will only be used to execute a single task within one application.

- Some of the benefits of microcontrollers include the following :
  - **Cost advantage :** The biggest advantage of microcontrollers against larger microprocessors is that the design and hardware costs are much lesser and can be kept to a minimum. A microcontroller is cheap to replace, while microprocessors are ten times more expensive.
  - **Lesser power usage :** Microcontrollers are generally built using a technology known as Complementary Metal Oxide Semiconductor (CMOS). This technology is a competent fabrication system that uses less power and is more immune to power spikes than other techniques.
  - **All-in-one :** A microcontroller usually comprises of a CPU, ROM, RAM and I/O ports, built within it to execute a single and dedicated task.

- On the other hand, a microprocessor generally does not have a RAM, ROM or J/O pins and generally uses its pins as a bus to interface to peripherals such as RAM, ROM, serial ports, digital and analog IO.The architecture of a typical microcontroller is complex and may include the following:
  - A CPU, ranging from simple 4-bit to complex 64-bit processors.

➢ Peripherals such as timers, event counters and watchdog.

➢ RAM (volatile memory) for data storage. The data is stored in the form of registers, and the general-purpose registers store information that interacts with the arithmetic logical unit (ALU).

➢ ROM, EPROM, EEPROM or flash memory for program and operating parameter storage.

➢ Programming capabilities.

➢ Serial input/output such as serial ports.

➢ A clock generator for resonator, quartz timing crystal or RC circuit.

➢ Analog-to-digital converters.

➢ Serial ports.

➢ Data bus to carry information.

Features of Microcontrollers :

1. **Architectural features:** Most microcontrollers built today are based on the CISC (Complex Instruction Set Computer) platform. A typical CISC microcontroller has over 80 instructions and it is quite common for the instructions to all behave quite differently. The main advantage of CISC architecture is that the instructions are macro-like, allowing the programmer to use one instruction in place of many simpler instructions.

2. **Advanced memory features :**

➢ **Electrically Erasable Programmable Read Only Memory (EEPROM) :** Many microcontrollers use the economic EEPROM for smaller amount of memory that have frequently changeable data. This type of memory is relatively slow, and the number of erase/write cycles allowed in its lifetime is limited.

➢ **FLASH (EPROM) :** Flash provides microcontrollers with a better solution than EEPROM for requirements of large amounts in non-volatile program memory. EPROM is faster and permits more erase/write cycles than EEPROM.

➢ **Power Management features :** A majority of microcontrollers usually support an operation of 3-5.5V. As consumer goods become trencher, compact and lighter, the focus is on microcontrollers to ensure that products with less power usage are efficiently built and then used by end-users.

5.1.10 Applications of Embedded System

• Microcontrollers are used in products that are controlled automatically.

• The various products that make use of microcontrollers in our everyday life are given :

- ➢ **Home**: Television, DVD player, Telephone, Fax machine, Cellular phones, Security systems, Camera, Sewing machine, Musical Instrument, Exercising machine, Video games, Computer, Microwave Oven.
- ➢ **Office**: Computers, Printers, Telephones, Fax machine, Security systems.

5.1.11 Criteria for Choosing a Microcontroller

- The most important factor is that the microcontroller should be cost-efficient and work capably to handle the dedicated task.
- Some questions that should be asked while deciding on a microcontroller are as follows:
  - ➢ What is the maximum speed of the microcontroller?
  - ➢ What is the amount of RAM and ROM on chip?
  - ➢ How easy it is to upgrade to higher upgrade or lower consumption version
  - ➢ Is the microcontroller readily available at cheaper rates?
  - ➢ What is the number of I/C pins and timer on the chip?

5.1.12 PIC Microcontroller

- Microcontroller is an inexpensive single-chip computer. The microcontroller's most important feature is its capabilities of STORING and RUNNING a program.
- Every Microcontroller (also MCU) consists of several major units:
  - ➢ Input/Output ports.
  - ➢ Control Pins: reset, power, dock.
  - ➢ Processor (CPU).
  - ➢ Memory (RAM, ROM, EEPROM).
  - ➢ Serial and parallel ports.
  - ➢ Timers.
  - ➢ Analog-to-digital (A/D) and digital-to-analog (D/A) converters.
- Microcontrollers PIC micro MCU from Microchip Company divided into large families.
- Each family has a variety of components that provide built-in special features:

5.1.12.1 The First Family, PIC1O (PIC1OFXXX) is called Low End

- The PIC1OFXXX devices from Microchip Technology are low-cost, high-performance, 8-bit, fully static, Flash-based CMOS microcontrollers.
- They employ RISC architecture with only 33 single-word single-cycle instructions. The 12-bit wide instructions are highly symmetrical.

- The easy-to-use and easy to remember instruction set reduces development time significantly.
- The PIC1OFXXX devices contain an 8-bit ALU and working register.

5.1.12.2 The Second Family, PICI2 (PICI2FXXX) is called Mid-Range

- The PIC12FXXX most popular among these starters their way in this field.
- Mid-Range devices feature 14-bit program word architecture and are available in 8 to 64-pin packages that offer an operating voltage range of 1.8-5.5V, small package footprints, interrupt handling an 8-level hardware stack, multiple A/D channels and ERPROM data memory.
- Mid-range devices offer a wide range of package options and a wide range of peripheral integration.
- These devices feature various serial analog and digital peripherals, such as: SPI, I^2CT, USART, LCD and A/D converters.

5.1.12.3 The Third Family is P1C16 (I6FXXX)

- With six variants ranging from 3.5K-14 Kbytes of Flash memory, up to 256 bytes of RAM and a mix of peripherals including EUSART, CCP and onboard analog comparators.
- These devices are well suited for designers with applications that need more code space or 110 than 14-pin variants supply, and are looking to increase system performance and code efficiency by employing hardware motor control and communications capability.

5.1.12.4 The Fourth Family is PIC 17/18(1 BFXXX)

- The PIC18 family utilizes 16-bit program word architecture and incorporates an advanced RISC architecture with 32 level-deep stacks, 8x8 hardware multiplier, and multiple internal and external interrupts.
- With the highest performance in Microchip's 8-bit portfolio, the PIC18 family provides up to 16 MIPS and linear memory.
- PIC18 is the most popular architecture for new 8-bit designs where customers want to program in C language.

5.1.13 How to Choose or Select a PIC Microcontroller?

- Each type of PIC microcontroller provides a different combination of features, thus the most suitable can be selected for any given application. Some of the main selection criteria are:

> ➢ Number of I/O pins available.
> ➢ Program memory size.
> ➢ Program memory type (ROM, EPROM, Flash).
> ➢ EEPROM data memory.
> ➢ Timers (8-bit or 16-bit), CCI.
> ➢ Interrupt sources.
> ➢ Analog inputs (8-bit or 10-bit).
> ➢ Serial communication interfaces (USART, SPI, I²C, CAN).
> ➢ Internal oscillator.
> ➢ In-circuit debugging.
> ➢ Package (DIP, SOIC, PLCC, QFP).
> ➢ Price.

5.1.14 Digital Signal Processor (DSP)

- A Digital Signal Processor is a special-purpose CPU (Central Processing Unit) that provides ultra-fast instruction sequences, such as shift and add, and multiply and add, which are commonly used in math-intensive signal processing applications.

- DSPs are not the same as typical microprocessors though. Microprocessors are typically general purpose devices that run large blocks of software.

- They are not often called upon for real-time computation and they work at a slower pace, choosing a course of action, and then waiting to finish the present job before responding to the next user command.

- A DSP, on the other hand, is often used as a type of embedded controller or processor that is built into another piece of equipment and is dedicated to a single group of tasks.

- In this environment, the DSP assists the general purpose host microprocessor.

5.1.14.1 Digital Signal Processing

- Digital Signal Processing is a technique that converts signals from real world sources (usually in analog form) into digital data that can then be analyzed.

- Analysis is performed in digital form because once a signal has been reduced to numbers; its components can be isolated, analyzed and rearranged more easily than in analog form.

- Eventually, when the DSP has finished its work, the digital data can be turned back into an analog signal, with improved quality.

- For example, a DSP can filter noise from a signal, remove interference, amplify frequencies and suppress others, encrypt information, or analyze a complex wave form into its spectral components.

- This process must be handled in real-time — which is often very quickly. For instance, stereo equipment handles sound signals of up to 20 kilohertz (20,000 cycles per second), requiring a DSP to perform hundreds of millions of operations per second.

5.1.14.2 Types of DSPs

- Because different applications have varying ranges of frequencies, different DSPs are required. DSPs are classified by their dynamic range, the spread of numbers that must be processed in the course of an application.

- This number is a function of the processor's data width (the number of bits it manipulates) and the type of arithmetic it performs (fixed or floating point).

- For example, a 32-bit processor has a wider dynamic range than a 24-bit processor, which has a wider range than 16-bit processor.

- Floating-point chips have wider ranges than fixed-point devices.

- Each type of processor is suited for a particular range of applications.

- Sixteen-bit fixed-point DSPs are used for voice-grade systems such as phones since they work with relative narrow range of sound frequency

- Hi-fidelity stereo sound has wider calling range fort 16 bit ADC and 24bit fixed point DSP Image processing, 3-D graphics and scientific simulations have a much wider dynamic range and require a 82-bit floating-point processor.

5.1.14.3 Uses of DSPs

- DSP chips are used in sound cards, fax machines, modems, cellular phones, high-capacity hard disks and digital TVs.

- According to Texas Instruments, DSPs are used as the engine in 70% of the world's digital cellular phones, and with the increase in wireless applications, this number will only increase.

- Digital signal processing is used in many fields including biomedicine, sonar, radar, seismology, speech and music processing, imaging and communications.

5.1.15 RISC and CISC Processors

- RISC and CISC are computing systems developed for computers.

- Difference between RISC and CISC is critical to understanding how a computer follows your instructions.

- These are commonly misunderstood terms and this article intends to clarify their meanings and concepts behind the two acronyms.

5.1.15.1 RISC (Reduced Instruction Set Computer)

- Pronounced same as RISK, it is an acronym for Reduced Instruction Set
- Computer. It is a type of microprocessor that has been designed to carry out few instructions at the same time.
- Till 1980's hardware manufacturers were trying to build CPU's that could carry out a large number of instructions at the same instant.
- But the trend was reversed and manufacturers decided to build computers that were capable of carrying out relatively very few instructions.
- Instructions being simple and few, CPU could execute them quickly.
- Another advantage of RISC is the use of fewer transistors making them inexpensive to produce.

5.1.15.2 Features of RISC

- Demands less decoding
- Uniform instruction set
- Identical general purpose registers used in any context
- Simple addressing modes
- Fewer data types in hardware

5.1.15.3 CISC (Complex Instruction Set Computer)

- CISC stands for Complex Instruction Set Computer. It is actually a CPU which is capable of executing many operations through a single instruction.
- These basic operations could be loading from memory, carrying out a mathematical operation etc.

5.1.15.4 Features of CISC

1. Complex instructions
2. More number of addressing modes
3. Highly pipelined
4. More data types in hardware
   - Over the period of time, the terms RISC and CISC have almost become meaningless as both RISC and CISC have undergone evolution and the distinction between the two has progressively become blurred with both being used in computer systems.

> ➢ Many of today RISC chips support as many instructions as yesterday's CISC chips.

> ➢ There are CISC chips using same tech that were earlier considered to be used for RISC chips only.

> ➢ However, basic differences between the two are easy to comprehend and are as follows.

> ➢ Talking of differences, RISC puts burden on software makers as they have to write more lines for same tasks.

> ➢ RISC is cheaper than CISC because of fewer transistors required. The speed of the computer is also higher with lesser instructions to follow at the same instant.

5.1.15.5 Difference between RISC and CISC Processor

Sr. No.	CISC	RISC
1.	A large number of instructions.	Many fewer instructions. Typically less than 100.
2.	Some instructions with long execution times. These include instructions that copy an entire block from one part of memory to another and others that copy multiple registers to and from memory.	No instruction with a long execution time. Some early RISC machines did not even have an integer multiply instruction, requiring compilers to implement multiplication as a sequence of additions.
3.	Variable-length encodings and instructions can range from 1 to 15 bytes.	Fixed-length encodings. Typically all instructions are encoded as 4 bytes.
4.	Multiple formats for special operands i.e. a memory operand specifier can have many different combinations of displacement, base and index registers, and scale factors.	Simple addressing formats. Typically just base and displacement addressing.
5.	Arithmetic and logical operations can be applied to both memory and register operands.	Arithmetic and logical operations only use register- operands. Memory referencing is only allowed by load instructions, reading from memory into a register, and store instructions, writing from a register to memory.

6.	Implementation artifacts hidden from machine level programs.	Implementation artifacts exposed to machine-level programs. Some RISC machines prohibit particular instruction sequences and have jumps that do not take effect until the following instruction is executed.
7.	Condition codes. Special flags are set as a side effect of instructions and then used for conditional branch testing	No condition codes. Instead, explicit test instructions store the test results in normal registers for use in conditional evaluation.
8.	Stack-intensive procedure linkage. The stack is used for procedure arguments and return addresses.	Register-intensive procedure linkage. Registers are used for procedure arguments and return addresses. Some procedures can thereby avoid any memory references. Typically, the processor has many more (up to 32)

5.1.16 John Von Neumann's and Harvard Architecture

- The heart of the von Neumann computer architecture is the Central Processing Unit (CPU), consisting of the control unit and the ALU (Arithmetic and Logic Unit).

- The CPU interacts with a memory and an input/output (I subsystem and executes a stream of instructions (the computer program) that process the data stored in memory and perform I/O operations.

- The key concept of the von Neumann architecture is that data and instructions are stored in the memory system in exactly the same way.

- The term "stored-program computer" is generally used to mean a computer of this design, although as modem computers are usually of this type, the term has fallen into disuse.

- One shared memory for instructions (program) and data with one data bus and one address bus between processor and memory.

- Instructions and data have to be fetched in sequential order (known as the Von Neumann Bottleneck), limiting the operation bandwidth.

- Its design is simpler than that of the Harvard architecture; it is mostly used to interface to external memory as shown in Fig. 5.2.

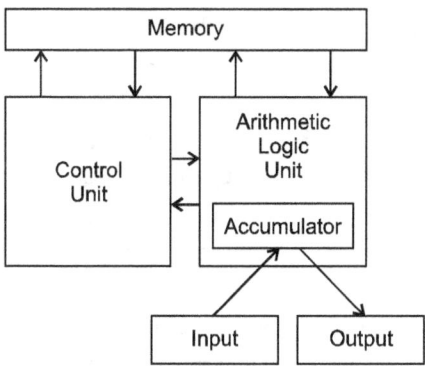

Fig. 5.2 : Von Neumann's Architecture

5.1.16.1 The Harvard Architecture

- The Harvard architecture uses physically separate memories for their instructions and data, requiring dedicated buses for each of them as shown in Fig. 5.3.

- Instructions and operands can therefore be fetched simultaneously.

- Different program and data bus widths are possible, allowing program and data memory to be better optimized to the architectural requirements.

- E.g. If the instruction format requires 14 bits then program bus and memory can be made 14-bit wide, while the data bus and data memory remain 8-bit wide.

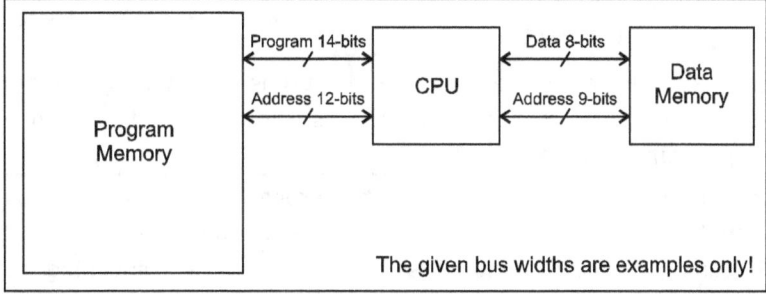

Fig. 5.3 : Harvard Architecture

- These early machines had limited data storage, entirely contained within the data processing unit, and provided no access to the instruction storage as data, making loading and modifying programs an entirely offline process.

- In Harvard architecture, there is no need to make the two memories share characteristics. In particular, the word width, timing, implementation technology, and memory address structure can differ.

- Instruction memory is often wider than data memory. In some systems, instructions can be stored in read-only memory while data memory generally requires read-write memory.

- In some systems, there is much more instruction memory than data memory so instruction addresses are much wider than data addresses.

- Harvard architectures are also frequently used in specialized digital signal processors, DSPs, commonly used in audio or video processing products. For example, Black fin processors by Analog Devices, Inc. use Harvard architecture.

- Most general purpose small microcontrollers used in many electronics applications, such as the PIC by Microchip Technology, Inc., and AVE by Atmel Corp.

- These processors are characterized by having small amounts of program and data memory, and take advantage of the Harvard architecture and reduced instruction sets (RISC) to ensure that most instructions can be executed within only one machine cycle, which is not necessarily one clock cycle.

- The separate storage means the program and data memories can have different bit depths.

- This a allow single instruction to contain a frill-size data constant. Other RISC architectures, for example the ARM, typically must use at least two instructions to load a full-size constant.

Sr. No.	John Von Neumann's Architecture	Harvard Architecture
1.	It has single storage system (memory) for storing data as well as program to be executed	It has two separate memories for storing data and program.
2.	Processor needs two clock cycles to complete an instruction so Pipelining the instructions is not possible with this architecture	Processor can complete an instruction in one cycle if appropriate pipelining strategies are implemented.
3.	In the first clock cycle the processor gets the instruction from memory and decodes it. In the next clock cycle the required data is taken from memory. For each instruction this cycle repeats and hence needs two cycles to complete an instruction.	In the first stage of pipeline the instruction to be executed can be taken from program memory. In the second stage of pipeline data is taken from the data memory using the decoded instruction or address.

| 4. | It is a relatively older architecture and was replaced by Harvard architecture, | Most of the modern computing architectures are based on Harvard Architecture. But the number of stages in the pipeline varies from system to system. |

5.1.17 Application Specific Integrated Circuits (ASICs)

- The term 'ASIC' stands for 'application-specific integrated circuit'. An ASIC s basically an integrated circuit designed specifically for a special purpose or aplication.

- Strictly speaking, this also implies that an ASIC is built only for one and only one customer.

- An example of an ASIC is an IC designed for a specific line of cellular phones of a company, whereby no other products can use it except the cell phones belonging to that product line.

- Aside from the nature of its application, an ASIC differs from a standard product in the nature of its availability.

- The intellectual property, design database, and deployment of an ASIC is usually controlled by just a single entity or company, which is generally the end-user of the ASIC too.

- Thus, an ASIC is proprietary by nature and not available to the general public. A standard product, on the other hand, is produced by the manufacturer for sale to the general public.

- Standard products are therefore readily available for use by anybody for a wider range of applications.

- The first ASIC known as uncommitted logic array or ULA's, utilized gate array technology.

- Having up to a few thousand gates, they were customized by varying the mask for metal interconnections.

- Thus, the functionality of such a device can be varied by modifying which nodes in the circuit are connected and which are not.

- Later versions became more generalized, customization of which involve variations in both the metal and polysilicon layers.

- ASIC's are usually classified into one of three categories:
  - ➢ full-custom,
  - ➢ semi- custom, and
  - ➢ structured.

5.1.17.1 Full-custom

- AS are those that are entirely tailor-fitted to a particular application from the very start.

- Since its ultimate design and functionality is pre-specified by the user, it is manufactured with all the photolithographic layers of the device already fully defined, just like most off-the-shelf general purpose IC.

- The use of predefined masks for manufacturing leaves no option for circuit modification during fabrication, except perhaps for some minor fine- tuning or calibration.

- This means that a full-custom ASIC cannot be modified to suit different applications, and is generally produced as a single, specific product for a particular application only.

5.1.17.2 Semi-custom

- Semi-custom ASIC on the other hand, can be partly customized to serve different functions within its general area of application.

- Unlike full-custom ASIC semi-custom ASIC are designed to allow a certain degree of modification during the manufacturing process.

- A semi-custom ASIC is manufactured with the masks for the diffused layers already fully defined, so the transistors and other active components of the circuit are already fixed for that semi-custom ASIC design.

- The customization of the final ASIC product to the intended application is done by varying the masks of the interconnection layers, e.g., the metallization layers.

- Structured or Platform ASIC's, which belong to a relatively new ASIC classification, are those which have been designed and produced from a tightly defined set of design methodologies, intellectual properties (IP's) and well-characterized silicon, aimed at shortening the design cycle and minimizing the development costs of the ASIC.

5.1.17.3 Examples of ASIC s include:

- An IC that encodes and decodes digital data using a proprietary encoding/decoding algorithm.

- A medical IC designed to monitor a specific human biometric parameter.

- An IC designed to serve a special function within a factory automation system.

- An amplifier IC designed to meet certain specifications not available in standard amplifier products.

- A proprietary system-on-a-chip (SOC)

- An IC that is custom-made for a particular automated test equipment.

5.1.18 Programmable Logic Devices (PLDS)

- In recent years programmable logic devices (PLDs) have all but replaced special-purpose logic devices such as AND gates, flip-flops, counters, multiplexers, etc.

- PLDs are chips that can be programmed, and often re-programmed, to implement different logic functions.

- The main reason for using programmable logic is to reduce total costs.

- This is due to a number of reasons: One important advantage is that design with PLDs is faster and this reduces the time required to bring a product to market. Programmable devices also reduce the risks associated with product development since they allow last-minute changes, often without having to redesign circuit boards.

- Since PLDs often replace several other special-purpose devices the design usually has fewer components and this reduces PCB, assembly, test and repair costs.

- Using PLDs also means fewer parts needs to be stocked and this reduces inventory costs.

- Since more of the logic is integrated into each chip the number of interconnections is decreased and this increases the reliability of the product.

- Of course, there are some disadvantages to using programmable logic.

- Design with PLDs requires additional development software and hardware which is often very expensive.

- Design staff often needs to be trained to use new design tools. In addition, parts must be programmed before they can be assembled into a final product.

- In spite of these disadvantages programmable logic usually makes economic sense except for very simple (e.g. bus buffers, latches, some decoders), very complex (e.g. CPU), or very high-speed circuits (e.g. DRAM controller).

- Even for one-of designs it's often easier to use PLDs if the development tools are available.

- Compared to ASICs (standard-cell or gate arrays) PLDs offer lower costs (zero vs. tens of thousands of dollars), fast (1 hour vs. several weeks) design turn-around, lower risk and simpler design tools.

- On the other hand, ASICs will operate at higher speeds and will be less expensive at very high volumes (typically many thousands of parts).

The PLD Advantages :

Advantages of using PLDs are :

  ➢ Less board space requires

  ➢ Faster in speed

- ➢ Lower power requirements (i.e., smaller power supplies)
- ➢ Less costly assembly processes,
- ➢ Higher reliability (fewer ICs and circuit connections means easier
- ➢ troubleshooting),
- ➢ Availability of design software.

5.1.19 Field-Programmable Gate Arrays (FPGAS)

- FPGAs (Field-Programmable Gate Arrays) are PLDs with large numbers of small macro-cells each of which can be interconnected to only a few neighboring cells.
- A typical FPGA might have 100 cells, each with only S inputs and 2 outputs.
- The output of each cell can be programmed to be an arbitrary function of its inputs.
- FPGAs typically have a large number of I/O pins. FPGA architectures vary in the complexity of their individual cells (simple cells are "fine-grained" and complex cells are "coarse-grained") and the flexibility of the interconnections between cells ("routing resources").
- Simple cells are arranged as simple ROM-like look-up tables (LUTs) while more complex cells such as the Xilinx CLBs (Configurable Logic Blocks) can include more specialized logic such as carry look-head generators for high speed adders and may include multiple levels of logic within the cell.
- A typical FPGA is the Xilinx XC4003. The XC4000 family is a coarse-grained architecture in which each CLB has 2 sets of 4 inputs, a second level of logic to combine the two intermediate outputs and 2 registered outputs.
- FPGAs are ideal for designs that require large amounts of logic since it's possible to integrate multiple storage registers, arithmetic and logic circuits, controllers, etc. on the same device.
- One disadvantage of FPGAs is the relatively large propagation delays. To complicate things, these delays are hard to predict before the circuit design is finished.
- This is due to the need to route signals through multiple levels of logic and interconnection blocks.
- Typical RAM-based FPGA circuits will have propagation delays of 20 to 50ns. Another disadvantage of FPGAs is the expensive ($3000 and up) and slow design software. FPGAs are typically designed using either schematic capture or HDLs.
- This is typically done with third-party tools (e.g. View logic schematic capture or Synopsys FPGA Compiler).

- These tools then output netlists 3 (lists of gates or cells and how they are to be logically interconnected).

- The components in the net list must then be assigned to specific cells on the device and the routing between cells laid out.

- This "place and route" process is a complex optimization problem winch typically includes constraints on propagation delay and the number of cells used.

- Although EEPROM and OTP (one-time programmable) FPGAs are available, the most popular designs use RAM to store their configuration.

- The device's configuration RAM thus has to be loaded each time it is powered up. Stand-alone designs can load their configuration from serial EPROMS while FPGAs in larger circuits can be loaded from another device such as a microprocessor.

- It should be noted that OW fuse-based FPGAs are considerably faster than RAM-based FPGAs because signals have to propagate through fewer gates.

- FPGAs cost between $10 and $300 depending on the number of cells, pins and speed.

5.1.20 Commercial Off-the Self Components (COTS)

- Industrial customers have long benefited from COTS products from the rapidly advancing commercial/industrial technology market to economically and reliably meet their most demanding application requirements.

- Commercial "off-the-shelf technology" (COTS) products enable our aerospace, military, scientific, and industrial customers to achieve a tremendous increase in price performance with reduced development costs and improved time-to-market.

- COTS (Commercial Off-the-Shell) products are products which are commercially available to the general public with published pricing and specifications.

- COTS products are typically used "as-is" and equivalent products based on industry standard specifications are readily available from multiple suppliers at competitive prices for immediate delivery from stock.

Reliable Quality Products :

- Industry standard mass-produced COTS products offer outstanding price/performance.

- Use them as delivered -- designed for quick start-up and easy installation.

- Use of rugged industrial-duty COTS products reduces overall project cost.
- Field proven COTS components reduce complexity and maximize system reliability.
- Open systems software is faster and cheaper to use than writing software from scratch.
- Standard operating systems ensure software migration and supportability.
- Changes in future application requirements can be met by upgrading with COTS.
- COTS components can be easily integrated into both new and legacy systems.

State of the Art Technology :

- Rapid prototyping facilitates the use of the latest commercial technological advances.
- COTS is backwards-compatible with systems incorporating standard components.
- Reduced development time enables the implementation of successive refinements.
- Shorter design cycles facilitate the continuous insertion of newer and higher Performance components at regular intervals over the life of a program.
- Early adaptation of state-of-the-art components helps maintain technological superiority.

Save Time :

- Industry-standard COTS products feature published pricing and specifications.
- Published pricing minimizes the need for bidding and lowers system acquisition costs.
- COTS helps avoid Non-Reoccurring Engineering (NRE) product development charges.
- Life cycle costs are lower due to availability of industry-standard replacement parts.

Save Money :

- Industry-standard COTS products feature published pricing and specifications.
- Published pricing minimizes the need for bidding and lowers system acquisition costs.
- COTS helps avoid Non-Reoccurring Engineering (NRE) product development charges.
- Life cycle costs are lower due to availability of industry-standard replacement parts.

Huge Selection :

- A large selection is available of standard, modified, and custom COTS products.

- COTS components with similar specifications are available from a variety of vendors.

- The addition of COTS vendors dramatically expands the available DOD supplier base.

- Cyber Research offers One-Stop-Shopping with over 4,000 COTS products available.

- One of the major advantages of COTS software, which is mass-produced, is its relatively low cost.

- Commercial off-the-shelf (COTS) software is a software package or solution that is purchased to support one or more business functions and information systems.

- One of the more common off the shelf solution is Enterprise Resource Planning software.

- Some of the major examples of ERP are SAP, PeopleSoft, Oracle Applications. These FEP solutions provide all the core information system functions for an entire business.

5.1.21 Software Embedded into Hardware System

- The software is the most important aspect, the brain of the embedded system.

- An embedded system processor and the system need software that is specific to a given application of that system. The processor of the system processes the instruction codes and data. In the final stage, these are placed in the memory (ROM) for all the tasks that have to be executed. The final stage software is also called ROM image. Why? Just as an image is a unique sequence and arrangement of pixels, embedded software is also a unique placement and arrangement of bytes for instructions and data.

- Each code or datum is available only in bits and byte(s) format. The system requires bytes at each ROM-address, according to the tasks being executed. A machine implement-able software file is therefore like a table of address and bytes at each address of the system memory. The table has to be readied as a ROM image for the targeted hardware. Fig. 1.5 shows the ROM image in a system memory. The image consists of the boot up program, stack (s) address pointer(s), program counter address pointer(s), application tasks, ISRs, RTOS, input data, and vector addresses.

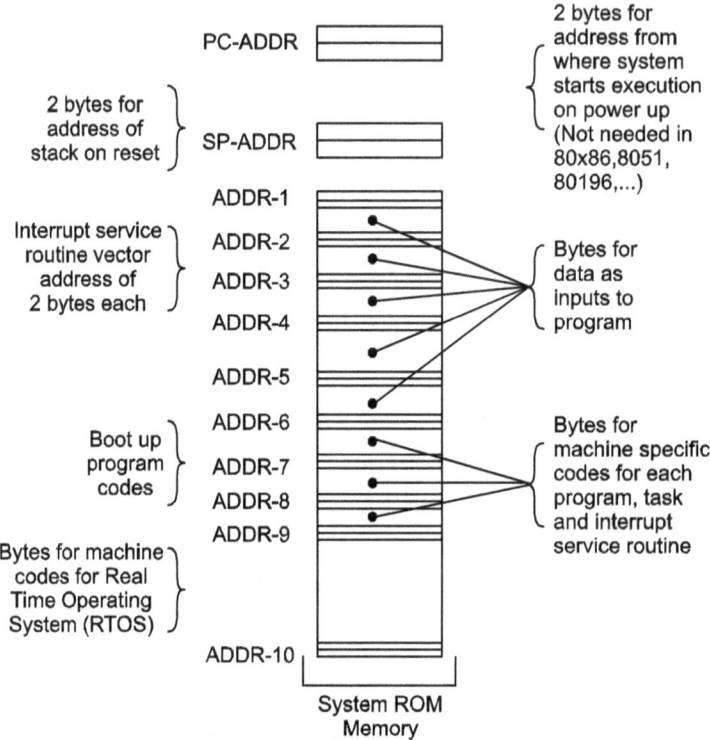

Fig. 5.4 : System ROM Memory embedding Software, RTOS, Data and Vector Address

5.1.21.1 Coding Software in Machine

* During coding in this format, the programmer defines the addresses and the corresponding bytes or bits at each address. In configuring some specific physical device or subsystem, machine code-based coding is used. For example, in a transceiver, placing certain machine code and bits can configure it to transmit at specific Mbps or Gbps, using a specific bus protocol and networking protocol.

* Another example is using certain codes for configuring a control register with the processor. During a specific code-section processing, the register can be configured to enable or disable use of its internal cache.

* However, coding in **machine implement-able codes** is done only in specific situations: **it is time consuming because the programmer must first understand** the processor instructions set and then memorize the instructions and their machine codes.

5.1.21.2 Software in processor specific Assembly Language

- When a programmer understands the processor and its instruction set thoroughly, a program or a small specific part can be coded in the **assembly language**. An example assembly language program in 8051 processor instruction set.

- Coding in assembly language is easy to learn for a designer who has gone through a microprocessor or microcontroller course. Coding is extremely useful for configuring physical devices like ports, a line-display interface, ADC and DAC and reading into or transmitting from a buffer.

- These codes can also be device driver codes. They are useful to run the processor or device specific features and provide an optimal coding solution.

- *Lack of knowledge of writing device driver codes or codes that utilize the processor-specific features-invoking codes in an embedded system design team can cost a lot. Vendors may not only charge for the API but also charge intellectual property fees for each system shipped out of the company.*

- To do all the coding in *assembly language* may, however, be very time consuming. Full coding in assembly may be done only for a few simple, small-scale systems, such as toys, automatic chocolate vending machine, robot or data acquisition system.

- **Fig.** shows the process of converting an *assembly language program* into the machine implement- able software file and then finally obtaining a ROM image file.

  ➢ An **assembler** translates the assembly software into the machine codes using a step called *assembling*.

  ➢ In the next step, called *linking,* a **linker** links these codes with the other required assembled codes. Linking is necessary because of the number of codes to be linked for the final binary file. For example, there are the standard codes to program a delay task for which there is a reference in the assembly language program. The codes for the delay must link with the assembled codes.

  ➢ The delay code is sequential from a certain beginning address. The assembly software code is also sequential from a certain beginning address. Both the codes have to at the distinct addresses as well as available addresses in the system.

  ➢ Linker links these. The linked file in binary for *run* on a computer is commonly known as executable file or simply '.exe' file. After linking, there has to be re-allocation of the sequences of placing the codes before actually placement of the codes in the memory.

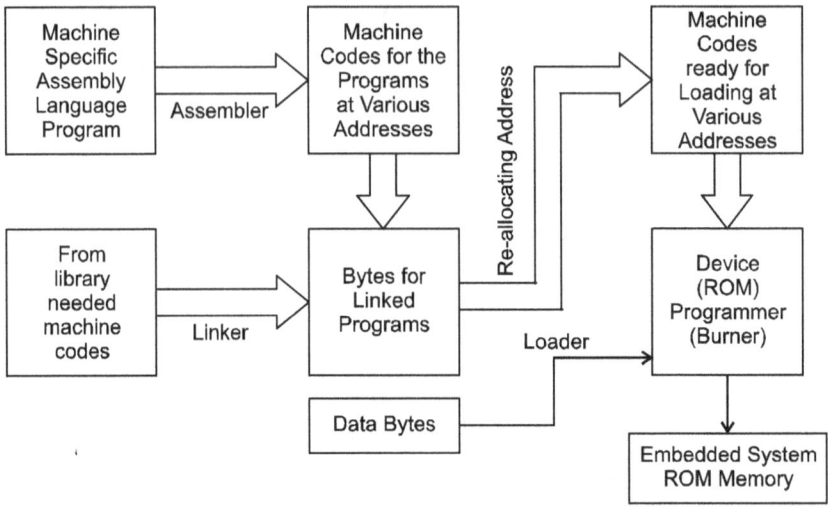

Fig. 5.5 : The process of converting an assembly language program into the machine codes and finally obtaining the ROM image

1. In the next step, the **loader** program performs the task of *reallocating* the codes after finding the physical RAM addresses available at a given instant. The loader is a part of the operating system and places codes into the memory after reading the '.exe' file. This step is necessary because the available memory addresses may not start from 0x0000, and binary codes have to be loaded at the different addresses during the run. The loader finds the appropriate start address. In a computer, the loader is used and it loads into a section of RAM the program that is ready to run.

2. The final step of the system design process is *locating* the codes as a ROM image and permanently placing them at the actually available addresses in the ROM. In embedded systems, there is no separate program to keep track of the available addresses at different times during the running, as in a computer. The designer has to define the available addresses to load and create files for permanently locating the codes. A program called **locator** reallocates the linked file and creates a file for permanent location of codes in a standard format. This format may be

3. Intel Hex file format or Motorola S-record format. Lastly, either

   (i) a laboratory system, called **device programmer,** takes as input the ROM image file and finally *burns* the image into the PROM or EPROM or

   (ii) at a foundry, a mask is created for the ROM of the embedded system from the image file. [The process of placing the codes in PROM or EPROM is also called burning.] **The** mask created from the image gives the ROM in IC chip form.

5.1.21.3 Software in High Level Language

- To do all the coding in *assembly language* may be very time consuming in most cases. Software is therefore developed in a high-level language, 'C' or 'C++' or 'Java'. Most of the times, 'C' is the preferred language.

- For coding, there is little need to understand assembly language instructions and the programmer does not have to know the machine code for any instruction at all. The programmer needs to understand only the hardware organization.

- As an example, consider the following problem :

  Add 127, 29 and 40 and print the square root.

  An example C language program for all the processors is as follows:

  ```
  # include <stdio.h>
  # include <math.h>
  void main (void)
  {
      int i1, i2, i3, a;
      float result;
      i1 = 127;
      i2 = 29;
      i3 = 40;
      a = i1 + i2 + i3;
      result = sqrt (a);
      printf (result);
  }
  ```

- This coding for square-root will need many lines of code and can be done only by an expert assembly language programmer. To write the program in a high level language is very simple compared to writing it in the assembly language. 'C' programs have a feature that adds the assembly instructions when using certain processor-specific features and coding for the specific section, for example, port device driver. Fig. 5.6 shows the different programming layers in a typical embedded 'C' software.

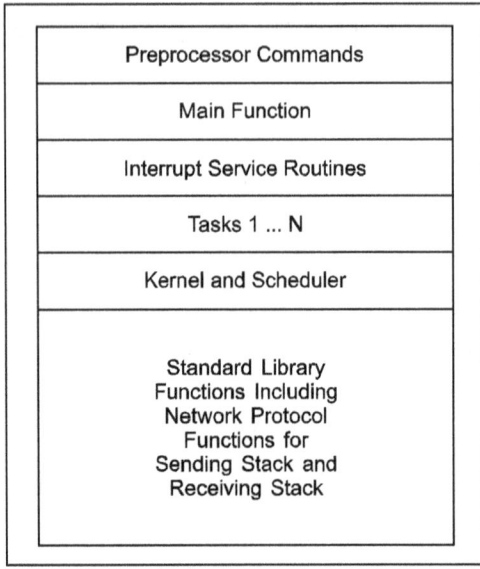

Fig. 5.6 : Different program layers in embedded software

- These layers are as follows :
  1. Processor Commands.
  2. Main Function.
  3. Interrupt Service Routine.
  4. Multiple tasks, say, 1 to N.
  5. Kernel and Scheduler.
  6. Standard library functions, protocol functions and stack allocation functions.

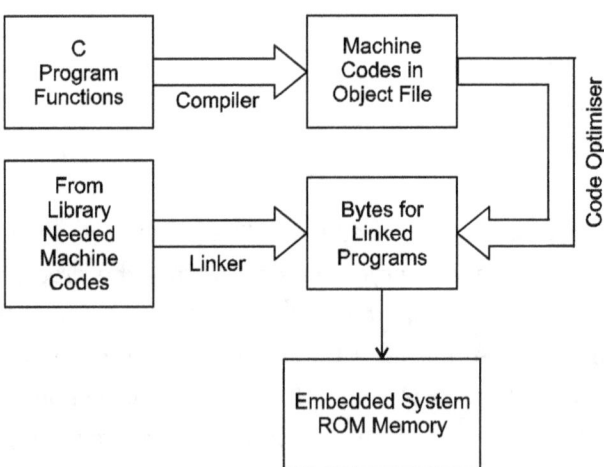

Fig. 5.7 : The process of Converting a C program into the file for Rom image

- Fig. 5.7 shows the process of converting a C *program* into the ROM image file. A **compiler** generates the object codes. The compiler assembles the codes according to the processor instruction set and other specifications. The 'C' compiler for embedded systems must, as a final step of compilation, use a *code-optimizer*. It optimizes the codes before linking.

- After compilation, the *linker* links the object codes with other needed codes. For example, the linker includes the codes for the functions, *printf* and *sqrt* codes. Codes for device management and driver (device control codes) also link at this stage: for example, printer device management and driver codes. After linking, the other steps for creating a file for ROM image are the same as shown earlier in Fig. 5.6.

5.1.21.4 Software for Device Driver and
Device Management using an Operating System

- In an embedded system, there are a number of *physical devices*. Exemplary physical devices are keyboard, display, disk, parallel port and network-card.

- *An innovative concept is use of virtual devices during programming. A v*irtual device example is a **file** (for reading and writing the stream of bytes or words) *or a* **pipe** (for buffering a stream of bytes).

- The term virtual device follows from the analogy that just as a keyboard gives an input to the processor on a *read*, a file also gives an input to the processor. The processor gives an output to a printer on a *write*. Similarly, the processor writes an output to the file. Most often, an embedded system is designed to perform multiple functions and has to control multiple physical and virtual devices.

- A **device** for the purpose of control, handling, reading and writing actions can be taken as consisting of three components. (i) Control Register or Word – It stores the bits that, on setting or resetting

- by a device driver, control the device actions. (ii) Status Register or Word – It provides the flags (bits) to show the device status. (iii) Device Mechanism that controls the device actions. There may be input data buffers and output data buffers at a device. Device action may be to get input into or send output from the buffer. (*The control registers, input data buffers, output data buffers and status registers form part of the device hardware.*)

- A **device driver** is software for controlling, receiving and sending a byte or a stream of bytes from or to a device. In case of physical devices, a driver uses the hardware status flags and control register bits that are in set and reset states. In case of virtual devices also, a driver uses the status and control words and the bits that exist in set and reset states.

- *Driver* controls three functions (i) Initializing that is activated by placing appropriate bits at the control register or word. (ii) Calling an ISR on interrupt or on setting a status flag in the status register and run (drive) the ISR (also called Interrupt Handler Routine). (iii) Resetting the status flag after interrupt service. A driver may be designed for asynchronous operations (multiple times use by tasks one after another) or synchronous operations (concurrent use by the tasks). This is because a device may get activated when an interrupt arises and the device driver routine services that.

- Using Operating System (OS) functions, a device driver coding can be made such that the underlying hardware is hidden as much as possible. An API then defines the hardware separately. This makes the driver usable when the device hardware changes in a system.

- A device driver accesses a parallel port or serial port, keyboard, mouse, disk, network, display, file, pipe and socket at specific addresses. An OS may also provide *Device driver* codes for the system port addresses and for the access mechanism (read, save, write) for the device hardware.

- *Device Management* software modules provide codes for detecting the presence of devices, for initializing these and for testing the devices that are present. The modules may also include software for allocating and registering port (in fact, it may be a register or memory) addresses for the various devices at distinctly different addresses, including codes for detecting any collision between these, if any. It ensures that any device accesses to one task at any given instant. It takes into account that virtual devices may have addresses that can be relocated by a *locator* (for PROM). [The actual physical or hardware devices have predefined fixed addresses (the addresses are not relocated by the locator)].

- An OS also provides and executes modules for managing devices that associate with an embedded system. The underlying principle is that at an instant, only one physical device should get access to or from one task only. The OS also provides and manages the virtual devices like pipes and sockets.

5.1.21.5 Software Design for Scheduling Multiple Task and Device using RTOS

- Most often, an embedded system is designed to perform scheduling of multiple functions while controlling multiple devices. An embedded system program is therefore designed as a multitasking system program.

- In a multitasking OS, *each process (task) has a distinct memory allocation of its own and a task has one or more functions or procedures for a specific job. A task may share the memory (data) with other tasks. A processor may process multiple tasks separately or concurrently.* The OS software includes scheduling features for the processes (tasks, ISRs and Device Drivers) *An OS or RTOS has a kernel.*

- *The kernel's important function is to schedule the transition of a task from a ready state to a running state.* It also schedules the transition of a task from a blocked state to the running state. The kernel may block a task to let a higher priority task be in running state. [It is called preemptive scheduling]. The *kernel* coordinates the use of the processor for the multiple tasks that are in ready state at any instant, such that only one task among many is in the running state. This is so because there is only one processor in the system. The kernel schedules and dispatches a task to a different state than the present. [For multiprocessor systems,

- scheduling and synchronization of various processors are also necessary]. The kernel controls the inter process (task) messaging and sharing of variables, queues and pipes.

- RTOS functions can thus be highly complex. In an embedded system, RTOS has to be scalable. *Scalable OS* is one in which memory is optimized by having only that part of features that are needed associate with the final system software.

- There are a number of popular and readily available RTOSs.

5.1.21.6 Software tools in designing of an Embedded System

- The applications of software tools for assembly language programming, high level language programming, RTOS, debugging and system integration tools are as follows:

- **Editor :** An editor is used for writing C codes or assembly mnemonics using the keyboard of the PC for entering the program. It allows the entry, addition, deletion, insert, appending previously written lines or files, merging record and files at the specific positions. It creates a source file that stores the edited file. It also has an appropriate name [provided by the programmer].

- **Interpreter :** The interpreter is used for expression-by-expression (line-by-line) translation to the machine executable codes.

- **Compiler :** The compiler uses the complete sets of the codes. It may also include the codes, functions and expressions from the library routines. It creates a file called object file.

- **Assembler :** An assembler is used for translating the assembly mnemonics into binary opcodes (instructions), i.e., into an executable file called a binary file. It also creates a list file that can be printed. The list file has address, source code (assembly language mnemonic) and hexadecimal object codes. The file has addresses that adjust during the actual run of the assembly language program.

- **Cross Assembler :** The cross compiler is used for converting object codes or executable codes for a processor to other codes for another processor and vice versa. The cross-assembler assembles the assembly codes of target processor as the assembly codes of the processor of the PC used in the system development. Later, it provides the object codes for the target processor. These codes will be the ones actually needed in the finally developed system.

- **Simulator :** The simulator is used to simulate all functions of an embedded system circuit including additional memory and peripherals. It is independent of a particular target system. It also simulates the processes that will execute when the codes execute on the targeted particular processor.

- **Source-code :** For source code comprehension, navigation and browsing, editing, debugging, configuring Engineering Software (disabling and enabling the C++ features) and compiling.

- **RTOS :** *Scalable OS* is one in which memory is optimized by having only that part of features that are needed associate with the final system software. Details of RTOS are in Last chapter.

- **Stethoscope :** The stethoscope is used for dynamically tracking the changes in any program variable. It tracks the changes in any parameter. It demonstrates the sequences of multiple processes (tasks, threads, service routines) that execute. It also records the entire time history.

- **Trace Scope :** The trace scope is used to help in tracing the changes in the modules and tasks with time on the X-axis. A list of actions also produces the desired time scales and the expected times for different tasks.

- **Integrated Development Environment Prototype :** Software and hardware environment that consists of simulators with editors, compilers, assemblers, RTOS, debuggers, stethoscope, tracer, emulators, logic analyzers, EPROM EEPROM application codes' burners for the integrated development of a system.

  For simulating, source code engineering including compiling, debugging and, on a Browser, summarizing the complete status of the final target system during the development phase.

- **Locator :** The locator uses cross-assembler output and a memory allocation map and provides the locator program output. It is the final step of software design process for the embedded system.

5.1.22 System on Chip

- A system on a chip or system on chip (SoC or SOC) is an Integrated Circuit (IC) that integrates all components of a computer or other electronic system into a single chip. It is a collection of all components and subcomponents of a system on to a single chip. SoC design allows high performance, good process technology, miniaturization, efficient battery life time and cost sensitivities.

- This revolution in design had been used by many designers of complex chips, as the performance, power consumption, cost, and size advantages of using the highest level of integration made available have proven to be extremely important for many designs.

- The emerging technologies in the field of semiconductors, along with the use of the System-on-Chip (SoC) design, have made this possible.

- System development based on the use of a core-based architecture, where the reusable cores are interconnected by means of a standard on-chip bus, which is the most common way to integrate the cores into the SoC.

- This design methodology has been proven to be very effective in terms of development time and productivity since it reuses existing Intellectual Property (IP) cores. In a SoC design which uses multi-million gates the design and test engineers face various problems such as signal integrity problems, heavy power consumption concerns and increase in testability challenges.

- The semiconductor industry has continued to make impressive improvements in the achievable density of very large-scale integrated circuits. In order to keep pace with the levels of integration available, design engineers have developed new methodologies and techniques to manage the increased complexity inherent in these large chips.

- One such emerging methodology is system-on-chip design, wherein predesigned blocks called Intellectual Property(IP) blocks, IP cores or virtual components are obtained from internal sources or third parties and combined into a single chip.

- These reusable IP cores may include embedded processors, memory blocks, interface blocks, analog blocks and components that handle application specific processing functions. The corresponding software components are also provided in a reusable form which includes real time operating systems, kernels, library functions and device drivers.

5.1.22.1 Inside SOC (System on Chip)

- **CPU** – the central processing unit, whether it is single- or multiple-core, this is what makes everything possible on your Smartphone. Most processors found inside the SoCs that we are going to look at will be based on ARM technology, but more on that later.

- **Memory** – just like in a computer, memory is required to perform the various tasks Smartphone and tablets are capable of, and therefore SoCs come with various memory architectures on board.

- **GPU** – the graphic processing unit is also an important component on the SoC, and it's responsible for handling those complex 3D games on the Smartphone or tablets. As you can expect, there are various GPU architectures available out there, and we're going to further detail them in what follows.

- **Northbridge** – this is a component that handles communications between the CPU and other components of the SoC including the Southbridge.

- **Southbridge** – a second chipset usually found on computers that handles various I/O functions. In some cases the Southbridge can be found on the SoC.

- **Cellular radios** – some SoCs also come with certain modems on board that are needed by mobile operators. Such is the case with the Snapdragon S4 from Qualcomm, which has an embedded LTE modem on board responsible for 4G LTE connectivity.

- **Other radios** – some SoCs may also have other components responsible for other types of connectivity, including Wi-Fi, GPS/GLONASS or Bluetooth. Again, the S4 is a good example in this regard.

- Other circuitry

5.1.22.2 Advantages of SOC

- Hybrid CPU/DSP integrated devices are supported by the same tool chain. In some cases, the complier seamlessly weaves together code instructions for the CPU and DSP.

- Once a particular SOC is fully debugged and functional, the developer can be assured that all devices in the SOC work as documented. Furthermore, all of the signals have been pre-qualified, so we know that the device is operating properly. This in turn means that most of the problems encountered will be related to software.

- With highly integrated SOCs, hard cores can be used to implement highly computational functions in hardware.

5.1.22.3 Disadvantages of SOC

- Obviously, with this highly integrated device, you can't simply replace a particular device; you must replace the entire SOC. For example, if the CCD controller isn't working properly, you can continue to develop without CCD functionality. Otherwise you must replace the SOC itself.

- Depending on the integrated device, you must be satisfied with how it was designed and integrated.

- Visibility into the SOC is limited.

5.1.23 Concept of Device Driver

- In computing, a device driver (commonly referred to as a driver) is a computer program that operates or controls a particular type of device that is attached to a computer. A driver provides a software interface to hardware devices, enabling operating systems and other computer programs to access hardware functions without needing to know precise details of the hardware being used.

- A driver typically communicates with the device through the computer bus or communications subsystem to which the hardware connects. When a calling program invokes a routine in the driver, the driver issues commands to the device. Once the device sends data back to the driver, the driver may invoke routines in the original calling program. Drivers are hardware-dependent and operating-system-specific. They usually provide the interrupt handling required for any necessary asynchronous time-dependent hardware interface.

- Device drivers simplify programming by acting as translator between a hardware device and the applications or operating systems that use it. Programmers can write the higher-level application code independently of whatever specific hardware the end-user is using.

- For example, a high-level application for interacting with a serial port may simply have two functions for "send data" and "receive data". At a lower level, a device driver implementing these functions would communicate to the particular serial port controller installed on a user's computer. The commands needed to control a16550 UART are much different from the commands needed to control an FTDI serial port converter, but each hardware-specific device driver abstracts these details into the same (or similar) software interface.

- Because of the diversity of modern hardware and operating systems, drivers operate in many different environments. Drivers may interface with:
  - Printers.
  - Video adapters.
  - Network cards.
  - Sound cards.
  - Local buses of various sorts—in particular, for bus mastering on modern systems.
  - Low-bandwidth I/O buses of various sorts (for pointing devices such as mice, key-boards, USB, etc.).
  - Computer storage devices such as hard disk, CD-ROM, and floppy disk buses (ATA, SATA, SCSI).

> ➢ Implementing support for different file systems.
> ➢ Image scanners.
> ➢ Digital cameras.

5.1.23.1 Embedded Device Driver

- Most embedded hardware requires some type of software initialization and management. The software that directly interfaces with and controls this hardware is called a device driver.

- All embedded systems that require software have, at the very least, device driver software in their system software layer. Device drivers are the software libraries that initialize the hardware and manage access to the hardware by higher layers of software.

- Device drivers are the liaison between the hardware and the operating system, middleware, and application layers. (See Fig. 5.8.)

- The reader must always check the details about the particular hardware if the hardware component is not 100% identical to what is currently supported by the embedded system.

- Never assume existing device drivers in the embedded system will be compatible for a particular hardware part—even if the hardware is the same type of hardware that the embedded device currently supports! So, it is very important when trying to understand device driver libraries that:

> ➢ Different types of hardware will have different device driver requirements that need to be met.

> ➢ Even the same type of hardware, such as Flash memory, that are created by different manufacturers can require substantially different device driver software libraries to support within the embedded device.

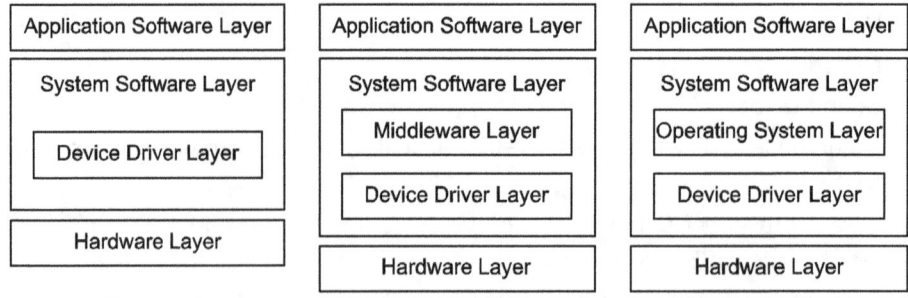

Fig. 5.8 : Embedded Systems Model and Device Drivers.

- The types of hardware components needing the support of device drivers vary from board to board, but they can be categorized according to the von Neumann model (see Fig. 5.9).

- The von Neumann model can be used as a software model as well as a hardware model in determining what device drivers are required within a particular platform. Specifically, this can include drivers for the master processor architecture-specific functionality, memory and memory management drivers, bus initialization and transaction drivers, and I/O (input/output) initialization and control drivers (such as for networking, graphics, input devices, storage devices, or debugging I/O) both at the board and master CPU level.

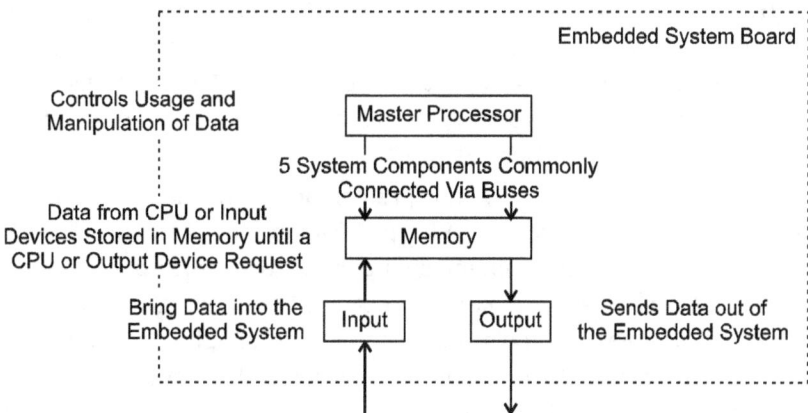

Fig. 5.9 : Embedded system board organization based upon the von Neumann architecture model

- Device drivers are typically considered either architecture-specific or generic. A device driver that is architecture-specific manages the hardware that is integrated into the master processor (the architecture). Examples of architecture-specific drivers that initialize and enable components within a master processor include on-chip memory, integrated memory managers (memory management units (MMUs)), and floating-point hardware.

- A device driver that is generic manages hardware that is located on the board and not integrated onto the master processor. In a generic driver, there are typically architecture-specific portions of source code, because the master processor is the central control unit and to gain access to anything on the board usually means going through the master processor.

- However, the generic driver also manages board hardware that is not specific to that particular processor, which means that a generic driver can be configured to run on a variety of architectures that contain the related board hardware for which the driver is written. Generic drivers include code that initializes and manages access to the remaining major components of the board, including board buses (I2C, PCI, PCMCIA, etc.), off-chip memory (controllers, level 2+ cache, Flash, etc.), and off-chip I/O (Ethernet, RS-232, display, mouse, etc.).

5.2 HARDWARE AND SOFTWARE DEVELOPMENT TOOLS

5.2.1 Integrated Development Environment (IDE)

- An **integrated development environment** (**IDE**) or **interactive development environment** is a software application that provides comprehensive facilities to computer programmers for software development. An IDE normally consists of a source code editor, build automation tools and a debugger. Most modern IDEs offer intelligent code completion feature.

- Some IDEs contain a compiler, interpreter, or both, such as Net Beans and Eclipse; others do not, such as Sharp Develop and Lazarus. The boundary between an integrated development environment and other parts of the broader *software development environment* is not well-defined. Sometimes a version control system and various tools are integrated to simplify the construction of a Graphical User Interface (GUI). Many modern IDEs also have a class browser, an object browser, and a class hierarchy diagram, for use in object-oriented software development.

5.2.2 Developing Embedded Systems - A Tools Introduction

- Developing software and hardware for microcontroller based systems involves the use of a range of tools that can include editors, assemblers, compilers, debuggers, simulators, emulators and Flash/OTP programmers. To the newcomer to microcontroller development it is often not clear how all of these different components play together in the development cycle and what differences there are for example between starter kits, emulators and simulators.

- To complicate matters more, there are quite a number of different approaches and technologies for emulation available that make it difficult for even seasoned embedded engineers to pick the right tools. With this article, I'll try to give a short explanation of the different tools involved in the microcontroller development cycle, with a particular focus on the different emulator types and their advantages and disadvantages.

- The typical microcontroller software development cycle with some of the software and hardware components involved:

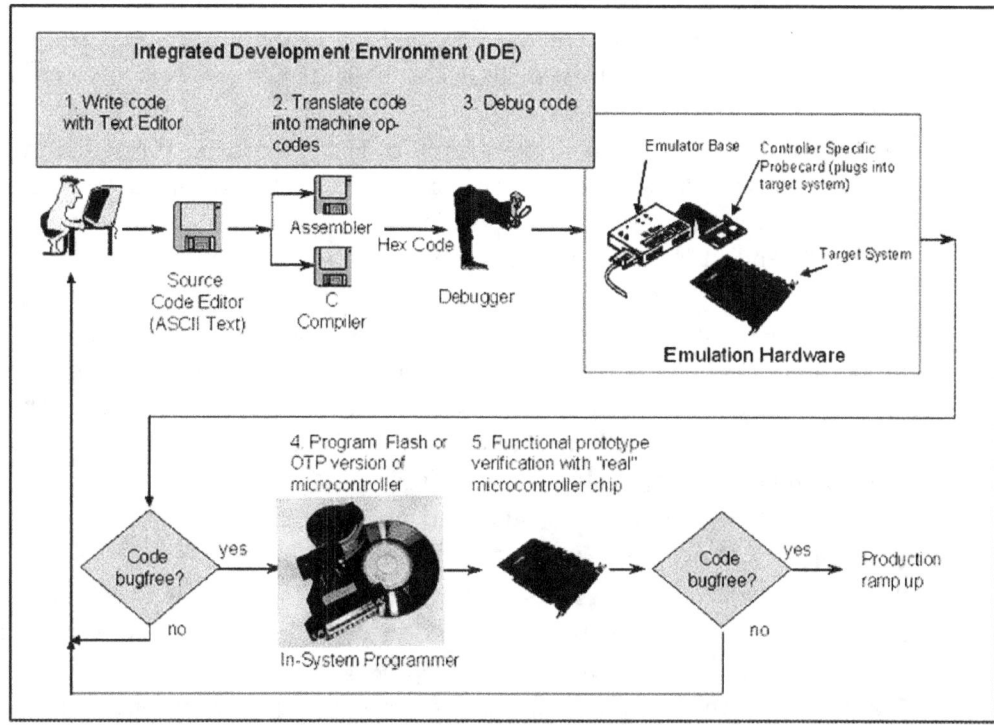

The Microcontroller Development Cycle

Fig. 5.10 : The microcontroller system development

- Above Fig. 5.10 shows the typical microcontrollers firmware development cycle, which involves:

  ➢ Writing the code.

  ➢ Translating the code.

  ➢ Debugging the code with the help of debugging tools, including emulators.

  ➢ Programming a Flash or OTP version of the microcontroller to build up a first functional prototype of your system.

  1. **Writing Microcontroller Code :** Software Code for a microcontroller is written in a programming language of choice (often Assembler or C). This source code is written with a standard **ASCII text editor** and saved as an ASCII text file. Programming in assembler involves learning a microcontroller's specific instruction set (assembler mnemonics), but results in the most compact and fastest code.

A higher level language like C is for the most part independent of a microcontroller's specific architecture, but still requires some controller specific extensions of the standard language to be able to control all of a chip's peripherals and functionality. The penalty for more portable code and faster program development is a larger code size (20%...40% compared to assembler).

2. **Translating the Code :** Next the source code needs to be translated into instructions the microcontroller can actually execute. A microcontroller's instruction set is represented by "op codes". Opcodes are a unique sequence of bits ("0" and "1") that are decoded by the controller's instruction decode logic and then executed.

   Instead of writing opcodes in bits, they are commonly represented as hexadecimal numbers, whereby one hex number represents 4 bits within a byte, so it takes two hex numbers to represent 8 bits or 1 byte. For that reason a microcontroller's firmware in machine readable form is also called Hex-Code and the file that stores that code Hex-File.

   Assemblers, Compilers, Linkers and Librarians

   Assemblers or (C-) Compilers translate the human readable source code into "hex code" that represents the machine instructions (op codes). To support modular code and reusable libraries of code, most assemblers and compilers today come with Linkers and Librarians.

   Linkers, link code modules saved in different files together into a single final program. At the same time they take care of a chip's memory allocation by assigning each instruction to a microcontroller memory addresses in such a way that different modules do not overlap.

   Librarians help you to manage, organize and revision control a library of re-usable code modules.

   Once the ASCII source code text file has been assembled (with an Assembler) or compiled (with a Compiler) and the files have been linked (with the Linker), the output results in a number of files that can be used for **debugging** the software and **programming** the actual microcontroller's memory.

3. **Debugging the Code :** A debugger is a piece of software running on the PC, which has to be tightly integrated with the emulator that you use to validate your code. For that reason all emulator manufacturers ship their own debugger software with their tools, but also compiler manufacturers frequently include debuggers, which work with certain emulators, into their development suites.

A **Debugger** allows you to download your code to the emulator's memory and then control all of the functions of the emulator from a PC. Common debugging features include the capability to examine and modify the microcontroller's on-chip registers, data- and program-memory; pausing or stopping program executing at defined program locations by setting breakpoints; single-stepping (execute one instruction at a time) through the code; and looking at a history of executed code (trace).

So far we've talked about several different pieces of software: Text Editor, Assembler or Compiler, Linkers, Librarians and Debugger. You can easily imagine that it can become quite a time-consuming challenge to alternate back and forth between all of these programs during the debugging process (discover a bug, edit the source code, compile it again, link it again, download the modified code to the emulator, etc.). This is where an integrated development environment (IDE) comes in.

An **Integrated Development Environment** puts all of the previously discussed software components under one common unified user interface, so that it becomes possible to make a code change and get the modified code loaded into the emulator with a few mouse clicks, instead of dozens. A good IDE allows you for example to click on a syntax error message produced by the compiler and have the source code with the highlighted offending instruction pop up for editing in the text editor.

One click of a button and the modified code gets retranslated, linked and downloaded to the emulator. An IDE allows you to store the configuration settings for a project - like compiler switches, or what flavor of chip to emulate - so you can easily recreate a project later on. Some IDEs are flexible enough to allow you to incorporate different choices of third party tools (like compilers and debuggers), others only work with a manufacturer's own tool chain.

5.2.3 Debugging Tools

* When it comes to debugging your code and testing your application there are several different tools you can utilize that differ greatly in terms of development time spend and debugging features available. In this section we take a look at simulators, microcontroller and emulators.

5.2.3.1 Simulators

* **Simulators** try to model the behavior of the complete microcontroller in software. Some simulators go even a step further and include the whole system

(simulation of peripherals outside of the microcontroller). No matter how fast your PC, there is no simulator on the market that can actually simulate a microcontroller's behavior in real-time. Simulating external events can become a time-consuming exercise, as you have to manually create "stimulus" files that tell the simulator what external waveforms to expect on which microcontroller pin. A simulator can also not talk to your target system, so functions that rely on external components are difficult to verify. For that reason simulators are best suited to test algorithms that run completely within the microcontroller (like a math routine for example). They are the perfect tool to complement expensive emulators for large development teams, where buying an emulator for each developer is financially not feasible.

5.2.4 Microcontroller Starter Kits

- **Starter Kits,** commonly bundle a hardware board and in-system programmer with some software components (assembler, linker, debugger, sometimes an IDE and a code-size limited "evaluation" version of a compiler), to allow for very basic emulation and debugging functions. These kits are most predominant with Flash based microcontrollers. The Flash memory allows an actual sample of the microcontroller to be used to "emulate" itself, by using the included in-system programmer to download the code into the Flash and execute it.

- To enable some basic debugging, those kits need to download a small piece of monitor code along with your own code. This monitor code allows you to stop execution (break) and examine memory and of course uses some of the microcontroller's resources (interrupts; stack-, code- and data-memory; some pins). That's why this approach is called **intrusive** or **non-transparent emulation.**

- Included with the starter kits is an **evaluation board,** whose main purpose it is to get you started on your development quickly without the need to develop your own hardware board. The board is typically equipped with a sample of a microcontroller to allow you to execute and evaluate your code. The kits also support the capability to hook up your own hardware if you prefer a setup closer to your final application.

- **Do not confuse the evaluation boards with a FLASH or OTP production programmer**. Even though the kits offer programming capability, the microcontroller sockets on the boards are not built to withstand hundreds or thousands of insertions and are also not equipped with a socket for all controller packages (sockets only for DIP/PLCC packages, but not for SO or QFP packages).

- A big advantage of these kits over simulators is that they work in real-time and thus allow for easy input/output functionality verification. Simulators on the other hand offer typically much more powerful debugging features that rival those of high-end emulators. Starter kits, however, are completely sufficient and the cheapest option to develop simple microcontroller projects.

5.2.5 Emulators

- An emulator is a piece of hardware that ideally behaves exactly like the real microcontroller chip with all its integrated functionality. It is the most powerful debugging tool of all. A microcontroller's functions are emulated in real-time and non-intrusively.

- All emulators contain 3 essential functions in different implementation forms:

  ➤ The emulator control logic, including emulation memory

  ➤ The actual emulation device

  ➤ A pin adapter that gives the emulator's target connector the same "package" and pin out as the microcontroller to be emulated

- Most emulators give you a range of choices of exchangeable pin adapters and emulation devices to build your own customized emulator that supports the exact derivative and package of your specific microcontroller.

- An emulator in my definition always works **transparent** or **non-intrusive** (of course some emulator manufacturers will disagree). This means none of a microcontroller's on-chip resources or I/O pins are lost due to emulation. If emulation is not transparent, then it's not an emulator, but an evaluation, development or starter kit. If you are developing projects of medium to large complexity, a non-intrusive emulator will save you lots of time and grey hair.

5.2.5.1 Emulation Memory

- Because, depending on memory technology, a microcontroller's program memory cannot (ROM) or only once (OTP) be programmed, an emulator uses external static RAM as the emulated micro's program memory. Even some Flash based microcontrollers can, depending on manufacturer, only be re-programmed 100 to 1000 times, which warrants the use of external RAM memory rather than the micro's integrated Flash for emulation. RAM memory allows for code to be changed quickly and an "indefinite" number of times during the software debugging process.

5.2.5.2 Bond-Out Emulation Chips versus PLD Implementations

- As higher-end emulators typically use external RAM memory as program memory, it becomes apparent that in some instances they cannot use a standard sample of the emulated microcontroller for emulation purposes. They need special **bond-out chips** of the microcontroller to be emulated. Those bond-out chips have additional pins that allow the emulator electronics to feed the externally stored program information to the microcontroller in place of the on-chip memory contents in real time; control the program execution flow; and access on-chip registers and data memory.

- Instead of special bond-out chips, some emulator manufacturers program a microcontroller's complete functional model into a PLD (programmable logic device). A drawback of this approach is that you never know how accurate the PLD model of the microcontroller is compared to the "real thing". It only works in real-time with models of less complex and slower microcontrollers. On the plus side such an emulator can easily be reconfigured to support many different derivatives of a microcontroller family.

5.2.5.3 Emulation Control Logic

- Contributing to the cost of emulators is the control logic required to recreate functions that might be lost due to the emulator using those resources (e.g. some standard I/O pins). By recreating such functions with additional logic, those emulators work truly transparent or non-intrusive, which means you have all the pins, all the memory and all the peripheral functions available like with the real microcontroller.

- Even more control logic is required to implement high-end emulator features like complex breakpoint trigger conditions, external event trigger conditions, loop counters, trace memory and in some cases even logic analyzer functions.

5.2.6 Technical Approaches to Emulation

- Existing emulators today use one of several approaches to emulation, which we will cover in the following sections.

5.2.6.1 Base Unit and Probecard

- Many emulators consist of a **base unit** and a **"probecard"**. The base unit is connected to a PC via the serial, parallel or USB port. It contains the majority of the emulator electronics, with the exception of the emulation chip itself. The emulation chip is a special bond-out version of the actual microcontroller and is mounted on a separate small PCB, called a probecard. This probecard connects via a ribbon cable to the base unit and has a pin adapter at the bottom, which allows the probecard to be plugged into a socket on the actual target application board in place of the actual microcontroller.

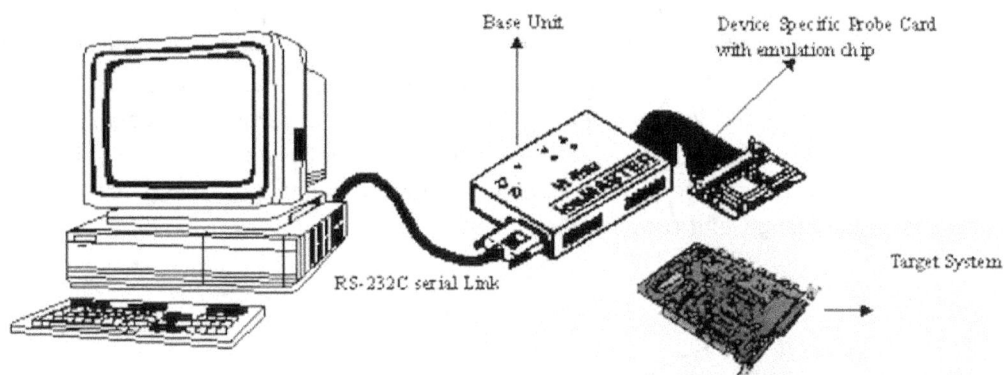

Fig. 5.11

- The advantage of partitioning the emulator into a base unit and separate probecard is that one and the same base unit can support many different derivatives of a given microcontroller architecture (e.g. all 8051 devices).

- By purchasing different probecards the emulator can then be changed to support all the on-chip features and packages of your specific microcontroller derivative(s) of choice. Another advantage is that the probecard can be kept relatively small, which makes it easier to plug it into the target in space constrained applications.

- The probecard approach also minimizes the physical distance of the emulation chip from the location of the final microcontroller, minimizing the impact of noise and additional capacitive/resistive loading that can become issues when analog peripherals need to be emulated.

5.2.6.2 Debug Board Modules (DBM)

- The "debug board" approach combines all of the emulator electronics and the actual emulation chip onto a single, larger sized PCB. This PCB is typically not housed in an enclosure to save cost.

- The connection to the target system is accomplished by ribbon cables, which provide, on one end, a connector that can plug into an actual chip package socket of the target system. This means that all pin signals for the microcontroller to be emulated are now routed via this ribbon cable that connects the target system with the debug board, including any analog signals to be measured by the microcontroller. This is a less than desirable solution if your micro has for example high resolution A/D converters and you'd like to make accurate measurements also during emulation.

* DBMs are in most cases dedicated to emulating a single specific microcontroller and cannot be modified to support other derivatives of a family. If you want to emulate a new derivative you have to buy a new DBM. On the plus side DBM's are typically priced lower than emulators using the probecard approach. DBM's emulation and debugging capabilities often range above starter kits, but below probecard based emulators, with certain exceptions being the rule (DBM has all the features of high-end probecard emulator).

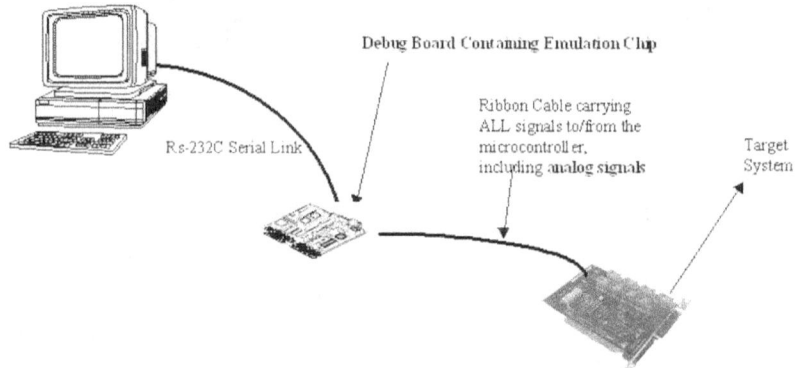

Fig. 5.12

5.2.6.3 Motherboards and Daughter cards

* There are several variations of the concepts discussed above on the market. One such variation is to put probe card and base unit into a single enclosure. The "base unit" in that case is a "**motherboard**" and the probe card a "**daughter card**" that connects onto the motherboard. This combination then directly plugs into the target board via a matching pin socket adapter at the bottom. These emulators can still be adapted to emulate different derivatives by exchanging the daughter card.

5.2.6.4 Dedicated Emulators

* Then there are several forms of the "dedicated emulator", which only supports a very narrow range of microcontroller devices (usually micros with identical functionality and pinout, but different memory sizes).

- In some implementations dedicated emulators are nothing more than a Debug Board Module, in others take the form of base unit and probe card with the probe card not being exchangeable. A third variant combines base and probe card onto a single non-exchangeable PCB (with or without enclosure) that can directly plug into the target system.

5.2.6.5 Emulators Using Microcontroller FLASH Memory

- With the advent of FLASH program memory a new approach in microcontroller emulation became possible. The electrical erase/write capability of FLASH program memory, in combination with emulation support circuitry and code embedded in the microcontroller, enable each such microcontroller to be its own emulator. Unfortunately this does not work with all FLASH micros on the market today; especially earlier generation FLASH devices lack the necessary on-chip emulation support circuitry.

- Flash microcontrollers that have the necessary on-chip emulation support can, regardless of package, be directly soldered into the target application. This, of course, means that now the microcontroller chip "sees" the exact same analog environment as the finalized application - a big advantage when it comes to accurately emulating on-chip analog peripherals.

- The only connection now required to enable PC based software debugging are a few fully digital I/O pins of the controller. The "normal" digital function of those I/Os is "recreated" on a small piece of hardware that sits between the PC and the target system, so that none of the controller's I/Os is lost.

- One common on-chip emulation interface for this kind of emulators is the JTAG interface, mostly found on 16-bit and higher microcontrollers. 8-bit devices frequently feature proprietary interfaces to save on cost.

- As opposed to emulators for ROM and OTP devices, Flash emulators do not require RAM memory to store the program code, but use the microcontroller's on-chip FLASH memory. This further saves cost and makes those emulators cheaper.

- A disadvantage of using the FLASH memory is that program downloads (required after every code change) take much longer. The microcontroller's FLASH memory life-time is limited. Depending on manufacturer, the number of write/erase cycles the memory can withstand varies anywhere between 100 and 100.000 cycles.

- On the plus side, FLASH emulators at the same time also double-function as a FLASH programmer, as the program code has to be downloaded into the chip's memory. Emulators for OTPs or ROMs (than can of course also support the FLASH version of a pin/function compatible device, but then in combination with external program memory), do not support any programming functions.

• Another advantage of FLASH emulators is the fact that one and the same emulator can support all Flash derivatives of a given microcontroller architecture. If a new device with new functionality comes out, all you need is a sample of that new device and an update of the debugger software. No more need to buy new probecards or debug modules for each new derivative.

5.2.7 OTP and Flash Programming

• It can't be stretched enough: A starter kit or emulator are no substitute for a production grade programmer. Using the microcontroller sockets on starter kit boards is ok to program one or two samples in the lab, but those sockets cannot withstand hundreds or thousands of insertions. You will also find that starter kits do not include any sockets for surface mount devices, as those sockets are extremely expensive.

5.2.7.1 Out-of-Circuit Programming

• OTP microcontrollers are typically programmed out-of-circuit. That means the microcontroller is programmed **before** being soldered on the target board. For that purpose production grade programmers offer a choice of optional, high quality, expensive, zero-insertion-force (ZIF) pin adapters to support different package flavors.

5.2.7.2 In-System Programming (ISP)

• FLASH microcontrollers can be programmed both in-circuit (in-system) and out-of-circuit.

• With in-circuit programming the microcontroller is already soldered into the target system and can be programmed via one of its communication interfaces (UART, SPI). This requires that you have the signals required for programming routed to an in-system-programming (ISP) connector to which an ISP programmer can be hooked up. The ISP connector required varies from manufacturer to manufacturer and microcontroller to microcontroller, so it is recommended that **before** you start your PCB layout, you decide on which ISP programmer you want to use and find out which ISP connector is required for it.

• As ISP programming is done via a serial interface it is slower than out-of-circuit programming that uses parallel data transfers - something you might want to consider if you have to program 100 000 devices.

- One big advantage of ISP programmers is the fact that they do not require expensive ZIF socket adapters. All you need is the ISP connector on your board and the microcontroller soldered onto the board to program even the most exotic package.

- Having an ISP connector on your board is a good idea - even if you use out-of-circuit programming for production. It enables you to do painless firmware updates or last minute bug fixes without having to de-solder the microcontroller first.

5.2.8 In-Circuit Emulator (ICE)

- An in-circuit emulator (ICE) is a hardware interface that allows a programmer to change or debug the software in an embedded system. The ICE is temporarily installed between the embedded system and an external terminal or personal computer so that the programmer can observe and alter what takes place in the embedded system, which has no display or keyboard of its own.

- An ICE serves as a "surrogate"(someone who takes the place of another) CPU (central processing unit) for the microcomputer in an embedded system. The ICE usually has a connector that fits the CPU socket in the system. If the connector provided with the ICE does not match the socket in the system, a suitable adapter can usually be found. An ICE can assist design engineers in product development, and also assist programmers or end users in product upgrading, modification, or maintenance.

- Using an ICE, technicians can test new, revised, or modified programming elements on an embedded system's hardware without committing to the change. Once they have optimized the embedded-system software by testing various versions using the ICE, technicians can modify the actual CPU program accordingly. This process ensures that the final product will function exactly as the vendor and consumer expect.

- More recently the term also covers JTAG based hardware debuggers which provide equivalent access using on-chip debugging hardware with standard production chips. Using standard chips instead of custom bond-out versions makes the technology ubiquitous and low cost, and eliminates most differences between the development and runtime environments. In this common case, the **in-circuit emulator** term is a misnomer, sometimes confusingly so, because emulation is no longer involved.

- Embedded systems present special problems for a programmer because they usually lack keyboards, monitors, disk drives and other user interfaces that are present on computers. These shortcomings make in-circuit software debugging tools essential for many common development tasks.

- **In-circuit emulation** can also refer to the use of hardware emulation, when the emulator is plugged into a system (not always embedded) in place of a yet-to-be-built chip (not always a processor). These in-circuit emulators provide a way to run the system with "live" data while still allowing relatively good debugging capabilities. It can be useful to compare this with an in-target probe (ITP) sometimes used on enterprise servers.

5.3 EMBEDDED SOFTWARE DEVELOPMENT CYCLE

- Software development is the computer programming, documenting, testing, and bug fixing involved in creating and maintaining applications and frameworks involved in a software release life cycle and resulting in a software product. The term refers to a process of writing and maintaining the source code, but in a broader sense of the term it includes all that is involved between the conception of the desired software through to the final manifestation of the software, ideally in a planned and structured process. Therefore, software development may include research, new development, prototyping, modification, reuse, re-engineering, maintenance, or any other activities that result in software products.

- Software can be developed for a variety of purposes, the three most common being to meet specific needs of a specific client/business (the case with custom software), to meet a perceived need of some set of potential users (the case with commercial and open source software), or for personal use (e.g. a scientist may write software to automate a mundane task). Embedded software development, that is, the development of embedded software such as used for controlling consumer products, requires the development process to be integrated with the development of the controlled physical product. System software underlies applications and the programming process itself, and is often developed separately.

- The need for better quality control of the software development process has given rise to the discipline of software engineering, which aims to apply the systematic approach exemplified in the engineering paradigm to the process of software development.

5.3.1 Software Development Life Cycle

- Following diagram represents the typical product life cycle and key functional areas of a Consumer Electronics OR Embedded Product :

1. Concept Phase:

> A comprehensive analysis of the market trends is done here in the concept phase. The phase involves brainstorming of innovative ideas driven by technology trends and customer inputs. The customer here could be strategic partners for an established company OR end- users of similar product in the market.

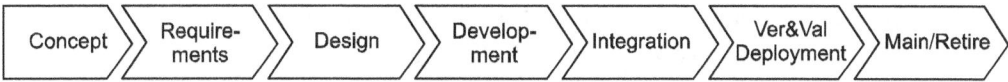

Fig. 5.13 : Embedded system development life cycle

> **Expected Deliverables:** Concept Paper.
> **Participants:** Idea Initiators (include VPs, Directors, Product Managers), Product Architecture Teams, Product Marketing and Management.

2. Requirements Gathering Phase:

> A critical stage for embedded product as it determines what kind of hardware and software support is required to satisfy the scenarios identified for the customer. The number of requirements will eventually determine the scope of the product and what problem areas are being addressed by your new version of the product. A detailed feasibility (technical and business) is done by soliciting feedback from all critical stake holders of this project.
> **Expected Deliverables:** Requirements Functional Spec OR PRDs, System Specifications.
> **Participants:** Idea Initiators (include VPs, Directors, Product Managers), Product Management and Systems Engineering.

3. Design Phase:

> During this phase, the product owner and design team will identify the relationship between input and output. A System Specification is written after investigating the overall behavior of the embedded system. All the required components to build the embedded product are identified and also how these components interact with each other. A functional design document is written to compile the findings of all the above components. A detailed Hardware and Software partitioning is determined. Rapid Prototyping is done in order to validate the identified and proposed design.
> Architecture viz. target processor architecture and Host O.S is also identified for the implementation purposes.

> **Expected Deliverables:** Architecture Doc, High Level Design, Low Level Design for HW and Software.

> **Participants:** Idea Initiators Limited Set (include VPs, Directors, Product Managers), Product Engineering Team (Development and Quality Assurance).

4. Development and Implementation Phase:

> Based on the specification of embedded system regarding functionality and power consumption and cost all the different hardware add on components are chosen and hardware (viz. ASIC) implementation will start in the first sub-phase of implementation. Then the software component, which deals with code running on a microcontroller running together on a RTOS is done as a next step in the development process. Some new development approaches recommend both the hardware implementation viz. VHDL programming and Software Implementation using C programming is done in parallel so that integration becomes easier.

> **Expected Deliverables:** Implemented Hardware and Software Components

> **Participants:** Product Engineering Team (Development and Quality Assurance).

5. Integration Phase:

> The next step in the implementation process is the testing of the entire embedded system. This will ensure whether the embedded system is complying with entire system specification defined above.

> **Expected Deliverables:** Implemented Embedded System – Beta and Working.

> **Participants:** Product Engineering Team (Development and Quality Assurance), Systems Engineering.

6. Verification and Validation Phase :

> The Validation phase is to ensure that the entire system is implemented as against the design and eventually against the requirements. Emulation based approaches can be followed for verification. Compliance testing and certification testing are carried on the target embedded system OR consumer device.

> **Expected Deliverables:** Implemented Embedded System – Beta and Working.

> **Participants:** Product Engineering Teams (Development and Quality Assurance), Systems Engineering, Partner Teams and Beta Customers.

7. Maintenance and Retire Phase :

> ➢ The Maintenance phase includes changes and additions as required by the users and also fixing bugs to keep the product up and running at the customer site.

> ➢ **Expected Deliverables:** Implemented Embedded System – Working

> ➢ **Participants:** Field Engineering, Product Engineering Teams (Development and Quality Assurance), Systems Engineering, Partner Teams and Beta Customers

5.3.2 Challenges in Developing an Embedded Product

1. Predicting product behavior with existing set of fuzzy requirements.
2. Difficulty in understanding the design change and implication across all disciplines.
3. Handling Distributed Software and Hardware Teams - Early identification of system level problems becomes challenging because of distributed teams.

Important Points

- **System** : A way of working, organizing or doing some task or series of tasks by following the fixed plan, program and set of rules.

- **Embedded system** : A sophisticated system that has a computer (hardware with application software and RTOS embedded in it) as one of its components. An embedded system is a dedicated computer-based system for an application or product.

- **Processor** : A processor implements a process or processes as per the command (instruction) given to it.

- **Process** : A program or task or thread that has a distinct memory allocation of its own and has be or more functions or procedures for specific job. The process may share the memory (data) with other tasks. A processor may run multiple processes separately or concurrently.

- **Microcontroller** : A unit with a processor. Memory, timers, watchdog timer, interrupt controller,

- **GPP (General-purpose processor)** : A processor from a number of families of processors, microcontrollers, embedded processors and digital signal processors (DSPs) having a general purpose instruction set and readily available compilers to enable programming in a high level language.

- **ASSP (Application Specific System Processor)** : A processing unit for specific tasks, for example, image compression, and that is integrated through the buses with the main processor n the embedded system.

- **ASIP (Application specific Instruction processor)** : A processor designed for specific application on a VLSI chip.

- **FPGA :** These are Field Programmable Gate Arrays on a chip. The chip has a large number of arrays with each element having fusable links. Each element of array consists of several XOR, AND, OR, multiplexer, demultiplexer and tristate gates. By appropriate programming of the fusable links, a design of a complex digital circuit is created on the chip.
- **Compiler :** A program that, according to the processor specification, generates machine codes from the high level language. The codes are called object codes.
- **Assembler :** A program that translates assembly language software into the machine codes placed in a file called '.exe' (executable) file.
- **Linker :** A program that links the compiled codes with the other codes and provides the input for a loader or locator.
- **Loader :** It is a program that reallocates the physical memory addresses for loading into the system RAM memory. Reallocation is necessary, as available memory may not start from 0x0000 at a given instant of processing in a computer. The loader is a part of the OS in a computer.
- **Locator :** It is a program to reallocate the linked files of the program application and the RTOS.
- codes at the actual addresses of the ROM memory. It creates a file in a standard format. File is called ROM image.
- **Device Programmer :** It takes the inputs from a file generated by the locator and burns the fusable link to actually store the data and codes at the ROM.
- **Device Driver :** Interrupt Service routine Software, which runs after the programming of the control register (or word) of a peripheral device (or virtual device) and to let the device get operated as per requirement.
- **VLSI chip :** A very large-scale integrated circuit made on silicon with ~ 1M transistors.
- **System on Chip :** A system on a VLSI chip that has all of needed analog as wells as digital circuits, for example, in a mobile phone.

MSBTE Questions

Summer 2012

1. List the parallel bus device protocols and describe any one.
2. Give any four applications of embedded system with their examples.
3. What do you mean by system on chip?
4. Draw the structural unit available in processor.
5. What do you meant by DMA? Describe the DMA process.
6. Enlist the processors available in the embedded system.
7. State the various types of memories available in embedded system. Also state the example of each.

8. Draw "DB-9" RS232 connector and describe any four signal.

9. Describe the software tools for designing an embedded system.

10. Compare serial and parallel communication.

11. What do you meant by Harvard architecture? Describe processor memory interface in it.

12. What do you meant by virtual device driver?

Winter 2012

1. Give the format of bits in RS232 bus used for serial communication with explanation.

2. Enlist the hardware and software components in the embedded system of mobile phone.

3. State two advantages and two limitations of I2C bus protocol. Describe the signals used in I2C bus protocol.

4. With a suitable diagram, explain the system on chip SOC in Embedded systems.

5. Describe DMA process with suitable diagram.

6. State the meaning of Device Driver with suitable example.

7. With a suitable figure describe the CAN bus format of bits.

8. Describe the processor and memory organization in Harvard architecture.

Summer 2013

1. State four applications of embedded systems.

2. With suitable figure describe data transfer in I2C bus.

3. Enlist the hardware and software components in the embedded system of digital camera.

4. With suitable diagram describe the DMA process.

5. Enlist the various forms of system memory.

6. Define the term device driver. State its features.

7. Describe the processor and memory organization in Harvard Architecture.

8. Elaborate the features of PCI bus which makes it suitable for distributed embedded devices.

9. Describe the stepwise procedure to convert C language program into a ROM image.

10. Elaborate features of CAN bus (any three). Explain the Arbitration field in a CAN frame.

11. State the various processors used in embedded system. Which features of processor are considered while carrying out selection in embedded system?

12. Which information must be collected by the programmer before writing the device driver program?

Winter 2013

1. Compare I2C bus with CAN bus.

2. List software components in embedded system and explain any one of them.

3. Describe different pins of RS232 connector.

4. Describe in detail, any two software development tools.

5. Explain the processor selection process with one example while designing an embedded system. Explain the concept of Direct Memory Access (DMA).

6. Draw and explain 'Software development cycle in embedded system.

7. List the serial protocols and explain I2C bus with diagram.

8. Describe hardware requirements of an embedded system with the help of an example.

9. Draw and describe the Harvard architecture.

10. State the need of DMA in embedded system and ways to implement it.

Summer 2014

1. Elaborate features of PCI bus which makes it suitable for embedded System.

2. Give 8 examples of embedded System.

3. Enlist hardware and software component in the embedded system of the mobile phone.

4. State advantages and disadvantages of I2c bus protocol? Describe signal in I2C bus protocol.

5. Draw and Describe DMA Process.

6. Explain different Hardware unit in embedded system.

7. Enlist structure unit in processor.

8. Explain on chip (SOC) in the embedded system.

9. Explain concept of device driver routine and Interrupt service routine.

10. What do you mean by Harvard architecture? Describe processor memory interface in it.

11. Enlist processor available in embedded system.

12. With suitable figure explain CAN bus format of bits.

Winter 2014

1. Draw the pin out of RS232.

2. Define Simulator and Debugger.

3. Describe PCI bus protocol.

4. Tell the steps to design an Embedded System.

5. Describe the working of DMA.

6. Discuss different types of memory used in Embedded System.

7. Enlist any four examples of embedded systems.

8. Describe structure unit in processor.

9. Describe CAN protocol.

10. Describe parallel port device driver with example

11. Demonstrate I2C protocol.

12. Show how to select processor for Embedded System.

13. What do you mean by device driver? Give example.

Chapter 6

RTOS & Inter-Process Communication

Weightage of Marks = 16, Teaching Hours = 08

Specific Objectives

➤ Students will be able to

❖ Understand the concepts of RTOS

❖ Know the concept multitasking, task synchronization

❖ Understand the concepts of deadlock, starvation.

6.1 INTRODUCTION

- Real time system is defines as a data processing system in which the time interval required to process and respond to inputs is so small that it controls the environment. Real time processing is always on line whereas on line system need not be real time. The time taken by the system to respond to an input and display of required updated information is termed as response time. So, in this method, response time is very less as compared to the online processing.

- Real-time systems are used when there are rigid time requirements on the operation of a processor or the flow of data and real-time systems can be used as a control device in a dedicated application. Real-time operating system has well-defined, fixed time constraints otherwise system will fail. For example Scientific experiments, medical imaging systems, industrial control systems, weapon systems, robots, and home-appliance controllers, Air traffic control system etc.

- There are two types of real-time operating systems.

6.1.1 Hard Real-Time Systems

- Hard real-time systems guarantee that critical tasks complete on time. In hard real-time systems secondary storage is limited or missing with data stored in ROM. In these systems virtual memory is almost never found.

6.1.2 Soft Real-Time Systems

- Soft real time systems are less restrictive. Critical real-time task gets priority over other tasks and retains the priority until it completes. Soft real-time systems have limited utility than hard real time systems. For example, multimedia, virtual reality, advanced scientific projects like undersea exploration and planetary rovers etc.

6.1.3 Soft Versus Hard Real Time

- Often, a distinction is made between hard and soft real time. A hard real-time constraint is one, for which there is no value to a computation, if it is late and where the effects of a late computation may be catastrophic. Simply put, a hard real-time system is one where all activities must be completed on time. A flight control system is a good example.

- On the other hand, soft real time is a property of the timeliness of a computation where the value diminishes according to its tardiness. A soft real-time system can tolerate some late answers to soft real time computations, as long as the value hasn't diminished to zero. Deadlines may be missed, but the number and frequency of such misses must typically comply with Quality of Service (QoS) metrics.

- Frequently, soft real time is erroneously applied to OSs that cannot guarantee computations will be completed on time. Such OSs are best described as quasi real time or pseudo real time OSs in that they execute real-time activities in preference to others whenever necessary, but don't adequately account for non-schedulable activities in the system. Put simply, soft real time shouldn't be confused with non real-time.

6.2 NECESSITY OF RTOS

- Real time is a sometimes misunderstood and misapplied property of operating systems. Moreover, there is often disagreement as to when a Real-Time Operating System (RTOS) is needed. For instance, when designing an industrial control system or medical instrument, most engineers and system designers would concur that an RTOS is necessary.

- However, questions arise, when it comes to other applications, such as tracking systems and a variety of in-vehicle devices. Is an RTOS needed here? Or would a general purpose OS such as Linux or Windows do the job? Often, such systems do require an RTOS, but the issue isn't recognized until later in the design phase. Therefore, it's important to understand why the real-time capabilities provided by an RTOS are not only beneficial, but necessary for a wide variety of embedded systems. For instance, consider a system where users expect or need immediate feedback to input.

- With an RTOS, a developer can ensure that the system always provides feedback in a timely fashion, even when the system is handling many other compute-intensive activities. The user is never left wondering whether the system has, in fact, accepted the button push or recognized the voice command. In a nutshell, an RTOS allows developers to control how long a system will take to perform a task or respond to critical events. Deadlines can be met within predictable, and wholly consistent, timelines, even under heavy system loads.

6.3 OPERATION OF RTOS

- The scheduler is one of the main functions of a real-time OS. How is it implemented in a real-time OS? Let's see how a task execution order is controlled.
- The OS chooses the next task to be executed according to specified rules. Creating a queue of tasks waiting for execution according to specified rules is called scheduling. The kernel, which is almost like the core of the OS, provides the scheduler functions, which handle the scheduling of tasks waiting for execution. The following describes commonly used task scheduling algorithms.

  - **First Come, First Served (FCFS) :** The task that enters the execution waiting state first is executed first. Waiting tasks are put in a queue in the order they enter the waiting state.

  - **Priority Based :** Each task is assigned a priority level, and tasks are executed in the order of priority as shown in Fig. 6.1.

- The algorithm for switching tasks at specified intervals and repeatedly executing them in turn is called round-robin scheduling. There are other scheduling algorithms, such as the deadline-driven scheduling algorithm, which assigns CPU execution to the task nearest to its deadline, and the shortest processing time first (SPT) algorithm, which assigns CPU execution to the task that requires the shortest processing time when the necessary time for each task is known.

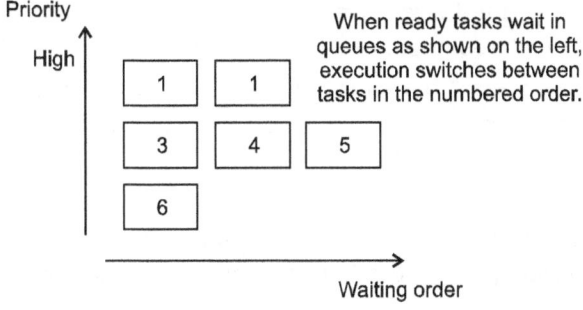

Fig. 6.1 : Priority Based Scheduling

- An embedded OS such as µITRON uses both priority-based and FCFS algorithms. The highest-priority task is executed first, and if multiple tasks have the same priority, they are executed in an FCFS manner. Tasks in the execution waiting queue (called the ready queue) can also be executed in a round-robin manner; that is, execution is cyclically switched among tasks at specified intervals.

When is Scheduler Activated?

- The scheduler is activated every time a task or a handler requests a service from the OS. This request to the OS is called a service call. When a service call is issued, control is shifted to the OS. After the OS has processed the requested service, the scheduler chooses the next task to be executed and switches execution to the task. Switching between tasks is called a task switch, and the act of switching is called dispatching. After dispatching, CPU execution is shifted to the chosen task. Necessary data is saved so that the previous task can continue execution when it is later dispatched. The data necessary for restarting execution is called a context as shown in Fig. 6.2.

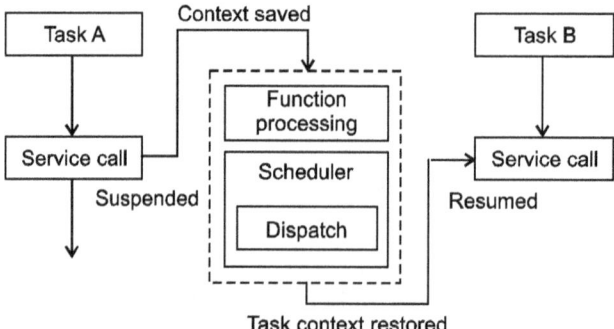

Fig. 6.2 : Context Switching

6.3.1 Difference Between Task and Handler

- As described earlier, the target of scheduling and dispatching is a task. A task is activated, suspended, resumed, or terminated by the OS.
- An interrupt program, however, is automatically activated without OS intervention when a dedicated signal is input to the microprocessor; it is a program that is not controlled by the OS.
- When this program issues a service call, control is shifted to the OS and tasks can be processed through the OS. This type of program is used when tasks should be processed upon generation of an event notified through an interrupt.
- A program that issues service calls but is not a task is called a handler. A handler that is activated by an interrupt is called an interrupt handler.

- In addition to interrupt handlers, there are cyclic handlers, which are activated at specified intervals, and alarm handlers, which are activated at a specified time or after a specified period as shown in Fig. 6.3.

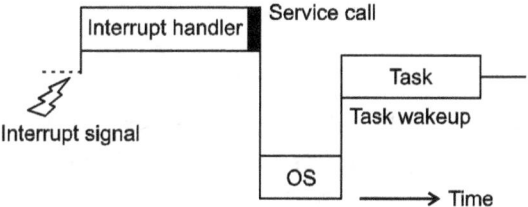

Fig. 6.3 : Flow from an Interrupt to Task Switching

Task State Transition :

- The scheduler described earlier determines which task in the execution-ready task queue should be executed. A task dynamically moves between various states; for example, a task being executed enters a waiting state or a waiting task enters an execution-ready state when the wait state is canceled upon generation of an event.

- The OS manages the state of each task. There are three basic task states as shown in the Fig. 6.4 below. RUNNING state is the state of a task being executed, which is entered when a task in READY state is chosen (dispatched) to be executed. When a RUNNING task is suspended (preempted), it enters READY state.

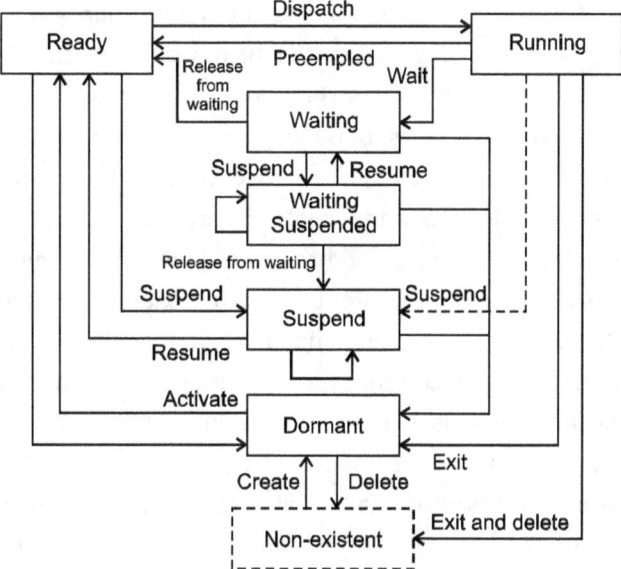

Fig. 6.4 : Task state transition

- In a single CPU, only one task can be in RUNNING state. Scheduling is the act of determining which task in READY state should be shifted to RUNNING. μITRON can handle six main states including DORMANT state, WAITING-SUSPENDED state, and SUSPENDED state.

Dividing the Task :

- What should we consider when dividing tasks? Let's look at some cases where processing should be divided into tasks from the viewpoint of task scheduling or pre-emption in the OS.

  ➢ **Dividing Tasks for Parallel Processing :** When some processes need to be executed in parallel (doing a process while doing another) within a specified period, execution should be switched between processes with wait conditions or at specified intervals and each process will continue intermittently. In this case, processes that need to be executed in parallel should be divided into separate tasks. Processes that are never executed in parallel need not be divided into tasks; in C language, such processes can be implemented through functions. It is important to consider which processes should work in parallel when dividing tasks. The fact that all processes within a single task have the same priority will also serve as a guideline for task division.

  ➢ **Dividing Tasks for Priority-Based Processing.** As shown in the earlier description of scheduling, tasks having the same priority are switched in the FCFS manner and a necessary task might not be executed first. When a task that needs to be preempted has the same priority as the current task being executed, the target task is not executed until the current task enters a waiting state. In other words, the processing to be preempted should be created as a separate task and a high priority level should be assigned to it. When different priority levels need to be assigned to multiple processes, they should be divided into separate tasks. In general, the highest priority is assigned to urgent processing needed to handle system failures and processing that will affect real-time operation if it is not executed in high speed; a low priority is assigned to processing that only needs to be executed during an unoccupied period, such as system log maintenance processing. The lowest-priority tasks are called idle tasks because they can be executed while no other task is being executed. Loop processing that performs no operation may be created for idling in some cases.

6.4 ARCHITECTURE OF RTOS

- The architecture of an RTOS is dependent on the complexity of its deployment. Good RTOSs are scalable to meet different sets of requirements for different applications.

- For simple applications, an RTOS usually comprises only a kernel. For more complex embedded systems, an RTOS can be a combination of various modules, including the kernel, networking protocol stacks, and other components as illustrated in Fig. 6.5.

6.4.1 Kernel

- An operating system generally consists of two parts: kernel space (kernel mode) and user space (user mode).

- Kernel is the smallest and central component of an operating system. Its services include managing memory and devices and also to provide an interface for software applications to use the resources.

- Additional services such as managing protection of programs and multitasking may be included depending on architecture of operating system.

- There are three broad categories of kernel models available, namely

    (1) monolithic kernel,

    (2) microkernel, and

    (3) exokernel.

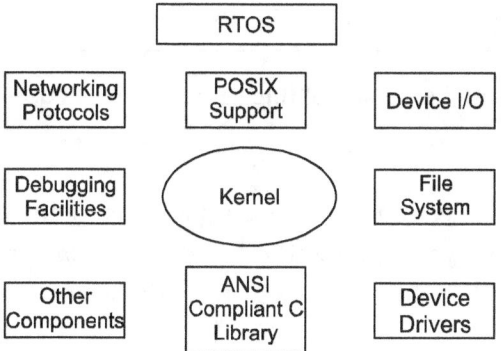

Fig. 6.5 : General architecture of RTOS

6.4.1.1 Monolithic Kernel

- It runs all basic system services (i.e. process and memory management, interrupt handling and I/O communication, file system, etc) in kernel space. As such, monolithic kernels provide rich and powerful abstractions of the underlying hardware.

- Amount of context switches and messaging involved are greatly reduced which makes it run faster than microkernel. Examples are Linux and Windows.

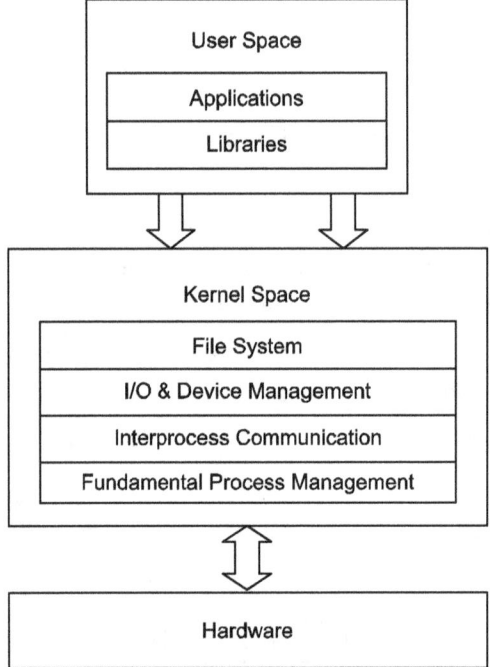

Fig. 6.6 : Monolithic kernel based RTOS

6.4.1.2 Microkernel

- It runs only basic process communication (messaging) and I/O control. The other system services (file system, networking, etc.) reside in user space in the form of daemons/servers. Thus, micro kernels provide a smaller set of simple hardware abstractions.

- It is more stable than monolithic as the kernel is unaffected even if the servers failed (i.e. File System). Examples are Amiga OS and QNX.

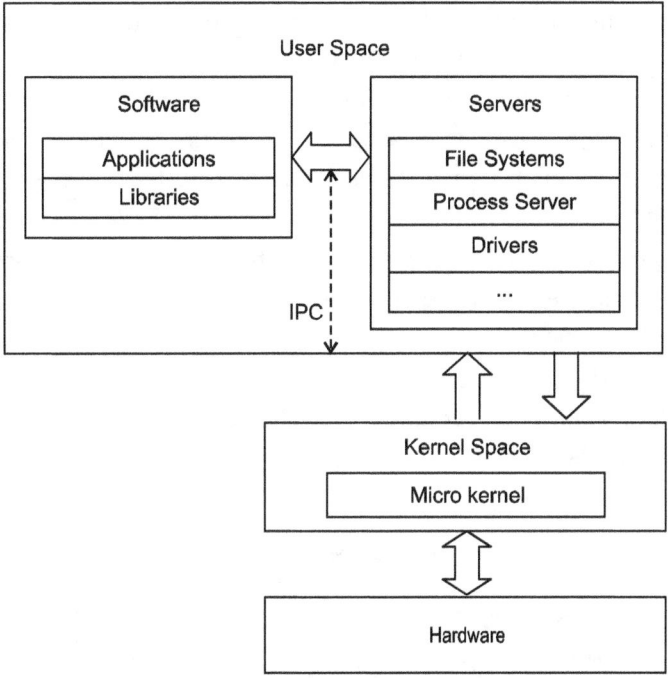

Fig. 6.7 : Microkernal based RTOS

6.4.1.3 Exokernel

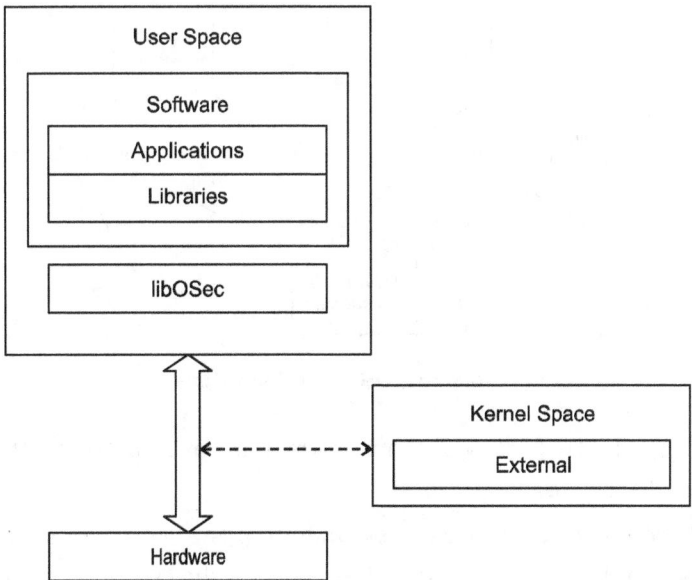

Fig. 6.8 : Exokernel based RTOS

- The concept is orthogonal to that of micro-vs. monolithic kernels by giving an application efficient control over hardware.

- It runs only services protecting the resources (i.e. tracking the ownership, guarding the usage, revoking access to resources, etc) by providing low-level interface for library operating systems (libOSes) and leaving the management to the application.

- An RTOS generally avoids implementing the kernel as a large monolithic program. The kernel is developed instead as a micro-kernel with added configurable functionalities.

- This implementation gives resulting benefit in increase system configurability, as each embedded application requires a specific set of system services with respect to its characteristics.

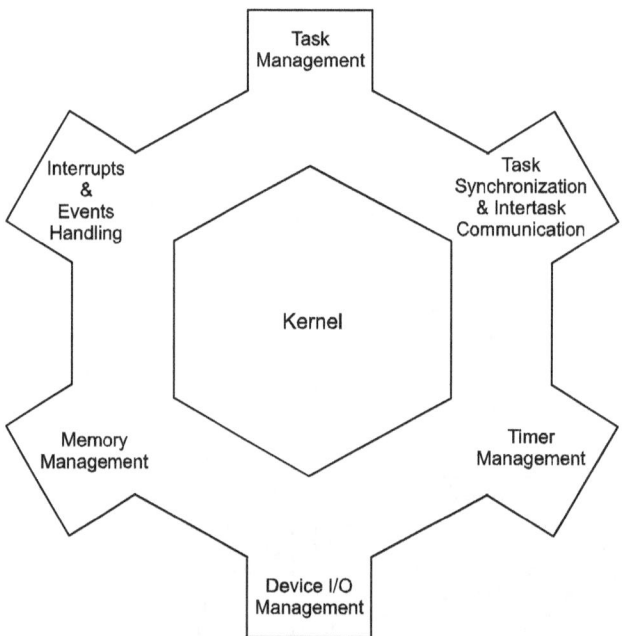

Fig. 6.9 : RTOS kernel services

- The kernel of an RTOS provides an abstraction layer between the application software and hardware.

- This abstraction layer comprises of six main types of common services provided by the kernel to the application software. Fig. 6.9 shows the six common services of an RTOS kernel.

6.5 TASK MANAGEMENT

- Task management allows programmers to design their software as a number of separate "chunks" of codes with each handling a distinct goal and deadline. This service encompasses mechanisms such as scheduler and dispatcher that create and maintain task objects.

6.5.1 Task Object

- To achieve concurrency in real-time application program, the application is decompose into small, schedulable, and sequential program units known as "Task".

- In real-time context, task is the basic unit of execution and is governed by three time-critical properties; release time, deadline and execution time. Release time refers to the point in time from which the task can be executed. Deadline is the point in time by which the task must complete. Execution time denotes the time the task takes to execute.

- A task object is defined by the following set of components:
  - Task control block (Task data structures residing in RAM and only accessible by RTOS)
  - Task Stack (Data defined in program residing in RAM and accessible by stack pointer)
  - Task Routine (Program code residing in ROM)

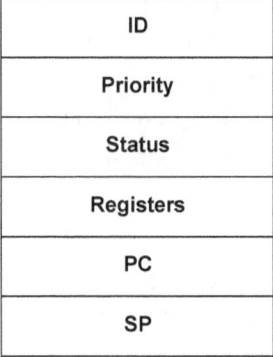

ID
Priority
Status
Registers
PC
SP

Fig. 6.10 : Task Control Block

- Each task may exist in any of the four states, including running, ready, or blocked and dormant as shown in Fig. 6.11.

- During the execution of an application program, individual tasks are continuously changing from one state to another. However, only one task is in the running mode (i.e. given CPU control) at any point of the execution.

- In the process where CPU control is change from one task to another, context of the to-be-suspended task will be saved while context of the to-be-executed task will be retrieved. This process of saving the context of a task being suspended and restoring the context of a task being resumed is called context switching.

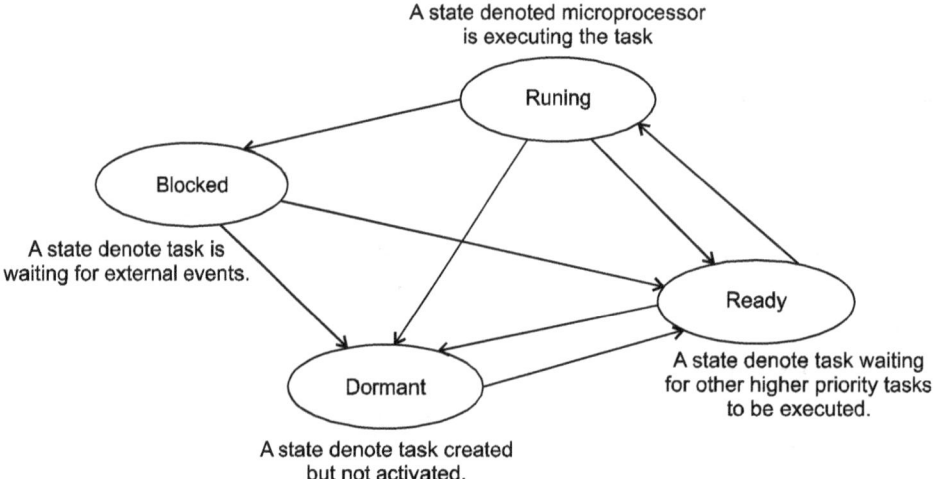

Fig. 6.11 : State transition of Task

6.5.1.1 Scheduler

- The scheduler keeps record of the state of each task and selects from among them that are ready to execute and allocates the CPU to one of them.

- A scheduler helps to maximize CPU utilization among different tasks in a multi-tasking program and to minimize waiting time.

- There are generally two types of schedulers :
  - ➢ non-preemptive and
  - ➢ priority-based preemptive.

- Non-preemptive scheduling or cooperative multitasking requires the tasks to cooperate with each other to explicitly give up control of the processor.

- When a task releases the control of the processor, the next most important task that is ready to run will be executed. A task that is newly assigned with a higher priority will only gain control of the processor when the current executing task voluntarily gives up the control.

- Fig. 6.12 gives an example of a non-preemptive scheduling.

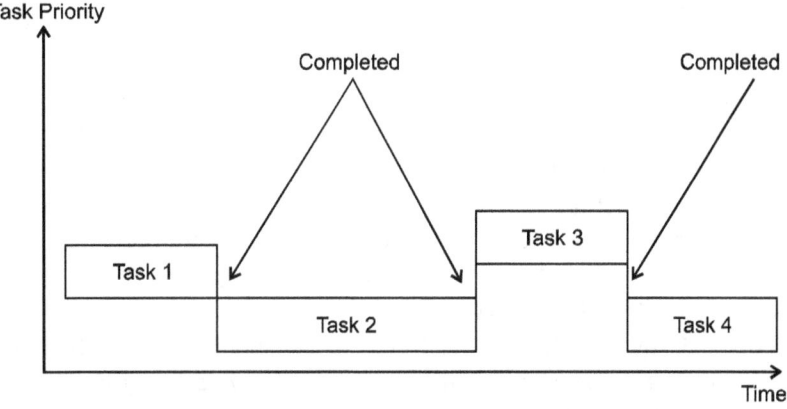

Fig. 6.12 : Non-preemptive task scheduling

- Priority-based preemptive scheduling requires control of the processor be given to the task of the highest priority at all time. In the event that makes a higher priority task ready to run, the current task is immediately suspended and the control of the processor is given to the higher priority task. Fig. 6.13 shows an example of a preemptive scheduling.

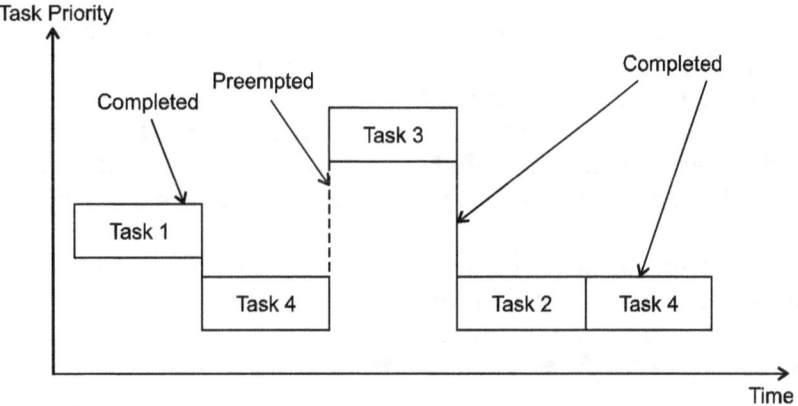

Fig. 6.13 : Preemptive task scheduling

6.5.1.2 Dispatcher

- The dispatcher gives control of the CPU to the task selected by the scheduler by performing context switching and changes the flow of execution. At any time an RTOS is running, the flow of execution passes through one of three areas: through the task program code, through an interrupt service routine, or through the kernel.

6.5.2 Memory Management

- An embedded RTOS usually strive to achieve small footprint by including only the functionality needed for the user's applications. There are two types of memory management in RTOSs. They are Stack and Heap managements.

- In a multi-tasking RTOS, each task needs to be allocated with an amount of memory for storing their contexts (i.e. volatile information such as registers contents, program counter, etc) for context switching. This allocation of memory is done using task-control block model. This set of memory is commonly known as kernel stack and the management process termed stack management.

- Upon the completion of a program initialization, physical memory of the MCU or MPU will usually be occupied with program code, program data and system stack. The remaining physical memory is called heap. This heap memory is typically used by the kernel for dynamic memory allocation of data space for tasks. The memory is divided into fixed size memory blocks, which can be requested by tasks. When a task finishes using a memory block it must return it to the pool. This process of managing the heap memory is known as heap management.

6.5.3 Timer Management

- In embedded systems, system and user tasks are often scheduled to perform after a specified duration. To provide such scheduling, there is a need for a periodical interrupt to keep track of time delays and timeout. Most RTOSs today offer both "relative timers" that work in units of ticks, and "absolute timers" that work with calendar date and time. For each kind of timer, RTOS provide a "task delay" service, and also a "task alert" service based on the signaling mechanism (for example, event flags). Another timer service provided is in meeting task deadline by cooperating with task schedulers to determine whether tasks have met or missed their real-time deadlines.

6.5.4 Interrupt and Event Handling

- An interrupt is a hardware mechanism used to inform the CPU that an asynchronous event has occurred. A fundamental challenge in RTOS design is supporting interrupts and thereby allowing asynchronous access to internal RTOS data structures. The interrupt and event handling mechanism of an RTOS provides the following functions :
  - ➢ Defining interrupt handler.
  - ➢ Creation and deletion of ISR.
  - ➢ Referencing the state of an ISR.
  - ➢ Enabling and disabling of an interrupt.

➢ Changing and referencing of an interrupt mask and help to ensure:

❖ Data integrity by restricting interrupts from occurring when modifying a data structure,

❖ Minimum interrupts latencies due to disabling of interrupts when RTOS is performing critical operations,

❖ Fastest possible interrupt responses that marked the preemptive performance of an RTOS,

❖ Shortest possible interrupt completion time with minimum overheads.

6.5.5 Device I/O Management

• An RTOS kernel is often equipped with a device I/O management service to provide a uniform framework (application programmer's interface-"API") and supervision facility for an embedded system to organize and access large numbers of diverse hardware device drivers. However, most device driver APIs and supervisors are "standard" only within a specific RTOS.

6.6 SELECTION OF RTOS

• RTOS tends to be a selection for many embedded projects. But is an RTOS always necessary? The answer lies on careful analysis in understanding what an application needs to deliver to determine whether implementing RTOS is a requirement or an extravagance.

• Most programmers are not familiar with RTOS constraints and requirements. An RTOS is usually chosen based on its performance or one's comfort and familiarity with the product. However, such a selection criteria is insufficient. To make matter worse, there is a wide variety of RTOS ranging from commercial RTOS, open-source RTOS to internally developed RTOS to choose from. Therefore, it is incumbent upon the programmers to exercise extra caution in the selection process.

• The selection criteria of RTOS can be broadly classified into two main areas; technical features of RTOS and commercial aspect of the implementation.

6.6.1 Technical Considerations

6.6.1.1 Scalability

• Size or memory footprint is an important consideration. Most RTOS are scalable in which only the code required is included in the final memory footprint. Looking for granular scalability in an RTOS is a worthwhile endeavor, as it minimizes memory usage.

6.6.1.2 Portability

- Often, a current application may outgrow the hardware it was originally designed for as the requirements of the product increases. An RTOS with such a capability can therefore be ported between processor architectures and between specific target systems.

6.6.1.3 Run-Time Facilities

- Run-time facilities refer to the services of the kernel (i.e. intertask communication, task synchronization, interrupts and events handling, etc). Different application systems have different sets of requirements. Comparison of RTOSs is frequently between the kernel-level facilities they provided.

6.6.1.4 Run-Time Performance

- Run-time performance of an RTOS is generally governed by the interrupt latency, context switching time and few other metric of kernel performance. This consideration is useful if the performance assessment of the application on a given RTOS is to prototype its performance-critical aspects on standard hardware.

6.6.1.5 Development Tools

- A sufficient set of development tools including debugger; compiler and performance profiler might help in shortening the development and debugging time, and improve the reliability of the coding. Commercial RTOSs usually have a complete set of tools for analyzing and optimizing the RTOSs' behavior whereas Open-Source RTOSs will not have.

6.7 COMMERCIAL CONSIDERATIONS

6.7.1 Costs

- Costs are a major consideration in selection of RTOS. There are currently more than 80 RTOS vendors.
- Some of the RTOS packages are complete operating systems including not only the real-time kernel but also an input/output manager, windowing systems, a file system, networking, language interface libraries, debuggers, and cross platform compilers. And the cost of an RTOS ranges from US$70 to over US$30,000.
- The RTOS vendor may also require royalties on a per-target-system basis, which may varies between USS5 to more than US$250 per unit. In addition, there will be maintenance required and that can easily cost between US$100 to US$5,000 per year.

6.7.2 License

- An RTOS vendor usually has a few license models for customers to choose from.

- A perpetual license enables customers to purchase the development set and pay an annual maintenance fee, which entitles he/her to upgrades and bug fixes.

- An alternative model, known as subscription model, allows customers to "rent" the development set whilst paying an annual renewal fee can escalate after many years.

6.7.3 Supplier Stability/Longevity

- Development with RTOS is not a problem free process. Reliable and consistent support from supplier is a critical factor in ensuring the prompt completion of a project. Supplier longevity thus helps to determine the availability of support.

6.8 SCHEDULING

- The task management module of RTOS is responsible for the scheduling of the multiple tasks. The scheduler is responsible for time sharing of CPU among tasks and keeps record of the state of each task and selects a task which is ready to execute by allocating the processor and resources to one of them.

- A scheduler is used to maximize processor utilization among different tasks in a multi-tasking and also minimize waiting time.

- Basically, there are two types of scheduler i.e.
  - ➤ Non-preemptive and
  - ➤ Priority based preemptive.

6.8.1 Non-Preemptive Scheduling

- In non-preemptive scheduling which is also called cooperative multitasking, the tasks in the system have to cooperate with each other to explicitly allocate control of the processor.

- When a task releases the control of the processor, the next scheduled task which is ready to run will be executed by taking the control of processor and resources needed.

- A task which is newly assigned a higher priority only gains control of the processor when the current executing task voluntarily gives the control processor and resources needed.

- Fig. 6.14 shows a non-preemptive scheduling of the task

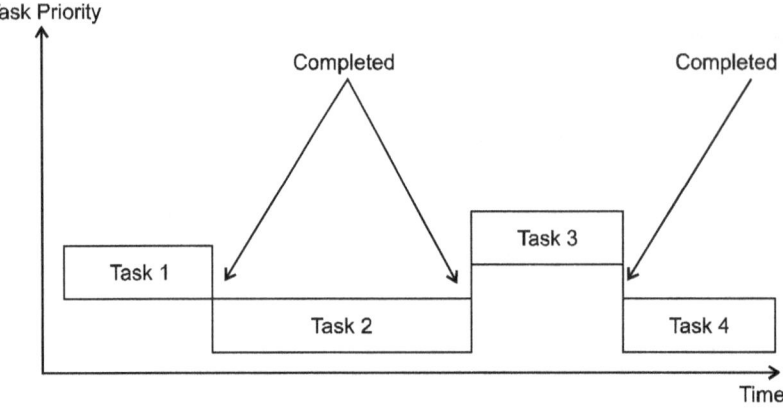

Fig. 6.14 : Non-preemptive scheduling

6.8.2 Priority Based Scheduling

*   In priority-based preemptive scheduling, the control of the processor and resources is given to the task of the highest priority at all time.

*   When a higher priority task ready to run, the current executing task is immediately suspended and the control of the processor and resources needed for execution is given to the higher priority task.

*   Fig. 6.15 shows a preemptive scheduling among tasks.

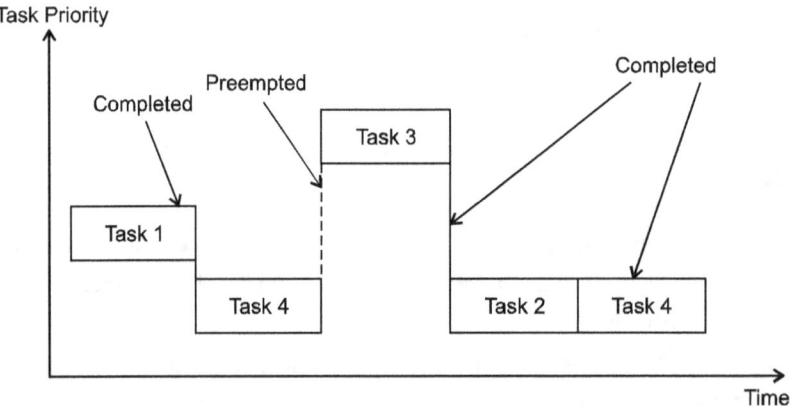

Fig. 6.15 : Preemptive scheduling

*   The dispatcher is module in task management which gives control of the CPU and resource needed to the task selected by the scheduler for the execution after performing context switching and changes the flow of execution.

- When RTOS is running, the flow of execution can be change by any one of three entities, i.e. through the task program code or through an interrupt service routine or through the kernel.
- While scheduling a task in real-time system, the following goals should be taken into consideration :
  1. Achieving the timing constraints of the system.
  2. Avoiding simultaneous access of shared resources and I/O devices.
  3. Achieving a high degree of utilization of system resources by satisfying the timing constraints of the system.
  4. Minimizing the timing of context switches introduced by pre-emption.
  5. Minimizing the communication time in real-time distributed systems.

6.8.3 Co-operative Scheduling

- In cooperative scheduling, all tasks are of equal priorities so every task is as important task i.e. non-preemptive.
- When the scheduler schedules a task for execution, then task gains the control of the processor and rims until it completes or reaches lot scheduling.
- During execution, a task cannot be block or wait for any event or resource needed or pause or allow another task to gain processor control.
- The RTOS using the cooperative scheduling s normally small and fast but must take care of one task doesn't starve one or more another tasks, hence cooperative scheduling cannot be used in hard real time requirement as it is difficult to meet deadlines.
- The cooperative scheduling is used in most of the soft real-time applications.

6.8.4 Round Robin Scheduling

- In Round Robin scheduling, the processor time is divided into equal parts called time slice and provides it to all the requesting tasks until the task has completed.
- In round robin scheduling, tasks are dispatched to FIFO pool consists of ready to run tasks waiting for the processor and all tasks are independent and compete for resources.
- If a task does not complete before its processor time slice expires, the processor is preempted and given to the next waiting task in the FIFO pool.
- The preempted task is then placed at the back of the ready list in FIFO pool.

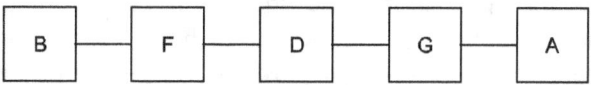

List of runnable tasks

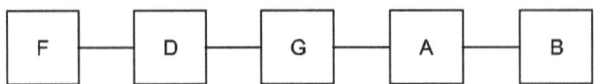

List of runnable tasks after B uses its quantum

Fig. 6.16 : Round robin scheduling

- Round Robin is used basically in timesharing environments where the system needs to give guaranteed reasonable response times for interactive users.
- The preemption overhead should be kept low by using the efficient context switching mechanisms and by providing sufficient memory for the tasks to reside in main storage.
- The issue with round robin is only the length of the time slice.
- Context switching needs some amount of tinu for switching from one task to another.
- The round robin scheduling is used mostly in t soil real-time applications.

6.8.5 Earliest Deadline First (EDF) Scheduling

- Earliest Deadline First (EDF) is a dynamic priority scheduling algorithm which places tasks in a priority queue.
- Whenever a current task finishes its execution, the queue is searched for the task which is closest to its deadline.
- If found then this task is the next to be scheduled for execution.
- EDF is an optimal scheduling algorithm on preemptive uni-processor systems.
- EDF has a utilization bound of 100% with scheduling periodic task which have deadlines equal to their periods.
- EDF can guarantee all deadlines are met if the total processor utilization is not more than 100% in the system at higher loading.
- But when the system is overloaded, the set of tasks which miss the deadlines are largely unpredictable.
- The algorithm is difficult to implement in hardware due to representing deadlines in different ranges and hence EDF is not commonly used in industrial real-time systems.

6.8.6 Rate-Monotonic or Fixed-Priority Preemptive Scheduling

- RM or Fixed-priority pre-emptive scheduling is commonly used in real-time systems in which the scheduler checks at any given time, the processor executes the highest priority task with shorter period of all those tasks that are currently ready to execute.

- Tasks with higher request rates i.e. shorter periods will have the higher priority.
- The pre-emptive scheduler has a clock interrupt task which provides with options to switch after the task has had a given the time slice.
- Fixed-priority pre-emptive scheduling has the advantage of making sure that no task acquires the processor for any time longer than the time slice.
- But this scheduling scheme also has a disadvantage as priority of execution is given to higher priority tasks where the lower priority tasks has to wait for indefinite amount of time.
- EM or Pre-emptive scheduling is different than the cooperative scheduling, in which a task runs continuously from start to end without preempting by other tasks.
- In this scheduling, deadlines should be equal to periods arid fixed priorities lead to starvation and deadlocks.

6.8.7 Scheduling Algorithms

- Each task in a real-time system has some timing properties that should be considered while scheduling tasks on a real-time system.
- The timing properties of a given task are :
    1. **Release time :** It defines the time at which the task is ready for execution.
    2. **Deadline** It defines the time by which execution of the task should be completed strictly, after the task is released.
    3. **Minimum delay:** It defines the minimum time elapse between the execution of the task is started and the task is released.
    4. **Maximum delay :** It defines the maximum allowed time that elapse between the execution of the task is started and the task is released.
    5. **Worst case execution time** It defines the maximum time taken to complete the task, after the task is released and also referred as the worst case response time.
    6. **Run time** It defines the time taken to complete the task without interruption, after the task is released.
    7. **Priority :** Relative emergency of the task.
- Now we will see the different scheduling algorithms one by one.
    1. Co-operative scheduling.
    2. Round Robin scheduling.
    3. Earliest Deadline First (EOF) scheduling.
    4. Rate or Fixed-priority preemptive scheduling.

6.9 MULTITASKING

- In RTOS, multitasking is technique in which multiple tasks share common processing resources such as a processor.

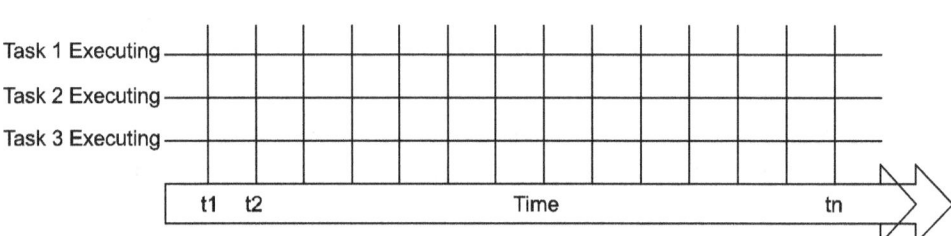

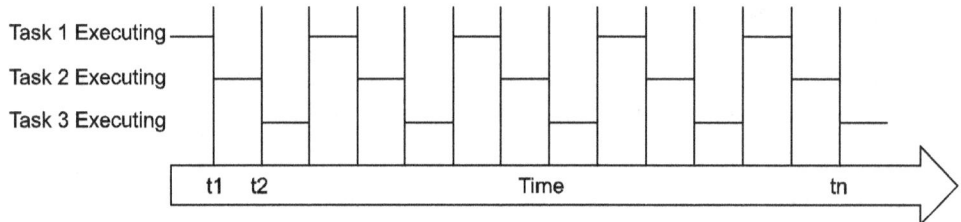

Fig. 6.17 : Multitasking

- Multitasking means running number of tasks simultaneously by the processor as shown in Fig. 6.19.In the single processor system, only one task can be executed at any point in time.

- Multitasking decides which task should be miming at any given time and when another task waiting task gets a turn.

- The assigning a processor from one task to another one is called a context switch.

- When context switches occur frequently then parallelism is achieved.

- On the system with more than one processor also called multiprocessor machines, multitasking is possible for more tasks to be run in parallel.

- A multitasking environment allows applications to be constructed as a set of independent tasks, each with a separate thread of execution and its own set of system resources.

- The inter-task communication facilities allow these tasks to synchronize and coordinate their activity.

- Multitasking provides the fundamental mechanism for an application to control and react to multiple, discrete real-world events and is therefore essential for many real-time applications.

- Multitasking creates the appearance of many threads of execution running concurrently when, in fact, the kernel interleaves their execution on the basis of a scheduling algorithm.

- This also leads to efficient utilization of the CPU time and is essential for many embedded applications where processors are limited in computing speed due to cost, power, silicon area and other constraints.

- In a multi-tasking operating system it is assumed that the various tasks are to cooperate to serve the requirements of the overall system. Co-operation will require that the tasks communicate with each other and share common data in an orderly and disciplined manner, without creating undue contention and deadlocks.

- The way in which tasks communicate and share data is to be regulated such that communication or shared data access error is prevented and data, which is private to a task, is protected. Further, tasks may be dynamically created and terminated by other tasks, as and when needed. To realize such a system, the following major functions are to be carried out.

  1. Process management :

  ➢ Interrupt handling.

  ➢ Task scheduling and dispatch.

  ➢ Create/delete, suspend/resume task.

  ➢ Manage scheduling information – priority, scheduling policy, etc.

  2. Interprocess communication and synchronization :

  ➢ Code, data and device sharing.

  ➢ Synchronization, coordination and data exchange mechanisms.

  ➢ Deadlock and Livelock detection.

  3. Memory management :

  ➢ Dynamic memory allocation.

  ➢ Memory locking.

  ➢ Services for file creation, deletion, reposition and protection.

  4. Input/Output management :

  ➢ Handles request and release functions and read, write functions for a variety of peripherals.

6.10 REQUIREMENTS OF RTOS

- The following are important requirements that an OS must meet to be considered an RTOS in the contemporary sense.

  ➢ The operating system must be multithreaded and preemptive. For example, handle multiple threads and be able to preempt tasks, if necessary.

  ➢ The OS must support priority of tasks and threads.

  ➢ A system of priority inheritance must exist. Priority inheritance is a mechanism to ensure that lower priority tasks cannot obstruct the execution of higher priority tasks.

  ➢ The OS must support various types of thread/task synchronization mechanisms.

  ➢ For predictable response :

    1. The time for every system function call to execute should be predictable and independent of the number of objects in the system.

    2. Non preemptable portions of kernel functions necessary for interprocess synchronization and communication are highly optimized, short and deterministic Non-preemptable portions of the interrupt handler routines are kept small and deterministic.

    3. Interrupt handlers are scheduled and executed at appropriate priority.

    4. The maximum time during which interrupts are masked by the OS and by device drivers must be known.

    5. The maximum time that device drivers use to process an interrupt, and specific IRQ information relating to those device drivers, must be known.

    6. The interrupt latency (the time from interrupt to task run) must be predictable and compatible with application requirements

  ➢ For fast response :

    1. Run-time overhead is decreased by reducing the unnecessary context switch.

    2. Important timings such as context switch time, interrupt latency, semaphore get/release latency must be minimum

6.11 SHARED DATA PROBLEM IN RTOS

- In RTOS some data is common to different tasks lot example time which is updated continuously by a task, 1 input data which is received by one task and further processed and analyzed by another task, memory buffer data which is stored by one task which may further read or deleted, processed and analyzed by another process.

- Suppose at an instant when the value of variable changes during the operations on it, only a part of the operation is completed and another part remains incomplete due to interrupt occurs.

- Hence whenever another task sharing the same partly operated data, then shared data problem arises.

- Suppose there is another task sharing the same variable the value of the variable may differ from the one expected if the earlier operation had been completed which had changed original value.

- Sharing data problem can be solved by using modifier variable or re-entrant function or putting shared variable in circular queue or disabling interrupt during the execution of critical section or using semaphore.

6.12 TASK SYNCHRONIZATION AND INTERTASK COMMUNICATION

- Task synchronization and intertask communications serves to enable information to be transmitted safely from one task to another. The service also makes it possible for tasks to coordinate and cooperate with one another.

6.12.1 Task Synchronization

- Synchronization is essential for tasks to share mutually exclusive resources (devices, buffers, etc) and/or allow multiple concurrent tasks to be executed (for example, Task A needs a result from task B, so task A can only run till task B produces it).

- Task synchronization is achieved using two types of mechanisms :
  1. Event objects, and
  2. Semaphores.

6.12.2 Event Objects

- Event objects are used when task synchronization is required without resource sharing. They allow one or more tasks to keep waiting for a specified event to occur. An event object can exist in either of two states: triggered and non-triggered.

- An event object in a triggered state indicates that a waiting task may resume. In contrast, if the event object is in a non-triggered state, a waiting task will need to stay suspended.

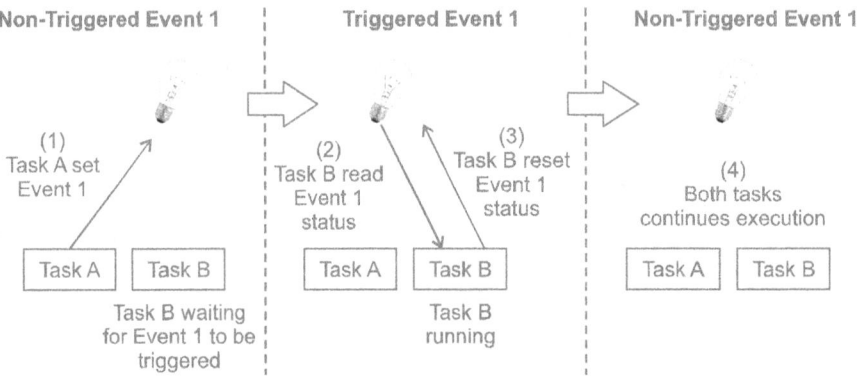

Fig. 6.18 : Working principle of event object

- Sharing of resource among tasks can be a problem when the coordination is not well done. For instance, if task A begins reading a set of data currently being updated by task B, task A might received corrupted data – mixture of new and existing data. To resolve this problem, RTOS kernels provide a semaphore object and associated semaphore services to ensure the integrity of data.

6.12.3 Semaphore

- A semaphore has an associated resource count and a wait queue. The resource count indicates availability of resource. RTOS kernels provide a semaphore to ensure the integrity of data during sharing the common data.

- Resource count and a wait queue is associated with semaphore where the resource çount shows availability of resource and the wait queue manages the tasks waiting for resources from the semaphore. The wait queue manages the tasks waiting for resources from the semaphore.

- A semaphore functions like a key or a manager that defines whether a task has the access to the resource.

- A task gets an access to the resource when it acquires the semaphore. The resource count of a semaphore determines the number of times the semaphore can be acquired.

- When a task acquires the semaphore, its count decrements by one. Likewise, its count increments by one, when a task releases the semaphore.

- The number of times the semaphore can be acquired by the task is determined by the resource count of a semaphore.

- The resource count is decremented by one, when a task acquires the semaphore and its resource count is incremented by one when a task releases the semaphore.

- Generally, there are three types of semaphore :

  ➤ Binary Semaphores (semaphore value of either 0 or 1 to indicate unavailability and availability respectively).

  ➤ Counting Semaphores (semaphore value of 0 or greater indicating it can be acquired/released multiple times).

  ➤ Mutually Exclusion Semaphores (semaphore value of 0 or 1 but lock count can be 0 or greater for recursive locking).

6.12.3.1 Binary Semaphore

- Binary semaphore uses value 0 or 1 to indicate unavailability and availability of semaphore respectively.

- Suppose task A attempts to acquire semaphore key to gain the access to shared resource.

- If semaphore count I indicates that it is available, task A acquires the shared resource and change semaphore count to 0 to indicate shared resource is not available for another task.

- Suppose at the same time, task B wants to acquire the shared resources, but task B cannot acquire the access to shared resource as semaphore count is C), i.e. semaphore is acquired by task A.

- When task A release a semaphore, the semaphore count is set to 1 and now task B attempts to acquire the shared resource as semaphore count is 1 as shown in Fig. 6.19.

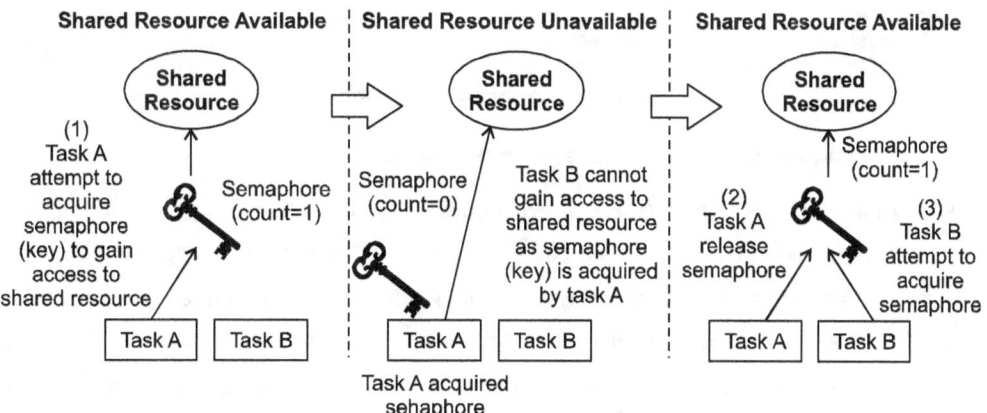

Fig. 6.19 : Binary semaphore

6.12.3.2 Count Semaphore

- In this semaphore, value 0 or greater indicates that the semaphore can be acquired or released many times.

- The blocking or running of the code of task is controlled by the value of semaphore.

- The counting semaphore is decremented each time when it is acquired by the task and is incremented when released by a task as shown in Fig. 6.20.

- Suppose task A already acquired the resource which gives semaphore count to 1 and task B attempts to acquire the shared resource.

- Now, task B acquires the shared resource as task A has been already acquired and decrement semaphore count by 1.

- When task A released the shared resource and task B is still acquired, then semaphore count is incremented by 1.

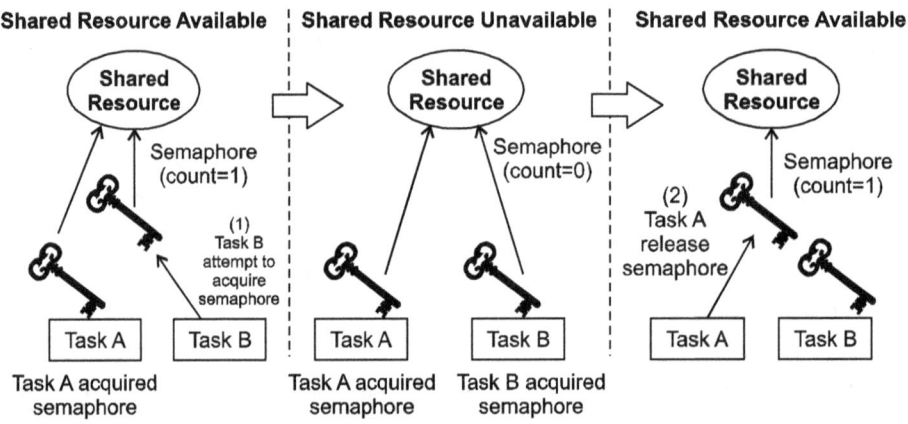

Fig. 6.20 : Counting semaphore

6.12.3.3 Mutually Exclusion (Mutex) Semaphore

- Semaphore uses value 0 or 1 to indicate unavailability and availability of semaphore respectively but lock count may be 0 or greater for recursive locking.

- In this method, a mutex key is used to lock the shared resource, lilt is acquired by the task, so that any other task cannot acquire until it is released.

- Suppose task A attempts to acquire shared resource if semaphore count is 1 and mutex lock count is 0.

- After acquiring the shared resource, semaphore count becomes U to indicate it has been already acquired by task A and mutex lock count becomes 1.

- Now suppose another task B wants to acquire shared resource, but task B cannot gain the access of shared resource as it is locked by task A.

- If task A locked shared resource again second time to gain recursive access, then mutex count becomes 2.

- So, task B cannot gain access to shared resources as it is locked again by task A as shown in Fig. 6.21.

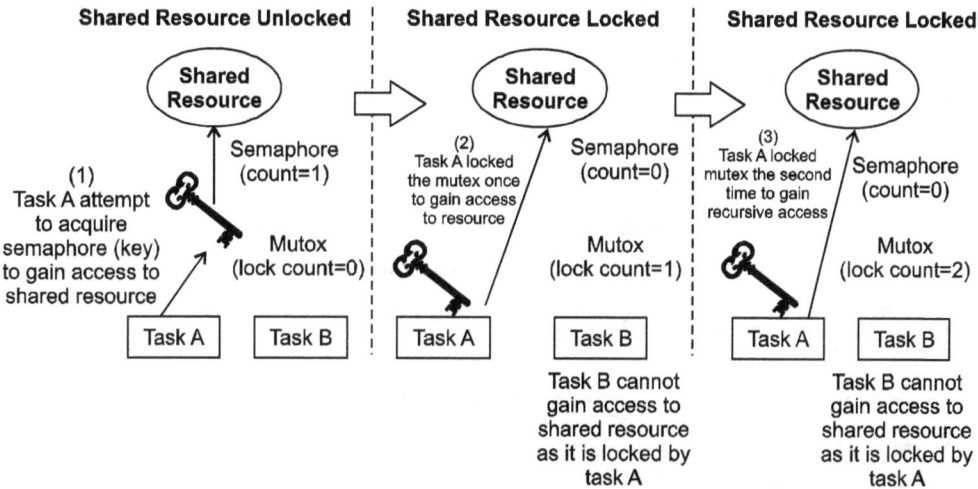

Fig. 6.21 : Mutual Exclusion (Mutex) Semaphore

6.13 DEADLOCK

- A deadlock is a situation in which two or more tasks or processes waiting for each other to release a resource, or more than two processes are waiting for resources in a circular chain and neither request can be satisfied.

- Deadlock is a common problem in multiprocessing and multitasking where numbers of tasks or processes share a specific type of mutually exclusive resource.

- Now a day, the computers or embedded systems designed for the time-sharing or real time are equipped with a hardware lock which provides exclusive access to processes, forcing serialized access.

- There is no general solution to avoid deadlocks.

- The example of traffic on square is shown in Fig. 6.22 which leads to deadlock.

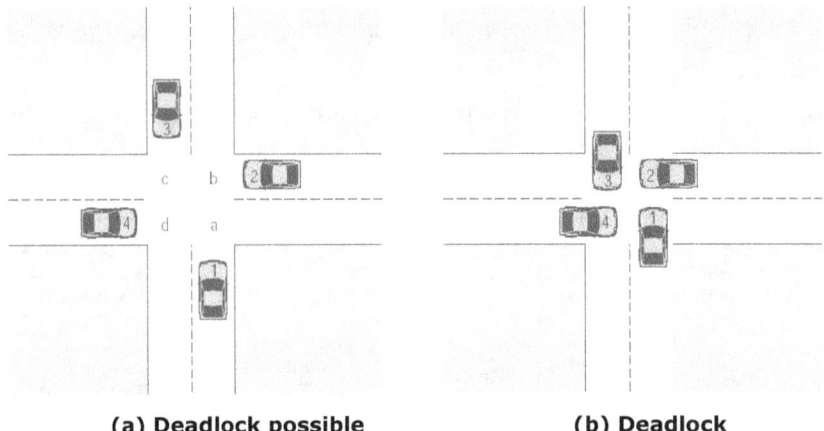

(a) Deadlock possible   **(b) Deadlock**

Fig. 6.22 : Deadlock example

6.13.1 Necessary Conditions

- There are four necessary conditions for a deadlock to occur:

  1. **Mutual exclusion :** A resource that cannot be used by more than one process at a time.

  2. **Hold and wait :** A process already holding resource may request new resource which is held by other processes.

  3. **No preemption :** There is only voluntary release of a resource by the process, no one can force a process to release a resource and resources can be released only by the explicit action of the process.

  4. **Circular wait :** Two or more processes form a circular chain where each process waits for a resource that the next process in the chain holds such as Process A waits for Process B waits for Process C waits for Process A.

6.13.2 Deadlock Prevention

- Deadlock can be prevented by not allowing one of the four conditions to occur as given below:

  1. **Mutual exclusion :** Removing the mutual exclusion condition i.e. process should not have exclusive access to a resource.

  2. **Hold and wait :** The "hold and wait" conditions must be removed i.e. acquire all resources before execution need before starting up and A particular resource can only be requested when no others are being held.

3. **No preemption** : Release any resource which is already being held if the process can't acquire an additional resource and allow preemption if a needed resource is held by another process, which is also waiting on some resource.

4. **Circular wait :**The circular wait condition can be prevented by disabling interrupts during critical section and requesting the number resources in ascending order.

6.13.3 Deadlock Avoidance

- Deadlock can be avoided, if certain information about processes is available in advance of resource allocation.

  ➢ For every resource request, the system is granting the request of resource means that the system is entering in an unsafe state that could result in deadlock.

  ➢ The system then only grants requests that leads to safe states if a sequence of processes exist in such way that there are enough resources for the first process to finish, and as each finishes and releases its resources there are enough for the next process to finish.

  ➢ To avoid the deadlock, the system should be able to determine either the next state is safe or unsafe and must know in advance at any time the number and type of all resources in existence, available, and requested.

  ➢ Banker's algorithm is used for deadlock avoidance which requires resource usage limit to be known in advance.

6.13.4 Deadlock Detection

- Instead of avoidance or prevention, deadlock detection, and process restart are used which tracks resource allocation and process states, and rolls back and restarts one or more of the processes in order to remove the deadlock.

- Detecting a deadlock which is already occurred is easily possible because the resources that each process has locked and/or currently requested are known to the resource scheduler.

- But detecting the deadlock before it occurs is man difficult and un-decidable, because the halting problem can be treated as a deadlock.

Approach	Resource Allocation Policy	Different schemes	Major advantages	Major disadvantages
Prevention	Conservative undercommits resources	Requesting all resources at once	• Works well for processes that perform a single burst of activity • No preemption necessary	• Inefficient • Delays process initiation • Future resource requirements must be known by processes
		Preemption	• Convenient when applied to resources whose state can be saved and restored easily	• Preempts more often than necessary
		Resource ordering	• Feasible to enforce via compile-time checks • Needs no run time computation since problem is solved in system design	• Disallows incremental resource requests
Avoidance	Midway between that of detection and prevention	Manipulate to find at least one safe path	• No preemption necessary	• Future resource requirements must be known by OS • Processes can be blocked for long periods
Detection	Very liberal; requested resources are granted where possible	Invoke periodically to test for deadlock	• Never delays process initiation • Facilitates online handling	• Inherent preemption losses

- However, deadlock detection may be decidable in specific environments, using specific ways of locking resources and using specific ways for resource allocation.

6.14 STARVATION, CAUSES AND REMEDIES

- Starvation is the name given to the indefinite postponement of a process because it requires some resource before it can run, but the resource, though available for allocation, is never allocated to this process.

- It is sometimes called livelock, though sometimes that name might be reserved for cases where the waiting process is doing something, but nothing useful, as in a spin lock.

- However it happens, starvation is self-evidently a bad thing; more formally, it's bad because we don't want a non-functional system.

- If starvation is possible in a system, then a process which enters the system can be held up for an arbitrary length of time.

- To avoid starvation, it is often said that we want the system's resources to be shared "fairly". This is an appealing suggestion, but in practice it isn't much use because it doesn't define what we mean by "fairly", so it is really more of a description of the problem than a contribution to its solution.

- It is more constructive to investigate the paths by which a system can reach a livelocked state, and try to control them.

6.14.1 Causes of Starvation

- Starvation is caused by failure to allocate some resource to a process, so to find the causes we must inspect the policies which the system uses in handling resources. Here are some possibilities.

  ➢ **Processes hand on resources to other processes without control**. If decisions about resource allocation are taken locally without considering the overall resource requirements of the system, anomalies can occur. If processes queue for a resource, and the resource is always handed on to the next process in the queue, it is essential that every process awaiting the resource must be placed in the queue.

  ➢ **Processes' priorities are strictly enforced**. If a process of worse priority requires a resource in competition with a constant stream of processes of better priority, it might wait forever.

  ➢ **"Random" selection is used**. If processes awaiting service are not queued, but an arbitrary process is selected whenever the resource becomes available, it is possible for some processes to wait for a very long time. In some circumstances, that doesn't matter too much – for example, if it is known that the average demand for resources is far less than the resource pool available, the congestion is almost certain to last for very short periods. The trouble with this strategy isn't usually that processes wait forever (unless your "random" number generator isn't), but that you just can't tell what will happen. A good example is the Ethernet communications technique, where processors use a common communications medium without overall synchronization, and resolve attempts to transmit simultaneously by delaying for an arbitrary interval and then trying again. Once the medium becomes moderately heavily used, quite long delays can be experienced.

➤ **Not enough resources**. This is commonly the real problem, so far as physical resources are concerned, though as its solution costs money it might be a hard one to solve. Provided that the supply of resource exceeds demand over a reasonable period of time, it should be possible to satisfy the demand, and strategies can be chosen to provide service to all processes which need it. On the other hand, if demand exceeds supply, no amount of ingenious trickery can serve everything, and under these conditions starvation can often occur.

• Starvation can happen at any organized scheduling level, though it is more likely in the automatic allocation processes than in the higher-level manual parts. (We assume that there is more intelligence and flexibility at the manual level; bureaucracy can defeat this assumption.)

6.14.2　Remedies for Starvation

• Cures for starvation are in general based on means of ensuring that the conditions for starvation can't happen. Here is a selection.

➤ **There must be an independent manager for each resource**, which must manage all allocations of its resource; this will guarantee that processes don't just pass resources around between themselves without making them available for general allocation.

➤ **Strict priorities should not be enforced**. A poor priority should be regarded as a weak claim, but not an over-rid able claim. There are at least two ways to achieve this end : - Improve the priority of a waiting process with time; then even a process with poor priority which has waited for a long time will eventually be able to compete successfully with a newly-arrived process of much better basic priority. Of course, the improved priority doesn't last – after allocation, the process's priorities revert to their original levels. - Implement priorities by rationing; regard the priorities not as indications of absolute importance, but as measures of the proportion of the resources which can be consumed.

➤ **Avoid random selections, uncontrolled competition**, etc. It is very unusual for random resource allocation techniques to have any intrinsic merit. After all, if a random technique will work, it doesn't matter which process receives the resource, so you might as well queue them and give the resource to the process at the head of the queue. If anything, the queue overhead is less, and you win by the closer approximation to a functional system.

➤ **Provide more resources**. This is the only satisfactory solution to continued congestion when demand approaches supply. If the supply and demand are closely balanced, even small fluctuations of demand can cause queues to form which can take a very long time to eliminate. Of course, if you have sufficient resource to reduce queuing to an acceptable minimum with any normal demand, you will have periods when the resource is standing idle.

6.15 INTERTASK COMMUNICATION

- Intertask communication is required for sharing of data among tasks by sharing a memory space, transfer of data from one task to another task but should be accessible by only one task at a time, i.e. when one task is writing or reading data then other task should not read or write it until the first task has finished reading or writing.
- Some of the mechanisms available for executing intertask communications are :
  1. Message queue.
  2. Pipes.
  3. Remote Procedure Call (RPC).

6.15.1 A Message Queue

- In inter-process communication, a message queue is an object used by the task to send or receive messages stored in a shared memory.
- Using services provided by the kernel, the Tasks and ISBs send or receive messages to the queue.
- A task reading a message from an empty queue is blocked either for some duration or till a message is received.
- The sending and receiving of messages to and from the queue may be in following way :
  1. First In First Out (FIFO).
  2. Last In First Out (LIF'O).
  3. Priority (PRI) Sequence.
- Usually a message queue contains the information such as Queue Control Block (QCB), name, unique 10, memory buffers, queue length, maximum message length and one or more task waiting lists.
- A message queue with a length of 1 is known as a mailbox.

6.15.2 Pipes

- A pipe is an object which provides communication path used for unstructured data exchange among different tasks.
- A pipe is a unidirectional data exchange facility which can be opened, closed, written to and read from.

- For reading and writing, there are two descriptors respectively at each end of the pipe.
- Data is written into the pipe as an unstructured byte stream through one descriptor and data is read from the pipe in the FIFO order from another descri11or.
- A pipe does not store multiple messages like message queue, but it stores stream of bytes and data flow from a pipe cannot be prioritized.

6.15.3 Remote Procedure Call (RPC)

- Remote Procedure Call (RPC) permits distributed computing environment and used for connecting two remotely placed functions or procedure by using a protocol for connecting the processes.
- The IPC permits a function or procedure to run at another address space of shared network or other remote computer.
- The client can make the call to the function or procedure which may be local or remote and the server response may be either remote or local in the call.
- Both systems should operate in the peer-to-peer communication network mode and each system in peer-to-peer communication network mode can make an RPc.
- In this way, an RPC allows remote invocation of the processes in the distributed systems.

6.16 DIFFERENCE BETWEEN GENERAL PURPOSE OS AND RTOS

- The whole purpose of this article is to outline the basic differences between a GPOS (General Purpose Operating System) or a Normal OS as many people call it and an RTOS (Real Time Operating System).

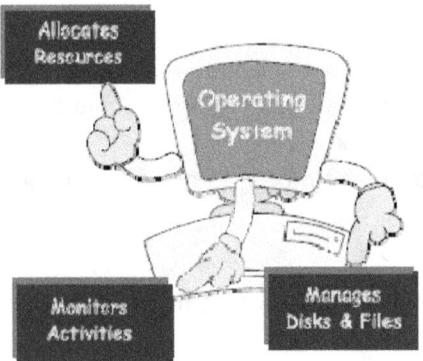

Fig. 6.23 : Feature of Operating System

- The basic difference of using a GPOS or an RTOS lies in the nature of the system – i.e. whether the system is *"time critical"* or not! A system can be of a single purpose or multiple purpose. Example of a "time critical system" is Automated Teller Machines (ATM). Here an ATM card user is supposed to get his money from the teller machine within 4 or 5 seconds from the moment he press the confirmation button. The card user will not wait 5 minutes at the ATM after he pressed the confirm button. So, an ATM is a time critical system; whereas a Personal Computer (PC) is not a time critical system. The purpose of a PC is multiple. A user can run many applications at the same time. After pressing the SAVE button of a finished document, there is no particular time limit that the doc should be saved within 5 seconds. It may take several minutes (in some cases) depending upon the number of tasks and processes running in parallel.

- A **GPOS** is used for systems/applications that are not time critical. **Example :** Windows, Linux, Unix etc.

- An **RTOS** is used for time critical systems. **Example:** VxWorks, uCos etc.

Task scheduling :

- In the case of a GPOS, task scheduling is not based on "priority" always! GPOS is programmed to handle scheduling in such a way that it manages to achieve high throughput. Here throughput means – the total number of processes that complete their execution per unit time. In such a case, sometimes execution of a high priority process will get delayed in order to serve 5 or 6 low priority tasks.

- High throughput is achieved by serving 5 low priority tasks than by serving a single high priority one; whereas in an RTOS – scheduling is always priority based. Most RTOS uses preemptive task scheduling method which is based on priority levels. Here a high priority process gets executed over the low priority ones. All **"low priority process execution"** will get paused.

- A high priority process execution will get override only if a request comes from an even high priority process.

Hardware and economical factors :

- An RTOS is usually designed for a low end, stand alone device like an ATM, Vending machines, Kiosks etc. RTOS is light weight and small in size compared to a GPOS.

- A GPOS is made for high end, general purpose systems like a personal computer, a work station, a server system etc. The basic difference between a low end system and high end system is in its hardware configuration.

- Now a days, a personal computer or even a smart phone comes with high speed processors (in the range of many Gigahertz), large RAMs (in the range 2 or 3 GBs and even higher) etc. But an embedded system works on low hardware configurations usually – speed in the range of Megahertz and RAM in the range of Megabytes.

- A GPOS being too heavy demands very high end hardware configurations. It is economical to port an RTOS to an embedded system of limited expectations and functionalities (Example: An ATM is supposed to do only certain functions like money transfer, Withdrawal, Balance check etc). So, it is more logical to use an RTOS inside the ATM with its limited hardware. It is not economical to improve the hardware of an ATM just to port a GPOS as its user interface.

Latency issues :

- Another major issue with a GPOS is unbounded dispatch latency, which most GPOS falls into. The more number of threads to schedule, latencies will get added up! An RTOS has no such issues because all the process and threads in it has got bounded latencies, which means a process/thread will get executed within a specified time limit.

Preemptible kernel :

- The kernel of an RTOS is preemptible; whereas a GPOS kernel is not preemptible. This is a major issue when it comes to serving high priority process/threads first. If kernel is not preemptible, then a request/call from kernel will override all other process and threads. For example, a request from a driver or some other system service comes in, it is treated as a kernel call which will be served immediately overriding all other process and threads.

- In an RTOS the kernel is kept very simple and only very important service requests are kept within the kernel call. All other service requests are treated as external processes and threads. All such service requests from kernel are associated with a bounded latency in an RTOS. This ensures highly predictable and quick response from an RTOS.

Important Points

- A regular OS focuses on computing throughput while an RTOS focuses on very fast response time.
- OSes are used in a wide variety of applications while RTOSes are generally embedded in devices that require real time response.
- OSes use a time sharing design to allow for multi-tasking while RTOSes either use a time sharing design or an even driven design.
- The coding of an RTOS is stricter compared to a standard OS.

Practice Questions

1. What are the functions of an operating system?
2. What is Real Time Operating System? Explain in brief.
3. Draw and explain the architecture of RTOS in brief.
4. What is task management? Explain with task state transition diagram.

5. What are the methods of task synchronization? Describe any one in detail. What is time management in RTOS? Explain in brief.

6. What is device I/O management in RTOS? Explain in brief. What is memory management in RTOS? Explain brief.

7. What is interrupt and event handling in RTOS? Explain in brief.

8. What are the scheduling algorithms of RTOS? Describe any one scheduling in brief?

9. What is cooperative scheduling? Explain in brief.

10. What is the Earliest Deadline First (EDE) Scheduling? Explain in brief.

11. What is the Earliest Rate-monotonic scheduling? Explain in brief?

12. what is multitasking? Explain in brief,

13. What is the shared data problem in RTOS?

14. What is semaphore? Explain binary semaphore in brief.

15. What is counting semaphore? Explain in brief.

16. What is mutex semaphore? Explain in brief.

17. What do you mean by deadlock? Explain with example.

18. What are necessary conditions for deadlock to occur?

19. How to prevent deadlock?

20. What are the mechanisms for executing intertask communication? Explain.

MSBTE Questions

Summer 2012

1. Describe the context switching mechanism with suitable diagram.
2. What do you meant by task Synchronization and mutual exclusion?
3. Enlist the scheduling algorithm and explain any one.
4. Describe the specifications of RTOS.
5. Define the term starvation and deadlock with respect to multiple process.
6. Describe various operating system functionalities in RTOS.
7. Define RTOS. Why RTOS is needed?

Winter 2012

1. State Need of Real Time System (RTOS).
2. Differentiate between RTOS and desktop OS.
3. State the methods of task synchronization and describe any one in detail.
4. Describe the context switching mechanism with suitable diagram.
5. Define task with respect to RTOS and give the five states in which task resides.
6. What is inter-process communication? State its working.

Summer 2013

1. Describe in detail the interrupt handling mechanism in real time operating system (RTOS).

2. Explain in detail context switching between two tasks in an operating system.

3. With suitable figure describe data transfer in I2C bus.

4. Enlist the hardware and software components in the embedded system of digital camera.

5. Enlist the various forms of system memory.

6. Describe Hard and Real time software.

7. Describe in brief, starvation an deadlock in an operating system.

8. Describe the various OS services in an RTOS software. Define task with respect to RTOS and give five states in which a task resides.

9. Which information must be collected by the programmer before writing the device driver program.

10. What do you mean by IPC? State various IPC functions.

11. State the methods of task synchronization and describe any one in detail.

Winter 2013

1. Describe the requirement and needs of RTOS in embedded system.

2. State task synchronization and mutual exclusion in an embedded system.

3. Compare RTOS with Desktop OS.

4. Explain in detail, concept of starvation in RTOS.

5. Explain interprocess communication in an operating system.

6. Describe the different OS services in RTOS.

Summer 2014

1. Define : (a) Starvation, (b) Deadlock.

2. Describe the context switching mechanism with suitable figure.

3. State the need of RTOS in embedded. State its four features.

4. What are the different problems of sharing data by multiple task routine?

5. Describe the specification of RTOS.

6. What is inter-process communication? State its working.

7. Differentiate between RTOS and OS.

8. State method of task synchronization and describe any one in detail.

Winter 2014

1. What do you mean by context switching?

2. Compare desktop OS with RTOS.

3. Describe starvation and deadlock.

4. Enlist any four specifications of RTOS.

5. Which are problems in inter-processors communication? How to solve it?

6. Define task. Which are different states of task?